中国社会科学院大学
University of Chinese Academy of Social Sciences

篤学 慎思　明辨 尚行

中国社会科学院大学系列教材

外国语言文学系列

美国短篇小说选读
与文本批评

杨 春 编著

American Short Stories:
A Critical Reading

社会科学文献出版社

SOCIAL SCIENCES ACADEMIC PRESS (CHINA)

本教材（编号：JCJS2022037）由中国社会科学院大学教材建设项目专项经费支持

前 言

小说学习、欣赏和研读对我们有着深远的意义。首先，通过学习小说，我们可以扩展自己的知识面和视野，了解不同文化和历史背景下人们的生活、思想和情感体验。小说作为文学形式之一，能够为我们提供丰富多彩的故事情节、人物形象和情感内核，让我们更加深入地理解人性和社会现实。

其次，欣赏小说能够给我们带来愉悦、启发和感悟。优秀的小说作品往往能触动我们的心灵，让我们共情和感同身受，体验到作者想要传达的情感和思想。欣赏小说可以使我们感受到文字的美感和力量，激发我们的想象力和审美情感。

最重要的是，研读小说可以帮助我们理解作品背后的深层含义、作者的创作意图以及作品与时代、文化背景的关系。透过对小说的深入研究，我们可以提升自己的文学素养和批评能力，培养批判性思维和文学审美，从而更好地认识自己、理解世界。研读小说也有助于我们提升阅读和写作能力，培养表达能力，丰富自己的内心世界，扩展认知领域，从而更好地适应和应对当下的社会挑战和生活压力。综上所述，小说学习、欣赏和研读对我们的成长与心灵体验丰富有着重要的意义。

《美国短篇小说选读与文本批评》（*American Short Stories: A Critical Reading*）将带领读者展开一次精彩纷呈的文学之旅，探索美国短篇小说的丰富历程。从华盛顿·欧文的《睡谷传说》（"The Legend of Sleepy Hollow"）开始，沿途经历爱伦·坡的诡谲之境、霍桑的历史超验、梅尔维尔的浪漫主义、吉尔曼的女性主义、朱厄特的深刻细腻、杰克·伦敦的自然主义、福克纳的现代主义、菲茨杰拉德的叙事技巧、贝娄的奇思妙想，直至巴塞尔姆的后现代主义，最终抵达雷蒙德·卡佛的"极简主义"写作风格。每个单元都承载着文学历史的精髓，提供了对文本的深入解读和对作家灵感的深入研究。

在本书中，我们通过作者简介、文学回顾、术语解析、情节概述、作品欣赏、补充文本阅读以及作品评论等内容，为读者提供了解美国短篇小说文学风格和主题的机会，帮助读者深刻感知每篇作品的内涵和价值所在。这种深入的研究和解读有助于读者更好地理解作品背后的意义和作者的创作意图，从而丰富其阅读体验并激发其对文学的深刻思考。

本书的独特之处不仅在于学术深度和广度，也就是说，它不仅仅是一部知识性的读物，更是一次关于文学热爱和思考的深刻体验。我们希望读者能在这本书中找到对文学的热情，体验到文学世界的多样性和魅力。

让我们一同踏上这次美国短篇小说之旅，感受文字背后的力量，让文学在我们的心中闪耀光芒，永不熄灭。愿本书能成为你探索文学世界的指南，让文字之美永存于你的心灵深处。愿我们共同领略文学的奇妙，从中汲取无尽的启迪与智慧。让我们携手走向文学之光，让心灵被文学的温暖抚慰。让我们成为字里行间的穿梭者，感受文学的魅力与力量。

中国社会科学院大学　杨　春

2024 年初春

Preface

The study, appreciation, and analysis of short stories hold profound significance for us. Firstly, through learning about short stories, we can broaden our knowledge and perspectives, gaining insights into the lives, thoughts, and emotional experiences of people from different cultures and historical backgrounds. As a literary form, short stories provide us with rich and colorful storylines, character portrayals, and emotional cores, allowing us to gain a deeper understanding of human nature and social realities.

Secondly, appreciating short stories can bring us joy, inspiration, and insight. Outstanding literary works often resonate with our hearts, allowing us to empathize and experience the emotions and thoughts the author intends to convey. Through the appreciation of short stories, we can feel the beauty and power of words, stimulating our imagination and aesthetic sensibility.

Most importantly, the in-depth study of short stories can help us understand the deeper meanings behind the works, the author's creative intentions, and the relationship between the works and their historical and cultural contexts. By delving into novels, we can enhance our literary literacy and critical thinking skills, cultivate critical thinking and literary appreciation, and thus better understand ourselves and the world around us. Studying novels also helps improve our reading and writing abilities, develope our abilities of expression, enrich our inner worlds, and expand our cognitive horizons, enabling us to better adapt to and cope with the challenges and pressures of contemporary society. In summary, the study, appreciation, and analysis of novels are of great importance for our growth and enriching our spiritual experiences.

American Short Stories: A Critical Reading will lead readers on an engaging literary journey, exploring the rich history of American short stories. Beginning with Washington Irving's "The Legend of Sleepy Hollow", we will traverse the eerie realms of Edgar Allan Poe, the historical transcendentalism of Nathaniel Hawthorne, the romanticism of Herman Melville, the feminism of Charlotte Perkins Gilman, the profound intricacies of Sarah Orne Jewett, the naturalism of Jack London, the modernism of William Faulkner, the narrative techniques of F. Scott Fitzgerald, the imaginative works of Saul Bellow, all the way to the postmodernism of Barthelme, and finally arriving at Raymond Carver's minimalist writing style. Each unit encapsulates the essence of literary history, providing in-depth interpretations of texts and explorations of the authors' inspirations.

In this book, we offer readers opportunities to explore the literary styles and themes of American short stories through author biographies, literary reviews, terminology analyses, plot summaries, work appreciations, supplementary readings, and critiques, helping readers to deeply perceive the connotation and value of each work. This in-depth research and interpretation help readers grasp the significance of each piece and the authors' creative intentions, enriching the reading experience and stimulating profound reflection on literature.

The uniqueness of this book lies not only in its academic depth and breadth; it is not merely an informative read but also a profound experience of literary passion and contemplation. We hope readers will find enthusiasm for literature within these pages and experience the diversity and charm of the literary world.

Let us embark together on this journey through American short stories, feeling the power behind the words and allowing literature to shine brightly in our hearts, never to fade. May this book become your guide in exploring the literary world, keeping the beauty of words alive deep within your soul. May we together appreciate the wonders of literature, drawing endless inspiration and wisdom from it. Let us walk towards the light of literature, allowing our hearts to be comforted by its warmth, becoming wanderers among the lines, experiencing the charm and power of literature.

Yang Chun,
University of Chinese Academy of Social Sciences
Early Spring 2024

CONTENTS

· Part I Romanticism and the American Short Story ·

· Part II Realism and the American Short Story ·

· Part III Modernism and the American Short Story ·

· Part IV Postmodernism and the American Short Story ·

· Supplementary Reading with Critical Essay ·

Part I
Romanticism and the American Short Story

Unit 1
Washington Irving: "The Legend of Sleepy Hollow"

About the Author

Washington Irving (1783–1859)

Washington Irving was a prominent American author and diplomat in the early 19th century. He was called the "first American man of letters" and he was the first to bring the American landscape to life in works of fiction. He is famous for his collection of short stories, including "The Legend of Sleepy Hollow" and "Rip Van Winkle". These stories have had a significant impact on the development of the American short story genre. "The Legend of Sleepy Hollow" takes place in a small town in New York's Hudson Valley and follows the adventures of Ichabod Crane, a superstitious schoolmaster. He is pursued by the Headless Horseman, the ghost of a Hessian soldier. This story is filled with supernatural elements like ghosts, witches, and mysterious creatures, contributing to its classification as American Gothic literature. It has been adapted into various forms of media, including movies, TV shows, and stage plays. In "Rip Van Winkle", the protagonist is a Dutch-American villager named Rip Van Winkle. He falls asleep in the Catskill Mountains and awakens 20 years later, having missed the American Revolution. Rip discovers that his friends and family have all passed away, and he struggles to fit into the new nation. The story takes place before and after the American Revolutionary War and is considered one of the earliest works of American fiction. It is widely beloved in American literature. As the inventor of the American story, Irving's success encouraged other Americans to explore the possibilities of short stories.

The Literary History

The Emergence and Development of the American Short Story

Washington Irving is often credited as the originator of the American short story, though this is not entirely accurate. Nevertheless, he is a monumental figure in

American literary history, being the first writer of fiction in the New World to gain an international reputation. Prior to Irving, hundreds of pieces of prose narrative had been published in newspapers and magazines, but his work brought a new artistic standard to the genre, combining narrative voice. These stories were immensely popular, providing amusement to a wide range of readers with their American settings, even when they were based on European myths. His writing style was humorous and graceful, with delicate character development that made his work relatable to those he was satirizing. However, his writing was better suited to sketches than to longer narratives, and he only wrote short stories.

Before Washington Irving's short stories, there were already many forms of prose that contained some of the features associated with the short story. These forms of storytelling were important in the evolution of the short story, but they did not quite match the modern definition of the short story due to the lack of thematic and technical development that is now seen as essential to this genre of literature. They have straightforward or clumsy plot development, lack consideration of narrative point of view, have minimal setting and characterization, and have an artificial, wordy, and awkward style.

Irving's short story is a masterpiece of literary artistry, featuring vivid characters, a well-defined setting, and a refined use of language. It is also the perfect medium for examining the implications of democracy in the newly established United States.

Literary Terms

Narratology

Narratology is the study of narrative structures and how they shape the way we interpret and understand stories. It involves the analysis of the elements that make up a narrative, such as plot, character, setting, point of view, and theme. Narratology seeks to understand the ways in which these elements work together to create meaning and communicate ideas. By studying the structure of narratives, narratologists aim to uncover the underlying patterns and conventions that shape our understanding of storytelling.

Setting

Setting refers to the general locale, historical time, social circumstance, and the particular physical location in which the narrative work takes place. Setting in the short story helps to create an appropriate atmosphere for the story, establish the background and conflict for action, arouse reader's expectations, reveal the personality of the character, and reinforce the theme of the story.

Character

Character applies to the individuals in a literary work, who are interpreted by the reader as being endowed with particular moral, intellectual, and emotional qualities. Types of character include protagonist & antagonist, flat & round character, and dynamic & static character.

Plot

The plot in narrative work is constituted by its events and actions, as these are rendered and ordered toward achieving particular artistic and emotional effects. Therefore, a plot is a plan for a story, based on conflicting human motivations, with the actions resulting from human response. The plot of traditional story often consists of exposition, complication, crisis, falling action and resolution.

Theme

Theme applies to a general concept or doctrine, whether implicit or asserted, which a literary work is designed to incorporate and make persuasive to the reader. Therefore, the theme is the central idea or statement about life that unifies and controls the total work.

Archetype

In literary criticism the term archetype denotes recurrent narrative designs, patterns of action, character-types, themes, and images which are identifiable in a wide variety of works of literature, as well as myths, dreams, and even social rituals. Such recurrent items are held to be the result of elemental and universal forms or patterns in the human psyche, whose effective embodiment in a literary work evokes a profound response from the attentive reader, because he or she shares the archetypes expressed by the author.

Defamiliarization

Defamiliarization is a literary technique in which an object, idea, or situation is presented in an unfamiliar or strange way in order to make the reader think about it in a new light. This technique is often used to challenge the reader's preconceived notions and to make them reconsider their assumptions. It can also be used to make the reader more be aware of the details of the setting, or to draw attention to a particular aspect of the story.

American Romanticism

American Romanticism was a literary movement in the early to mid-19th century that celebrated the beauty of nature and the power of the individual. It was characterized by a focus on emotion and individualism, as well as glorification of all the past and nature, preferring the pastoral to the commercial. American Romantic writers often focused on the mysterious, the supernatural, and the exotic, and often used symbols, metaphors, and allegories in their works. They also tended to value intuition and emotion over reason, and imagination over science. Distinctive characteristics of American Romantic literature include an emphasis on individualism and the adulation of the individual as well as a deep reverence for nature's beauty and its capacity to inspire. Furthermore, this literary movement prioritized emotions and intuition over reason and logic, utilizing symbolism and imagery to convey profound meanings. Another notable element of American Romanticism was a fascination with the supernatural and mysterious, with love, death, and nature recurring as prevalent themes. Writers probed the inner self and explored the human condition, employing exaggeration and hyperbole to emphasize their points.

The Story

The Legend of Sleepy Hollow[1]:
Found Among the Papers of the Late Diedrich Knickerbocker

> *A pleasing land of drowsy head it was,*
> *Of dreams that wave before the half-shut eye;*
> *And of gay castles in the clouds that pass,*
> *Forever flushing round a summer sky.*
> CASTLE OF INDOLENCE[2]

IN the bosom of one of those spacious coves which indent the eastern shore of the Hudson, at that broad expansion of the river denominated by the ancient Dutch navigators the Tappan Zee[3], and where they always prudently shortened sail and implored the protection of St. Nicholas when they crossed, there lies a small market town or rural port, which by some is called Greensburgh, but which is more generally and properly known by the name of Tarry Town[4]. This name was given, we are told, in former days, by the good housewives of the adjacent country, from the inveterate propensity of their husbands to linger about the village tavern on market days. Be that as it may, I do not vouch for the fact, but merely advert to it, for the sake of being precise and authentic. Not far from this village, perhaps about two miles, there is a little valley or rather lap of land among high hills, which is one of the quietest places in the whole world.

---

1   Washington Irving, *The Sketch Book of Geoffrey Crayon, Gent* (Penguin Classics, 2004), pp.23–46.
2   CASTLE OF INDOLENCE is an allegorical poem written by James Thompson (1700–1748) in 1748.
3   Tappan Zee is the spacious part of the Hudson River near Tarrytown in southeastern New York.
4   Now Tarry Town, about fifteen miles above New York City limits.

A small brook glides through it, with just murmur enough to lull one to repose; and the occasional whistle of a quail or tapping of a woodpecker is almost the only sound that ever breaks in upon the uniform tranquility.

I recollect that, when a stripling, my first exploit in squirrel-shooting was in a grove of tall walnut-trees that shades one side of the valley. I had wandered into it at noontime, when all nature is peculiarly quiet, and was startled by the roar of my own gun, as it broke the Sabbath stillness around and was prolonged and reverberated by the angry echoes. If ever I should wish for a retreat whither I might steal from the world and its distractions, and dream quietly away the remnant of a troubled life, I know of none more promising than this little valley.

From the listless repose of the place, and the peculiar character of its inhabitants, who are descendants from the original Dutch settlers, this sequestered glen has long been known by the name of SLEEPY HOLLOW, and its rustic lads are called the Sleepy Hollow Boys throughout all the neighboring country. A drowsy, dreamy influence seems to hang over the land, and to pervade the very atmosphere. Some say that the place was bewitched by a High German doctor, during the early days of the settlement; others, that an old Indian chief, the prophet or wizard of his tribe, held his powwows there before the country was discovered by Master Hendrick Hudson. Certain it is, the place still continues under the sway of some witching power, that holds a spell over the minds of the good people, causing them to walk in a continual reverie. They are given to all kinds of marvelous beliefs, are subject to trances and visions, and frequently see strange sights, and hear music and voices in the air. The whole neighborhood abounds with local tales, haunted spots, and twilight superstitions; stars shoot and meteors glare oftener across the valley than in any other part of the country, and the nightmare, with her whole nine fold[1], seems to make it the favorite scene of her gambols.

The dominant spirit, however, that haunts this enchanted region, and seems to be commander-in-chief of all the powers of the air, is the apparition of a figure on horseback, without a head. It is said by some to be the ghost of a Hessian trooper[2], whose head had been carried away by a cannon-ball, in some nameless battle during the Revolutionary War, and who is ever and anon seen by the country folk hurrying along in the gloom of night, as if on the wings of the wind.

His haunts are not confined to the valley, but extend at times to the adjacent roads, and especially to the vicinity of a church at no great distance. Indeed, certain of the most authentic historians of those parts, who have been careful in collecting and collating the floating facts concerning this specter, allege that the body of the trooper having been buried in the churchyard, the ghost rides forth to the scene of battle in

---

1   Read "the nightmare and her nine fold" in Shakespeare's *King Lear*, Act III, Scene 4, L. 128. The nightmare, in folk superstition, was a demon; her nine foals (offspring of a mare) were imps.

2   German mercenary soldiers hired by the British.

nightly quest of his head, and that the rushing speed with which he sometimes passes along the Hollow, like a midnight blast, is owing to his being belated, and in a hurry to get back to the churchyard before daybreak.

Such is the general purport of this legendary superstition, which has furnished materials for many a wild story in that region of shadows; and the specter is known at all the country firesides, by the name of the Headless Horseman of Sleepy Hollow.

It is remarkable that the visionary propensity I have mentioned is not confined to the native inhabitants of the valley, but is unconsciously imbibed by every one who resides there for a time. However wide awake they may have been before they entered that sleepy region, they are sure, in a little time, to inhale the witching influence of the air, and begin to grow imaginative, to dream dreams, and see apparitions.

I mention this peaceful spot with all possible laud, for it is in such little retired Dutch valleys, found here and there embosomed in the great State of New York, that population, manners, and customs remain fixed, while the great torrent of migration and improvement, which is making such incessant changes in other parts of this restless country, sweeps by them unobserved. They are like those little nooks of still water, which border a rapid stream, where we may see the straw and bubble riding quietly at anchor, or slowly revolving in their mimic harbor, undisturbed by the rush of the passing current. Though many years have elapsed since I trod the drowsy shades of Sleepy Hollow, yet I question whether I should not still find the same trees and the same families vegetating in its sheltered bosom.

In this by-place of nature there abode, in a remote period of American history, that is to say, some thirty years since, a worthy wight[1] of the name of Ichabod Crane, who sojourned, or, as he expressed it, "tarried," in Sleepy Hollow, for the purpose of instructing the children of the vicinity.

He was a native of Connecticut, a State which supplies the Union with pioneers for the mind as well as for the forest, and sends forth yearly its legions of frontier woodmen and country schoolmasters. The cognomen of Crane was not inapplicable to his person. He was tall, but exceedingly lank, with narrow shoulders, long arms and legs, hands that dangled a mile out of his sleeves, feet that might have served for shovels, and his whole frame most loosely hung together. His head was small, and flat at top, with huge ears, large green glassy eyes, and a long snipe nose, so that it looked like a weather-cock perched upon his spindle neck to tell which way the wind blew. To see him striding along the profile of a hill on a windy day, with his clothes bagging and fluttering about him, one might have mistaken him for the genius of famine descending upon the earth, or some scarecrow eloped from a cornfield.

His schoolhouse was a low building of one large room, rudely constructed of logs; the windows partly glazed, and partly patched with leaves of old copybooks. It was

---

1   a wight=a person.

most ingeniously secured at vacant hours, by a withe twisted in the handle of the door, and stakes set against the window shutters; so that though a thief might get in with perfect ease, he would find some embarrassment in getting out, an idea most probably borrowed by the architect, Yost Van Houten, from the mystery of an eelpot. The schoolhouse stood in a rather lonely but pleasant situation, just at the foot of a woody hill, with a brook running close by, and a formidable birch-tree growing at one end of it. From hence the low murmur of his pupils' voices, conning over their lessons, might be heard in a drowsy summer's day, like the hum of a beehive; interrupted now and then by the authoritative voice of the master, in the tone of menace or command, or, peradventure, by the appalling sound of the birch, as he urged some tardy loiterer along the flowery path of knowledge. Truth to say, he was a conscientious man, and ever bore in mind the golden maxim, "Spare the rod and spoil the child." Ichabod Crane's scholars certainly were not spoiled.

I would not have it imagined, however, that he was one of those cruel potentates of the school who joy in the smart of their subjects; on the contrary, he administered justice with discrimination rather than severity; taking the burden off the backs of the weak, and laying it on those of the strong.

Your mere puny stripling, that winced at the least flourish of the rod, was passed by with indulgence; but the claims of justice were satisfied by inflicting a double portion on some little tough wrong-headed, broad-skirted Dutch urchin, who sulked and swelled and grew dogged and sullen beneath the birch. All this he called "doing his duty by their parents"; and he never inflicted a chastisement without following it by the assurance, so consolatory to the smarting urchin, that "he would remember it and thank him for it the longest day he had to live".

When school hours were over, he was even the companion and playmate of the larger boys; and on holiday afternoons would convoy some of the smaller ones home, who happened to have pretty sisters, or good housewives for mothers, noted for the comforts of the cupboard. Indeed, it behooved him to keep on good terms with his pupils. The revenue arising from his school was small, and would have been scarcely sufficient to furnish him with daily bread, for he was a huge feeder, and, though lank, had the dilating powers of an anaconda; but to help out his maintenance, he was, according to country custom in those parts, boarded and lodged at the houses of the farmers whose children he instructed. With these he lived successively a week at a time, thus going the rounds of the neighborhood, with all his worldly effects tied up in a cotton handkerchief.

That all this might not be too onerous on the purses of his rustic patrons, who are apt to consider the costs of schooling a grievous burden, and schoolmasters as mere drones, he had various ways of rendering himself both useful and agreeable. He assisted the farmers occasionally in the lighter labors of their farms, helped to make hay, mended the fences, took the horses to water, drove the cows from pasture, and cut wood for the winter fire. He laid aside, too, all the dominant dignity and absolute sway with which he lorded it in his little empire, the school, and became wonderfully gentle and ingratiating. He found favor in the eyes of the mothers by petting the children, particularly the youngest; and like the lion bold, which whilom so magnanimously the lamb did hold, he would sit with a child on one knee, and rock a cradle with his foot for whole hours together.

In addition to his other vocations, he was the singing-master of the neighborhood, and picked up many bright shillings by instructing the young folks in psalmody. It was a matter of no little vanity to him on Sundays, to take his station in front of the church gallery, with a band of chosen singers; where, in his own mind, he completely carried away the palm from the parson. Certain it is, his voice resounded far above all the rest of the congregation; and there are peculiar quavers still to be heard in that church, and which may even be heard half a mile off, quite to the opposite side of the millpond, on a still Sunday morning, which are said to be legitimately descended from the nose of Ichabod Crane. Thus, by divers little makeshifts, in that ingenious way which is commonly denominated "by hook and by crook", the worthy pedagogue got on tolerably enough, and was thought, by all who understood nothing of the labor of headwork, to have a wonderfully easy life of it.

The schoolmaster is generally a man of some importance in the female circle of a rural neighborhood; being considered a kind of idle, gentlemanlike personage, of vastly superior taste and accomplishments to the rough country swains, and, indeed, inferior in learning only to the parson. His appearance, therefore, is apt to occasion some little stir at the tea-table of a farmhouse, and the addition of a supernumerary dish of cakes or sweetmeats, or, peradventure, the parade of a silver teapot. Our man of letters, therefore, was peculiarly happy in the smiles of all the country damsels. How he would figure among them in the churchyard, between services on Sundays; gathering grapes for them from the wild vines that overran the surrounding trees; reciting for their amusement all the epitaphs on the tombstones; or sauntering, with a whole bevy of them, along the banks of the adjacent millpond; while the more bashful country bumpkins hung sheepishly back, envying his superior elegance and address.

From his half-itinerant life, also, he was a kind of travelling gazette, carrying the whole budget of local gossip from house to house, so that his appearance was always greeted with satisfaction. He was, moreover, esteemed by the women as a man of great erudition, for he had read several books quite through, and was a perfect master of Cotton Mather's "History of New England Witchcraft", in which, by the way, he most firmly and potently believed.

He was, in fact, an odd mixture of small shrewdness and simple credulity. His appetite for the marvelous, and his powers of digesting it, were equally extraordinary; and both had been increased by his residence in this spell-bound region. No tale was too gross or monstrous for his capacious swallow. It was often his delight, after his school was dismissed in the afternoon, to stretch himself on the rich bed of clover bordering the little brook that whimpered by his schoolhouse, and there con over old Mather's direful tales, until the gathering dusk of evening made the printed page a mere mist before his eyes. Then, as he wended his way by swamp and stream and awful woodland, to the farmhouse where he happened to be quartered, every sound of nature, at that witching hour, fluttered his excited imagination, the moan of the whip-poor-will from the hillside, the boding cry of the tree toad, that harbinger of storm, the dreary hooting of the screech owl, or the sudden rustling in the thicket of birds frightened from their roost. The fireflies, too, which sparkled most vividly in the darkest places, now and then startled him, as one of uncommon brightness would stream across his path; and if, by chance, a huge blockhead of a beetle came winging his blundering flight against him, the poor varlet was ready to give up the ghost, with the idea that he was struck with a witch's token. His only resource on such occasions, either to drown thought or drive away evil spirits, was to sing psalm tunes and the good people of Sleepy Hollow, as they sat by their doors of an evening, were often filled with awe at hearing his nasal melody, "in linked sweetness long drawn out", floating from the distant hill, or along the dusky road.

Another of his sources of fearful pleasure was to pass long winter evenings with the old Dutch wives, as they sat spinning by the fire, with a row of apples roasting and spluttering along the hearth, and listen to their marvelous tales of ghosts and goblins, and haunted fields, and haunted brooks, and haunted bridges, and haunted houses, and particularly of the headless horseman, or Galloping Hessian of the Hollow, as they sometimes called him. He would delight them equally by his anecdotes of witchcraft, and of the direful omens and portentous sights and sounds in the air, which prevailed in the earlier times of Connecticut; and would frighten them woefully with speculations upon comets and shooting stars; and with the alarming fact that the world did absolutely turn round, and that they were half the time topsy-turvy!

But if there was a pleasure in all this, while snugly cuddling in the chimney corner of a chamber that was all of a ruddy glow from the crackling wood fire, and where, of course, no specter dared to show its face, it was dearly purchased by the terrors of his subsequent walk homewards. What fearful shapes and shadows beset his path, amidst the dim and ghastly glare of a snowy night! With what wistful look did he eye every trembling ray of light streaming across the waste fields from some distant window! How often was he appalled by some shrub covered with snow, which, like a sheeted specter, beset his very path! How often did he shrink with curdling awe at the sound of his own steps on the frosty crust beneath his feet; and dread to look over his shoulder, lest he should behold some uncouth being tramping close behind him! And how often was he thrown into complete dismay by some rushing blast, howling among the trees, in the idea that it was the Galloping Hessian on one of his nightly scourings!

All these, however, were mere terrors of the night, phantoms of the mind that walk in darkness; and though he had seen many specters in his time, and been more than once beset by Satan in divers shapes, in his lonely perambulations, yet daylight put an end to all these evils; and he would have passed a pleasant life of it, in despite of the Devil and all his works, if his path had not been crossed by a being that causes more perplexity to mortal man than ghosts, goblins, and the whole race of witches put together, and that was—a woman.

Among the musical disciples who assembled, one evening in each week, to receive his instructions in psalmody, was Katrina Van Tassel, the daughter and only child of a substantial Dutch farmer. She was a blooming lass of fresh eighteen; plump as a partridge; ripe and melting and rosy-cheeked as one of her father's peaches, and universally famed, not merely for her beauty, but her vast expectations. She was withal a little of a coquette, as might be perceived even in her dress, which was a mixture of ancient and modern fashions, as most suited to set off her charms. She wore the ornaments of pure yellow gold, which her great-great-grandmother had brought over from Saardam[1]; the tempting stomacher of the olden time, and withal a provokingly short petticoat, to display the prettiest foot and ankle in the country round.

Ichabod Crane had a soft and foolish heart towards the sex; and it is not to be wondered at that so tempting a morsel soon found favor in his eyes, more especially after he had visited her in her paternal mansion. Old Baltus Van Tassel was a perfect picture of a thriving, contented, liberal-hearted farmer. He seldom, it is true, sent either his eyes or his thoughts beyond the boundaries of his own farm; but within those everything was snug, happy and well-conditioned. He was satisfied with his wealth, but not proud of it; and piqued himself upon[2] the hearty abundance, rather than the style in which he lived. His stronghold was situated on the banks of the Hudson, in one of those green, sheltered, fertile nooks in which the Dutch farmers are so fond of nestling. A great elm tree spread its broad branches over it, at the foot of which bubbled up a spring of the softest and sweetest water, in a little well-formed of a barrel; and then stole sparkling away through the grass, to a neighboring brook, that babbled along among alders and dwarf willows. Hard by the farmhouse was a vast barn, that might have served for a church; every window and crevice of which seemed bursting forth with the treasures of the farm; the flail was busily resounding within it from morning to night; swallows and martins skimmed twittering about the eaves; and rows of pigeons, some with one eye turned up, as if watching the weather, some with their heads under their wings or buried in their bosoms, and others swelling, and cooing, and bowing about their dames, were enjoying the sunshine on the roof. Sleek unwieldy porkers were grunting in the repose and abundance of their pens, from whence sallied forth, now and then, troops of sucking pigs, as if to snuff the air. A stately squadron of snowy

---

1   Modern Zaandam, four miles from Amsterdam, Holland.

2   piqued himself upon=prided himself upon.

geese were riding in an adjoining pond, convoying whole fleets of ducks; regiments of turkeys were gobbling through the farmyard, and Guinea fowls fretting about it, like ill-tempered housewives, with their peevish, discontented cry. Before the barn door strutted the gallant cock, that pattern of a husband, a warrior and a fine gentleman, clapping his burnished wings and crowing in the pride and gladness of his heart, sometimes tearing up the earth with his feet, and then generously calling his ever-hungry family of wives and children to enjoy the rich morsel which he had discovered.

The pedagogue's mouth watered as he looked upon this sumptuous promise of luxurious winter fare. In his devouring mind's eye, he pictured to himself every roasting-pig running about with a pudding in his belly, and an apple in his mouth; the pigeons were snugly put to bed in a comfortable pie, and tucked in with a coverlet of crust; the geese were swimming in their own gravy; and the ducks pairing cosily in dishes, like snug married couples, with a decent competency of onion sauce. In the porkers he saw carved out the future sleek side of bacon, and juicy relishing ham; not a turkey but he beheld daintily trussed up, with its gizzard under its wing, and, peradventure, a necklace of savory sausages; and even bright chanticleer himself lay sprawling on his back, in a side dish, with uplifted claws, as if craving that quarter which his chivalrous spirit disdained to ask while living.

As the enraptured Ichabod fancied all this, and as he rolled his great green eyes over the fat meadow lands, the rich fields of wheat, of rye, of buckwheat, and Indian corn, and the orchards burdened with ruddy fruit, which surrounded the warm tenement[1] of Van Tassel, his heart yearned after the damsel who was to inherit these domains, and his imagination expanded with the idea, how they might be readily turned into cash, and the money invested in immense tracts of wild land, and shingle palaces in the wilderness. Nay, his busy fancy already realized his hopes, and presented to him the blooming Katrina, with a whole family of children, mounted on the top of a wagon loaded with household trumpery, with pots and kettles dangling beneath; and he beheld himself bestriding a pacing mare, with a colt at her heels, setting out for Kentucky, Tennessee, or the Lord knows where!

When he entered the house, the conquest of his heart was complete. It was one of those spacious farmhouses, with high-ridged but lowly sloping roofs, built in the style handed down from the first Dutch settlers; the low projecting eaves forming a piazza along the front, capable of being closed up in bad weather. Under this were hung flails, harness, various utensils of husbandry, and nets for fishing in the neighboring river. Benches were built along the sides for summer use; and a great spinning-wheel at one end, and a churn at the other, showed the various uses to which this important porch might be devoted. From this piazza the wondering Ichabod entered the hall, which formed the center of the mansion, and the place of usual residence.

---

1   tenement=residence.

Here rows of resplendent pewter, ranged on a long dresser, dazzled his eyes. In one corner stood a huge bag of wool, ready to be spun; in another, a quantity of linsey-woolsey just from the loom; ears of Indian corn, and strings of dried apples and peaches, hung in gay festoons along the walls, mingled with the gaud of red peppers; and a door left ajar gave him a peep into the best parlor, where the claw-footed chairs and dark mahogany tables shone like mirrors; andirons, with their accompanying shovel and tongs, glistened from their covert of asparagus tops; mock-oranges and conch-shells decorated the mantelpiece; strings of various-colored birds eggs were suspended above it; a great ostrich egg was hung from the center of the room, and a corner cupboard, knowingly left open, displayed immense treasures of old silver and well-mended china.

From the moment Ichabod laid his eyes upon these regions of delight, the peace of his mind was at an end, and his only study was how to gain the affections of the peerless daughter of Van Tassel. In this enterprise, however, he had more real difficulties than generally fell to the lot of a knight-errant of yore, who seldom had anything but giants, enchanters, fiery dragons, and such like easily conquered adversaries, to contend with and had to make his way merely through gates of iron and brass, and walls of adamant to the castle keep, where the lady of his heart was confined; all which he achieved as easily as a man would carve his way to the center of a Christmas pie; and then the lady gave him her hand as a matter of course. Ichabod, on the contrary, had to win his way to the heart of a country coquette, beset with a labyrinth of whims and caprices, which were forever presenting new difficulties and impediments; and he had to encounter a host of fearful adversaries of real flesh and blood, the numerous rustic admirers, who beset every portal to her heart, keeping a watchful and angry eye upon each other, but ready to fly out in the common cause against any new competitor.

Among these, the most formidable was a burly, roaring, roystering blade, of the name of Abraham, or, according to the Dutch abbreviation, Brom Van Brunt, the hero of the country round, which rang with his feats of strength and hardihood. He was broad-shouldered and double-jointed, with short curly black hair, and a bluff but not unpleasant countenance, having a mingled air of fun and arrogance. From his Herculean frame and great powers of limb he had received the nickname of BROM BONES, by which he was universally known.

He was famed for great knowledge and skill in horsemanship, being as dexterous on horseback as a Tartar. He was foremost at all races and cock fights; and, with the ascendancy which bodily strength always acquires in rustic life, was the umpire in all disputes, setting his hat on one side, and giving his decisions with an air and tone that admitted of no gainsay or appeal. He was always ready for either a fight or a frolic; but had more mischief than ill-will in his composition; and with all his overbearing roughness, there was a strong dash of waggish good humor at bottom. He had three or four boon companions, who regarded him as their model, and at the head of whom he scoured the country, attending every scene of feud or merriment for miles round. In cold weather he was distinguished by a fur cap, surmounted with a flaunting fox's tail; and when the folks at a country gathering descried this well-known crest at a distance, whisking about among a squad of hard riders, they always stood by for a squall. Sometimes his crew would be heard dashing along past the farmhouses at midnight, with whoop and halloo, like a troop of Don Cossacks; and the old dames, startled out of their sleep, would listen for a moment till the hurry-scurry had clattered by, and then exclaim, "Ay, there goes Brom Bones and his gang!" The neighbors looked upon him with a mixture of awe, admiration, and good-will; and, when any madcap prank or rustic brawl occurred in the vicinity, always shook their heads, and warranted Brom Bones was at the bottom of it.

This rantipole hero had for some time singled out the blooming Katrina for the object of his uncouth gallantries, and though his amorous toyings were something like the gentle caresses and endearments of a bear, yet it was whispered that she did not altogether discourage his hopes. Certain it is, his advances were signals for rival candidates to retire, who felt no inclination to cross a lion in his amours; insomuch, that when his horse was seen tied to Van Tassel's paling, on a Sunday night, a sure sign that his master was courting, or, as it is termed, "sparking," within, all other suitors passed by in despair, and carried the war into other quarters.

Such was the formidable rival with whom Ichabod Crane had to contend, and, considering all things, a stouter man than he would have shrunk from the competition, and a wiser man would have despaired. He had, however, a happy mixture of pliability and perseverance in his nature; he was in form and spirit like a supple-jack—yielding, but tough; though he bent, he never broke; and though he bowed beneath the slightest pressure, yet, the moment it was away—jerk!—he was as erect, and carried his head as high as ever.

To have taken the field openly against his rival would have been madness; for he was not a man to be thwarted in his amours, any more than that stormy lover, Achilles. Ichabod, therefore, made his advances in a quiet and gently insinuating manner. Under cover of his character of singing-master, he made frequent visits at the farmhouse; not that he had anything to apprehend from the meddlesome interference of parents, which is so often a stumbling-block in the path of lovers. Balt Van Tassel was an easy indulgent soul; he loved his daughter better even than his pipe, and, like a reasonable man and an excellent father, let her have her way in everything. His notable little wife, too, had enough to do to attend to her housekeeping and manage her poultry; for, as she sagely observed, ducks and geese are foolish things, and must be looked after, but girls can take care of themselves. Thus, while the busy dame bustled about the house, or plied her spinning-wheel at one end of the piazza, honest Balt would sit smoking his evening pipe at the other, watching the achievements of a little wooden warrior, who, armed with a sword in each hand, was most valiantly fighting the wind on the pinnacle of the barn. In the meantime, Ichabod would carry on his suit with the daughter by the side of the spring under the great elm, or sauntering along in the twilight, that hour so favorable to the lover's eloquence.

I profess not to know how women's hearts are wooed and won. To me they have always been matters of riddle and admiration. Some seem to have but one vulnerable point, or door of access; while others have a thousand avenues, and may be captured in a thousand different ways. It is a great triumph of skill to gain the former, but a still greater proof of generalship to maintain possession of the latter, for man must battle for his fortress at every door and window.

He who wins a thousand common hearts is therefore entitled to some renown; but he who keeps undisputed sway over the heart of a coquette is indeed a hero. Certain it is, this was not the case with the redoubtable Brom Bones; and from the moment Ichabod Crane made his advances, the interests of the former evidently declined: his horse was no longer seen tied to the palings on Sunday nights, and a deadly feud gradually arose between him and the preceptor of Sleepy Hollow.

Brom, who had a degree of rough chivalry in his nature, would fain have carried matters to open warfare and have settled their pretensions to the lady, according to the mode of those most concise and simple reasoners, the knights-errant of yore—by single combat; but Ichabod was too conscious of the superior might of his adversary to enter the lists against him; he had overheard a boast of Bones, that he would "double the schoolmaster up, and lay him on a shelf of his own schoolhouse;" and he was too wary to give him an opportunity. There was something extremely provoking in this obstinately pacific system; it left Brom no alternative but to draw upon the funds of rustic waggery in his disposition, and to play off boorish practical jokes upon his rival. Ichabod became the object of whimsical persecution to Bones and his gang of rough riders. They harried his hitherto peaceful domains; smoked out his singing school by stopping up the chimney; broke into the schoolhouse at night, in spite of its formidable fastenings of withe and window stakes, and turned everything topsy-turvy, so that the poor schoolmaster began to think all the witches in the country held their meetings there. But what was still more annoying, Brom took all opportunities of turning him into ridicule in presence of his mistress, and had a scoundrel dog whom he taught to whine in the most ludicrous manner, and introduced as a rival of Ichabod's, to instruct her in psalmody.

In this way matters went on for some time, without producing any material effect on the relative situations of the contending powers. On a fine autumnal afternoon, Ichabod, in pensive mood, sat enthroned on the lofty stool from whence he usually watched all the concerns of his little literary realm. In his hand he swayed a ferule[1], that scepter of despotic power; the birch of justice reposed on three nails behind the throne, a constant terror to evil doers, while on the desk before him might be seen sundry contraband

---

1   ferule=ferula.

articles and prohibited weapons, detected upon the persons of idle urchins, such as half-munched apples, popguns, whirligigs, fly-cages, and whole legions of rampant little paper gamecocks. Apparently there had been some appalling act of justice recently inflicted, for his scholars were all busily intent upon their books, or slyly whispering behind them with one eye kept upon the master; and a kind of buzzing stillness reigned throughout the schoolroom. It was suddenly interrupted by the appearance of a negro in tow-cloth jacket and trowsers, a round-crowned fragment of a hat, like the cap of Mercury, and mounted on the back of a ragged, wild, half-broken colt, which he managed with a rope by way of halter. He came clattering up to the school door with an invitation to Ichabod to attend a merry-making or "quilting frolic", to be held that evening at Mynheer Van Tassel's; and having delivered his message with that air of importance, and effort at fine language, which a negro is apt to display on petty embassies of the kind, he dashed over the brook, and was seen scampering away up the hollow, full of the importance and hurry of his mission.

All was now bustle and hubbub in the late quiet schoolroom. The scholars were hurried through their lessons without stopping at trifles; those who were nimble skipped over half with impunity, and those who were tardy had a smart application now and then in the rear, to quicken their speed or help them over a tall word. Books were flung aside without being put away on the shelves, inkstands were overturned, benches thrown down, and the whole school was turned loose an hour before the usual time, bursting forth like a legion of young imps, yelping and racketing about the green in joy at their early emancipation.

The gallant Ichabod now spent at least an extra half hour at his toilet, brushing and furbishing up his best, and indeed only suit of rusty black, and arranging his locks by a bit of broken looking-glass that hung up in the schoolhouse. That he might make his appearance before his mistress in the true style of a cavalier, he borrowed a horse from the farmer with whom he was domiciliated, a choleric old Dutchman of the name of Hans Van Ripper, and, thus gallantly mounted, issued forth like a knight-errant in quest of adventures.

But it is meet I should, in the true spirit of romantic story, give some account of the looks and equipments of my hero and his steed. The animal he bestrode was a broken-down plow-horse, that had outlived almost everything but its viciousness. He was gaunt and shagged, with a ewe neck, and a head like a hammer; his rusty mane and tail were tangled and knotted with burs; one eye had lost its pupil, and was glaring and spectral, but the other had the gleam of a genuine devil in it. Still he must have had fire and mettle in his day, if we may judge from the name he bore of Gunpowder. He had, in fact, been a favorite steed of his master's, the choleric Van Ripper, who was a furious rider, and had infused, very probably, some of his own spirit into the animal; for, old and broken-down as he looked, there was more of the lurking devil in him than in any young filly in the country.

Ichabod was a suitable figure for such a steed. He rode with short stirrups, which brought his knees nearly up to the pommel of the saddle; his sharp elbows stuck out like grasshoppers'; he carried his whip perpendicularly in his hand, like a scepter, and as his horse jogged on, the motion of his arms was not unlike the flapping of a pair of wings. A small wool hat rested on the top of his nose, for so his scanty strip of forehead might be called, and the skirts of his black coat fluttered out almost to the horses tail. Such was the appearance of Ichabod and his steed as they shambled out of the gate of Hans Van Ripper, and it was altogether such an apparition as is seldom to be met with in broad daylight.

It was, as I have said, a fine autumnal day; the sky was clear and serene, and nature wore that rich and golden livery which we always associate with the idea of abundance. The forests had put on their sober brown and yellow, while some trees of the tenderer kind had been nipped by the frosts into brilliant dyes of orange, purple, and scarlet. Streaming files of wild ducks began to make their appearance high in the air; the bark of the squirrel might be heard from the groves of beech and hickory-nuts, and the pensive whistle of the quail at intervals from the neighboring stubble field.

The small birds were taking their farewell banquets. In the fullness of their revelry, they fluttered, chirping and frolicking from bush to bush, and tree to tree, capricious from the very profusion and variety around them. There was the honest cock robin, the favorite game of stripling sportsmen, with its loud querulous note; and the twittering blackbirds flying in sable clouds; and the golden-winged woodpecker with his crimson crest, his broad black gorget, and splendid plumage; and the cedar bird, with its red-tipt[1] wings and yellow-tipt tail and its little monteiro cap[2] of feathers; and the blue jay, that noisy coxcomb, in his gay light blue coat and white underclothes, screaming and chattering, nodding and bobbing and bowing, and pretending to be on good terms with every songster of the grove.

As Ichabod jogged slowly on his way, his eye, ever open to every symptom of culinary abundance, ranged with delight over the treasures of jolly autumn. On all sides he beheld vast store of apples; some hanging in oppressive opulence on the trees; some gathered into baskets and barrels for the market; others heaped up in rich piles for the cider-press. Farther on he beheld great fields of Indian corn, with its golden ears peeping from their leafy coverts, and holding out the promise of cakes and hasty-pudding; and the yellow pumpkins lying beneath them, turning up their fair round bellies to the sun, and giving ample prospects of the most luxurious of pies; and anon he passed the fragrant buckwheat fields breathing the odor of the beehive, and as he beheld them, soft anticipations stole over his mind of dainty slapjacks, well buttered,

---

1   tipt=tipped.

2   monteiro cap=montero (Spanish), a hunting cap with flaps; here referring to the crest of the cedar wax wing.

and garnished with honey or treacle, by the delicate little dimpled hand of Katrina Van Tassel.

Thus feeding his mind with many sweet thoughts and "sugared suppositions," he journeyed along the sides of a range of hills which look out upon some of the goodliest scenes of the mighty Hudson. The sun gradually wheeled his broad disk down in the west. The wide bosom of the Tappan Zee lay motionless and glassy, excepting that here and there a gentle undulation waved and prolonged the blue shadow of the distant mountain. A few amber clouds floated in the sky, without a breath of air to move them. The horizon was of a fine golden tint, changing gradually into a pure apple green, and from that into the deep blue of the mid-heaven. A slanting ray lingered on the woody crests of the precipices that overhung some parts of the river, giving greater depth to the dark gray and purple of their rocky sides.

A sloop was loitering in the distance, dropping slowly down with the tide, her sail hanging uselessly against the mast; and as the reflection of the sky gleamed along the still water, it seemed as if the vessel was suspended in the air.

It was toward evening that Ichabod arrived at the castle of the Heer Van Tassel, which he found thronged with the pride and flower of the adjacent country. Old farmers, a spare leathern-faced race, in homespun coats and breeches, blue stockings, huge shoes, and magnificent pewter buckles. Their brisk, withered little dames, in close-crimped caps, long-waisted short gowns, homespun petticoats, with scissors and pincushions, and gay calico pockets hanging on the outside. Buxom lasses, almost as antiquated as their mothers, excepting where a straw hat, a fine ribbon, or perhaps a white frock, gave symptoms of city innovation. The sons, in short square-skirted coats, with rows of stupendous brass buttons, and their hair generally queued in the fashion of the times, especially if they could procure an eel-skin for the purpose, it being esteemed throughout the country as a potent nourisher and strengthener of the hair.

Brom Bones, however, was the hero of the scene, having come to the gathering on his favorite steed Daredevil, a creature, like himself, full of mettle and mischief, and which no one but himself could manage. He was, in fact, noted for preferring vicious animals, given to all kinds of tricks which kept the rider in constant risk of his neck, for he held a tractable, well-broken horse as unworthy of a lad of spirit.

Fain would I pause[1] to dwell upon the world of charms that burst upon the enraptured gaze of my hero, as he entered the state parlor of Van Tassel's mansion. Not those of the bevy of buxom lasses, with their luxurious display of red and white; but the ample charms of a genuine Dutch country tea-table, in the sumptuous time of autumn. Such heaped up platters of cakes of various and almost indescribable kinds, known only to experienced Dutch housewives! There was the doughty doughnut, the tender oly koek [a cake fried in deep fat], and the crisp and crumbling cruller; sweet cakes and short

---

1   Fain would I pause=I would like to pause.

cakes, ginger cakes and honey cakes, and the whole family of cakes. And then there were apple pies, and peach pies, and pumpkin pies; besides slices of ham and smoked beef; and moreover delectable dishes of preserved plums, and peaches, and pears, and quinces; not to mention broiled shad and roasted chickens; together with bowls of milk and cream, all mingled higgledy-piggledy, pretty much as I have enumerated them, with the motherly teapot sending up its clouds of vapor from the midst—Heaven bless the mark! I want breath and time to discuss this banquet as it deserves, and am too eager to get on with my story. Happily, Ichabod Crane was not in so great a hurry as his historian, but did ample justice to every dainty.

He was a kind and thankful creature, whose heart dilated in proportion as his skin was filled with good cheer, and whose spirits rose with eating, as some men's do with drink. He could not help, too, rolling his large eyes round him as he ate, and chuckling with the possibility that he might one day be lord of all this scene of almost unimaginable luxury and splendor. Then, he thought, how soon he'd turn his back upon the old schoolhouse; snap his fingers in the face of Hans Van Ripper, and every other niggardly patron, and kick any itinerant pedagogue out of doors that should dare to call him comrade!

Old Baltus Van Tassel moved about among his guests with a face dilated with content and good humor, round and jolly as the harvest moon. His hospitable attentions were brief, but expressive, being confined to a shake of the hand, a slap on the shoulder, a loud laugh, and a pressing invitation to "fall to, and help themselves."

And now the sound of the music from the common room, or hall, summoned to the dance. The musician was an old gray-headed negro, who had been the itinerant orchestra of the neighborhood for more than half a century. His instrument was as old and battered as himself. The greater part of the time he scraped on two or three strings, accompanying every movement of the bow with a motion of the head; bowing almost to the ground, and stamping with his foot whenever a fresh couple were to start.

Ichabod prided himself upon his dancing as much as upon his vocal powers. Not a limb, not a fibre about him was idle; and to have seen his loosely hung frame in full motion, and clattering about the room, you would have thought St. Vitus[1] himself, that blessed patron of the dance, was figuring before you in person. He was the admiration of all the negroes; who, having gathered, of all ages and sizes, from the farm and the neighborhood, stood forming a pyramid of shining black faces at every door and window, gazing with delight at the scene, rolling their white eyeballs, and showing grinning rows of ivory from ear to ear. How could the flogger of urchins be otherwise than animated and joyous? The lady of his heart was his partner in the dance, and smiling graciously in reply to all his amorous oglings; while Brom Bones, sorely smitten with love and jealousy, sat brooding by himself in one corner.

---

1   "St. Vitus' dance" is a nervous disorder, characterized by involuntary twitching.

When the dance was at an end, Ichabod was attracted to a knot of the sager folks, who, with Old Van Tassel, sat smoking at one end of the piazza, gossiping over former times, and drawing out long stories about the war.

This neighborhood, at the time of which I am speaking, was one of those highly favored places which abound with chronicle and great men. The British and American line had run near it during the war; it had, therefore, been the scene of marauding and infested with refugees, cowboys, and all kinds of border chivalry. Just sufficient time had elapsed to enable each storyteller to dress up his tale with a little becoming fiction, and, in the indistinctness of his recollection, to make himself the hero of every exploit.

There was the story of Doffue Martling, a large blue-bearded Dutchman, who had nearly taken a British frigate with an old iron nine-pounder from a mud breastwork, only that his gun burst at the sixth discharge. And there was an old gentleman who shall be nameless, being too rich a mynheer[1] to be lightly mentioned, who, in the battle of White Plains, being an excellent master of defence, parried a musket-ball with a small sword, insomuch that he absolutely felt it whiz round the blade, and glance off at the hilt; in proof of which he was ready at any time to show the sword, with the hilt a little bent. There were several more that had been equally great in the field, not one of whom but was persuaded that he had a considerable hand in bringing the war to a happy termination.

But all these were nothing to the tales of ghosts and apparitions that succeeded. The neighborhood is rich in legendary treasures of the kind. Local tales and superstitions thrive best in these sheltered, long-settled retreats; but are trampled under foot by the shifting throng that forms the population of most of our country places. Besides, there is no encouragement for ghosts in most of our villages, for they have scarcely had time to finish their first nap and turn themselves in their graves, before their surviving friends have travelled away from the neighborhood; so that when they turn out at night to walk their rounds, they have no acquaintance left to call upon. This is perhaps the reason why we so seldom hear of ghosts except in our long-established Dutch communities.

The immediate cause, however, of the prevalence of supernatural stories in these parts, was doubtless owing to the vicinity of Sleepy Hollow. There was a contagion in the very air that blew from that haunted region; it breathed forth an atmosphere of dreams and fancies infecting all the land. Several of the Sleepy Hollow people were present at Van Tassel's, and, as usual, were doling out their wild and wonderful legends. Many dismal tales were told about funeral trains, and mourning cries and wailings heard and seen about the great tree where the unfortunate Major André was taken, and which stood in the neighborhood. Some mention was made also of the woman in white, that haunted the dark glen at Raven Rock, and was often heard to shriek on winter nights before a storm, having perished there in the snow. The chief part of the stories,

---

1   mynheer=mister or sir.

however, turned upon the favorite specter of Sleepy Hollow, the Headless Horseman, who had been heard several times of late, patrolling the country; and, it was said, tethered his horse nightly among the graves in the churchyard.

The sequestered situation of this church seems always to have made it a favorite haunt of troubled spirits. It stands on a knoll, surrounded by locust-trees and lofty elms, from among which its decent, whitewashed walls shine modestly forth, like Christian purity beaming through the shades of retirement. A gentle slope descends from it to a silver sheet of water, bordered by high trees, between which, peeps may be caught at the blue hills of the Hudson. To look upon its grass-grown yard, where the sunbeams seem to sleep so quietly, one would think that there at least the dead might rest in peace. On one side of the church extends a wide woody dell, along which raves a large brook among broken rocks and trunks of fallen trees.

Over a deep black part of the stream, not far from the church, was formerly thrown a wooden bridge; the road that led to it, and the bridge itself, were thickly shaded by overhanging trees, which cast a gloom about it, even in the daytime; but occasioned a fearful darkness at night. Such was one of the favorite haunts of the Headless Horseman, and the place where he was most frequently encountered. The tale was told of old Brouwer, a most heretical disbeliever in ghosts, how he met the Horseman returning from his foray into Sleepy Hollow, and was obliged to get up behind him; how they galloped over bush and brake, over hill and swamp, until they reached the bridge; when the Horseman suddenly turned into a skeleton, threw old Brouwer into the brook, and sprang away over the tree-tops with a clap of thunder.

This story was immediately matched by a thrice marvelous adventure of Brom Bones, who made light of the Galloping Hessian as an arrant jockey[1]. He affirmed that on returning one night from the neighboring village of Sing Sing, he had been overtaken by this midnight trooper; that he had offered to race with him for a bowl of punch, and should have won it too, for Daredevil beat the goblin horse all hollow, but just as they came to the church bridge, the Hessian bolted, and vanished in a flash of fire.

All these tales, told in that drowsy undertone with which men talk in the dark, the countenances of the listeners only now and then receiving a casual gleam from the glare of a pipe, sank deep in the mind of Ichabod. He repaid them in kind with large extracts from his invaluable author, Cotton Mather, and added many marvelous events that had taken place in his native State of Connecticut, and fearful sights which he had seen in his nightly walks about Sleepy Hollow.

The revel now gradually broke up. The old farmers gathered together their families in their wagons, and were heard for some time rattling along the hollow roads, and over the distant hills. Some of the damsels mounted on pillions behind their favorite swains,

---

1   Current slang: a cheat or a trickster.

and their light-hearted laughter, mingling with the clatter of hoofs, echoed along the silent woodlands, sounding fainter and fainter, until they gradually died away, —and the late scene of noise and frolic was all silent and deserted. Ichabod only lingered behind, according to the custom of country lovers, to have a tête-à-tête with the heiress; fully convinced that he was now on the high road to success. What passed at this interview I will not pretend to say, for in fact I do not know. Something, however, I fear me[1], must have gone wrong, for he certainly sallied forth, after no very great interval, with an air quite desolate and chapfallen. Oh, these women! these women! Could that girl have been playing off any of her coquettish tricks? Was her encouragement of the poor pedagogue all a mere sham to secure her conquest of his rival? Heaven only knows, not I! Let it suffice to say, Ichabod stole forth with the air of one who had been sacking a henroost, rather than a fair lady's heart. Without looking to the right or left to notice the scene of rural wealth, on which he had so often gloated, he went straight to the stable, and with several hearty cuffs and kicks roused his steed most uncourteously from the comfortable quarters in which he was soundly sleeping, dreaming of mountains of corn and oats, and whole valleys of timothy and clover.

It was the very witching time of night that Ichabod, heavy-hearted and crestfallen, pursued his travels homewards, along the sides of the lofty hills which rise above Tarry Town, and which he had traversed so cheerily in the afternoon. The hour was as dismal as himself. Far below him the Tappan Zee spread its dusky and indistinct waste of waters, with here and there the tall mast of a sloop, riding quietly at anchor under the land. In the dead hush of midnight, he could even hear the barking of the watchdog from the opposite shore of the Hudson; but it was so vague and faint as only to give an idea of his distance from this faithful companion of man. Now and then, too, the long-drawn crowing of a cock, accidentally awakened, would sound far, far off, from some farmhouse away among the hills—but it was like a dreaming sound in his ear. No signs of life occurred near him, but occasionally the melancholy chirp of a cricket, or perhaps the guttural twang of a bullfrog from a neighboring marsh, as if sleeping uncomfortably and turning suddenly in his bed.

All the stories of ghosts and goblins that he had heard in the afternoon now came crowding upon his recollection. The night grew darker and darker; the stars seemed to sink deeper in the sky, and driving clouds occasionally hid them from his sight. He had never felt so lonely and dismal. He was, moreover, approaching the very place where many of the scenes of the ghost stories had been laid.

In the center of the road stood an enormous tulip-tree, which towered like a giant above all the other trees of the neighborhood, and formed a kind of landmark. Its limbs were gnarled and fantastic, large enough to form trunks for ordinary trees, twisting down almost to the earth, and rising again into the air. It was connected with the

---

1   I fear me=I'm afraid.

tragical story of the unfortunate André, who had been taken prisoner hard by; and was universally known by the name of Major André's tree. The common people regarded it with a mixture of respect and superstition, partly out of sympathy for the fate of its ill-starred namesake, and partly from the tales of strange sights, and doleful lamentations, told concerning it.

As Ichabod approached this fearful tree, he began to whistle; he thought his whistle was answered; it was but a blast sweeping sharply through the dry branches. As he approached a little nearer, he thought he saw something white, hanging in the midst of the tree: he paused and ceased whistling but, on looking more narrowly, perceived that it was a place where the tree had been scathed by lightning, and the white wood laid bare. Suddenly he heard a groan—his teeth chattered, and his knees smote against the saddle: it was but the rubbing of one huge bough upon another, as they were swayed about by the breeze. He passed the tree in safety, but new perils lay before him.

About two hundred yards from the tree, a small brook crossed the road, and ran into a marshy and thickly-wooded glen, known by the name of Wiley's Swamp. A few rough logs, laid side by side, served for a bridge over this stream. On that side of the road where the brook entered the wood, a group of oaks and chestnuts, matted thick with wild grape-vines, threw a cavernous gloom over it. To pass this bridge was the severest trial. It was at this identical spot that the unfortunate André was captured, and under the covert of those chestnuts and vines were the sturdy yeomen concealed who surprised him. This has ever since been considered a haunted stream, and fearful are the feelings of the schoolboy who has to pass it alone after dark.

As he approached the stream, his heart began to thump; he summoned up, however, all his resolution, gave his horse half a score of kicks in the ribs, and attempted to dash briskly across the bridge; but instead of starting forward, the perverse old animal made a lateral movement, and ran broadside against the fence.

Ichabod, whose fears increased with the delay, jerked the reins on the other side, and kicked lustily with the contrary foot: it was all in vain; his steed started, it is true, but it was only to plunge to the opposite side of the road into a thicket of brambles and alder bushes. The schoolmaster now bestowed both whip and heel upon the starveling ribs of old Gunpowder, who dashed forward, snuffling and snorting, but came to a stand just by the bridge, with a suddenness that had nearly sent his rider sprawling over his head. Just at this moment a plashy tramp by the side of the bridge caught the sensitive ear of Ichabod. In the dark shadow of the grove, on the margin of the brook, he beheld something huge, misshapen and towering. It stirred not, but seemed gathered up in the gloom, like some gigantic monster ready to spring upon the travelers.

The hair of the affrighted pedagogue rose upon his head with terror. What was to be done? To turn and fly was now too late; and besides, what chance was there of escaping ghost or goblin, if such it was, which could ride upon the wings of the wind? Summoning up, therefore, a show of courage, he demanded in stammering accents,

"Who are you?" He received no reply. He repeated his demand in a still more agitated voice. Still there was no answer. Once more he cudgelled the sides of the inflexible Gunpowder, and, shutting his eyes, broke forth with involuntary fervor into a psalm tune. Just then the shadowy object of alarm put itself in motion, and with a scramble and a bound stood at once in the middle of the road. Though the night was dark and dismal, yet the form of the unknown might now in some degree be ascertained. He appeared to be a horseman of large dimensions, and mounted on a black horse of powerful frame. He made no offer of molestation or sociability, but kept aloof on one side of the road, jogging along on the blind side of old Gunpowder, who had now got over his fright and waywardness.

Ichabod, who had no relish for this strange midnight companion, and bethought himself of the adventure of Brom Bones with the Galloping Hessian, now quickened his steed in hopes of leaving him behind. The stranger, however, quickened his horse to an equal pace. Ichabod pulled up, and fell into a walk, thinking to lag behind, the other did the same. His heart began to sink within him; he endeavored to resume his psalm tune, but his parched tongue clove to the roof of his mouth, and he could not utter a stave. There was something in the moody and dogged silence of this pertinacious companion that was mysterious and appalling. It was soon fearfully accounted for.

On mounting a rising ground, which brought the figure of his fellow-travelers in relief against the sky, gigantic in height, and muffled in a cloak, Ichabod was horror-struck on perceiving that he was headless! —but his horror was still more increased on observing that the head, which should have rested on his shoulders, was carried before him on the pommel of his saddle! His terror rose to desperation; he rained a shower of kicks and blows upon Gunpowder, hoping by a sudden movement to give his companion the slip; but the specter started full jump with him. Away, then, they dashed through thick and thin; stones flying and sparks flashing at every bound. Ichabod's flimsy garments fluttered in the air, as he stretched his long lank body away over his horse's head, in the eagerness of his flight.

They had now reached the road which turns off to Sleepy Hollow; but Gunpowder, who seemed possessed with a demon, instead of keeping up it, made an opposite turn, and plunged headlong downhill to the left. This road leads through a sandy hollow shaded by trees for about a quarter of a mile, where it crosses the bridge famous in goblin story; and just beyond swells the green knoll on which stands the whitewashed church.

As yet the panic of the steed had given his unskillful rider an apparent advantage in the chase, but just as he had got half way through the hollow, the girths of the saddle gave way, and he felt it slipping from under him. He seized it by the pommel, and endeavored to hold it firm, but in vain; and had just time to save himself by clasping old Gunpowder round the neck, when the saddle fell to the earth, and he heard it trampled underfoot by his pursuer. For a moment the terror of Hans Van Ripper's wrath passed across his mind, —for it was his Sunday saddle; but this was no time for petty fears; the goblin was hard on his haunches; and (unskillful rider that he was!) he had much ado to maintain his seat; sometimes slipping on one side, sometimes on another, and sometimes jolted on the high ridge of his horse's backbone, with a violence that he verily feared would cleave him asunder.

An opening in the trees now cheered him with the hopes that the church bridge was at hand. The wavering reflection of a silver star in the bosom of the brook told him that he was not mistaken. He saw the walls of the church dimly glaring under the trees beyond. He recollected the place where Brom Bones's ghostly competitor had disappeared.

"If I can but reach that bridge," thought Ichabod, "I am safe." Just then he heard the black steed panting and blowing close behind him; he even fancied that he felt his hot breath. Another convulsive kick in the ribs, and old Gunpowder sprang upon the bridge; he thundered over the resounding planks; he gained the opposite side; and now Ichabod cast a look behind to see if his pursuer should vanish, according to rule, in a flash of fire and brimstone. Just then he saw the goblin rising in his stirrups, and in the very act of hurling his head at him. Ichabod endeavored to dodge the horrible missile, but too late. It encountered his cranium with a tremendous crash, —he was tumbled headlong into the dust, and Gunpowder, the black steed, and the goblin rider, passed by like a whirlwind.

The next morning the old horse was found without his saddle, and with the bridle under his feet, soberly cropping the grass at his master's gate. Ichabod did not make his appearance at breakfast; dinner-hour came, but no Ichabod. The boys assembled at the schoolhouse, and strolled idly about the banks of the brook; but no schoolmaster. Hans Van Ripper now began to feel some uneasiness about the fate of poor Ichabod, and his saddle. An inquiry was set on foot, and after diligent investigation they came upon his traces. In one part of the road leading to the church was found the saddle trampled in the dirt; the tracks of horses' hoofs deeply dented in the road, and evidently at furious speed, were traced to the bridge, beyond which, on the bank of a broad part of the brook, where the water ran deep and black, was found the hat of the unfortunate Ichabod, and close beside it a shattered pumpkin.

The brook was searched, but the body of the schoolmaster was not to be discovered. Hans Van Ripper as executor of his estate, examined the bundle which contained all his worldly effects. They consisted of two shirts and a half; two stocks for the neck; a pair or two of worsted stockings; an old pair of corduroy small-clothes; a rusty razor; a book of psalm tunes full of dog's-ears; and a broken pitch-pipe. As to the books and furniture of the schoolhouse, they belonged to the community, excepting Cotton Mather's "History of Witchcraft", a "New England Almanac", and a book of dreams and fortune-telling; in which last was a sheet of foolscap much scribbled and blotted in several fruitless attempts to make a copy of verses in honor of the heiress of Van Tassel.

These magic books and the poetic scrawl were forthwith consigned to the flames by Hans Van Ripper; who, from that time forward, determined to send his children no more to school, observing that he never knew any good come of this same reading and writing. Whatever money the schoolmaster possessed, and he had received his quarter's pay but a day or two before, he must have had about his person at the time of his disappearance.

The mysterious event caused much speculation at the church on the following Sunday. Knots of gazers and gossips were collected in the churchyard, at the bridge, and at the spot where the hat and pumpkin had been found. The stories of Brouwer, of Bones, and a whole budget of others were called to mind; and when they had diligently considered them all, and compared them with the symptoms of the present case, they shook their heads, and came to the conclusion that Ichabod had been carried off by the Galloping Hessian. As he was a bachelor, and in nobody's debt, nobody troubled his head any more about him; the school was removed to a different quarter of the hollow, and another pedagogue reigned in his stead.

It is true, an old farmer, who had been down to New York on a visit several years after, and from whom this account of the ghostly adventure was received, brought home the intelligence that Ichabod Crane was still alive; that he had left the neighborhood partly through fear of the goblin and Hans Van Ripper, and partly in mortification at having been suddenly dismissed by the heiress; that he had changed his quarters to a distant part of the country; had kept school and studied law at the same time; had been admitted to the bar; turned politician; electioneered; written for the newspapers; and finally had been made a justice of the Ten Pound Court[1]. Brom Bones, too, who, shortly after his rival's disappearance conducted the blooming Katrina in triumph to the altar, was observed to look exceedingly knowing whenever the story of Ichabod was related, and always burst into a hearty laugh at the mention of the pumpkin; which led some to suspect that he knew more about the matter than he chose to tell.

The old country wives, however, who are the best judges of these matters, maintain to this day that Ichabod was spirited away by supernatural means; and it is a favorite story often told about the neighborhood round the winter evening fire. The bridge became more than ever an object of superstitious awe; and that may be the reason why the road has been altered of late years, so as to approach the church by the border of the millpond. The schoolhouse being deserted soon fell to decay, and was reported to be haunted by the ghost of the unfortunate pedagogue and the plowboy, loitering homeward of a still summer evening, has often fancied his voice at a distance, chanting a melancholy psalm tune among the tranquil solitudes of Sleepy Hollow.

---

1   A petty magistrate's court, limited to cases involving no more than £10.

Plot Summary

"The Legend of Sleepy Hollow" tells the story of Ichabod Crane, a superstitious schoolmaster who moves to the small town of Sleepy Hollow in the Hudson Valley of New York. Ichabod is a superstitious man who believes in ghosts and superstitions, and he is soon confronted with the legend of the Headless Horseman, a ghostly figure who is said to haunt the area. Ichabod is also in competition for the affections of the beautiful Katrina Van Tassel, the daughter of a wealthy farmer. She is also pursued by the town's rowdy young men, including the handsome and wealthy Brom Bones. Brom is determined to win Katrina's heart, and he uses the legend of the Headless Horseman to scare Ichabod away. One night, Ichabod is riding home from a party at the Van Tassel's when he is chased by the Headless Horseman. He is terrified and manages to escape, but his hat and a shattered pumpkin are found the next day. Ichabod is never seen again, and the townspeople believe that he was taken by the Headless Horseman.

Language Exercises

Choose the item that best replaces or explains the underlined part of the sentence.

1. If ever I should wish for a retreat whither I might steal from the world and its distractions, and dream quietly away the <u>remnant</u> of a troubled life, I know of none more promising than this little valley.

   A. replicate   B. reminiscence   C. remains   D. reign

2. His haunts are not confined to the valley, but extend at times to the adjacent roads, and especially to the <u>vicinity</u> of a church at no great distance.

   A. conjunction   B. cover   C. far-reaching   D. nearby region

3. … and on holiday afternoons would <u>convoy</u> some of the smaller one's home, who happened to have pretty sisters, or good housewives for mothers, noted for the comforts of the cupboard.

   A. escort   B. discharge   C. delegate   D. assemble

4. Thus, by divers little makeshifts, in that <u>ingenious</u> way which is commonly denominated "by hook and by crook", the worthy pedagogue got on tolerably enough, and was thought, by all who understood nothing of the labor of headwork, to have a wonderfully easy life of it.

   A. visionary   B. cunning   C. promising   D. genuine

5. How often did he shrink with curdling awe at the sound of his own steps on the frosty crust beneath his feet; and <u>dread</u> to look over his shoulder, lest he should behold some uncouth being tramping close behind him!

   A. frightened   B. sacred   C. respectable   D. oncoming

6. The pedagogue's mouth watered as he looked upon this <u>sumptuous</u> promise of

luxurious winter fare.

    A. picturesque   B. tedious   C. grand   D. torrential

7. He was famed for great knowledge and skill in horsemanship, being as <u>dexterous</u> on horseback as a Tartar.

    A. clumsy   B. vigilant   C. skillful   D. arduous

8. Such was the formidable rival with whom Ichabod Crane had to contend, and, considering all things, a <u>stouter</u> man than he would have shrunk from the competition, and a wiser man would have despaired.

    A. more masculine   B. more stubborn

    C. more determined   D. more chivalric

9. To have taken the field openly against his rival would have been madness; for he was not a man to be <u>thwarted</u> in his amours, any more than that stormy lover, Achilles.

    A. defeated   B. indulged   C. immersed   D. addicted

10. A small wool hat rested on the top of his nose, for so his scanty strip of forehead might be called, and the skirts of his black coat <u>fluttered</u> out almost to the horses tail.

    A. hang loosely   B. fly highly

    C. shine brightly   D. move lightly and quickly

11. The small birds were taking their farewell banquets. In the fullness of their revelry, they fluttered, chirping and frolicking from bush to bush, and tree to tree, <u>capricious</u> from the very profusion and variety around them.

    A. intriguing   B. formidable   C. changeable   D. predictable

12. He was a kind and thankful creature, whose heart <u>dilated</u> in proportion as his skin was filled with good cheer, and whose spirits rose with eating, as some men's do with drink.

    A. expanded   B. pumped   C. vibrated   D. accumulated

13. The immediate cause, however, of the <u>prevalence</u> of supernatural stories in these parts, was doubtless owing to the vicinity of Sleepy Hollow.

    A. simplicity   B. serenity   C. prosperity   D. popularity

14. The <u>sequestered</u> situation of this church seems always to have made it a favorite haunt of troubled spirits.

    A. suppressed   B. tranquil   C. secluded   D. discarded

15. The next morning the old horse was found without his saddle, and with the bridle under his feet, <u>soberly</u> cropping the grass at his master's gate.

    A. calmly and leisurely   B. solitarily

    C. impatiently   D. abruptly

Topics for Discussion

1. Discuss the characters of Ichabod Crane and Brom Bones.

2.   Some critics say that as the sturdy Brom Bones competes with the ambitious schoolmaster, Ichabod Crane, for the love of Katrian Van Tassel, Irving emphasizes two underlying sets of values that are inherently in conflict. What do you think are the two underlying sets of values that are inherently in conflict? Find proofs in the fiction to certify your ideas.

3.   How do you understand Irving's skillful use of the supernatural in the story?

4.   Humor abounds in the story. Can you find some examples to illustrate this point?

5.   Comment on the writing style of the fiction.

6.   What is the theme of "The Legend of Sleepy Hollow"?

7.   One of the most striking features of the story is the long passages of rich descriptive details. Find some examples to illustrate this point.

8.   Explore the various aspects of the evil in Ichabod Crane's personality and actions that necessitates Ichabod's eventual expulsion from the community.

9.   Research the status of African Americans in New York during the end of the eighteenth century. Analyze Irving's casual disrespect for the "Negro" characters in his story in terms of how his contemporary readers would have responded to it, and in terms of how modern readers might respond.

10. Find a copy of "The Castle of Indolence", a poem from 1748 written by the Scottish poet James Thomson. Why might Irving have attached four lines of this poem to his own story? What do the two pieces have in common?

Discussion Tips

"The Legend of Sleepy Hollow" is set in the quaint rural valley of Sleepy Hollow, New York, nestled near Tarry Town in the picturesque Catskill Mountains. This timeless tale, inspired by German folklore but uniquely American in its setting, delves into the classic conflict between urban and rural life, and between intellect and physical strength. Ichabod Crane's courtship of Katrina Van Tassel is disrupted by his rival, Brom Bones, who cleverly disguises himself as the menacing headless horseman to frighten Crane away. The story showcases Washington Irving's renowned humor and his gift for creating vivid, evocative imagery.

A prevalent theme in American literature and folklore is the clash between the city and the countryside, civilization and the untamed wilderness. This dichotomy is often portrayed in two contrasting ways: the city as a bastion of beauty, wealth, cleanliness, and safety, with the country depicted as rugged, dirty, and perilous; or the city as a den of deceit and danger, inhabited by swindlers preying on the gentle denizens of the idyllic countryside. In the folklore of nineteenth-century America, the latter interpretation often takes precedence. Settlers took pride in the untamed wilderness and reveled in its challenges, and their stories celebrated the skills and qualities necessary for survival on the frontier.

Irving skillfully crafts a confrontation between these opposing forces, and it is clear to any reader of American folklore how the conflict will unfold. Crane's erudition pales in comparison to Brom's natural wit, his slight frame and clumsy horsemanship no match for Brom's strength and skill. Ultimately, Katrina chooses the rugged and robust Brom over the refined and delicate Crane. Neither man is inherently unlikable, but in the context of a young country with a wild frontier to be conquered, the values of the countryside triumph over those of the city.

"The Legend of Sleepy Hollow" serves as a microcosm of the broader American ethos, reflecting the nation's reverence for the untamed wilderness and the rugged, self-reliant spirit it engenders. It embodies the enduring narrative of the triumph of the rural over the urban, the strength of the wilderness over the trappings of civilization, and the celebration of the qualities needed to thrive in the vast, uncharted expanses of the American frontier.

Unit 2
Edgar Allen Poe: "The Fall of the House of Usher"

About the Author

Edgar Allen Poe (1809–1849)

Edgar Allan Poe was an American writer, poet, editor, and literary critic. He is best known for his poetry and short stories, particularly his tales of mystery and the macabre. He is widely regarded as a central figure of Romanticism in the United States and of American literature as a whole, and he was one of the country's earliest practitioners of the short story. He is also generally considered the inventor of the detective fiction genre. Poe was born in Boston, Massachusetts, in 1809 to two traveling actors. He was orphaned at the age of two and was taken in by John and Frances Allan of Richmond, Virginia. He attended the University of Virginia for one semester but left due to lack of money. After enlisting in the Army and later failing as an officer's cadet at West Point, he began to focus on his writing career. Poe's works, which combined elements of horror, mystery, and the macabre, were greatly influential in both literature and popular culture. He is also credited with contributing to the emerging genre of science fiction. His most famous works include the poem "The Raven" (1845) and the short stories "The Pit and the Pendulum" (1842), "The Tell-Tale Heart" (1843), and "The Cask of Amontillado" (1846). Poe died in Baltimore, Maryland, in 1849 at the age of 40. His cause of death is disputed and has been variously attributed to alcohol, drugs, cholera, rabies, suicide, and other agents.

The Literary History

Allen Poe and the American Short Story

Edgar Allan Poe was an American writer, poet, and critic of the early 19th century who is best known for his Gothic horror stories and is often credited as having helped to popularize the short story form in American literature. His contributions to American literature, particularly the American short story, were significant, and his impact on subsequent writers and popular culture has been enduring.

Poe's contribution to the development of the American short story cannot be overstated. During his lifetime, the short story was not considered a significant genre in American literature. However, Poe's imaginative and macabre tales, like "The Fall of the House of Usher", "The Cask of Amontillado", and "The Murders in the Rue Morgue", revolutionized the form and earned him a reputation as a master of the craft.

One of the key elements of Poe's success was his unique style of writing. He often used unconventional narrative techniques, such as non-linear storytelling, to create tension and suspense in his stories. He also employed vivid imagery and metaphors to evoke emotions and create a sense of atmosphere. Poe's use of suspense and horror in his writing was particularly influential, leading many later writers to imitate his style.

Poe's influence on the American short story can also be seen in his emphasis on psychological realism. In many of his stories, he explored the inner workings of the human mind, focusing on themes like guilt, obsession, and insanity. Indeed, his story "The Tell-Tale Heart" is often seen as one of the first examples of psychological horror in American literature. This emphasis on the inner workings of the mind would be echoed in the works of later writers, like Herman Melville and William Faulkner.

Poe also helped create the modern detective story with "The Murders in the Rue Morgue", which introduced the character of C. Auguste Dupin, a brilliant detective who uses logic and deduction to solve crimes. This story is often regarded as the first of its kind, and it inspired many later writers, including Sir Arthur Conan Doyle, who created the iconic detective Sherlock Holmes.

Finally, Poe's influence can be seen in the way he inspired subsequent writers to experiment with the short story form. His use of narrative structure and imagery inspired writers like Nathaniel Hawthorne, who experimented with allegory and symbolism in his stories. More contemporary writers, like Gabriel Garcia Marquez, also cite Poe as an influence, particularly in his use of magical realism.

Literary Terms

Gothic romance

Gothic romance is a type of prose fiction which was inaugurated by Horace Walpole's *The Castle of Otranto: A Gothic Story* (1764), and flourished through the early nineteenth century. It is a genre of romantic literature that combines elements of horror and suspense with romance. It typically involves a mysterious atmosphere, dark settings, and characters who are troubled by their pasts. It often focuses on themes of forbidden love, death, and the supernatural.

Unity of effect

In his review of Hawthorne's Twice-Told Tales, Poe advocated his writing strategy "unity of effect" as he wrote: "We need only here say, upon this topic that, in almost all classes of composition, the unity of effect or impression is a point of the greatest importance. It is clear, moreover, that, this unity cannot be thoroughly preserved in productions whose perusal cannot be completed at one setting." The short story must be of such length as to be read at one sitting (brevity), so as to ensure the totality of impression. No word should be used which does not contribute to the "pre-established" design of the work. Short story should be of brevity, totality, single effect, compression and finality. Allen Poe's "unity of effect" is the idea that a work of literature should have a single, unified emotional effect on the reader. He believed that this effect should be created by the use of carefully chosen words, images, and structure.

Aestheticism

Aestheticism refers to a philosophical and artistic movement that emerged in the late 19th century. It is characterized by the pursuit of beauty and the rejection of traditional morality and social norms. Aestheticism is closely associated with the works of Oscar Wilde, who was a leading figure in the movement. At its core, Aestheticism is a celebration of beauty, art, and the pleasures of the senses. It is a rejection of the idea that art should have a moral or social purpose, and that it should be used to convey a message or serve a particular agenda. Instead, Aestheticism sees art as an end in itself, and values it for its intrinsic beauty and aesthetic qualities. Aestheticism is also characterized by a certain decadence and a rejection of conventional values. This can be seen in the movement's emphasis on luxury, extravagance, and hedonism. Aestheticism celebrates the pleasures of life and the pursuit of beauty, and sees these as the ultimate goals of human existence. The art produced by Aestheticism is also characterized by certain features. These include a focus on form over content, an emphasis on beauty and decoration, and a preference for exotic and sensual subjects. Aestheticism also often incorporates symbolism and allusion into its works.

The Story

The Fall of the House of Usher[1]

Son cœur est un luth suspendu;
Sitôt qu'on le touche il résonne.

— De Béranger

During the whole of a dull, dark, and soundless day in the autumn of the year, when the clouds hung oppressively low in the heavens, I had been passing alone, on

---

1   Edgar Allan Poe, *Tales of the Grotesque and Arabesque* (Dover Publications, 2001), pp. 1–20.

horseback, through a singularly dreary tract of country, and at length found myself, as the shades of the evening drew on, within view of the melancholy House of Usher. I know not how it was—but, with the first glimpse of the building, a sense of insufferable gloom pervaded my spirit. I say insufferable; for the feeling was unrelieved by any of that half-pleasurable, because poetic, sentiment, with which the mind usually receives even the sternest natural images of the desolate or terrible. I looked upon the scene before me—upon the mere house, and the simple landscape features of the domain— upon the bleak walls—upon the vacant eye-like windows—upon a few rank sedges— and upon a few white trunks of decayed trees—with an utter depression of soul which I can compare to no earthly sensation more properly than to the after-dream of the reveller upon opium—the bitter lapse into every-day life—the hideous dropping off of the veil. There was an iciness, a sinking, a sickening of the heart—an unredeemed dreariness of thought which no goading of the imagination could torture into aught of the sublime. What was it—I paused to think—what was it that so unnerved me in the contemplation of the House of Usher? It was a mystery all insoluble; nor could I grapple with the shadowy fancies that crowded upon me as I pondered. I was forced to fall back upon the unsatisfactory conclusion, that while, beyond doubt, there *are* combinations of very simple natural objects which have the power of thus affecting us, still the analysis of this power lies among considerations beyond our depth. It was possible, I reflected, that a mere different arrangement of the particulars of the scene, of the details of the picture, would be sufficient to modify, or perhaps to annihilate its capacity for sorrowful impression; and, acting upon this idea, I reined my horse to the precipitous brink of a black and lurid tarn that lay in unruffled lustre by the dwelling, and gazed down—but with a shudder even more thrilling than before—upon the re-modelled and inverted images of the gray sedge, and the ghastly tree-stems, and the vacant and eye-like windows.

Nevertheless, in this mansion of gloom I now proposed to myself a sojourn of some weeks. Its proprietor, Roderick Usher, had been one of my boon companions in boyhood; but many years had elapsed since our last meeting. A letter, however, had lately reached me in a distant part of the country—a letter from him—which, in its wildly importunate nature, had admitted of no other than a personal reply. The MS. gave evidence of nervous agitation. The writer spoke of acute bodily illness—of a mental disorder which oppressed him—and of an earnest desire to see me, as his best and indeed his only personal friend, with a view of attempting, by the cheerfulness of my society, some alleviation of his malady. It was the manner in which all this, and much more, was said—it was the apparent *heart* that went with his request—which allowed me no room for hesitation; and I accordingly obeyed forthwith what I still considered a very singular summons.

Although, as boys, we had been even intimate associates, yet I really knew little of my friend. His reserve had been always excessive and habitual. I was aware, however, that his very ancient family had been noted, time out of mind, for a peculiar sensibility of temperament, displaying itself, through long ages, in many works of exalted art, and manifested, of late, in repeated deeds of munificent yet unobtrusive charity, as well as in a passionate devotion to the intricacies, perhaps even more than to the orthodox and easily recognizable beauties, of musical science. I had learned, too, the very remarkable fact, that the stem of the Usher race, all time-honored as it was, had put forth, at no period, any enduring branch; in other words, that the entire family lay in the direct line of descent, and had always, with very trifling and very temporary variation, so lain. It was this deficiency, I considered, while running over in thought the perfect keeping of the character of the premises with the accredited character of the people, and while speculating upon the possible influence which the one, in the long lapse of centuries, might have exercised upon the other—it was this deficiency, perhaps, of collateral issue, and the consequent undeviating transmission, from sire to son, of the patrimony with the name, which had, at length, so identified the two as to merge the original title of the estate in the quaint and equivocal appellation of the "House of Usher"—an appellation which seemed to include, in the minds of the peasantry who used it, both the family and the family mansion.

I have said that the sole effect of my somewhat childish experiment—that of looking down within the tarn—had been to deepen the first singular impression. There can be no doubt that the consciousness of the rapid increase of my superstition—for why should I not so term it? —served mainly to accelerate the increase itself. Such, I have long known, is the paradoxical law of all sentiments having terror as a basis. And it might have been for this reason only, that, when I again uplifted my eyes to the house itself, from its image in the pool, there grew in my mind a strange fancy—a fancy so ridiculous, indeed, that I but mention it to show the vivid force of the sensations which oppressed me. I had so worked upon my imagination as really to believe that about the whole mansion and domain there hung an atmosphere peculiar to themselves and their immediate vicinity—an atmosphere which had no affinity with the air of heaven, but which had reeked up from the decayed trees, and the gray wall, and the silent tarn—a pestilent and mystic vapor, dull, sluggish, faintly discernible, and leaden-hued.

Shaking off from my spirit what *must* have been a dream, I scanned more narrowly the real aspect of the building. Its principal feature seemed to be that of an excessive antiquity. The discoloration of ages had been great. Minute fungi overspread the whole exterior, hanging in a fine tangled web-work from the eaves. Yet all this was apart from any extraordinary dilapidation. No portion of the masonry had fallen; and there appeared to be a wild inconsistency between its still perfect adaptation of parts, and the crumbling condition of the individual stones. In this there was much that reminded me of the specious totality of old wood-work which has rotted for long years in some neglected vault, with no disturbance from the breath of the external air. Beyond this indication of extensive decay, however, the fabric gave little token of instability.

36

Perhaps the eye of a scrutinizing observer might have discovered a barely perceptible fissure, which, extending from the roof of the building in front, made its way down the wall in a zigzag direction, until it became lost in the sullen waters of the tarn.

Noticing these things, I rode over a short causeway to the house. A servant in waiting took my horse, and I entered the Gothic archway of the hall. A valet, of stealthy step, thence conducted me, in silence, through many dark and intricate passages in my progress to the *studio* of his master. Much that I encountered on the way contributed, I know not how, to heighten the vague sentiments of which I have already spoken. While the objects around me—while the carvings of the ceilings, the sombre tapestries of the walls, the ebony blackness of the floors, and the phantasmagoric armorial trophies which rattled as I strode, were but matters to which, or to such as which, I had been accustomed from my infancy—while I hesitated not to acknowledge how familiar was all this—I still wondered to find how unfamiliar were the fancies which ordinary images were stirring up. On one of the staircases, I met the physician of the family. His countenance, I thought, wore a mingled expression of low cunning and perplexity. He accosted me with trepidation and passed on. The valet now threw open a door and ushered me into the presence of his master.

The room in which I found myself was very large and lofty. The windows were long, narrow, and pointed, and at so vast a distance from the black oaken floor as to be altogether inaccessible from within. Feeble gleams of encrimsoned light made their way through the trellised panes, and served to render sufficiently distinct the more prominent objects around; the eye, however, struggled in vain to reach the remoter angles of the chamber, or the recesses of the vaulted and fretted ceiling. Dark draperies hung upon the walls. The general furniture was profuse, comfortless, antique, and tattered. Many books and musical instruments lay scattered about, but failed to give any vitality to the scene. I felt that I breathed an atmosphere of sorrow. An air of stern, deep, and irredeemable gloom hung over and pervaded all.

Upon my entrance, Usher rose from a sofa on which he had been lying at full length, and greeted me with a vivacious warmth which had much in it, I at first thought, of an overdone cordiality—of the constrained effort of the *ennuyé* man of the world. A glance, however, at his countenance convinced me of his perfect sincerity. We sat down; and for some moments, while he spoke not, I gazed upon him with a feeling half of pity, half of awe. Surely, man had never before so terribly altered, in so brief a period, as had Roderick Usher! It was with difficulty that I could bring myself to admit the identity of the man being before me with the companion of my early boyhood. Yet the character of his face had been at all times remarkable. A cadaverousness of complexion; an eye large, liquid, and luminous beyond comparison; lips somewhat thin and very pallid, but of a surpassingly beautiful curve; a nose of a delicate Hebrew model, but with a breadth of nostril unusual in similar formations; a finely moulded chin, speaking, in its want of prominence, of a want of moral energy; hair of a more than web-like softness and tenuity; —these features, with an inordinate expansion above the regions of the temple, made up altogether a countenance not easily to be forgotten. And now in the mere exaggeration of the prevailing character of these features, and of the expression they were wont to convey, lay so much of change that I doubted to whom I spoke. The now ghastly pallor of the skin, and the now miraculous lustre of the eye, above all things startled and even awed me. The silken hair, too, had been suffered to grow all unheeded, and as, in its wild gossamer texture, it floated rather than fell about the face, I could not, even with effort, connect its Arabesque expression with any idea of simple humanity.

In the manner of my friend, I was at once struck with an incoherence—an inconsistency; and I soon found this to arise from a series of feeble and futile struggles to overcome an habitual trepidancy—an excessive nervous agitation. For something of this nature, I had indeed been prepared, no less by his letter, than by reminiscences of certain boyish traits, and by conclusions deduced from his peculiar physical conformation and temperament. His action was alternately vivacious and sullen. His voice varied rapidly from a tremulous indecision (when the animal spirits seemed utterly in abeyance) to that species of energetic concision—that abrupt, weighty, unhurried, and hollow-sounding enunciation—that leaden, self-balanced and perfectly modulated guttural utterance, which may be observed in the lost drunkard, or the irreclaimable eater of opium, during the periods of his most intense excitement.

It was thus that he spoke of the object of my visit, of his earnest desire to see me, and of the solace he expected me to afford him. He entered, at some length, into what he conceived to be the nature of his malady. It was, he said, a constitutional and a family evil, and one for which he despaired to find a remedy—a mere nervous affection, he immediately added, which would undoubtedly soon pass off. It displayed itself in a host of unnatural sensations. Some of these, as he detailed them, interested and bewildered me; although, perhaps, the terms and the general manner of the narration had their weight. He suffered much from a morbid acuteness of the senses; the most insipid food was alone endurable; he could wear only garments of certain texture; the odors of all flowers were oppressive; his eyes were tortured by even a faint light; and there were but peculiar sounds, and these from stringed instruments, which did not inspire him with horror.

To an anomalous species of terror, I found him a bounden slave. "I shall perish," said he, "I *must* perish in this deplorable folly. Thus, thus, and not otherwise, shall I be lost. I dread the events of the future, not in themselves, but in their results. I shudder at the thought of any, even the most trivial, incident, which may operate upon this intolerable agitation of soul. I have, indeed, no abhorrence of danger, except in its absolute effect—in terror. In this unnerved, in this pitiable, condition I feel that the period will sooner or later arrive when I must abandon life and reason together, in some struggle with the grim phantasm, FEAR."

I learned, moreover, at intervals, and through broken and equivocal hints, another singular feature of his mental condition. He was enchained by certain superstitious impressions in regard to the dwelling which he tenanted, and whence, for many years, he had never ventured forth—in regard to an influence whose supposititious force was conveyed in terms too shadowy here to be re-stated—an influence which some peculiarities in the mere form and substance of his family mansion had, by dint of long sufferance, he said, obtained over his spirit—an effect which the *physique* of the gray walls and turrets, and of the dim tarn into which they all looked down, had, at length, brought about upon the *morale* of his existence.

He admitted, however, although with hesitation, that much of the peculiar gloom which thus afflicted him could be traced to a more natural and far more palpable origin—to the severe and long-continued illness—indeed to the evidently approaching dissolution—of a tenderly beloved sister, his sole companion for long years, his last and only relative on earth. "Her decease," he said, with a bitterness which I can never forget, "would leave him (him the hopeless and the frail) the last of the ancient race of the Ushers." While he spoke, the lady Madeline (for so was she called) passed slowly through a remote portion of the apartment, and, without having noticed my presence, disappeared. I regarded her with an utter astonishment not unmingled with dread; and yet I found it impossible to account for such feelings. A sensation of stupor oppressed me as my eyes followed her retreating steps. When a door, at length, closed upon her, my glance sought instinctively and eagerly the countenance of the brother; but he had buried his face in his hands, and I could only perceive that a far more than ordinary wanness had overspread the emaciated fingers through which trickled many passionate tears.

The disease of the lady Madeline had long baffled the skill of her physicians. A settled apathy, a gradual wasting away of the person, and frequent although transient affections of a partially cataleptical character were the unusual diagnosis. Hitherto she had steadily borne up against the pressure of her malady, and had not betaken herself finally to bed; but on the closing in of the evening of my arrival at the house, she succumbed (as her brother told me at night with inexpressible agitation) to the prostrating power of the destroyer; and I learned that the glimpse I had obtained of her person would thus probably be the last I should obtain—that the lady, at least while living, would be seen by me no more.

For several days ensuing, her name was unmentioned by either Usher or myself; and during this period I was busied in earnest endeavors to alleviate the melancholy of my friend. We painted and read together, or I listened, as if in a dream, to the wild improvisations of his speaking guitar. And thus, as a closer and still closer intimacy admitted me more unreservedly into the recesses of his spirit, the more bitterly did I perceive the futility of all attempt at cheering a mind from which darkness, as if an inherent positive quality, poured forth upon all objects of the moral and physical universe in one unceasing radiation of gloom.

I shall ever bear about me a memory of the many solemn hours I thus spent alone with the master of the House of Usher. Yet I should fail in any attempt to convey an idea of the exact character of the studies, or of the occupations, in which he involved me, or led me the way. An excited and highly distempered ideality threw a sulphureous lustre over all. His long-improvised dirges will ring forever in my ears. Among other things, I hold painfully in mind a certain singular perversion and amplification of the wild air of the last waltz of Von Weber[1]. From the paintings over which his elaborate fancy brooded, and which grew, touch by touch, into vagueness at which I shuddered the more thrillingly, because I shuddered knowing not why—from these paintings (vivid as their images now are before me) I would in vain endeavor to educe more than a small portion which should lie within the compass of merely written words. By the utter simplicity, by the nakedness of his designs, he arrested and overawed attention. If ever mortal painted an idea, that mortal was Roderick Usher. For me at least, in the circumstances then surrounding me, there arose out of the pure abstractions which the hypochondriac contrived to throw upon his canvas, an intensity of intolerable awe, no shadow of which felt I ever yet in the contemplation of the certainly glowing yet too concrete reveries of Fuseli[2].

One of the phantasmagoric conceptions of my friend, partaking not so rigidly of the spirit of abstraction, may be shadowed forth, although feebly, in words. A small picture presented the interior of an immensely long and rectangular vault or tunnel, with low walls, smooth, white, and without interruption or device. Certain accessory points of the design served well to convey the idea that this excavation lay at an exceeding depth below the surface of the earth. No outlet was observed in any portion of its vast extent, and no torch or other artificial source of light was discernible; yet a flood of intense rays rolled throughout, and bathed the whole in a ghastly and inappropriate splendor.

I have just spoken of that morbid condition of the auditory nerve which rendered all music intolerable to the sufferer, with the exception of certain effects of stringed instruments. It was, perhaps, the narrow limits to which he thus confined himself upon the guitar which gave birth, in great measure, to the fantastic character of the performances. But the fervid *facility* of his *impromptus* could not be so accounted for. They must have been, and were, in the notes, as well as in the words of his wild fantasias (for he not unfrequently accompanied himself with rhymed verbal improvisations), the result of that intense mental collectedness and concentration to which I have previously alluded as observable only in particular moments of the highest artificial excitement. The words of one of these rhapsodies I have easily remembered.

---

1   Carl Maria von Weber (1786–1826), a German composer, conductor, and critic of the early Romantic period.
2   Henry Fuseli (1741–1825), a Swiss painter who made his reputation in London, noted for his interest in the supernatural.

I was, perhaps, the more forcibly impressed with it as he gave it, because, in the under or mystic current of its meaning, I fancied that I perceived, and for the first time, a full consciousness on the part of Usher of the tottering of his lofty reason upon her throne. The verses, which were entitled "The Haunted Palace", ran very nearly, if not accurately, thus:

I.

In the greenest of our valleys,
   By good angels tenanted,
Once a fair and stately palace—
   Radiant palace—reared its head.
In the monarch Thought's dominion—
   It stood there!
Never seraph spread a pinion
Over fabric half so fair.

II.

Banners yellow, glorious, golden,
   On its roof did float and flow;
(This—all this—was in the olden
   Time long ago);
And every gentle air that dallied,
   In that sweet day,
Along the ramparts plumed and pallid,
   A winged odor went away.

III.

Wanderers in that happy valley
   Through two luminous windows saw
Spirits moving musically
   To a lute's well-tunèd law;
Round about a throne, where sitting
   (Porphyrogene!)
In state his glory well befitting,
   The ruler of the realm was seen.

IV.

And all with pearl and ruby glowing
   Was the fair palace door,
Through which came flowing, flowing, flowing

41

And sparkling evermore,
A troop of Echoes whose sweet duty
    Was but to sing,
In voices of surpassing beauty,
    The wit and wisdom of their king.

                    V.
But evil things, in robes of sorrow,
    Assailed the monarch's high estate;
(Ah, let us mourn, for never morrow
    Shall dawn upon him, desolate!)
And, round about his home, the glory
    That blushed and bloomed
Is but a dim-remembered story
    Of the old time entombed.

                    VI.
And travellers now within that valley,
    Through the red-litten windows see
Vast forms that move fantastically
    To a discordant melody;
While, like a rapid ghastly river,
    Through the pale door,
A hideous throng rush out forever,
And laugh—but smile no more.

I well remember that suggestions arising from this ballad, led us into a train of thought wherein there became manifest an opinion of Usher's which I mention not so much on account of its novelty (for other men have thought thus), as on account of the pertinacity with which he maintained it. This opinion, in its general form, was that of the sentience of all vegetable things. But, in his disordered fancy, the idea had assumed a more daring character, and trespassed, under certain conditions, upon the kingdom of inorganization. I lack words to express the full extent, or the earnest *abandon* of his persuasion. The belief, however, was connected (as I have previously hinted) with the gray stones of the home of his forefathers. The conditions of the sentience had been here, he imagined, fulfilled in the method of collocation of these stones—in the order of their arrangement, as well as in that of the many *fungi* which overspread them, and of the decayed trees which stood around—above all, in the long undisturbed endurance of this arrangement, and in its reduplication in the still waters of the tarn. Its evidence—the evidence of the sentience—was to be seen, he said (and I here started as he spoke), in the gradual yet certain condensation of an atmosphere of their own about the waters and the walls. The result was discoverable, he added, in that silent yet importunate and terrible influence which for centuries had moulded the destinies of his family, and which made *him* what I now saw him—what he was. Such opinions need no comment, and I will make none.

Our books—the books which, for years, had formed no small portion of the mental existence of the invalid—were, as might be supposed, in strict keeping with this character of phantasm. We pored together over such works as the "Ververt et Chartreuse" of Gresset; the "Belphegor" of Machiavelli; the "Heaven and Hell" of Swedenborg; the "Subterranean Voyage of Nicholas Klimm" by Holberg; the "Chiromancy" of Robert Flud, of Jean D'Indaginé, and of De la Chambre; the "Journey into the Blue Distance" of Tieck; and the "City of the Sun" of Campanella. One favorite volume was a small octavo edition of the "Directorium Inquisitorium," by the Dominican Eymeric de Gironne; and there were passages in Pomponius Mela, about the old African Satyrs and Ægipans, over which Usher would sit dreaming for hours. His chief delight, however, was found in the perusal of an exceedingly rare and curious book in quarto Gothic—the manual of a forgotten church—the *Vigiliæ Mortuorum Secundum Chorum Ecclesiæ Maguntinæ.*

I could not help thinking of the wild ritual of this work, and of its probable influence upon the hypochondriac, when, one evening, having informed me abruptly that the lady Madeline was no more, he stated his intention of preserving her corpse for a fortnight (previously to its final interment), in one of the numerous vaults within the main walls of the building. The worldly reason, however, assigned for this singular proceeding, was one which I did not feel at liberty to dispute. The brother had been led to his resolution (so he told me) by consideration of the unusual character of the malady of the deceased, of certain obtrusive and eager inquiries on the part of her medical men, and of the remote and exposed situation of the burial-ground of the family. I will not deny that when I called to mind the sinister countenance of the person whom I met upon the staircase, on the day of my arrival at the house, I had no desire to oppose what I regarded as at best but a harmless, and by no means an unnatural, precaution.

At the request of Usher, I personally aided him in the arrangements for the temporary entombment. The body having been encoffined, we two alone bore it to its rest. The vault in which we placed it (and which had been so long unopened that our torches, half smothered in its oppressive atmosphere, gave us little opportunity for investigation) was small, damp, and entirely without means of admission for light; lying, at great depth, immediately beneath that portion of the building in which was my own sleeping apartment. It had been used, apparently, in remote feudal times, for the worst purposes of a donjon-keep, and, in later days, as a place of deposit for powder, or some other highly combustible substance, as a portion of its floor, and the whole interior of a long archway through which we reached it, were carefully sheathed with copper. The door, of massive iron, had been, also, similarly protected. Its immense weight caused an unusually sharp, grating sound, as it moved upon its hinges.

Having deposited our mournful burden upon tressels within this region of horror, we partially turned aside the yet unscrewed lid of the coffin, and looked upon the face of the tenant. A striking similitude between the brother and sister now first arrested my attention; and Usher, divining, perhaps, my thoughts, murmured out some few words from which I learned that the deceased and himself had been twins, and that sympathies of a scarcely intelligible nature had always existed between them. Our glances, however, rested not long upon the dead—for we could not regard her unawed. The disease which had thus entombed the lady in the maturity of youth, had left, as usual in all maladies of a strictly cataleptical character, the mockery of a faint blush upon the bosom and the face, and that suspiciously lingering smile upon the lip which is so terrible in death. We replaced and screwed down the lid, and, having secured the door of iron, made our way, with toil, into the scarcely less gloomy apartments of the upper portion of the house.

And now, some days of bitter grief having elapsed, an observable change came over the features of the mental disorder of my friend. His ordinary manner had vanished. His ordinary occupations were neglected or forgotten. He roamed from chamber to chamber with hurried, unequal, and objectless step. The pallor of his countenance had assumed, if possible, a more ghastly hue—but the luminousness of his eye had utterly gone out. The once occasional huskiness of his tone was heard no more; and a tremulous quaver, as if of extreme terror, habitually characterized his utterance. There were times, indeed, when I thought his unceasingly agitated mind was laboring with some oppressive secret, to divulge which he struggled for the necessary courage. At times, again, I was obliged to resolve all into the mere inexplicable vagaries of madness, for I beheld him gazing upon vacancy for long hours, in an attitude of the profoundest attention, as if listening to some imaginary sound. It was no wonder that his condition terrified—that it infected me. I felt creeping upon me, by slow yet certain degrees, the wild influences of his own fantastic yet impressive superstitions.

It was, especially, upon retiring to bed late in the night of the seventh or eighth day after the placing of the lady Madeline within the donjon, that I experienced the full power of such feelings. Sleep came not near my couch—while the hours waned and waned away. I struggled to reason off the nervousness which had dominion over me. I endeavored to believe that much, if not all of what I felt, was due to the bewildering influence of the gloomy furniture of the room—of the dark and tattered draperies, which, tortured into motion by the breath of a rising tempest, swayed fitfully to and fro upon the walls, and rustled uneasily about the decorations of the bed. But my efforts were fruitless. An irrepressible tremor gradually pervaded my frame; and, at length, there sat upon my very heart an incubus of utterly causeless alarm. Shaking this off with a gasp and a struggle, I uplifted myself upon the pillows, and, peering earnestly within the intense darkness of the chamber, hearkened—I know not why, except that an instinctive spirit prompted me—to certain low and indefinite sounds which came, through the pauses of the storm, at long intervals, I knew not whence. Overpowered by an intense sentiment of horror, unaccountable yet unendurable, I threw on my clothes with haste (for I felt that I should sleep no more during the night), and endeavored to arouse myself from the pitiable condition into which I had fallen, by pacing rapidly to and fro through the apartment.

I had taken but few turns in this manner, when a light step on an adjoining staircase arrested my attention. I presently recognized it as that of Usher. In an instant afterward he rapped, with a gentle touch, at my door, and entered, bearing a lamp. His countenance was, as usual, cadaverously wan—but, moreover, there was a species of mad hilarity in his eyes—an evidently restrained *hysteria* in his whole demeanor. His air appalled me—but anything was preferable to the solitude which I had so long endured, and I even welcomed his presence as a relief.

"And you have not seen it?" he said abruptly, after having stared about him for some moments in silence— "you have not then seen it? —but, stay! you shall." Thus speaking, and having carefully shaded his lamp, he hurried to one of the casements, and threw it freely open to the storm.

The impetuous fury of the entering gust nearly lifted us from our feet. It was, indeed, a tempestuous yet sternly beautiful night, and one wildly singular in its terror and its beauty. A whirlwind had apparently collected its force in our vicinity; for there were frequent and violent alterations in the direction of the wind; and the exceeding density of the clouds (which hung so low as to press upon the turrets of the house) did not prevent our perceiving the life-like velocity with which they flew careering from all points against each other, without passing away into the distance. I say that even their exceeding density did not prevent our perceiving this—yet we had no glimpse of the moon or stars, nor was there any flashing forth of the lightning. But the under surfaces of the huge masses of agitated vapor, as well as all terrestrial objects immediately around us, were glowing in the unnatural light of a faintly luminous and distinctly visible gaseous exhalation which hung about and enshrouded the mansion.

"You must not—you shall not behold this!" said I, shuddering, to Usher, as I led him, with a gentle violence, from the window to a seat. "These appearances, which bewilder you, are merely electrical phenomena not uncommon—or it may be that they have their ghastly origin in the rank miasma of the tarn. Let us close this casement; —the air is chilling and dangerous to your frame. Here is one of your favorite romances. I will read, and you shall listen—and so we will pass away this terrible night together."

The antique volume which I had taken up was the "Mad Trist" of Sir Launcelot Canning; but I had called it a favorite of Usher's more in sad jest than in earnest; for, in truth, there is little in its uncouth and unimaginative prolixity which could have

45

had interest for the lofty and spiritual ideality of my friend. It was, however, the only book immediately at hand; and I indulged a vague hope that the excitement which now agitated the hypochondriac, might find relief (for the history of mental disorder is full of similar anomalies) even in the extremeness of the folly which I should read. Could I have judged, indeed, by the wild overstrained air of vivacity with which he hearkened, or apparently hearkened, to the words of the tale, I might well have congratulated myself upon the success of my design.

I had arrived at that well-known portion of the story where Ethelred, the hero of the Trist, having sought in vain for peaceable admission into the dwelling of the hermit, proceeds to make good an entrance by force. Here, it will be remembered, the words of the narrative run thus:

"And Ethelred, who was by nature of a doughty heart, and who was now mighty withal, on account of the powerfulness of the wine which he had drunken, waited no longer to hold parley with the hermit, who, in sooth, was of an obstinate and maliceful turn, but, feeling the rain upon his shoulders, and fearing the rising of the tempest, uplifted his mace outright, and, with blows, made quickly room in the plankings of the door for his gauntleted hand; and now pulling therewith sturdily, he so cracked, and ripped, and tore all asunder, that the noise of the dry and hollow-sounding wood alarumed and reverberated throughout the forest."

At the termination of this sentence I started and, for a moment, paused; for it appeared to me (although I at once concluded that my excited fancy had deceived me)—it appeared to me that, from some very remote portion of the mansion, there came, indistinctly to my ears, what might have been, in its exact similarity of character, the echo (but a stifled and dull one certainly) of the very cracking and ripping sound which Sir Launcelot had so particularly described. It was, beyond doubt, the coincidence alone which had arrested my attention; for, amid the rattling of the sashes of the casements, and the ordinary commingled noises of the still increasing storm, the sound, in itself, had nothing, surely, which should have interested or disturbed me. I continued the story:

"But the good champion Ethelred, now entering within the door, was sore enraged and amazed to perceive no signal of the maliceful hermit; but, in the stead thereof, a dragon of a scaly and prodigious demeanor, and of a fiery tongue, which sat in guard before a palace of gold, with a floor of silver; and upon the wall there hung a shield of shining brass with this legend enwritten—

> Who entereth herein, a conqueror hath bin;
> Who slayeth the dragon, the shield he shall win.

And Ethelred uplifted his mace, and struck upon the head of the dragon, which fell before him, and gave up his pesty breath, with a shriek so horrid and harsh, and withal so piercing, that Ethelred had fain to close his ears with his hands against the dreadful noise of it, the like whereof was never before heard."

Here again I paused abruptly, and now with a feeling of wild amazement—for there could be no doubt whatever that, in this instance, I did actually hear (although from what direction it proceeded I found it impossible to say) a low and apparently distant, but harsh, protracted, and most unusual screaming or grating sound—the exact counterpart of what my fancy had already conjured up for the dragon's unnatural shriek as described by the romancer.

Oppressed, as I certainly was, upon the occurrence of this second and most extraordinary coincidence, by a thousand conflicting sensations, in which wonder and extreme terror were predominant, I still retained sufficient presence of mind to avoid exciting, by any observation, the sensitive nervousness of my companion. I was by no means certain that he had noticed the sounds in question; although, assuredly, a strange alteration had, during the last few minutes, taken place in his demeanor. From a position fronting my own, he had gradually brought round his chair, so as to sit with his face to the door of the chamber; and thus I could but partially perceive his features, although I saw that his lips trembled as if he were murmuring inaudibly. His head had dropped upon his breast—yet I knew that he was not asleep, from the wide and rigid opening of the eye as I caught a glance of it in profile. The motion of his body, too, was at variance with this idea—for he rocked from side to side with a gentle yet constant and uniform sway. Having rapidly taken notice of all this, I resumed the narrative of Sir Launcelot, which thus proceeded:

"And now, the champion, having escaped from the terrible fury of the dragon, bethinking himself of the brazen shield, and of the breaking up of the enchantment which was upon it, removed the carcass from out of the way before him, and approached valorously over the silver pavement of the castle to where the shield was upon the wall; which in sooth tarried not for his full coming, but fell down at his feet upon the silver floor, with a mighty great and terrible ringing sound."

No sooner had these syllables passed my lips, than—as if a shield of brass had indeed, at the moment, fallen heavily upon a floor of silver—I became aware of a distinct, hollow, metallic, and clangorous, yet apparently muffled, reverberation. Completely unnerved, I leaped to my feet; but the measured rocking movement of Usher was undisturbed. I rushed to the chair in which he sat. His eyes were bent fixedly before him, and throughout his whole countenance there reigned a stony rigidity. But, as I placed my hand upon his shoulder, there came a strong shudder over his whole person; a sickly smile quivered about his lips; and I saw that he spoke in a low, hurried, and gibbering murmur, as if unconscious of my presence. Bending closely over him, I at length drank in the hideous import of his words.

"Not hear it? —yes, I hear it, and *have* heard it. Long—long—long—many minutes, many hours, many days, have I heard it—yet I dared not—oh, pity me, miserable wretch that I am! — I dared not—I *dared* not speak! *We have put her living in the tomb!* Said I not that my senses were acute? I *now* tell you that I heard her first feeble movements in the hollow coffin. I heard them—many, many days ago—yet I dared not—*I dared not speak!* And now—to-night—Ethelred—ha! ha! —the breaking of the hermit's door, and the death-cry of the dragon, and the clangor of the shield! —say, rather, the rending of her coffin, and the grating of the iron hinges of her prison, and her struggles within the coppered archway of the vault! Oh! whither shall I fly? Will she not be here anon? Is she not hurrying to upbraid me for my haste? Have I not heard her footstep on the stair? Do I not distinguish that heavy and horrible beating of her heart? Madman!"—here he sprang furiously to his feet, and shrieked out his syllables, as if in the effort he were giving up his soul —*"Madman! I tell you that she now stands without the door!"*

As if in the superhuman energy of his utterance there had been found the potency of a spell, the huge antique panels to which the speaker pointed threw slowly back, upon the instant, their ponderous and ebony jaws. It was the work of the rushing gust—but then without those doors there *did* stand the lofty and enshrouded figure of the lady Madeline of Usher. There was blood upon her white robes, and the evidence of some bitter struggle upon every portion of her emaciated frame. For a moment she remained trembling and reeling to and fro upon the threshold—then, with a low moaning cry, fell heavily inward upon the person of her brother, and in her violent and now final death-agonies, bore him to the floor a corpse, and a victim to the terrors he had anticipated.

From that chamber, and from that mansion, I fled aghast. The storm was still abroad in all its wrath as I found myself crossing the old causeway. Suddenly there shot along the path a wild light, and I turned to see whence a gleam so unusual could have issued; for the vast house and its shadows were alone behind me. The radiance was that of the full, setting, and blood-red moon which now shone vividly through that once barely-discernible fissure of which I have before spoken as extending from the roof of the building, in a zigzag direction, to the base. While I gazed, this fissure rapidly widened—there came a fierce breath of the whirlwind—the entire orb of the satellite burst at once upon my sight—my brain reeled as I saw the mighty walls rushing asunder—there was a long tumultuous shouting sound like the voice of a thousand waters—and the deep and dank tarn at my feet closed sullenly and silently over the fragments of the *"House of Usher."*

Plot Summary

"The Fall of the House of Usher" is a hauntingly tragic tale written by Edgar Allan Poe. The story follows an unnamed narrator who receives a distressing letter from his childhood friend, Roderick Usher. Concerned for his friend's well-being, the narrator travels to the decaying Usher mansion, a symbol of the family's deteriorating state. Upon arrival, the narrator is greeted by Roderick, whose appearance unsettles him. Roderick explains that the Usher family is cursed and plagued by a range of physical and mental ailments. The narrator also learns that Roderick's twin sister, Madeline, is gravely ill and near death. As time passes, the atmosphere within the mansion grows increasingly eerie and oppressive. The narrator spends his days engaging in idle conversation with Roderick and his nights plagued by vivid nightmares. The narrator becomes fixated on an artistic representation of the deteriorating Usher mansion, which he believes reflects Roderick's deteriorating mental state. Soon, Madeline's condition worsens, and she is pronounced dead. Roderick insists on placing her body in a temporary crypt within the mansion to protect it from outside forces. Over the following days, strange events unfold—loud noises at night, ethereal sounds, and ghostly apparitions. The narrator becomes increasingly terrified as he witnesses Roderick's descent into madness. In an intense climax, Madeline, who is not dead but, in a trance-like state, breaks free from her tomb and confronts Roderick. The two siblings fall to the floor, lifeless, as the entire House of Usher collapses into a murky lake surrounding the estate. The story concludes with the narrator fleeing from the crumbling mansion, barely escaping the clutches of the doomed Usher bloodline. He watches as the once-majestic house sinks into the lake, forever lost in history.

Language Exercises

Choose the item that best replaces or explains the underlined part of the sentence.

1. … I had been passing alone, on horseback, through a singularly dreary tract of country, and at length found myself, as the shades of the evening drew on, within view of the <u>melancholy</u> House of Usher.
    A. tranquil   B. elliptical   C. infertile   D. somber
2. It was a mystery all insoluble; nor could I <u>grapple with</u> the shadowy fancies that crowded upon me as I pondered.
    A. overcome   B. master   C. grasp   D. cling to
3. He suffered much from a <u>morbid</u> acuteness of the senses; the most insipid food was alone endurable; he could wear only garments of certain texture; …
    A. unpredictable   B. diseased   C. appalling   D. pathetic
4. I learned, moreover, at intervals, and through broken and <u>equivocal</u> hints, another singular feature of his mental condition.
    A. hesitant   B. alternate   C. vague   D. hysterical
5. A settled apathy, a gradual wasting away of the person, and frequent although <u>transient</u> affections of a partially cataleptical character were the unusual diagnosis.
    A. permanent   B. arbitrary   C. fleeting   D. profound

6. For several days ensuing, her name was unmentioned by either Usher or myself; and during this period, I was busied in earnest endeavors to <u>alleviate</u> the melancholy of my friend.
   A. relieve   B. afflict   C. fling   D. dodge

7. There were times, indeed, when I thought his unceasingly agitated mind was laboring with some oppressive secret, to <u>divulge</u> which he struggled for the necessary courage.
   A. burst   B. disclose   C. transmit   D. assail

8. An irrepressible <u>tremor</u> gradually pervaded my frame; and, at length, there sat upon my very heart an incubus of utterly causeless alarm.
   A. flutter   B. hover   C. torture   D. quiver

9. But the under surfaces of the huge masses of agitated vapor, as well as all terrestrial objects immediately around us, were glowing in the unnatural light of a faintly <u>luminous</u> and distinctly visible gaseous exhalation which hung about and enshrouded the mansion.
   A. producing vapor   B. giving out a gas
   C. shining in the dark   D. absorbing energy

10. Could I have judged, indeed, by the wild overstrained air of <u>vivacity</u> with which he hearkened, or apparently hearkened, to the words of the tale, I might well have congratulated myself upon the success of my design.
    A. vitality   B. vanity   C. infinity   D. tranquility

11. I was by no means certain that he had noticed the sounds in question; although, assuredly, a strange alteration had, during the last few minutes, taken place in his <u>demeanor</u>.
    A. ritual   B. behavior   C. etiquette   D. custom

12. … as if a shield of brass had indeed, at the moment, fallen heavily upon a floor of silver—I became aware of a distinct, hollow, metallic, and clangorous, yet apparently <u>muffled</u>, reverberation.
    A. distinct   B. distant   C. immersed   D. dull

13. … and I saw that he spoke in a low, hurried, and <u>gibbering</u> murmur, as if unconscious of my presence.
    A. incoherent and confused   B. incessant and agitated
    C. excited and nervous   D. eager and anxious

14. There was blood upon her white robes, and the evidence of some bitter struggle upon every portion of her <u>emaciated</u> frame.
    A. flexible   B. feeble   C. frugal   D. fugitive

15. … there was a long <u>tumultuous</u> shouting sound like the voice of a thousand waters—and the deep and dank tarn at my feet closed sullenly and silently over the fragments of the *"House of Usher."*
    A. calm and tender   B. indifferent and aloof

C. detached and distant   D. loud and violent

Topics for Discussion

1. Edgar Allan Poe likes to create a mood in the short stories. Describe the mood of "The Fall of the House of Usher".
2. "The Fall of the House of Usher", written by Poe in 1839, is regarded as an early and supreme example of the Gothic horror story. How does Poe create a Gothic terror through his use of language?
3. How many characters are there in the story? Who are they? Try to describe them.
4. From what point of view is the story told? How does the narrator tell the story?
5. Try to discuss the narrative technology in the story.
6. The story exhibits Poe's practice of "art for art's sake". Describe the artistic effect produced in the story.
7. The Usher mansion is the most important symbol in the story. What is the symbolic meaning of it?
8. Read the short story "The Yellow Wallpaper" (1892) by Charlotte Perkins Oilman and compare and contrast the portrayal of mental breakdown in each story.
9. Examine the lyric "The Haunted Palace" written by Roderick Usher in "The Fall of the House of Usher" and discuss how it reflects Roderick's mental and emotional state.
10. Poe's fictional works and critical theories greatly impacted nineteenth-century literature, particularly the French symbolist movement. Research and discuss Poe's influence in literary history.

Discussion Tips

"The Fall of the House of Usher", penned by Edgar Allan Poe in 1839, is often considered an early and exemplary specimen of Gothic horror literature. While Poe referred to such works as "arabesque", emphasizing their ornate and flowery prose, the story is renowned for its supernatural elements, which have been subject to diverse interpretations by critics. It embodies Poe's concept of "art for art's sake", advocating that a narrative should be devoid of explicit social, political, or moral messages, instead focusing on evoking a specific mood—in this case, terror—through the masterful use of language.

The atmosphere of terror in "The Fall of the House of Usher" is primarily rooted in the theme of the unknown. The narrator encounters enigmatic and inexplicable occurrences throughout the story, fostering a pervasive sense of uncertainty and dread that instills fear and unease in the reader. The setting, a dilapidated and sinister mansion, further contributes to the atmosphere of apprehension and foreboding. Psychological terror is heightened by the presence of the mysterious figure of Madeline, who appears to be a specter from the past, intensifying the sense of fear and disquietude for both the narrator and the reader.

Moreover, the mood of terror in the narrative is intricately woven into its atmospheric elements. The narrator's vivid portrayal of the house and its environs cultivates an aura of unease and foreboding, accentuated by the peculiar behavior of the Usher family. The narrator's disquietude is compounded by the mysterious ailment of Madeline Usher, eerie sounds and visions, and the increasingly irrational conduct of Roderick Usher, collectively creating an escalating sense of fear and apprehension throughout the tale.

Additionally, the narrator's own psychological state plays a pivotal role in the exploration of fear within the narrative. His initial apprehension is compounded by unsettling auditory and visual experiences within the house, such as melancholic music and disturbing tales shared with Roderick, blurring the boundaries between reality and the supernatural. This fusion of experiences contributes to the prevailing sense of disquiet and dread that permeates the story.

Unit 3
Nathaniel Hawthorne: "Young Goodman Brown"

About the Author

Nathaniel Hawthorne (1804–1864)

Nathaniel Hawthorne, an American novelist and short-story writer, was born in 1804 in Salem, Massachusetts. His ancestors included both of the judges in the witchcraft trials (John Hathorne) and a revolutionary war hero (Daniel Hathorne). After graduating from Bowdoin College in 1825, Hawthorne decided to pursue a career as a writer. He is best known for his novels *The Scarlet Letter* (1850) and *The House of Seven Gables* (1851), as well as his collections of short stories *Twice-Told Tales* (1837) and *Mosses from an Old Manse* (1846). Throughout his lifetime, Nathaniel Hawthorne felt guilt over certain actions of his ancestors. Critics view Hawthorne's preoccupation with Puritanism in his literature as an outgrowth of these familial roots. Hawthorne's own father, a ship's captain, passed away when Hawthorne was only four years old, further contributing to his exploration of the idea of original sin in works. Nathaniel Hawthorne's short story "Young Goodman Brown" is widely regarded as one of the most powerful literary works to address the hysteria surrounding the Salem Witch Trials of 1692. Hawthorne is also remembered for his contribution to the development of the short story as a respected form of literature, as well as for his use of moral lessons in his writing.

The Literary History

Towards History and Beyond: Hawthorne and the American Short Story

Nathaniel Hawthorne made great contributions to the American short story in the early nineteenth century. By combining Gothic elements with psychological depth, he revolutionized the historical tale into a respected literary genre. His status as a short story writer today is largely due to his historical tales from the 1830s, such as "Young Goodman Brown" (1835) and "The Minister's Black Veil" (1836), which are two of his most renowned and widely anthologized works. Nathaniel Hawthorne crafted a unique form of short story writing that enabled him to delve into moral issues, psychological trauma, and historical facts. His works, which often draw on his Puritan upbringing, use allegory and symbolism to examine the wrongs of the past, the hardships of humanity, and the concepts of guilt, sin, and morality. His story, "Young Goodman Brown", is a prime example of his exploration of the "fortunate fall", which suggests that recognizing one's own faults can lead to greater understanding of others, self-forgiveness, and an appreciation of the complexity of human nature.

Nathaniel Hawthorne is renowned for revolutionizing the short story genre in America. In a mere two decades, he shifted the focus of fiction away from European mythological tales and onto American legendary figures and ideas, which he explored through unprecedented psychological depth, moral insight, and stylistic integrity. His legacy is especially evident in three influential collections: *Twice-Told Tales* (1837), *Mosses from an Old Manse* (1846), and *The Snow Image, and Other Twice-Told Tales* (1852). These volumes helped establish American Romanticism as a legitimate form of artistic expression, garnering international recognition for its intellectual and aesthetic value.

Literary Terms

Allegory

Allegory is a narrative, either in prose or verse, in which the characters and events are used to represent a deeper, underlying meaning. The term "allegory" comes from the Greek word "allegoria" which means "speaking otherwise". The primary level of signification is complemented by a second, correlated order of meaning. In allegorical works, abstract concepts such as virtues, vices, mental states, lifestyles, and character types are often personified. John Bunyan's *The Pilgrim's Progress* uses this technique to illustrate the Christian doctrine of salvation. It tells the story of a character named Christian, who is warned by Evangelist to flee the City of Destruction and make his way to the Celestial City. Along the way, he meets characters with names like Faithful, Hopeful, and Giant Despair, and passes through places like the Slough of Despond, the Valley of the Shadow of Death, and Vanity Fair.

Symbolism

Symbolism is the use of symbols to represent ideas, emotions, and qualities in literature, art, and other forms of expression. Symbols are often used to give a deeper meaning to a piece of work, and can be used to evoke certain feelings or emotions in the audience.

Initiation story

An initiation story is a narrative that focuses on the protagonist's transition from innocence to experience, often marked by significant life events or rites of passage. This genre explores themes of personal growth, self-discovery, and the complexities of human relationships as the character confronts challenges that reshape their understanding of themselves and the world around them. Classic examples include J.D. Salinger's *The Catcher in the Rye*, where Holden Caulfield grapples with his transition into adulthood amid disillusionment, and Harper Lee's *To Kill a Mockingbird*, which portrays Scout Finch's awakening to social injustices through her childhood experiences. Key elements of initiation story include rites of passage, transformation, loss of innocence, and emotional journey. Initiation stories can be found in many cultures and are used to teach lessons, share wisdom, and pass on traditions.

Dark Romanticism

Dark romanticism is a literary movement that emerged in the 19th century in response to the optimistic views of the transcendentalist movement. It is characterized by a focus on the darker aspects of human nature, the power of evil, and the macabre. Dark romanticism often delves into themes of guilt, sin, and the supernatural, as well as the psychological effects of guilt and sin on human mind. Writers associated with this movement include Edgar Allan Poe, Nathaniel Hawthorne, and Mary Shelley, who created works that explored the complexities of the human experience in more morbid and haunting ways. Dark romanticism is often seen as a reaction against the idealism and optimism of the transcendentalist movement, challenging the notion of innate human goodness and instead exploring the complexities of the human soul and the darker aspects of human existence.

The Story

Young Goodman Brown[1]

Young Goodman Brown came forth at sunset into the street at Salem village[2]; but put his head back, after crossing the threshold, to exchange a parting kiss with his young wife. And Faith, as the wife was aptly named, thrust her own pretty head into the street, letting the wind play with the pink ribbons of her cap while she called to Goodman Brown.

"Dearest heart," whispered she, softly and rather sadly, when her lips were close to his ear, "prithee put off your journey until sunrise and sleep in your own bed to-night.

---

1   Nathaniel Hawthorne, *Mosses from an Old Manse* (Penguin Classics, 2005), pp. 75–92.

2   Salem village: Today's Danvers, hometown of Hawthorne. Hawthorne often used this place as the setting of his tales.

A lone woman is troubled with such dreams and such thoughts that she's afeard[1] of herself sometimes. Pray tarry with me this night, dear husband, of all nights in the year."

"My love and my Faith," replied young Goodman Brown, "of all nights in the year, this one night must I tarry away from thee. My journey, as thou callest it, forth and back again, must needs be done 'tuix wixt now and sunrise. What, my sweet, pretty wife, dost thou doubt me already, and we but three months married?"

"Then God bless you!" said Faith, with the pink ribbons, "and may you find all well when you come back."

"Amen!" cried Goodman Brown. "Say thy prayers, dear Faith, and go to bed at dusk, and no harm will come to thee."

So they parted; and the young man pursued his way until, being about to turn the corner by the meeting-house[2], he looked back and saw the head of Faith still peeping after him with a melancholy air, in spite of her pink ribbons.

"Poor little Faith!" thought he, for his heart smote him. "What a wretch am I to leave her on such an errand! She talks of dreams, too. Methought as she spoke there was trouble in her face, as if a dream had warned her what work is to be done tonight. But no, no; 't would kill her to think it. Well, she's a blessed angel on earth; and after this one night I'll cling to her skirts and follow her to heaven."

With this excellent resolve for the future, Goodman Brown felt himself justified in making more haste on his present evil purpose[3]. He had taken a dreary road, darkened by all the gloomiest trees of the forest, which barely stood aside to let the narrow path creep through, and closed immediately behind. It was all as lonely as could be; and there is this peculiarity in such a solitude, that the traveller knows not who may be concealed by the innumerable trunks and the thick boughs overhead; so that with lonely footsteps he may yet be passing through an unseen multitude.

"There may be a devilish Indian behind every tree," said Goodman Brown to himself, and he glanced fearfully behind him as he added, "What if the devil himself should be at my very elbow!"

His head being turned back, he passed a crook of the road, and, looking forward again, beheld the figure of a man, in grave and decent attire, seated at the foot of an old tree. He arose at Goodman Brown's approach and walked onward side by side with him.

"You are late, Goodman Brown," said he. "The clock of the Old South[4] was striking as I came through Boston, and that is full fifteen minutes agone[5]."

---

1   afeard=afraid.

2   meeting-house: the place for religious activities and official business.

3   evil purpose: refer to Goodman Brown's purpose of meeting with Devil.

4   Old South: the Old South Church in Boston, established in 1729.

5   agone=ago.

"Faith kept me back a while," replied the young man, with a tremor in his voice, caused by the sudden appearance of his companion, though not wholly unexpected.

It was now deep dusk in the forest, and deepest in that part of it where these two were journeying. As nearly as could be discerned, the second traveller was about fifty years old, apparently in the same rank of life as Goodman Brown, and bearing a considerable resemblance to him, though perhaps more in expression than features. Still they might have been taken for father and son. And yet, though the elder person was as simply clad as the younger, and as simple in manner too, he had an indescribable air of one who knew the world, and who would not have felt abashed at the governor's dinner table or in King William's court, were it possible that his affairs should call him thither. But the only thing about him that could be fixed upon as remarkable was his staff, which bore the likeness of a great black snake, so curiously wrought that it might almost be seen to twist and wriggle itself like a living serpent. This, of course, must have been an ocular deception, assisted by the uncertain light.

"Come, Goodman Brown," cried his fellow-traveller, "this is a dull pace for the beginning of a journey. Take my staff, if you are so soon weary."

"Friend," said the other, exchanging his slow pace for a full stop, "having kept covenant by meeting thee here, it is my purpose now to return whence I came. I have scruples touching the matter thou wot'st of[1]."

"Sayest thou so[2]?" replied he of the serpent, smiling apart. "Let us walk on, nevertheless, reasoning as we go; and if I convince thee not thou shalt turn back. We are but a little way in the forest yet."

"Too far! too far!" exclaimed the goodman, unconsciously resuming his walk. "My father never went into the woods on such an errand, nor his father before him. We have been a race of honest men and good Christians since the days of the martyrs[3]; and shall I be the first of the name of Brown that ever took this path and kept"

"Such company, thou wouldst say," observed the elder person, interpreting his pause. "Well said, Goodman Brown! I have been as well acquainted with your family as with ever a one among the Puritans; and that's no trifle to say. I helped your grandfather, the constable, when he lashed the Quaker woman so smartly through the streets of Salem; and it was I that brought your father a pitch-pine knot, kindled at my own hearth, to set fire to an Indian village, in King Philip's war. They were my good friends, both; and many a pleasant walk have we had along this path, and returned merrily after midnight. I would fain be friends with you for their sake."

"If it be as thou sayest," replied Goodman Brown, "I marvel they never spoke of

---

1   wot'st of=know of.

2   Sayest thou so?=Do you say so?

3   days of the martyrs: also called "Bloody Mary" for the persecution of Protestants during the reign of the Catholic Mary Tudor of England (1553–1558).

these matters; or, verily, I marvel not, seeing that the least rumor of the sort would have driven them from New England. We are a people of prayer, and good works to boot, and abide no such wickedness."

"Wickedness or not," said the traveller with the twisted staff, "I have a very general acquaintance here in New England. The deacons of many a church have drunk the communion wine with me; the selectmen of divers towns make me their chairman; and a majority of the Great and General Court[1] are firm supporters of my interest. The governor and I, too—But these are state secrets."

"Can this be so?" cried Goodman Brown, with a stare of amazement at his undisturbed companion. "Howbeit, I have nothing to do with the governor and council; they have their own ways, and are no rule for a simple husbandman[2] like me. But, were I to go on with thee, how should I meet the eye of that good old man, our minister, at Salem village? Oh, his voice would make me tremble both Sabbath day and lecture day."

Thus far the elder traveller had listened with due gravity; but now burst into a fit of irrepressible mirth, shaking himself so violently that his snake-like staff actually seemed to wriggle in sympathy.

"Ha! ha! ha!" shouted he again and again; then composing himself, "Well, go on, Goodman Brown, go on; but, prithee, don't kill me with laughing."

"Well, then, to end the matter at once," said Goodman Brown, considerably nettled, "there is my wife, Faith. It would break her dear little heart; and I'd rather break my own."

"Nay, if that be the case," answered the other, "e'en[3] go thy ways, Goodman Brown. I would not for twenty old women like the one hobbling before us that Faith should come to any harm."

As he spoke, he pointed his staff at a female figure on the path, in whom Goodman Brown recognized a very pious and exemplary dame, who had taught him his catechism in youth, and was still his moral and spiritual adviser, jointly with the minister and Deacon Gookin.

"A marvel, truly, that Goody Cloyse should be so far in the wilderness at nightfall," said he. "But with your leave, friend, I shall take a cut through the woods until we have left this Christian woman behind. Being a stranger to you, she might ask whom I was consorting with and whither I was going."

"Be it so," said his fellow-traveller. "Betake you to the woods, and let me keep the path."

Accordingly, the young man turned aside, but took care to watch his companion,

---

1   the Great and General Court: the legislative body of the Colonial Massachusetts.

2   husbandman: usually, farmer; here, man of ordinary status.

3   e'en=just.

who advanced softly along the road until he had come within a staff's length of the old dame. She, meanwhile, was making the best of her way, with singular speed for so aged a woman, and mumbling some indistinct words—a prayer, doubtless—as she went. The traveller put forth his staff and touched her withered neck with what seemed the serpent's tail.

"The devil!" screamed the pious old lady.

"Then Goody Cloyse knows her old friend?" observed the traveller, confronting her and leaning on his writhing stick.

"Ah, forsooth, and is it your worship indeed?" cried the good dame. "Yea, truly is it, and in the very image of my old gossip, Goodman Brown, the grandfather of the silly fellow that now is. But—would your worship believe it?—my broomstick hath strangely disappeared, stolen, as I suspect, by that unhanged witch, Goody Cory[1], and that, too, when I was all anointed with the juice of smallage, and cinquefoil, and wolf's bane"

"Mingled with fine wheat and the fat of a new-born babe," said the shape of old Goodman Brown.

"Ah, your worship knows the recipe," cried the old lady, cackling aloud. "So, as I was saying, being all ready for the meeting, and no horse to ride on, I made up my mind to foot it; for they tell me there is a nice young man to be taken into communion to-night. But now your good worship will lend me your arm, and we shall be there in a twinkling."

"That can hardly be," answered her friend. "I may not spare you my arm, Goody Cloyse; but here is my staff, if you will."

So saying, he threw it down at her feet, where, perhaps, it assumed life, being one of the rods which its owner had formerly lent to the Egyptian magi[2]. Of this fact, however, Goodman Brown could not take cognizance[3]. He had cast up his eyes in astonishment, and, looking down again, beheld neither Goody Cloyse nor the serpentine staff, but his fellow-traveller alone, who waited for him as calmly as if nothing had happened.

"That old woman taught me my catechism," said the young man; and there was a world of meaning in this simple comment.

They continued to walk onward, while the elder traveller exhorted his companion to make good speed and persevere in the path, discoursing so aptly that his arguments seemed rather to spring up in the bosom of his auditor than to be suggested by himself. As they went, he plucked a branch of maple to serve for a walking stick, and began to strip it of the twigs and little boughs, which were wet with evening dew. The moment his fingers touched them they became strangely withered and dried up as with a week's

---

1   unhanged witch, Goody Cory: the damned witch who had not been hanged in Salem case, here the lady use it to scold her neighbor Cory.

2   magi=magicians.

3   take cognizance=take notice.

sunshine. Thus the pair proceeded, at a good free pace, until suddenly, in a gloomy hollow of the road, Goodman Brown sat himself down on the stump of a tree and refused to go any farther.

"Friend," said he, stubbornly, "my mind is made up. Not another step will I budge on this errand. What if a wretched old woman do choose to go to the devil when I thought she was going to heaven: is that any reason why I should quit my dear Faith and go after her?"

"You will think better of this by and by," said his acquaintance, composedly. "Sit here and rest yourself a while; and when you feel like moving again, there is my staff to help you along."

Without more words, he threw his companion the maple stick, and was as speedily out of sight as if he had vanished into the deepening gloom. The young man sat a few moments by the roadside, applauding himself greatly, and thinking with how clear a conscience he should meet the minister in his morning walk, nor shrink from the eye of good old Deacon Gookin[1]. And what calm sleep would be his that very night, which was to have been spent so wickedly, but so purely and sweetly now, in the arms of Faith! Amidst these pleasant and praiseworthy meditations, Goodman Brown heard the tramp of horses along the road, and deemed it advisable to conceal himself within the verge of the forest, conscious of the guilty purpose that had brought him thither, though now so happily turned from it.

On came the hoof tramps and the voices of the riders, two grave old voices, conversing soberly as they drew near. These mingled sounds appeared to pass along the road, within a few yards of the young man's hiding-place; but, owing doubtless to the depth of the gloom at that particular spot, neither the travellers nor their steeds were visible. Though their figures brushed the small boughs by the wayside, it could not be seen that they intercepted, even for a moment, the faint gleam from the strip of bright sky athwart which they must have passed. Goodman Brown alternately crouched and stood on tiptoe, pulling aside the branches and thrusting forth his head as far as he durst without discerning so much as a shadow. It vexed him the more, because he could have sworn, were such a thing possible, that he recognized the voices of the minister and Deacon Gookin, jogging along quietly, as they were wont to do, when bound to some ordination or ecclesiastical council. While yet within hearing, one of the riders stopped to pluck a switch.

"Of the two, reverend sir," said the voice like the deacon's, "I had rather miss an ordination dinner than to-night's meeting. They tell me that some of our community are to be here from Falmouth and beyond, and others from Connecticut and Rhode Island,

---

1   Deacon Gookin: possibly Daniel Gookin (1616–1687), a colonial Puritan magistrate and missionary to the Indians.

besides several of the Indian powwows[1], who, after their fashion, know almost as much deviltry as the best of us. Moreover, there is a goodly young woman to be taken into communion."

"Mighty well, Deacon Gookin!" replied the solemn old tones of the minister. "Spur up, or we shall be late. Nothing can be done, you know, until I get on the ground."

The hoofs clattered again; and the voices, talking so strangely in the empty air, passed on through the forest, where no church had ever been gathered or solitary Christian prayed. Whither, then, could these holy men be journeying so deep into the heathen wilderness? Young Goodman Brown caught hold of a tree for support, being ready to sink down on the ground, faint and overburdened with the heavy sickness of his heart. He looked up to the sky, doubting whether there really was a heaven above him. Yet there was the blue arch, and the stars brightening in it.

"With heaven above and Faith below, I will yet stand firm against the devil!" cried Goodman Brown.

While he still gazed upward into the deep arch of the firmament and had lifted his hands to pray, a cloud, though no wind was stirring, hurried across the zenith and hid the brightening stars. The blue sky was still visible, except directly overhead, where this black mass of cloud was sweeping swiftly northward. Aloft in the air, as if from the depths of the cloud, came a confused and doubtful sound of voices. Once the listener fancied that he could distinguish the accents of towns-people of his own, men and women, both pious and ungodly, many of whom he had met at the communion table[2], and had seen others rioting at the tavern. The next moment, so indistinct were the sounds, he doubted whether he had heard aught but the murmur of the old forest, whispering without a wind. Then came a stronger swell of those familiar tones, heard daily in the sunshine at Salem village, but never until now from a cloud of night. There was one voice of a young woman, uttering lamentations, yet with an uncertain sorrow, and entreating for some favor, which, perhaps, it would grieve her to obtain; and all the unseen multitude, both saints and sinners, seemed to encourage her onward.

"Faith!" shouted Goodman Brown, in a voice of agony and desperation; and the echoes of the forest mocked him, crying, "Faith! Faith!" as if bewildered wretches were seeking her all through the wilderness.

The cry of grief, rage, and terror was yet piercing the night, when the unhappy husband held his breath for a response. There was a scream, drowned immediately in a louder murmur of voices, fading into far-off laughter, as the dark cloud swept away, leaving the clear and silent sky above Goodman Brown. But something fluttered lightly

---

1   Indian powwows: medicine men.
2   the communion table: the table for the Holy Communion, the Christian ceremony based on Christ's last supper.

down through the air and caught on the branch of a tree. The young man seized it, and beheld a pink ribbon.

"My Faith is gone!" cried he, after one stupefied moment. "There is no good on earth; and sin is but a name. Come, devil; for to thee is this world given."

And, maddened with despair, so that he laughed loud and long, did Goodman Brown grasp his staff and set forth again, at such a rate that he seemed to fly along the forest path rather than to walk or run. The road grew wilder and drearier and more faintly traced, and vanished at length, leaving him in the heart of the dark wilderness, still rushing onward with the instinct that guides mortal man to evil. The whole forest was peopled with frightful sounds—the creaking of the trees, the howling of wild beasts, and the yell of Indians; while sometimes the wind tolled like a distant church bell, and sometimes gave a broad roar around the traveller, as if all Nature were laughing him to scorn. But he was himself the chief horror of the scene, and shrank not from its other horrors.

"Ha! ha! ha!" roared Goodman Brown when the wind laughed at him.

"Let us hear which will laugh loudest. Think not to frighten me with your deviltry. Come witch, come wizard, come Indian powwow, come devil himself, and here comes Goodman Brown. You may as well fear him as he fears you."

In truth, all through the haunted forest there could be nothing more frightful than the figure of Goodman Brown. On he flew among the black pines, brandishing his staff with frenzied gestures, now giving vent to an inspiration of horrid blasphemy, and now shouting forth such laughter as set all the echoes of the forest laughing like demons around him. The fiend in his own shape is less hideous than when he rages in the breast of man. Thus sped the demoniac on his course, until, quivering among the trees, he saw a red light before him, as when the felled trunks and branches of a clearing have been set on fire, and throw up their lurid blaze against the sky, at the hour of midnight. He paused, in a lull of the tempest that had driven him onward, and heard the swell of what seemed a hymn, rolling solemnly from a distance with the weight of many voices. He knew the tune; it was a familiar one in the choir of the village meeting-house. The verse died heavily away, and was lengthened by a chorus, not of human voices, but of all the sounds of the benighted wilderness pealing in awful harmony together. Goodman Brown cried out, and his cry was lost to his own ear by its unison with the cry of the desert.

In the interval of silence, he stole forward until the light glared full upon his eyes. At one extremity of an open space, hemmed in by the dark wall of the forest, arose a rock, bearing some rude, natural resemblance either to an alter or a pulpit, and surrounded by four blazing pines, their tops aflame, their stems untouched, like candles at an evening meeting. The mass of foliage that had overgrown the summit of the rock was all on fire, blazing high into the night and fitfully illuminating the whole field. Each pendent twig and leafy festoon was in a blaze. As the red light arose and fell, a numerous congregation alternately shone forth, then disappeared in shadow, and again grew, as it were, out of the darkness, peopling the heart of the solitary woods at once.

"A grave and dark-clad company," quoth Goodman Brown.

In truth they were such. Among them, quivering to and fro between gloom and splendor, appeared faces that would be seen next day at the council board of the province, and others which, Sabbath after Sabbath, looked devoutly heavenward, and benignantly over the crowded pews, from the holiest pulpits in the land. Some affirm that the lady of the governor was there. At least there were high dames well known to her, and wives of honored husbands, and widows, a great multitude, and ancient maidens, all of excellent repute, and fair young girls, who trembled lest their mothers should espy them. Either the sudden gleams of light flashing over the obscure field bedazzled Goodman Brown, or he recognized a score of the church members of Salem village famous for their especial sanctity. Good old Deacon Gookin had arrived, and waited at the skirts of that venerable saint, his revered pastor. But, irreverently consorting with these grave, reputable, and pious people, these elders of the church, these chaste dames and dewy virgins, there were men of dissolute lives and women of spotted fame, wretches given over to all mean and filthy vice, and suspected even of horrid crimes. It was strange to see that the good shrank not from the wicked, nor were the sinners abashed by the saints. Scattered also among their pale-faced enemies were the Indian priests, or powwows, who had often scared their native forest with more hideous incantations than any known to English witchcraft.

"But where is Faith?" thought Goodman Brown; and, as hope came into his heart, he trembled.

Another verse of the hymn arose, a slow and mournful strain, such as the pious love, but joined to words which expressed all that our nature can conceive of sin, and darkly hinted at far more. Unfathomable to mere mortals is the lore of fiends. Verse after verse was sung; and still the chorus of the desert swelled between like the deepest tone of a mighty organ; and with the final peal of that dreadful anthem there came a sound, as if the roaring wind, the rushing streams, the howling beasts, and every other voice of the unconcerted wilderness were mingling and according with the voice of guilty man in homage to the prince of all. The four blazing pines threw up a loftier flame, and obscurely discovered shapes and visages of horror on the smoke wreaths above the impious assembly. At the same moment the fire on the rock shot redly forth and formed a glowing arch above its base, where now appeared a figure. With reverence be it spoken, the figure bore no slight similitude, both in garb and manner, to some grave divine of the New England churches.

"Bring forth the converts!" cried a voice that echoed through the field and rolled into the forest.

At the word, Goodman Brown stepped forth from the shadow of the trees and approached the congregation, with whom he felt a loathful brotherhood by the sympathy of all that was wicked in his heart. He could have well-nigh sworn that the shape of his own dead father beckoned him to advance, looking downward from a smoke wreath, while a woman, with dim features of despair, threw out her hand to warn him back. Was it his mother? But he had no power to retreat one step, nor to resist, even in thought, when the minister and good old Deacon Gookin seized his arms and led him to the blazing rock. Thither came also the slender form of a veiled female, led between Goody Cloyse, that pious teacher of the catechism, and Martha Carrier[1], who had received the devil's promise to be queen of hell. A rampant hag was she. And there stood the proselytes beneath the canopy of fire.

"Welcome, my children," said the dark figure, "to the communion of your race. Ye have found thus young your nature and your destiny. My children, look behind you!"

They turned; and flashing forth, as it were, in a sheet of flame, the fiend worshippers were seen; the smile of welcome gleamed darkly on every visage.

"There," resumed the sable form[2], "are all whom ye have reverenced from youth. Ye deemed them holier than yourselves, and shrank from your own sin, contrasting it with their lives of righteousness and prayerful aspirations heavenward. Yet here are they all in my worshipping assembly. This night it shall be granted you to know their secret deeds: how hoary-bearded elders of the church have whispered wanton words to the young maids of their households; how many a woman, eager for widows' weeds[3], has given her husband a drink at bedtime and let him sleep his last sleep in her bosom; how beardless youths have made haste to inherit their fathers' wealth; and how fair damsels[4]—blush not, sweet ones—have dug little graves in the garden, and bidden me, the sole guest to an infant's funeral. By the sympathy of your human hearts for sin ye shall scent out all the places—whether in church, bedchamber, street, field, or forest—where crime has been committed, and shall exult to behold the whole earth one stain of guilt, one mighty blood spot. Far more than this. It shall be yours to penetrate, in every bosom, the deep mystery of sin, the fountain of all wicked arts, and which inexhaustibly supplies more evil impulses than human power—than my power at its utmost—can make manifest in deeds. And now, my children, look upon each other."

They did so; and, by the blaze of the hell-kindled torches, the wretched man beheld his Faith, and the wife her husband, trembling before that unhallowed altar.

"Lo, there ye stand, my children," said the figure, in a deep and solemn tone, almost sad with its despairing awfulness, as if his once angelic nature could yet mourn for our miserable race. "Depending upon one another's hearts, ye had still hoped that virtue were not all a dream. Now are ye undeceived. Evil is the nature of mankind. Evil must

---

1   Martha Carrier: hanged as a witch at Salem, 1962. She had confessed that the devil had promised she would be "queen of hell".

2   the sable form: the dark figure, i.e. the Satan.

3   widow's weeds=widows' immortal life.

4   damsels=young noble woman.

be your only happiness. Welcome again, my children, to the communion of your race."

"Welcome," repeated the fiend worshippers, in one cry of despair and triumph.

And there they stood, the only pair, as it seemed, who were yet hesitating on the verge of wickedness in this dark world. A basin was hollowed, naturally, in the rock. Did it contain water, reddened by the lurid light? or was it blood? or, perchance, a liquid flame? Herein did the shape of evil dip his hand and prepare to lay the mark of baptism upon their foreheads, that they might be partakers of the mystery of sin, more conscious of the secret guilt of others, both in deed and thought, than they could now be of their own. The husband cast one look at his pale wife, and Faith at him. What polluted wretches would the next glance show them to each other, shuddering alike at what they disclosed and what they saw!

"Faith! Faith!" cried the husband, "look up to heaven, and resist the wicked one."

Whether Faith obeyed he knew not. Hardly had he spoken when he found himself amid calm night and solitude, listening to a roar of the wind which died heavily away through the forest. He staggered against the rock, and felt it chill and damp; while a hanging twig, that had been all on fire, besprinkled his cheek with the coldest dew.

The next morning young Goodman Brown came slowly into the street of Salem village, staring around him like a bewildered man. The good old minister was taking a walk along the graveyard to get an appetite for breakfast and meditate his sermon, and bestowed a blessing, as he passed, on Goodman Brown. He shrank from the venerable saint as if to avoid an anathema[1]. Old Deacon Gookin was at domestic worship, and the holy words of his prayer were heard through the open window. "What God doth the wizard pray to?" quoth Goodman Brown. Goody Cloyse, that excellent old Christian, stood in the early sunshine at her own lattice, catechizing a little girl who had brought her a pint of morning's milk. Goodman Brown snatched away the child as from the grasp of the fiend himself. Turning the corner by the meeting-house, he spied the head of Faith, with the pink ribbons, gazing anxiously forth, and bursting into such joy at sight of him that she skipped along the street and almost kissed her husband before the whole village. But Goodman Brown looked sternly and sadly into her face, and passed on without a greeting.

Had Goodman Brown fallen asleep in the forest and only dreamed a wild dream of a witch-meeting?

Be it so if you will; but, alas! it was a dream of evil omen for young Goodman Brown. A stern, a sad, a darkly meditative, a distrustful, if not a desperate man did he become from the night of that fearful dream. On the Sabbath day, when the congregation were singing a holy psalm, he could not listen because an anthem of sin rushed loudly upon his ear and drowned all the blessed strain. When the minister spoke from the pulpit with power and fervid eloquence, and, with his hand on the open Bible,

---

1   anathema=curse.

of the sacred truths of our religion, and of saint-like lives and triumphant deaths, and of future bliss or misery unutterable, then did Goodman Brown turn pale, dreading lest the roof should thunder down upon the gray blasphemer and his hearers. Often, waking suddenly at midnight, he shrank from the bosom of Faith; and at morning or eventide, when the family knelt down at prayer, he scowled and muttered to himself, and gazed sternly at his wife, and turned away. And when he had lived long, and was borne to his grave a hoary corpse, followed by Faith, an aged woman, and children and grandchildren, a goodly procession, besides neighbors not a few, they carved no hopeful verse upon his tombstone, for his dying hour was gloom.

Plot Summary

Goodman Brown is a young Puritan man living in Salem, Massachusetts. He is about to embark on a journey into the forest, and his wife, Faith, pleads with him to stay. He insists on going, and she reluctantly lets him go. Once in the forest, Goodman Brown meets the mysterious figure, who reveals himself to be the devil. The devil tells Goodman Brown that he has been chosen to witness the evil deeds of the people of Salem. He leads Goodman Brown to a clearing in the forest, where he sees many of the townspeople, including his own family, participating in a black mass. Goodman Brown is horrified by what he sees, and he flees in terror. He returns to Salem, but he is a changed man. He no longer trusts anyone, and he sees the evil in everyone. He becomes a bitter, cynical man, and he never recovers from the shock of what he witnessed in the forest. The story is a parable about the dangers of losing faith in humanity. Goodman Brown's journey into the forest symbolizes his journey into adulthood, and his experience in the forest symbolizes the disillusionment that often accompanies adulthood. The story serves as a warning to readers to be wary of the darkness that lies within us all.

Language Exercises

Choose the item that best replaces or explains the underlined part of the sentence.

1. And Faith, as the wife was <u>aptly</u> named, thrust her own pretty head into the street, letting the wind play with the pink ribbons of her cap while she called to Goodman Brown.

   A. piously   B. keenly   C. abruptly   D. suitably

2. … he looked back and saw the head of Faith still peeping after him with a <u>melancholy</u> air, in spite of her pink ribbons.

   A. depressed   B. melodious   C. melodramatic   D. reclusive

3. But the only thing about him that could be fixed upon as remarkable was his staff, which bore the likeness of a great black snake, so curiously wrought that it might almost be seen to twist and <u>wriggle</u> itself like a living serpent.

    A. dodge   B. squirm   C. thrust   D. shudder

4. Being a stranger to you, she might ask whom I was <u>consorting</u> with and whither I was going.

    A. comforting   B. talking   C. connecting   D. associating

5. They continued to walk onward, while the elder traveller <u>exhorted</u> his companion to make good speed and persevere in the path, discoursing so aptly that his arguments seemed rather to spring up in the bosom of his auditor than to be suggested by himself.

    A. urged   B. spurred   C. manipulated   D. simulated

6. "You will think better of this by and by," said his acquaintance, <u>composedly</u>.

    A. prominently   B. initially   C. collectedly   D. punctually

7. There was one voice of a young woman, uttering lamentations, yet with an uncertain sorrow, and <u>entreating</u> for some favor, which, perhaps, it would grieve her to obtain; …

    A. impelling   B. inducing   C. imploring   D. persuading

8. The fiend in his own shape is less <u>hideous</u> than when he rages in the breast of man.

    A. pleasant   B. horrific   C. dramatic   D. fierce

9. In the <u>interval</u> of silence, he stole forward until the light glared full upon his eyes.

    A. currency   B. access   C. essence   D. break

10. Each <u>pendent</u> twig and leafy festoon was in a blaze.

    A. pealike   B. hanging   C. pendulous   D. penetrable

11. … and others which, Sabbath after Sabbath, looked <u>devoutly</u> heavenward, and benignantly over the crowded pews, from the holiest pulpits in the land.

    A. ravenously   B. dexterously   C. devotedly   D. sincerely

12. Either the sudden gleams of light flashing over the <u>obscure</u> field bedazzled Goodman Brown, or he recognized a score of the church members of Salem village famous for their especial sanctity.

    A. unknown   B. arbitrary   C. secret   D. unique

13. <u>Unfathomable</u> to mere mortals is the lore of fiends.

    A. Compatible   B. Inscrutable   C. Convincible   D. Inconceivable

14. A <u>rampant</u> hag was she. And there stood the proselytes beneath the canopy of fire.

    A. rambling   B. unrestrained   C. growing   D. running

15. A stern, a sad, a darkly <u>meditative</u>, a distrustful, if not a desperate man did he become from the night of that fearful dream.

    A. pensive   B. indifferent   C. solitary   D. tranquil

Topics for Discussion

1. The story's mode lies somewhere between ghostly tale and parable. What is the meaning of this story?

2. Hawthorne explores the dark side of Brown's nature; can you describe it? What do you think is the author's opinion of "original sin"?

3. Comment on the whole structure. Is it compact, tense or loose? What is the writing style of the story?

4. Hawthorne comprehensively employs realism, allegory and symbolism in the story; find out the description of each means and analyze them.

5. There are several binary oppositions reflected in the story. What are they?

6. Some critics treat the fiction as an initiation story, do you agree or disagree? Why?

7. What does Goodman Brown mean when he says "Faith kept me back a while", after the Devil comments on his lack of punctuality?

8. Was Goodman Brown's brush with evil real or imagined? Read other works of literature in which the line between reality and imagination is blurred, such as "The Fall of the House of Usher" by Edgar Allan Poe. What are some of the reasons why authors might use this technique?

9. Investigate the dictates of Puritan culture. How is contemporary American culture different? How is it the same?

10. What effects did the Salem Witch Trials have on the nation as a whole? Cite specific historic examples.

Discussion Tips

"Young Goodman Brown", written in 1835 by Nathaniel Hawthorne, stands as a compelling portrayal of seventeenth-century Puritan society, renowned for its exploration of the human experience and the pervasive themes of sin and morality. It serves as a thought-provoking exploration of the human psyche, delving into the complexities of morality, the inevitability of sin, and the enduring struggle to reconcile the darker aspects of human nature.

The story follows the journey of a young Puritan man, Goodman Brown, who becomes entangled in a pact with the Devil. His idealized perceptions of the goodness of his community are shattered when he discovers that many of his fellow townspeople, including religious leaders and even his own wife, are participating in a sinister Black Mass. The tale concludes with an ambiguous ending, leaving the reader questioning whether Brown's ordeal was a nightmare or reality. Nevertheless, the outcome remains unchanged—Brown is unable to reconcile the potential for evil within his loved ones, leading him to a life of desolate loneliness and despair.

While a work of fiction, "Young Goodman Brown" is widely regarded as a poignant commentary on the hysteria surrounding the Salem Witch Trials of 1692. Hawthorne is also celebrated for his role in elevating the short story as a respected literary form and for infusing moral lessons into his writing. Throughout his life, Hawthorne grappled with the guilt stemming from the actions of his ancestors. Critics perceive his literary preoccupation with Puritanism as an extension of his familial heritage. The first Hawthorne to immigrate to Massachusetts, William, was a magistrate who ordered the public punishment of a Quaker woman. Subsequently, William's son, John, served as a judge in the Salem Witch Trials. Hawthorne's own father, a ship's captain, passed away when he was just four years old. Consequently, Hawthorne infused much of his work, including "Young Goodman Brown" with themes exploring human malevolence and the concept of original sin.

In "Young Goodman Brown", Hawthorne presents sin as an inevitable aspect of human nature. The notion that Goodman Brown embarks on his journey into the malevolent forest only once suggests that the spiritual quest is a rite of passage that all individuals must undergo at some point in their lives. However, Brown proves himself incapable of accepting this facet of the human condition, consequently becoming paralyzed and unable to progress in his life. Conversely, his wife, Faith, symbolically embraces her name by exhibiting unwavering trust and love, welcoming her husband back with open arms after his inexplicable absence. In contrast, Brown gazes at her with a sorrowful and stern countenance, refusing to acknowledge her. While Faith embraces the inevitable fallen nature of humanity and continues to thrive, Brown, entrenched in absolutism, is unable to reconcile this truth and remains ensnared in a state of suspicion and bitterness. Through these contrasting reactions, Hawthorne not only comments on the rigid, black-and-white Puritan perspective of good and evil, but also illustrates the multifaceted nature of malevolence.

Unit 4
Herman Melville: "Bartleby, the Scrivener"

About the Author

Herman Melville (1819–1891)

Herman Melville (1819–1891), best known for his novel *Moby-Dick* (1851), a tremendous work about a whaling voyage, was born in New York City. By the time he was in his early twenties, he went off to sea, sailing first to Liverpool, England, then to the Marquesas Islands and areas in the South Seas on a whaling ship. Based on his experiences, he wrote the novels *Typee* (1846) and *Omoo* (1847). *Redburn*, an autobiographical novel based on his first voyage, appeared in 1849. Largely self-educated, Melville read widely, especially William Shakespeare and Ralph Waldo Emerson, both of whom influenced Melville's legendary novel, *Moby-Dick*. In the book, Melville's narrator, Ishmael, tells of the epic quest of Captain Ahab after the white whale. Now widely regarded as one of the greatest novels of American literature for its gripping epic adventure and its profound metaphysical journey. Although Melville is most known for his novels, later in his life he also wrote poems and many fine stories, including "Bartleby, the Scrivener", which reflects his experience of working on Wall Street.

The Literary History

Melville and American Short Stories

The Span (1828–1865) from the Jacksonian era to the Civil War, often identified as the Romantic Period in America, marks the full coming of age of a distinctively American literature. American romanticism reached its peak with the appearance of the major authors of the 19th century, such as Edgar Allan Poe, Walt Whitman and Emily Dickinson in poetry, and Nathaniel Hawthorne and Herman Melville in fiction.

Herman Melville is best known as the author of *Moby-Dick*, a novel which reveals his epic powers of observation and analysis, while "Bartleby, the Scrivener" and "Billy Budd", two enduring works of short stories that have secured a lasting place in the

American literary canon. Like *Moby-Dick*, these shorter works reflect many of the issues central to 19th-century society and continue to illuminate contemporary social concerns. Compared with early romantics like Irving, who, generally speaking, were naive, experimental, conformist, self-conscious and imitative, which were picturesque, but lacked a deeper power, Melville presented the dark side of humanity. Symbolic richness, irony, vicious satire and metaphysical metaphor abound in his short fiction. The themes of his stories usually concern alienation, loneliness, suicidal individualism, rejection and quest, confrontation of innocence and evil, and the loss of faith and the sense of futility and meaninglessness. "Bartleby, the Scrivener", the story recounts how a scrivener, a copier of legal records, progressively withdrew from his duties and from all activities of normal life, staring out the window at a brick wall, and eventually starved to death in a prison. What gives the narrative substance is that it is told, in retrospect, by the lawyer who employed Bartleby, and although he needs the services of all of his employees, he finds something deeply intriguing in the sense of emptiness, pointlessness, and resignation that the scrivener exhibits. An intelligent man, the lawyer is capable of searching his own mind and recognizing the degree to which Bartleby is but an exaggeration of the impulses that seem to invest his own life and, perhaps, that of all mankind. That interest in the tale has remained strong over all of the decades since it was originally published, the lawyer would seem to have been right: there is a universal appeal in Bartleby's strange and yet touching hopelessness.

Literary Terms

Nihilism

Nihilism (from Latin nihil, "nothing"), originally a philosophy of moral and epistemological skepticism that arose in 19th-century Russia during the early years of the reign of Tsar Alexander II. The term was famously used by Friedrich Nietzsche to describe the disintegration of traditional morality in Western society. In the 20th century, nihilism encompassed a variety of philosophical and aesthetic stances that, in one sense or another, denied the existence of genuine moral truths or values, rejected the possibility of knowledge or communication, and asserted the ultimate meaninglessness or purposelessness of life or of the universe.

Alienation

Alienation is a theoretical concept developed by Karl Marx that describes the isolating, dehumanizing, and disenchanting effects of working within a capitalist system of production. Per Marx, its cause is the economic system itself. The concept of alienation has a long and complex history as it has been used in Judeo-Christian theology, Roman law, medieval concepts of insanity, German Idealism especially in

Hegel, in the dialectical materialism of Marx, and more recently, in Frankfurt School Critical Theory and in existentialism. As adopted and adapted to different disciplines, alienation serves to convey an understanding of voluntary and involuntary withdrawal from the full realization of capabilities. Thus, alienation bears a variety of meanings, ranging from its usage as a term for the general malaise of the human condition to its usage as a detailed description of the specifics of oppression through mechanisms of wage labor.

The Story

Bartleby, the Scrivener: The Story of Wall Street[1]

I am a rather elderly man. The nature of my avocations, for the last thirty years, has brought me into more than ordinary contact with what would seem an interesting and somewhat singular set of men, of whom, as yet, nothing, that I know of, has ever been written—I mean, the law-copyists, or scriveners. I have known very many of them, professionally and privately, and, if I pleased, could relate diverse histories, at which good-natured gentlemen might smile, and sentimental souls might weep. But I waive the biographies of all other scriveners, for a few passages in the life of Bartleby, who was a scrivener, the strangest I ever saw, or heard of. While, of other law-copyists, I might write the complete life, of Bartleby nothing of that sort can be done. I believe that no materials exist, for a full and satisfactory biography of this man. It is an irreparable loss to literature. Bartleby was one of those beings of whom nothing is ascertainable, except from the original sources, and, in his case, those are very small. What my own astonished eyes saw of Bartleby, that is all I know of him, except, indeed, one vague report, which will appear in the sequel.

Ere[2] introducing the scrivener, as he first appeared to me, it is fit I make some mention of myself, my employes, my business, my chambers, and general surroundings, because some such description is indispensable to an adequate understanding of the chief character about to be presented.

Imprimis[3]: I am a man who, from his youth upwards, has been filled with a profound conviction that the easiest way of life is the best. Hence, though I belong to a profession proverbially energetic and nervous, even to turbulence, at times, yet nothing of that sort have I ever suffered to invade my peace. I am one of those unambitious lawyers who never address a jury, or in any way draw down public applause; but, in the cool tranquility of a snug retreat, do a snug business among rich men's bonds, and mortgages, and title-deeds. All who know me, consider me an eminently safe man. The

---

1   Herman Melville, *The Piazza Tales* (Penguin Classics, 1986), pp. 3–30.

2   Ere=before.

3   Imprimis=in the first place.

late John Jacob Astor[1], a personage little given to poetic enthusiasm, had no hesitation in pronouncing my first grand point to be prudence; my next, method. I do not speak it in vanity, but simply record the fact, that I was not unemployed in my profession by the late John Jacob Astor; a name which, I admit, I love to repeat; for it hath a rounded and orbicular sound to it, and rings like unto bullion. I will freely add, that I was not insensible to the late John Jacob Astor's good opinion.

Some time prior to the period at which this little history begins, my avocations had been largely increased. The good old office, now extinct in the State of New York, of a Master in Chancery, had been conferred upon me. It was not a very arduous office, but very pleasantly remunerative. I seldom lose my temper; much more seldom indulge in dangerous indignation at wrongs and outrages; but I must be permitted to be rash here and declare, that I consider the sudden and violent abrogation of the office of Master in Chancery, by the new Constitution, as a-premature act; inasmuch as I had counted upon a life-lease of the profits, whereas I only received those of a few short years. But this is by the way.

My chambers were upstairs, at No. —Wall Street. At one end, they looked upon the white wall of the interior of a spacious skylight shaft, penetrating the building from top to bottom. This view might have been considered rather tame than otherwise, deficient in what landscape painters call "life." But, if so, the view from the other end of my chambers offered, at least, a contrast, if nothing more. In that direction, my windows commanded an unobstructed view of a lofty brick wall, black by age and everlasting shade; which wall required no spyglass to bring out its lurking beauties, but, for the benefit of all near-sighted spectators, was pushed up to within ten feet of my window-panes. Owing to the great height of the surrounding buildings, and my chambers being on the second floor, the interval between this wall and mine not a little resembled a huge square cistern.

At the period just preceding the advent of Bartleby, I had two persons as copyists in my employment, and a promising lad as an office-boy. First, Turkey; second, Nippers; third, Ginger Nut. These may seem names, the like of which are not usually found in the Directory. In truth, they were nicknames, mutually conferred upon each other by my three clerks, and were deemed expressive of their respective persons or characters. Turkey was a short, pursy Englishman, of about my own age—that is, somewhere not far from sixty. In the morning, one might say, his face was of a fine florid hue, but after twelve o'clock, meridian—his dinner hour—it blazed like a grate full of Christmas coals; and continued blazing—but, as it were, with a gradual wane—till six o'clock, P.M., or thereabouts; after which, I saw no more of the proprietor of the face, which, gaining its meridian with the sun, seemed to set with it, to rise, culminate, and decline

---

1　John Jacob Astor: United States capitalist (born in Germany) who made a fortune in fur trading (1763–1848).

the following day, with the like regularity and undiminished glory. There are many singular coincidences I have known in the course of my life, not the least among which was the fact, that, exactly when Turkey displayed his fullest beams from his red and radiant countenance, just then, too, at that critical moment, began the daily period when I considered his business capacities as seriously disturbed for the remainder of the twenty-four hours. Not that he was absolutely idle, or averse to business then; far from it. The difficulty was, he was apt to be altogether too energetic. There was a strange, inflamed, flurried, flighty recklessness of activity about him. He would be incautious in dipping his pen into his inkstand. All his blots upon my documents were dropped there after twelve o'clock, meridian. Indeed, not only would he be reckless, and sadly given to making blots in the afternoon, but, some days, he went further, and was rather noisy. At such times, too, his face flamed with augmented blazonry, as if cannel coal had been heaped on anthracite. He made an unpleasant racket with his chair; spilled his sand-box; in mending his pens, impatiently split them all to pieces, and threw them on the floor in a sudden passion; stood up, and leaned over his table, boxing his papers about in a most indecorous manner, very sad to behold in an elderly man like him. Nevertheless, as he was in many ways a most valuable person to me, and all the time before twelve o'clock, meridian, was the quickest, steadiest creature, too, accomplishing a great deal of work in a style not easily to be matched—for these reasons, I was willing to overlook his eccentricities, though, indeed, occasionally, I remonstrated with him. I did this very gently, however, because, though the civilest, nay, the blandest and most reverential of men in the morning, yet, in the afternoon, he was disposed, upon provocation, to be slightly rash with his tongue—in fact, insolent. Now, valuing his morning services as I did, and resolved not to lose them—yet, at the same time, made uncomfortable by his inflamed ways after twelve o'clock—and being a man of peace, unwilling by my admonitions to call forth unseemly retorts from him, I took upon me, one Saturday noon (he was always worse on Saturdays) to hint to him, very kindly, that, perhaps, now that he was growing old, it might be well to abridge his labors; in short, he need not come to my chambers after twelve o'clock, but, dinner over, had best go home to his lodgings, and rest himself till tea-time. But no; he insisted upon his afternoon devotions. His countenance became intolerably fervid, as he oratorically assured me—gesticulating with a long ruler at the other end of the room—that if his services in the morning were useful, how indispensable, then, in the afternoon?

"With submission, sir," said Turkey, on this occasion, "I consider myself your right-hand man. In the morning I but marshal and deploy my columns; but in the afternoon I put myself at their head, and gallantly charge the foe, thus"—and he made a violent thrust with the ruler.

"But the blots, Turkey," intimated I.

"True; but, with submission, sir, behold these hairs! I am getting old. Surely, sir, a blot or two of a warm afternoon is not to be severely urged against gray hairs. Old age—even if it blot the page—is honorable. With submission, sir, we both are getting old."

This appeal to my fellow-feeling was hardly to be resisted. At all events, I saw that go he would not. So, I made up my mind to let him stay, resolving, nevertheless, to see to it that, during the afternoon, he had to do with my less important papers.

Nippers, the second on my list, was a whiskered, sallow, and, upon the whole, rather piratical-looking young man, of about five-and-twenty. I always deemed him the victim of two evil powers—ambition and indigestion. The ambition was evinced by a certain impatience of the duties of a mere copyist, an unwarrantable usurpation of strictly professional affairs such as the original drawing up of legal documents. The indigestion seemed betokened in an occasional nervous testiness and grinning irritability, causing the teeth to audibly grind together over mistakes committed in copying; unnecessary maledictions, hissed, rather than spoken, in the heat of business; and especially by a continual discontent with the height of the table where he worked. Though of a very ingenious mechanical turn, Nippers could never get this table to suit him. He put chips under it, blocks of various sorts, bits of pasteboard, and at last went so far as to attempt an exquisite adjustment, by final pieces of folded blotting-paper. But no invention would answer. If, for the sake of easing his back, he brought the table-lid at a sharp angle well up towards his chin, and wrote there like a man using the steep roof of a Dutch house for his desk, then he declared that it stopped the circulation in his arms. If now he lowered the table to his waistbands, and stooped over it in writing, then there was a sore aching in his back. In short, the truth of the matter was, Nippers knew not what he wanted. Or, if he wanted anything, it was to be rid of a scrivener's table altogether. Among the manifestations of his diseased ambition was a fondness he had for receiving visits from certain ambiguous-looking fellows in seedy coats, whom he called his clients. Indeed, I was aware that not only was he, at times, considerable of a ward-politician, but he occasionally did a little business at the justices' courts, and was not unknown on the steps of the Tombs. I have good reason to believe, however, that one individual who called upon him at my chambers, and who, with a grand air, he insisted was his client, was no other than a dun, and the alleged title-deed, a bill. But, with all his failings, and the annoyances he caused me, Nippers, like his compatriot Turkey, was a very useful man to me; wrote a neat, swift hand; and, when he chose, was not deficient in a gentlemanly sort of deportment. Added to this, he always dressed in a gentlemanly sort of way; and so, incidentally, reflected credit upon my chambers. Whereas, with respect to Turkey, I had much ado to keep him from being a reproach to me. His clothes were apt to look oily, and smell of eating-houses. He wore his pantaloons very loose and baggy in summer. His coats were execrable, his hat not to be handled. But while the hat was a thing of indifference to me, inasmuch as his natural civility and deference, as a dependent Englishman, always led him to doff it the moment he entered the room, yet his coat was another matter. Concerning his coats, I reasoned with him; but with no effect. The truth was, I suppose, that a man with so small an income could not afford to sport such a lustrous face and a lustrous coat at one and the same time. As Nippers once observed, Turkey's money went chiefly for red ink. One winter day, I presented Turkey with a highly respectable-looking coat of my own—a padded gray coat, of a most comfortable warmth, and which buttoned straight up from the knee to the neck. I thought Turkey would appreciate the favor, and abate his rashness and obstreperousness of afternoons. But no; I verily believe that buttoning himself up in so downy and blanket-like a coat had a pernicious effect upon him—upon the same principle that too much oats are bad for horses. In fact, precisely as a rash, restive horse is said to feel his oats, so Turkey felt his coat. It made him insolent. He was a man whom prosperity harmed.

Though, concerning the self-indulgent habits of Turkey, I had my own private surmises, yet, touching Nippers, I was well persuaded that, whatever might be his faults in other respects, he was, at least, a temperate young man. But indeed, nature herself seemed to have been his vintner, and, at his birth, charged him so thoroughly with an irritable, brandy-like disposition, that all subsequent potations were needless. When I consider how, amid the stillness of my chambers, Nippers would sometimes impatiently rise from his seat, and stooping over his table, spread his arms wide apart, seize the whole desk, and move it, and jerk it, with a grim, grinding motion on the floor, as if the table were a perverse voluntary agent, intent on thwarting and vexing him, I plainly perceive that, for Nippers, brandy-and-water were altogether superfluous.

It was fortunate for me that, owing to its peculiar cause—indigestion—the irritability and consequent nervousness of Nippers were mainly observable in the morning, while in the afternoon he was comparatively mild. So that, Turkey's paroxysms only coming on about twelve o'clock, I never had to do with their eccentricities at one time. Their fits relieved each other, like guards. When Nippers' was on, Turkey's was off; and vice versa. This was a good natural arrangement, under the circumstances.

Ginger Nut, the third on my list, was a lad, some twelve years old. His father was a carman, ambitious of seeing his son on the bench instead of a cart, before he died. So he sent him to my office, as student at law, errand-boy, cleaner, and sweeper, at the rate of one dollar a week. He had a little desk to himself, but he did not use it much. Upon inspection, the drawer exhibited a great array of the shells of various sorts of nuts. Indeed, to this quick-witted youth, the whole noble science of the law was contained in a nutshell. Not the least among the employments of Ginger Nut, as well as one which he discharged with the most alacrity, was his duty as cake and apple purveyor for Turkey and Nippers. Copying lawpapers being proverbially a dry, husky sort of business, my two scriveners were fain to moisten their mouths very often with

Spitzenbergs[1], to be had at the numerous stalls nigh the Custom House and Post Office. Also, they sent Ginger Nut very frequently for that peculiar cake—small, flat, round, and very spicy—after which he had been named by them. Of a cold morning, when business was but dull, Turkey would gobble up scores of these cakes, as if they were mere wafers—indeed, they sell them at the rate of six or eight for a penny—the scrape of his pen blending with the crunching of the crisp particles in his mouth. Of all the fiery afternoon blunders and flurried rashness of Turkey, was his once moistening a ginger-cake between his lips, and clapping it on to a mortgage, for a seal. I came within an ace of dismissing him then. But he mollified me by making an oriental bow, and saying—

"With submission, sir, it was generous of me to find you in stationery on my own account."

Now my original business—that of a conveyancer and title hunter, and drawer-up of recondite documents of all sorts—was considerably increased by receiving the Master's office. There was now great work for scriveners. Not only must I push the clerks already with me, but I must have additional help.

In answer to my advertisement, a motionless young man one morning stood upon my office threshold, the door being open, for it was summer. I can see that figure now—pallidly neat, pitiably respectable, incurably forlorn! It was Bartleby.

After a few words touching his qualifications, I engaged him, glad to have among my corps of copyists a man of so singularly sedate an aspect, which I thought might operate beneficially upon the flighty temper of Turkey, and the fiery one of Nippers.

I should have stated before that ground-glass folding-doors divided my premises into two parts, one of which was occupied by my scriveners, the other by myself. According to my humor, I threw open these doors, or closed them. I resolved to assign Bartleby a corner by the folding-doors, but on my side of them, so as to have this quiet man within easy call, in case any trifling thing was to be done. I placed his desk close up to a small side-window in that part of the room, a window which originally had afforded a lateral view of certain grimy brickyards and bricks, but which, owing to subsequent erections, commanded at present no view at all, though it gave some light. Within three feet of the panes was a wall, and the light came down from far above, between two lofty buildings, as from a very small opening in a dome. Still further to a satisfactory arrangement, I procured a high green folding screen, which might entirely isolate Bartleby from my sight, though not remove him from my voice. And thus, in a manner, privacy and society were conjoined.

---

1   Spitzenberg is a variety of apple that originated in the United States and is primarily grown in the Hudson Valley region of New York State. The skin of the fruit is deep red with occasional yellowish spots. The name Spitzenberg comes from the German language and means "sharp peak mountain", possibly indicating its origins in the Shawangunk Mountains region of New York.

At first, Bartleby did an extraordinary quantity of writing. As if long famishing for something to copy, he seemed to gorge himself on my documents. There was no pause for digestion. He ran a day and night line, copying by sunlight and by candlelight. I should have been quite delighted with his application, had he been cheerfully industrious. But he wrote on silently, palely, mechanically.

It is, of course, an indispensable part of a scrivener's business to verify the accuracy of his copy, word by word. Where there are two or more scriveners in an office, they assist each other in this examination, one reading from the copy, the other holding the original. It is a very dull, wearisome, and lethargic affair. I can readily imagine that, to some sanguine temperaments, it would be altogether intolerable. For example, I cannot credit that the mettlesome poet, Byron, would have contentedly sat down with Bartleby to examine a law document of, say five hundred pages, closely written in a crimpy hand.

Now and then, in the haste of business, it had been my habit to assist in comparing some brief document myself, calling Turkey or Nippers for this purpose. One object I had, in placing Bartleby so handy to me behind the screen, was, to avail myself of his services on such trivial occasions. It was on the third day, I think, of his being with me, and before any necessity had arisen for having his own writing examined, that, being much hurried to complete a small affair I had in hand, I abruptly called to Bartleby. In my haste and natural expectancy of instant compliance, I sat with my head bent over the original on my desk, and my right hand sideways, and somewhat nervously extended with the copy, so that, immediately upon emerging from his retreat, Bartleby might snatch it and proceed to business without the least delay.

In this very attitude did I sit when I called to him, rapidly stating what it was I wanted him to do—namely, to examine a small paper with me. Imagine my surprise, nay, my consternation, when, without moving from his privacy, Bartleby, in a singularly mild, firm voice, replied, "I would prefer not to."

I sat awhile in perfect silence, rallying my stunned faculties. Immediately it occurred to me that my ears had deceived me, or Bartleby had entirely misunderstood my meaning. I repeated my request in the clearest tone I could assume; but in quite as clear a one came the previous reply, "I would prefer not to."

"Prefer not to," echoed I, rising in high excitement, and crossing the room with a stride. "What do you mean? Are you moonstruck? I want you to help me compare this sheet here—take it," and I thrust it towards him.

"I would prefer not to," said he.

I looked at him steadfastly. His face was leanly composed; his gray eye dimly calm. Not a wrinkle of agitation rippled him. Had there been the least uneasiness, anger, impatience, or impertinence in his manner; in other words, had there been anything ordinarily human about him, doubtless I should have violently dismissed him from the premises. But as it was, I should have as soon thought of turning my pale plaster-of-paris bust of Cicero out of doors. I stood gazing at him awhile, as he went on with his own writing, and then reseated myself at my desk. This is very strange, thought I. What had one best do? But my business hurried me. I concluded to forget the matter for the present, reserving it for my future leisure. So, calling Nippers from the other room, the paper was speedily examined.

A few days after this, Bartleby concluded four lengthy documents, being quadruplicates of a week's testimony taken before me in my High Court of Chancery. It became necessary to examine them. It was an important suit, and great accuracy was imperative. Having all things arranged, I called Turkey, Nippers, and Ginger Nut, from the next room, meaning to place the four copies in the hands of my four clerks, while I should read from the original. Accordingly, Turkey, Nippers, and Ginger Nut had taken their seats in a row, each with his document in his hand, when I called to Bartleby to join this interesting group.

"Bartleby! quick, I am waiting."

I heard a slow scrape of his chair legs on the uncarpeted floor, and soon he appeared standing at the entrance of his hermitage. "What is wanted?" said he, mildly.

"The copies, the copies," said I, hurriedly. "We are going to examine them. There"—and I held towards him the fourth quadruplicate.

"I would prefer not to," he said, and gently disappeared behind the screen.

For a few moments I was turned into a pillar of salt, standing at the head of my seated column of clerks. Recovering myself, I advanced towards the screen, and demanded the reason for such extraordinary conduct.

"Why do you refuse?"

"I would prefer not to."

With any other man I should have flown outright into a dreadful passion, scorned all further words, and thrust him ignominiously from my presence. But there was something about Bartleby that not only strangely disarmed me, but, in a wonderful manner, touched and disconcerted me. I began to reason with him.

"These are your own copies we are about to examine. It is labor saving to you, because one examination will answer for your four papers. It is common usage. Every copyist is bound to help examine his copy. Is it not so? Will you not speak? Answer!"

"I prefer not to," he replied in a flute-like tone. It seemed to me that, while I had been addressing him, he carefully revolved every statement that I made; fully comprehended the meaning; could not gainsay the irresistible conclusion; but, at the same time, some paramount consideration prevailed with him to reply as he did.

"You are decided, then, not to comply with my request—a request made according to common usage and common sense?"

He briefly gave me to understand, that on that point my judgment was sound. Yes: his decision was irreversible.

It is not seldom the case that, when a man is browbeaten in some unprecedented and violently unreasonable way, he begins to stagger in his own plainest faith. He begins, as it were, vaguely to surmise that, wonderful as it may be, all the justice and all the reason is on the other side. Accordingly, if any disinterested persons are present, he turns to them for some reinforcement for his own faltering mind.

"Turkey," said I, "what do you think of this? Am I not right?"

"With submission, sir," said Turkey, in his blandest tone, "I think that you are."

"Nippers," said I, "what do you think of it?"

"I think I should kick him out of the office."

(The reader of nice perceptions will have perceived that, it being morning, Turkey's answer is couched in polite and tranquil terms, but Nippers replies in ill-tempered ones. Or, to repeat a previous sentence, Nippers' ugly mood was on duty, and Turkey's off.)

"Ginger Nut," said I, willing to enlist the smallest suffrage in my behalf, "what do you think of it?"

"I think, sir, he's a little luny" replied Ginger Nut, with a grin.

"You hear what they say," said I, turning towards the screen, "come forth and do 50 your duty."

But he vouchsafed no reply. I pondered a moment in sore perplexity. But once more business hurried me. I determined again to postpone the consideration of this dilemma to my future leisure. With a little trouble we made out to examine the papers without Bartleby, though at every page or two Turkey deferentially dropped his opinion, that this proceeding was quite out of the common; while Nippers, twitching in his chair with a dyspeptic nervousness, ground out, between his set teeth, occasional hissing maledictions against the stubborn oaf behind the screen. And for his (Nippers') part, this was the first and the last time he would do another man's business without pay.

Meanwhile Bartleby sat in his hermitage, oblivious to everything but his own peculiar business there.

Some days passed; the scrivener being employed upon another lengthy work. His late remarkable conduct led me to regard his ways narrowly. I observed that he never went to dinner; indeed, that he never went anywhere. As yet I had never, of my personal knowledge, known him to be outside of my office. He was a perpetual sentry in the corner. At about eleven o'clock though, in the morning, I noticed that Ginger Nut would advance toward the opening in Bartleby's screen, as if silently beckoned thither by a gesture invisible to me where I sat. The boy would then leave the office, jingling a few pence, and reappear with a handful of ginger-nuts, which he delivered in the hermitage, receiving two of the cakes for his trouble.

He lives, then, on ginger-nuts, thought I; never eats a dinner, properly speaking; he must be a vegetarian, then, but no; he never eats even vegetables, he eats nothing but ginger-nuts. My mind then ran on in reveries concerning the probable effects upon the human constitution of living entirely on ginger-nuts. Ginger-nuts are so called, because they contain ginger as one of their peculiar constituents, and the final flavoring one.

Now, what was ginger? A hot, spicy thing. Was Bartleby hot and spicy? Not at all. Ginger, then, had no effect upon Bartleby. Probably he preferred it should have none.

Nothing so aggravates an earnest person as a passive resistance. If the individual so resisted be of a not inhumane temper, and the resisting one perfectly harmless in his passivity, then, in the better moods of the former, he will endeavor charitably to construe to his imagination what proves impossible to be solved by his judgment. Even so, for the most part, I regarded Bartleby and his ways. Poor fellow! thought I, he means no mischief; it is plain he intends no insolence; his aspect sufficiently evinces that his eccentricities are involuntary. He is useful to me. I can get along with him. If I turn him away, the chances are he will fall in with some less indulgent employer, and then he will be rudely treated, and perhaps driven forth miserably to starve. Yes. Here I can cheaply purchase a delicious self-approval. To befriend Bartleby; to humor him in his strange willfulness, will cost me little or nothing, while I lay up in my soul what will eventually prove a sweet morsel for my conscience. But this mood was not invariable with me. The passiveness of Bartleby sometimes irritated me. I felt strangely goaded on to encounter him in new opposition—to elicit some angry spark from him answerable to my own. But, indeed, I might as well have essayed to strike fire with my knuckles against a bit of Windsor soap. But one afternoon the evil impulse in me mastered me, and the following little scene ensued:

"Bartleby," said I, "when those papers are all copied, I will compare them with you."

"I would prefer not to."

"How? Surely you do not mean to persist in that mulish vagary?" No answer.

I threw open the folding-doors nearby, and turning upon Turkey and Nippers, 60 exclaimed:

"Bartleby a second time says, he won't examine his papers. What do you think of it, Turkey?"

It was afternoon, be it remembered. Turkey sat glowing like a brass boiler; his bald head steaming; his hands reeling among his blotted papers.

"Think of it?" roared Turkey. "I think I'll just step behind his screen, and black his eyes for him!"

So saying, Turkey rose to his feet and threw his arms into a pugilistic position. He was hurrying away to make good his promise, when I detained him, alarmed at the effect of incautiously rousing Turkey's combativeness after dinner.

"Sit down, Turkey," said I, "and hear what Nippers has to say. What do you think of it, Nippers? Would I not be justified in immediately dismissing Bartleby?"

"Excuse me, that is for you to decide, sir. I think his conduct quite unusual, and, indeed, unjust, as regards Turkey and myself. But it may only be a passing whim."

"Ah," exclaimed I, "you have strangely changed your mind, then—you speak very gently of him now."

"All beer," cried Turkey; "gentleness is effects of beer—Nippers and I dined together

81

to-day. You see how gentle I am, sir. Shall I go and black his eyes?"

"You refer to Bartleby, I suppose. No, not to-day, Turkey," I replied; "pray, put up your fists."

I closed the doors, and again advanced towards Bartleby. I felt additional incentives tempting me to my fate. I burned to be rebelled against again. I remembered that Bartleby never left the office.

"Bartleby," said I, "Ginger Nut is away; just step around to the Post Office, won't you?" (it was but a three minutes' walk) "and see if there is anything for me."

"I would prefer not to."

"You will not?"

"I prefer not."

I staggered to my desk, and sat there in a deep study. My blind inveteracy returned. Was there any other thing in which I could procure myself to be ignominiously repulsed by this lean, penniless wight?—my hired clerk? What added thing is there, perfectly reasonable, that he will be sure to refuse to do?

"Bartleby!"

No answer.

"Bartleby," in a louder tone. No answer.

"Bartleby," I roared. Like a very ghost, agreeably to the laws of magical invocation, at the third summons, he appeared at the entrance of his hermitage.

"Go to the next room, and tell Nippers to come to me."

"I prefer not to," he respectfully and slowly said, and mildly disappeared.

"Very good, Bartleby," said I, in a quiet sort of serenely-severe self-possessed tone, intimating the unalterable purpose of some terrible retribution very close at hand. At the moment I half intended something of the kind. But upon the whole, as it was drawing towards my dinner-hour, I thought it best to put on my hat and walk home for the day, suffering much from perplexity and distress of mind.

Shall I acknowledge it? The conclusion of this whole business was, that it soon 85 became a fixed fact of my chambers, that a pale young scrivener, by the name of Bartleby, had a desk there; that he copied for me at the usual rate of four cents a folio (one hundred words); but he was permanently exempt from examining the work done by him, that duty being transferred to Turkey and Nippers, out of compliment, doubtless, to their superior acuteness; moreover, said Bartleby was never, on any account, to be dispatched on the most trivial errand of any sort; and that even if entreated to take upon him such a matter, it was generally understood that he would "prefer not to"—in other words, that he would refuse point-blank.

As days passed on, I became considerably reconciled to Bartleby. His steadiness, his freedom from all dissipation, his incessant industry (except when he chose to throw himself into a standing revery behind his screen), his great stillness, his unalterableness of demeanor under all circumstances, made him a valuable acquisition. One prime thing was this—he was always there—first in the morning, continually through the day, and the last at night. I had a singular confidence in his honesty. I felt my most precious papers perfectly safe in his hands. Sometimes, to be sure, I could not, for the very soul of me, avoid falling into sudden spasmodic passions with him. For it was exceeding difficult to bear in mind all the time those strange peculiarities, privileges, and unheard-of exemptions, forming the tacit stipulations on Bartleby's part under which he remained in my office. Now and then, in the eagerness of dispatching pressing business, I would inadvertently summon Bartleby, in a short, rapid tone, to put his finger, say, on the incipient tie of a bit of red tape with which I was about compressing some papers. Of course, from behind the screen the usual answer, "I prefer not to," was sure to come; and then, how could a human creature, with the common infirmities of our nature, refrain from bitterly exclaiming upon such perverseness—such unreasonableness? However, every added repulse of this sort which I received only tended to lessen the probability of my repeating the inadvertence.

Here it must be said, that, according to the custom of most legal gentlemen occupying chambers in densely populated law buildings, there were several keys to my door. One was kept by a woman residing in the attic, which person weekly scrubbed and daily swept and dusted my apartments. Another was kept by Turkey for convenience sake. The third I sometimes carried in my own pocket. The fourth I knew not who had.

Now, one Sunday morning I happened to go to Trinity Church, to hear a celebrated preacher, and finding myself rather early on the ground I thought I would walk round to my chambers for a while. Luckily I had my key with me; but upon applying it to the lock, I found it resisted by something inserted from the inside. Quite surprised, I called out; when to my consternation a key was turned from within; and thrusting his lean visage at me, and holding the door ajar, the apparition of Bartleby appeared, in his shirt-sleeves, and otherwise in a strangely tattered deshabille, saying quietly that he was sorry, but he was deeply engaged just then, and—preferred not admitting me at present. In a brief word or two, he moreover added, that perhaps I had better walk round the block two or three times, and by that time he would probably have concluded his affairs.

Now, the utterly unsurmised appearance of Bartleby, tenanting my law-chambers of a Sunday morning, with his cadaverously gentlemanly nonchalance, yet withal firm and self-possessed, had such a strange effect upon me, that incontinently I slunk away from my own door, and did as desired. But not without sundry twinges of impotent rebellion against the mild effrontery of this unaccountable scrivener. Indeed, it was his wonderful mildness chiefly, which not only disarmed me, but unmanned me, as it were. For I consider that one, for the time, is sort of unmanned when he tranquilly permits his hired clerk to dictate to him, and order him away from his own premises. Furthermore, I was full of uneasiness as to what Bartleby could possibly be doing in my office in his shirt-sleeves, and in an otherwise dismantled condition of a Sunday morning. Was anything amiss going on? Nay, that was out of the question. It was not to be thought of for a moment that Bartleby was an immoral person. But what could he be doing there? —copying? Nay again, whatever might be his eccentricities, Bartleby was an eminently decorous person. He would be the last man to sit down to his desk in any state approaching to nudity. Besides, it was Sunday; and there was something about Bartleby that forbade the supposition that he would by any secular occupation violate the proprieties of the day.

Nevertheless, my mind was not pacified; and full of a restless curiosity, at last I 90 returned to the door. Without hindrance I inserted my key, opened it, and entered. Bartleby was not to be seen. I looked round anxiously, peeped behind his screen; but it was very plain that he was gone. Upon more closely examining the place, I surmised that for an indefinite period Bartleby must have ate, dressed, and slept in my office, and that too without plate, mirror, or bed. The cushioned seat of a rickety old sofa in one corner bore the faint impress of a lean, reclining form. Rolled away under his desk, I found a blanket; under the empty grate, a blacking box and brush; on a chair, a tin basin, with soap and a ragged towel; in a newspaper a few crumbs of ginger-nuts and a morsel of cheese. Yes, thought I, it is evident enough that Bartleby has been making his home here, keeping bachelor's hall all by himself. Immediately then the thought came sweeping across me, what miserable friendlessness and loneliness are here revealed! His poverty is great; but his solitude, how horrible! Think of it. Of a Sunday, Wall Street is deserted as Petra; and every night of every day it is an emptiness. This building, too, which of week-days hums with industry and life, at nightfall echoes with sheer vacancy, and all through Sunday is forlorn. And here Bartleby makes his home; sole spectator of a solitude which he has seen all populous—a sort of innocent and transformed Marius brooding among the ruins of Carthage?

For the first time in my life a feeling of overpowering stinging melancholy seized me. Before, I had never experienced aught but a not unpleasing sadness. The bond of a common humanity now drew me irresistibly to gloom. A fraternal melancholy! For both I and Bartleby were sons of Adam. I remembered the bright silks and sparkling faces I had seen that day, in gala trim, swan-like sailing down the Mississippi of Broadway; and I contrasted them with the pallid copyist, and thought to myself, Ah, happiness courts the light, so we deem the world is gay; but misery hides aloof, so we deem that misery there is none. These sad fancyings—chimeras, doubtless, of a sick and silly brain—led on to other and more special thoughts, concerning the eccentricities of Bartleby. Presentiments of strange discoveries hovered round me. The scrivener's pale form appeared to me laid out, among uncaring strangers, in its shivering winding-sheet.

Suddenly I was attracted by Bartleby's closed desk, the key in open sight left in the lock.

I mean no mischief, seek the gratification of no heartless curiosity, thought I; besides, the desk is mine, and its contents, too, so I will make bold to look within. Everything was methodically arranged, the papers smoothly placed. The pigeonholes were deep, and removing the files of documents, I groped into their recesses. Presently I felt something there, and dragged it out. It was an old bandanna handkerchief, heavy and knotted. I opened it, and saw it was a savings' bank.

I now recalled all the quiet mysteries which I had noted in the man. I remembered that he never spoke but to answer; that, though at intervals he had considerable time to himself, yet I had never seen him reading—no, not even a newspaper; that for long periods he would stand looking out, at his pale window behind the screen, upon the dead brick wall; I was quite sure he never visited any refectory or eating-house; while his pale face clearly indicated that he never drank beer like Turkey; or tea and coffee even, like other men; that he never went anywhere in particular that I could learn; never went out for a walk, unless, indeed, that was the case at present; that he had declined telling who he was, or whence he came, or whether he had any relatives in the world; that though so thin and pale, he never complained of ill-health. And more than all, I remembered a certain unconscious air of pallid—how shall I call it?—of pallid haughtiness, say, or rather an austere reserve about him, which had positively awed me into my tame compliance with his eccentricities, when I had feared to ask him to do the slightest incidental thing for me, even though I might know, from his long-continued motionlessness, that behind his screen he must be standing in one of those dead-wall reveries of his.

Revolving all these things, and coupling them with the recently discovered fact, that he made my office his constant abiding place and home, and not forgetful of his morbid moodiness; revolving all these things, a prudential feeling began to steal over me. My first emotions had been those of pure melancholy and sincerest pity; but just in proportion as the forlornness of Bartleby grew and grew to my imagination, did that same melancholy merge into fear, that pity into repulsion. So true it is, and so terrible, too, that up to a certain point the thought or sight of misery enlists our best affections; but, in certain special cases, beyond that point it does not. They err who would assert that invariably this is owing to the inherent selfishness of the human heart. It rather proceeds from a certain hopelessness of remedying excessive and organic ill. To a sensitive being, pity is not seldom pain. And when at last it is perceived that such pity cannot lead to effectual succor, common sense bids the soul be rid of it. What I saw that morning persuaded me that the scrivener was the victim of innate and incurable disorder. I might give alms to his body; but his body did not pain him; it was his soul that suffered, and his soul I could not reach.

I did not accomplish the purpose of going to Trinity Church that morning. Somehow, the things I had seen disqualified me for the time from church-going. I walked homeward, thinking what I would do with Bartleby. Finally, I resolved upon this— I would put certain calm questions to him the next morning, touching his history, etc., and if he declined to answer them openly and unreservedly (and I supposed he would prefer not), then to give him a twenty dollar bill over and above whatever I might owe him, and tell him his services were no longer required; but that if in any other way I could assist him, I would be happy to do so, especially if he desired to return to his native place, wherever that might be, I would willingly help to defray the expenses. Moreover, if, after reaching home, he found himself at any time in want of aid, a letter from him would be sure of a reply.

The next morning came.

"Bartleby," said I, gently calling to him behind his screen. No reply.

"Bartleby," said I, in a still gentler tone, "come here; I am not going to ask you to 100 do anything you would prefer not to do—I simply wish to speak to you." Upon this he noiselessly slid into view. "Will you tell me, Bartleby, where you were born?" "I would prefer not to." "Will you tell me anything about yourself?"

"I would prefer not to."

"But what reasonable objection can you have to speak to me? I feel friendly towards you."

He did not look at me while I spoke, but kept his glance fixed upon my bust of Cicero, which, as I then sat, was directly behind me, some six inches above my head.

"What is your answer, Bartleby?" said I, after waiting a considerable time for a reply, during which his countenance remained immovable, only there was the faintest conceivable tremor of the white attenuated mouth.

"At present I prefer to give no answer," he said, and retired into his hermitage.

It was rather weak in me I confess, but his manner, on this occasion, nettled 110 me. Not only did there seem to lurk in it a certain calm disdain, but his perverseness seemed ungrateful, considering the undeniable good usage and indulgence he had received from me.

Again, I sat ruminating what I should do. Mortified as I was at his behavior, and resolved as I had been to dismiss him when I entered my office, nevertheless I strangely felt something superstitious knocking at my heart, and forbidding me to carry out my purpose, and denouncing me for a villain if I dared to breathe one bitter word against this forlornest of mankind. At last, familiarly drawing my chair behind his screen, I sat down and said: "Bartleby, never mind, then, about revealing your history; but let me entreat you, as a friend, to comply as far as may be with the usages of this office. Say now, you will help to examine papers tomorrow or next day: in short, say now, that in a day or two you will begin to be a little reasonable:—say so, Bartleby."

"At present I would prefer not to be a little reasonable," was his mildly cadaverous reply.

Just then the folding-doors opened, and Nippers approached. He seemed suffering from an unusually bad night's rest, induced by severer indigestion than common. He overheard those final words of Bartleby.

"Prefer not, eh?" gritted Nippers—"I'd prefer him, if I were you, sir," addressing me— "I'd prefer him; I'd give him preferences, the stubborn mule! What is it, sir, pray, that he prefers not to do now?"

Bartleby moved not a limb.

"Mr. Nippers," said I, "I'd prefer that you would withdraw for the present."

Somehow, of late, I had got into the way of involuntarily using this word "prefer" upon all sorts of not exactly suitable occasions. And I trembled to think that my contact with the scrivener had already and seriously affected me in a mental way. And what further and deeper aberration might it not yet produce? This apprehension had not been without efficacy in determining me to summary measures.

As Nippers, looking very sour and sulky, was departing, Turkey blandly and deferentially approached.

"With submission, sir," said he, "yesterday I was thinking about Bartleby here, and I think that if he would but prefer to take a quart of good ale every day, it would do much towards mending him, and enabling him to assist in examining his papers."

"So you have got the word, too," said I, slightly excited.

"With submission, what word, sir?" asked Turkey, respectfully crowding himself into the contracted space behind the screen, and by so doing, making me jostle the scrivener. "What word, sir?"

"I would prefer to be left alone here," said Bartleby, as if offended at being mobbed in his privacy.

"That's the word, Turkey," said I—"that's it."

"Oh, prefer? oh yes—queer word. I never use it myself. But, sir, as I was saying, if he would but prefer—"

"Turkey," interrupted I, "you will please withdraw."

"Oh certainly, sir, if you prefer that I should."

As he opened the folding-door to retire, Nippers at his desk caught a glimpse of me, and asked whether I would prefer to have a certain paper copied on blue paper or white. He did not in the least roguishly accent the word "prefer." It was plain that it involuntarily rolled from his tongue. I thought to myself, surely, I must get rid of a demented man, who already has in some degree turned the tongues, if not the heads of myself and clerks. But I thought it prudent not to break the dismission at once.

The next day I noticed that Bartleby did nothing but stand at his window in his dead-wall revery. Upon asking him why he did not write, he said that he had decided upon doing no more writing.

"Why, how now? what next?" exclaimed I, "do no more writing?"

"No more."

"And what is the reason?"

"Do you not see the reason for yourself?" he indifferently replied.

I looked steadfastly at him, and perceived that his eyes looked dull and glazed. Instantly it occurred to me, that his unexampled diligence in copying by his dim window for the first few weeks of his stay with me might have temporarily impaired his vision.

I was touched. I said something in condolence with him. I hinted that of course he did wisely in abstaining from writing for a while; and urged him to embrace that opportunity of taking wholesome exercise in the open air. This, however, he did not do. A few days after this, my other clerks being absent, and being in a great hurry to dispatch certain letters by the mail, I thought that, having nothing else earthly to do, Bartleby would surely be less inflexible than usual, and carry these letters to the Post Office. But he blankly declined. So, much to my inconvenience, I went myself.

Still added days went by. Whether Bartleby's eyes improved or not, I could not say. To all appearance, I thought they did. But when I asked him if they did, he vouchsafed no answer. At all events, he would do no copying. At last, in replying to my urgings, he informed me that he had permanently given up copying.

"What!" exclaimed I, "Suppose your eyes should get entirely well—better than ever before—would you not copy then?"

"I have given up copying," he answered, and slid aside.

He remained as ever, a fixture in my chamber. Nay—if that were possible—he became still more of a fixture than before. What was to be done? He would do nothing in the office; why should he stay there? In plain fact, he had now become a millstone to me, not only useless as a necklace, but afflictive to bear. Yet I was sorry for him. I speak less than truth when I say that, on his own account, he occasioned me uneasiness. If he would but have named a single relative or friend, I would instantly have written, and urged their taking the poor fellow away to some convenient retreat. But he seemed alone, absolutely alone in the universe. A bit of wreck in the mid-Atlantic. At length, necessities connected with my business tyrannized over all other considerations. Decently as I could, I told Bartleby that in six days' time he must unconditionally leave the office. I warned him to take measures, in the interval, for procuring some other abode. I offered to assist him in this endeavor, if he himself would but take the first step towards a removal. "And when you finally quit me, Bartleby," added I, "I shall see that you go not away entirely unprovided. Six days from this hour, remember."

At the expiration of that period, I peeped behind the screen, and lo! Bartleby was there.

I buttoned up my coat, balanced myself; advanced slowly towards him, touched his shoulder, and said, "The time has come; you must quit this place; I am sorry for you; here is money; but you must go."

"I would prefer not," he replied, with his back still towards me.

"You must."

He remained silent.

Now I had an unbounded confidence in this man's common honesty. He had frequently restored to me sixpences and shillings carelessly dropped upon the floor, for

I am apt to be very reckless in such shirt-button affairs. The proceeding, then, which followed will not be deemed extraordinary.

"Bartleby," said I, "I owe you twelve dollars on account; here are thirty-two, the odd twenty are yours—Will you take it?" and I handed the bills towards him.

But he made no motion.

"I will leave them here, then," putting them under a weight on the table. Then taking my hat and cane and going to the door, I tranquilly turned and added—" After you have removed your things from these offices, Bartleby, you will of course lock the door—since every one is now gone for the day but you—and if you please, slip your key underneath the mat, so that I may have it in the morning. I shall not see you again; so good-bye to you. If, hereafter, in your new place of abode, I can be of any service to you, do not fail to advise me by letter. Good-bye, Bartleby, and fare you well."

But he answered not a word; like the last column of some ruined temple, he remained standing mute and solitary in the middle of the otherwise deserted room.

As I walked home in a pensive mood, my vanity got the better of my pity. I could not but highly plume myself on my masterly management in getting rid of Bartleby. Masterly I call it, and such it must appear to any dispassionate thinker. The beauty of my procedure seemed to consist in its perfect quietness. There was no vulgar bullying, no bravado of any sort, no choleric hectoring, and striding to and fro across the apartment, jerking out vehement commands for Bartleby to bundle himself off with his beggarly traps. Nothing of the kind. Without loudly bidding Bartleby depart—as an inferior genius might have done—I assumed the ground that depart he must; and upon that assumption built all I had to say. The more I thought over my procedure, the more I was charmed with it. Nevertheless, next morning, upon awakening, I had my doubts—I had somehow slept off the fumes of vanity. One of the coolest and wisest hours a man has, is just after he awakes in the morning. My procedure seemed as sagacious as ever—but only in theory. How it would prove in practice—there was the rub. It was truly a beautiful thought to have assumed Bartleby's departure; but, after all, that assumption was simply my own, and none of Bartleby's. The great point was, not whether I had assumed that he would quit me, but whether he would prefer to do so. He was more a man of preferences than assumptions.

After breakfast, I walked down town, arguing the probabilities pro and con. One 150 moment I thought it would prove a miserable failure, and Bartleby would be found all alive at my office as usual; the next moment it seemed certain that I should find his chair empty. And so I kept veering about. At the corner of Broadway and Canal Street, I saw quite an excited group of people standing in earnest conversation.

"I'll take odds he doesn't," said a voice as I passed.

"Doesn't go?—done!" said I, "put up your money."

I was instinctively putting my hand in my pocket to produce my own, when I remembered that this was an election day. The words I had overheard bore no reference

89

to Bartleby, but to the success or non-success of some candidate for the mayoralty. In my intent frame of mind, I had, as it were, imagined that all Broadway shared in my excitement, and were debating the same question with me. I passed on, very thankful that the uproar of the street screened my momentary absent-mindedness.

As I had intended, I was earlier than usual at my office door. I stood listening for a moment. All was still. He must be gone. I tried the knob. The door was locked. Yes, my procedure had worked to a charm; he indeed must be vanished. Yet a certain melancholy mixed with this: I was almost sorry for my brilliant success. I was fumbling under the door mat for the key, which Bartleby was to have left there for me, when accidentally my knee knocked against a panel, producing a summoning sound, and in response a voice came to me from within—" Not yet; I am occupied."

It was Bartleby.

I was thunderstruck. For an instant I stood like the man who, pipe in mouth, was killed one cloudless afternoon long ago in Virginia, by summer lightning; at his own warm open window he was killed, and remained leaning out there upon the dreamy afternoon, till some one touched him, when he fell.

"Not gone!" I murmured at last. But again obeying that wondrous ascendancy which the inscrutable scrivener had over me, and from which ascendancy, for all my chafing, I could not completely escape, I slowly went down stairs and out into the street, and while walking round the block, considered what I should next do in this unheard-of perplexity. Turn the man out by an actual thrusting I could not; to drive him away by calling him hard names would not do; calling in the police was an unpleasant idea; and yet, permit him to enjoy his cadaverous triumph over me—this, too, I could not think of. What was to be done? or, if nothing could be done, was there anything further that I could assume in the matter? Yes, as before I had prospectively assumed that Bartleby would depart, so now I might retrospectively assume that departed he was. In the legitimate carrying out of this assumption, I might enter my office in a great hurry, and pretending not to see Bartleby at all, walk straight against him as if he were air. Such a proceeding would in a singular degree have the appearance of a home-thrust. It was hardly possible that Bartleby could withstand such an application of the doctrine of assumption. But upon second thoughts the success of the plan seemed rather dubious. I resolved to argue the matter over with him again.

"Bartleby," said I, entering the office, with a quietly severe expression, "I am seriously displeased. I am pained, Bartleby. I had thought better of you. I had imagined you of such a gentlemanly organization, that in any delicate dilemma a slight hint would suffice—in short, an assumption. But it appears I am deceived. Why," I added, unaffectedly starting, "you have not even touched that money yet," pointing to it, just where I had left it the evening previous.

He answered nothing.

"Will you, or will you not, quit me?" I now demanded in a sudden passion, advancing close to him.

"I would prefer not to quit you," he replied, gently emphasizing the not. "What earthly right have you to stay here? Do you pay any rent? Do you pay my taxes? Or is this property yours?" He answered nothing.

"Are you ready to go on and write now? Are your eyes recovered? Could you copy a small paper for me this morning? or help examine a few lines? or step round to the Post Office? In a word, will you do anything at all, to give a coloring to your refusal to depart the premises?"

He silently retired into his hermitage.

I was now in such a state of nervous resentment that I thought it but prudent to check myself at present from further demonstrations. Bartleby and I were alone. I remembered the tragedy of the unfortunate Adams and the still more unfortunate Colt6 in the solitary office of the latter; and how poor Colt, being dreadfully incensed by Adams, and imprudently permitting himself to get wildly excited, was at unawares hurried into his fatal act—an act which certainly no man could possibly deplore more than the actor himself. Often it had occurred to me in my ponderings upon the subject that had that altercation taken place in the public street, or at a private residence, it would not have terminated as it did. It was the circumstance of being alone in a solitary office, upstairs, of a building entirely unhallowed by humanizing domestic associations— an uncarpeted office, doubtless, of a dusty, haggard sort of appearance— this it must have been, which greatly helped to enhance the irritable desperation of the hapless Colt.

But when this old Adam of resentment rose in me and tempted me concerning Bartleby, I grappled him and threw him. How? Why, simply by recalling the divine injunction: "A new commandment give I unto you, that ye love one another." Yes, this it was that saved me. Aside from higher considerations, charity often operates as a vastly wise and prudent principle—a great safeguard to its possessor. Men have committed murder for jealousy's sake, and anger's sake, and hatred's sake, and selfishness' sake, and spiritual pride's sake; but no man, that ever I heard of, ever committed a diabolical murder for sweet charity's sake. Mere self-interest, then, if no better motive can be enlisted, should, especially with high-tempered men, prompt all beings to charity and philanthropy. At any rate, upon the occasion in question, I strove to drown my exasperated feelings towards the scrivener by benevolently construing his conduct. Poor fellow, poor fellow! thought I, he don't mean anything; and besides, he has seen hard times, and ought to be indulged.

I endeavored, also, immediately to occupy myself, and at the same time to comfort my despondency. I tried to fancy, that in the course of the morning, at such time as might prove agreeable to him, Bartleby, of his own free accord, would emerge from his hermitage and take up some decided line of march in the direction of the door. But no. Half-past twelve o'clock came; Turkey began to glow in the face, overturn his inkstand,

and become generally obstreperous; Nippers abated down into quietude and courtesy; Ginger Nut munched his noon apple; and Bartleby remained standing at his window in one of his profoundest dead-wall reveries. Will it be credited? Ought I to acknowledge it? That afternoon I left the office without saying one further word to him.

Some days now passed, during which, at leisure intervals I looked a little into "Edwards on the Will," and "Priestley on Necessity" Under the circumstances, those books induced a salutary feeling. Gradually I slid into the persuasion that these troubles of mine, touching the scrivener, had been all predestined from eternity, and Bartleby was billeted upon me for some mysterious purpose of an all-wise Providence, which it was not for a mere mortal like me to fathom. Yes, Bartleby, stay there behind your screen, thought I; I shall persecute you no more; you are harmless and noiseless as any of these old chairs; in short, I never feel so private as when I know you are here. At last I see it, I feel it; I penetrate to the predestined purpose of my life. I am content. Others may have loftier parts to enact; but my mission in this world, Bartleby, is to furnish you with office-room for such period as you may see fit to remain.

I believe that this wise and blessed frame of mind would have continued with me, had it not been for the unsolicited and uncharitable remarks obtruded upon me by my professional friends who visited the rooms. But thus it often is, that the constant friction of illiberal minds wears out at last the best resolves of the more generous. Though to be sure, when I reflected upon it, it was not strange that people entering my office should be struck by the peculiar aspect of the unaccountable Bartleby, and so be tempted to throw out some sinister observations concerning him. Sometimes an attorney, having business with me, and calling at my office, and finding no one but the scrivener there, would undertake to obtain some sort of precise information from him touching my whereabouts; but without heeding his idle talk, Bartleby would remain standing immovable in the middle of the room. So after contemplating him in that position for a time, the attorney would depart, no wiser than he came.

Also, when a reference was going on, and the room full of lawyers and witnesses, and business driving fast, some deeply-occupied legal gentleman present, seeing Bartleby wholly unemployed, would request him to run round to his (the legal gentleman's) office and fetch some papers for him. Thereupon, Bartleby would tranquilly decline, and yet remain idle as before. Then the lawyer would give a great stare, and turn to me. And what could I say? At last I was made aware that all through the circle of my professional acquaintance, a whisper of wonder was running round, having reference to the strange creature I kept at my office. This worried me very much. And as the idea came upon me of his possibly turning out a long-lived man, and keeping occupying my chambers, and denying my authority; and perplexing my visitors; and scandalizing my professional reputation; and casting a general gloom over the premises; keeping soul and body together to the last upon his savings (for doubtless he spent but half a dime a day), and in the end perhaps outlive me, and claim possession of my office by right of his perpetual occupancy: as all these dark anticipations crowded upon me more and more, and my friends continually intruded their relentless remarks upon the apparition in my room; a great change was wrought in me. I resolved to gather all my faculties together, and forever rid me of this intolerable incubus.

Ere revolving any complicated project, however, adapted to this end, I first simply suggested to Bartleby the propriety of his permanent departure. In a calm and serious tone, I commended the idea to his careful and mature consideration. But, having taken three days to meditate upon it, he apprised me, that his original determination remained the same; in short, that he still preferred to abide with me.

What shall I do? I now said to myself, buttoning up my coat to the last button. What shall I do? what ought I to do? what does conscience say I should do with this man, or, rather, ghost. Rid myself of him, I must; go, he shall. But how? You will not thrust him, the poor, pale, passive mortal—you will not thrust such a helpless creature out of your door? you will not dishonor yourself by such cruelty? No, I will not, I cannot do that. Rather would I let him live and die here, and then mason up his remains in the wall. What, then, will you do? For all your coaxing, he will not budge. Bribes he leaves under your own paper-weight on your table; in short, it is quite plain that he prefers to cling to you.

Then something severe, something unusual must be done. What! surely you will not have him collared by a constable, and commit his innocent pallor to the common jail? And upon what ground could you procure such a thing to be done?—a vagrant, is he? What! he a vagrant, a wanderer, who refuses to budge? It is because he will not be a vagrant, then, that you seek to count him as a vagrant. That is too absurd. No visible means of support: there I have him. Wrong again: for indubitably he does support himself, and that is the only unanswerable proof that any man can show of his possessing the means so to do. No more, then. Since he will not quit me, I must quit him. I will change my offices; I will move elsewhere, and give him fair notice, that if I find him on my new premises I will then proceed against him as a common trespasser.

Acting accordingly, next day I thus addressed him: "I find these chambers too far from the City Hall; the air is unwholesome. In a word, I propose to remove my offices next week, and shall no longer require your services. I tell you this now, in order that you may seek another place."

He made no reply, and nothing more was said.

On the appointed day I engaged carts and men, proceeded to my chambers, and having but little furniture, everything was removed in a few hours. Throughout, the scrivener remained standing behind the screen, which I directed to be removed the last thing. It was withdrawn; and, being folded up like a huge folio, left him the motionless occupant of a naked room. I stood in the entry watching him a moment, while something from within me upbraided me.

I re-entered, with my hand in my pocket—and—and my heart in my mouth.

"Good-bye, Bartleby; I am going—good-bye, and God some way bless you; and take that," slipping something in his hand. But it dropped upon the floor, and then—strange to say—I tore myself from him whom I had so longed to be rid of.

Established in my new quarters, for a day or two I kept the door locked, and 180 started at every footfall in the passages. When I returned to my rooms, after any little absence, I would pause at the threshold for an instant, and attentively listen, ere applying my key. But these fears were needless. Bartleby never came nigh me.

I thought all was going well, when a perturbed-looking stranger visited me, inquiring whether I was the person who had recently occupied rooms at No.-Wall Street.

Full of forebodings, I replied that I was.

"Then, sir," said the stranger, who proved a lawyer, "you are responsible for the man you left there. He refuses to do any copying; he refuses to do anything; he says he prefers not to; and he refuses to quit the premises."

"I am very sorry, sir," said I, with assumed tranquility, but an inward tremor, "but, really, the man you allude to is nothing to me—he is no relation or apprentice of mine, that you should hold me responsible for him."

"In mercy's name, who is he?"

"I certainly cannot inform you. I know nothing about him. Formerly I employed him as a copyist; but he has done nothing for me now for some time past."

"I shall settle him, then—good morning, sir."

Several days passed, and I heard nothing more; and, though I often felt a charitable prompting to call at the place and see poor Bartleby, yet a certain squeamish-ness, of I know not what, withheld me.

All is over with him, by this time, thought I, at last, when, through another week, no further intelligence reached me. But, coming to my room the day after, I found several persons waiting at my door in a high state of nervous excitement.

"That's the man—here he comes," cried the foremost one, whom I recognized 190 as the lawyer who had previously called upon me alone.

"You must take him away, sir, at once," cried a portly person among them, advancing upon me, and whom I knew to be the landlord of No. — Wall Street. "These gentlemen, my tenants, cannot stand it any longer; Mr. B —," pointing to the lawyer, "has turned him out of his room, and he now persists in haunting the building generally, sitting upon the banisters of the stairs by day, and sleeping in the entry by night. Everybody is concerned; clients are leaving the offices; some fears are entertained of a mob; something you must do, and that without delay."

Aghast at this torrent, I fell back before it, and would fain have locked myself in my new quarters. In vain I persisted that Bartleby was nothing to me—no more than to any one else. In vain—I was the last person known to have anything to do with him, and they held me to the terrible account. Fearful, then, of being exposed in the papers (as one person present obscurely threatened), I considered the matter, and, at length, said, that if the lawyer would give me a confidential interview with the scrivener, in his (the lawyer's) own room, I would, that afternoon, strive my best to rid them of the nuisance they complained of.

Going up stairs to my old haunt, there was Bartleby silently sitting upon the banister at the landing.

"What are you doing here, Bartleby?" said I.

"Sitting upon the banister," he mildly replied. I motioned him into the lawyer's room, who then left us. "Bartleby," said I, "are you aware that you are the cause of great tribulation to me, by persisting in occupying the entry after being dismissed from the office?" No answer.

"Now one of two things must take place. Either you must do something, or something must be done to you. Now what sort of business would you like to engage in? Would you like to re-engage in copying for some one?"

"No; I would prefer not to make any change."

"Would you like a clerkship in a dry-goods store?"

"There is too much confinement about that. No, I would not like a clerkship; but I am not particular."

"Too much confinement," I cried, "why, you keep yourself confined all the time!"

"I would prefer not to take a clerkship," he rejoined, as if to settle that little item at once.

"How would a bar-tender's business suit you? There is no trying of the eye-sight in that."

"I would not like it at all; though, as I said before, I am not particular." His unwonted wordiness inspirited me. I returned to the charge. "Well, then, would you like to travel through the country collecting bills for the merchants? That would improve your health."

"No, I would prefer to be doing something else."

"How, then, would going as a companion to Europe, to entertain some young gentleman with your conversation—how would that suit you?"

"Not at all. It does not strike me that there is anything definite about that. I like to be stationary. But I am not particular."

"Stationary you shall be, then," I cried, now losing all patience, and, for the first time in all my exasperating connection with him, fairly flying into a passion. "If you do not go away from these premises before night, I shall feel bound—indeed, I am bound—to—to quit the premises myself !" I rather absurdly concluded, knowing not with what possible threat to try to frighten his immobility into compliance. Despairing of all further efforts, I was precipitately leaving him, when a final thought occurred to me—one which had not been wholly unindulged before.

"Bartleby," said I, in the kindest tone I could assume under such exciting circumstances, "will you go home with me now—not to my office, but my dwelling—and remain there till we can conclude upon some convenient arrangement for you at our leisure? Come, let us start now, right away."

"No, at present I would prefer not to make any change at all."

I answered nothing; but, effectually dodging every one by the suddenness and rapidity of my flight, rushed from the building, ran up Wall Street towards Broadway, and, jumping into the first omnibus, was soon removed from pursuit. As soon as tranquility returned, I distinctly perceived that I had now done all that I possibly could, both in respect to the demands of the landlord and his tenants, and with regard to my own desire and sense of duty, to benefit Bartleby, and shield him from rude persecution. I now strove to be entirely care-free and quiescent; and my conscience justified me in the attempt; though, indeed, it was not so successful as I could have wished. So fearful was I of being again hunted out by the incensed landlord and his exasperated tenants, that, surrendering my business to Nippers, for a few days, I drove about the upper part of the town and through the suburbs, in my rockaway; crossed over to Jersey City and Hoboken, and paid fugitive visits to Manhattanville and Astoria. In fact, I almost lived in my rockaway for the time.

When again I entered my office, lo, a note from the landlord lay upon the desk. I opened it with trembling hands. It informed me that the writer had sent to the police, and had Bartleby removed to the Tombs as a vagrant. Moreover, since I knew more about him than any one else, he wished me to appear at that place, and make a suitable statement of the facts. These tidings had a conflicting effect upon me. At first I was indignant; but, at last, almost approved. The landlord's energetic, summary disposition, had led him to adopt a procedure which I do not think I would have decided upon myself; and yet, as a last resort, under such peculiar circumstances, it seemed the only plan.

As I afterwards learned, the poor scrivener, when told that he must be conducted to the Tombs, offered not the slightest obstacle, but, in his pale, unmoving way, silently acquiesced.

Some of the compassionate and curious by-standers joined the party; and headed by one of the constables arm-in-arm with Bartleby, the silent procession filed its way through all the noise, and heat, and joy of the roaring thoroughfares at noon.

The same day I received the note, I went to the Tombs, or, to speak more properly, the Halls of Justice. Seeking the right officer, I stated the purpose of my call, and was informed that the individual I described was, indeed, within. I then assured the functionary that Bartleby was a perfectly honest man, and greatly to be compassionated, however unaccountably eccentric. I narrated all I knew, and closed by suggesting the idea of letting him remain in as indulgent confinement as possible, till something less harsh might be done—though, indeed, I hardly knew what. At all events, if nothing else could be decided upon, the almshouse must receive him. I then begged to have an interview.

Being under no disgraceful charge, and quite serene and harmless in all his ways, they had permitted him freely to wander about the prison, and, especially, in the enclosed grass-platted yards thereof. And so I found him there, standing all alone in the quietest of the yards, his face towards a high wall, while all around, from the narrow slits of the jail windows, I thought I saw peering out upon him the eyes of murderers and thieves.

"Bartleby!"

"I know you," he said, without looking round—"and I want nothing to say to you."

"It was not I that brought you here, Bartleby," said I, keenly pained at his implied suspicion. "And to you, this should not be so vile a place. Nothing reproachful attaches to you by being here. And see, it is not so sad a place as one might think. Look, there is the sky, and here is the grass."

"I know where I am," he replied, but would say nothing more, and so I left him.

As I entered the corridor again, a broad meat-like man, in an apron, accosted me, and, jerking his thumb over his shoulder, said—"Is that your friend?"

"Yes."

"Does he want to starve? If he does, let him live on the prison fare, that's all"

"Who are you?" asked I, not knowing what to make of such an unofficially speaking person in such a place.

"I am the grub-man. Such gentlemen as have friends here, hire me to provide them with something good to eat."

"Is this so?" said I, turning the turnkey.

He said it was.

"Well, then," said I, slipping some silver into the grub-man's hands (for so they called him), "I want you to give particular attention to my friend there; let him have the best dinner you can get. And you must be as polite to him as possible."

"Introduce me, will you?" said the grub-man, looking at me with an expression which seemed to say he was all impatience for an opportunity to give a specimen of his breeding.

Thinking it would prove of benefit to the scrivener, I acquiesced; and, asking the grub-man his name, went up with him to Bartleby.

"Bartleby, this is a friend; you will find him very useful to you."

"Your sarvant, sir, your sarvant," said the grub-man, making a low salutation behind his apron. "Hope you find it pleasant here, sir; nice grounds—cool apartments—hope you'll stay with us some time—try to make it agreeable. What will you have for dinner to-day?"

"I prefer not to dine to-day," said Bartleby, turning away. "It would disagree with me; I am unused to dinners." So saying, he slowly moved to the other side of the inclosure, and took up a position fronting the dead wall.

"How's this?" said the grub-man, addressing me with a stare of astonishment. "He's odd, ain't he?"

"I think he is a little deranged," said I, sadly.

"Deranged? deranged is it? Well, now, upon my word, I thought that friend of your was a gentleman forger; they are always pale and genteel-like, them forgers. I can't help pity 'em—can't help it, sir. Did you know Monroe Edwards?" he added, touchingly, and paused. Then, laying his hand piteously on my shoulder, sighed, "he died of consumption at Sing-Sing. So you weren't acquainted with Monroe?"

"No, I was never socially acquainted with any forgers. But I cannot stop longer. Look to my friend yonder. You will not lose by it. I will see you again."

Some few days after this, I again obtained admission to the Tombs, and went through the corridors in quest of Bartleby; but without finding him.

"I saw him coming from his cell not long ago," said a turnkey, "may be he's gone to loiter in the yards."

So I went in that direction.

"Are you looking for the silent man?" said another turnkey, passing me. "Yonder he lies — sleeping in the yard there. 'Tis not twenty minutes since I saw him lie down."

The yard was entirely quiet. It was not accessible to the common prisoners. The surrounding walls, of amazing thickness, kept off all sounds behind them. The Egyptian character of the masonry weighed upon me with its gloom. But a soft imprisoned turf grew under foot. The heart of the eternal pyramids, it seemed, wherein, by some strange magic, through the clefts, grass-seed, dropped by birds, had sprung.

Strangely huddled at the base of the wall, his knees drawn up, and lying on his side, his head touching the cold stones, I saw the wasted Bartleby. But nothing stirred. I paused; then went close up to him; stooped over, and saw that his dim eyes were open; otherwise he seemed profoundly sleeping. Something prompted me to touch him. I felt his hand, when a tingling shiver ran up my arm and down my spine to my feet.

The round face of the grub-man peered upon me now. "His dinner is ready. Won't he dine to-day, either? Or does he live without dining?" "Lives without dining," said I, and closed the eyes.

"Eh!—He's asleep, ain't he?"

"With kings and counselors," murmured I.

There would seem little need for proceeding further in this history. Imagination will readily supply the meagre recital of poor Bartleby's interment. But, ere parting with the reader, let me say, that if this little narrative has sufficiently interested him, to awaken curiosity as to who Bartleby was, and what manner of life he led prior to the present narrator's making his acquaintance, I can only reply, that in such curiosity I fully share, but am wholly unable to gratify it. Yet here I hardly know whether I should divulge one little item of rumor, which came to my ear a few months after the scrivener's decease. Upon what basis it rested, I could never ascertain; and hence, how true it is I cannot now tell. But, inasmuch as this vague report has not been without a certain suggestive interest to me, however sad, it may prove the same with some others; and so I will briefly mention it. The report was this: that Bartleby had been a subordinate clerk in the Dead Letter Office at Washington, from which he had been suddenly removed by a change in the administration. When I think over this rumor, hardly can I express the emotions which seize me. Dead letters! does it not sound like dead men? Conceive a man by nature and misfortune prone to a pallid hopelessness, can any business seem more fitted to heighten it than that of continually handling these dead letters, and assorting them for the flames? For by the cart-load they are annually burned. Sometimes from out the folded paper the pale clerk takes a ring—the finger it was meant for, perhaps, moulders in the grave; a bank-note sent in swiftest charity— he whom it would relieve, nor eats nor hungers any more; pardon for those who died despairing; hope for those who died unhoping; good tidings for those who died stifled by unrelieved calamities. On errands of life, these letters speed to death.

Ah, Bartleby! Ah, humanity!

Plot Summary

"Bartleby, the Scrivener" is a short story by Herman Melville that follows the narrator, a lawyer, and his interactions with a strange scrivener named Bartleby. The lawyer is a successful and well-respected man who runs a law office in New York City. He hires Bartleby, a scrivener, to help with the workload. Bartleby is a strange man who is very quiet and does not seem to have any friends or family. At first, Bartleby is a model employee. He is diligent and efficient, and the lawyer is pleased with his work. However, as time passes, Bartleby begins to refuse to do certain tasks. He refuses to proofread documents, and when the lawyer asks him to do something, he simply responds with "I would prefer not to." The lawyer is perplexed by Bartleby's behavior and tries to reason with him, but Bartleby remains unmoved. The lawyer eventually decides to fire Bartleby, but he is unable to do so because he feels sorry for him. He allows Bartleby to stay in the office and continues to pay him, even though Bartleby does no work. As time passes, Bartleby's behavior becomes increasingly strange. He stops eating and sleeping, and he spends all of his time in the office, staring out the window. The lawyer eventually decides to move his office and tells Bartleby that he must leave. Bartleby refuses and the lawyer is forced to have him removed by the police. Bartleby is taken to a prison, where he dies a few days later. The lawyer is saddened by Bartleby's death and reflects on his strange behavior. He realizes that Bartleby was a man who had been broken by life and had simply given up.

Language Exercises

Choose the item that best replaces or explains the underlined part of the sentence.

1. But I <u>waive</u> the biographies of all other scriveners, for a few passages in the life of Bartleby, who was a scrivener, the strangest I ever saw, or heard of.
   A. facilitate   B. forbid   C. forgo   D. forge

2. Ere introducing the scrivener, as he first appeared to me, it is fit I make some mention of myself, my employes, my business, my chambers, and general surroundings, because some such description is <u>indispensable</u> to an adequate understanding of the chief character about to be presented.
   A. influential   B. essential   C. incompatible   D. eminent

3. … after which, I saw no more of the proprietor of the face, which, gaining its meridian with the sun, seemed to set with it, to rise, <u>culminate</u>, and decline the following day, with the like regularity and undiminished glory.
   A. climax   B. rotate   C. cumulate   D. resolve

4. … in mending his pens, impatiently split them all to pieces, and threw them on the floor in a sudden passion; stood up, and leaned over his table, boxing his papers about in a most <u>indecorous</u> manner, very sad to behold in an elderly man like him.
   A. inconceivable   B. inconvenient   C. immersive   D. indecent

5. The truth was, I suppose, that a man with so small an income could not afford to sport such a lustrous face and a <u>lustrous</u> coat at one and the same time.
   A. luxurious   B. shiny   C. shabby   D. shattered

6. I came within an ace of dismissing him then. But he <u>mollified</u> me by making an oriental bow, and saying—"With submission, sir, it was generous of me to find you in stationery on my own account."
   A. pacified   B. flattered   C. marginalized   D. delighted

7. I can see that figure now—pallidly neat, pitiably respectable, incurably <u>forlorn</u>! It was Bartleby.
   A. nervous and timid   B. lonely and unhappy
   C. embarrassed and reserved   D. ambitious and arrogant

8. After a few words touching his qualifications, I engaged him, glad to have among my corps of copyists a man of so singularly <u>sedate</u> an aspect, which I thought might operate beneficially upon the flighty temper of Turkey, and the fiery one of Nippers.
   A. indifferent   B. aloof   C. detached   D. composed

9. I can readily imagine that, to some <u>sanguine</u> temperaments, it would be altogether intolerable.
   A. solitary   B. aggressive   C. optimistic   D. pessimistic

10. Imagine my surprise, nay, my <u>consternation</u>, when, without moving from his

privacy, Bartleby, in a singularly mild, firm voice, replied, "I would prefer not to."

    A. dismay   B. astonishment   C. numbness   D. tranquility

11. With any other man I should have flown outright into a dreadful passion, scorned all further words, and thrust him <u>ignominiously</u> from my presence.

    A. reverently   B. solemnly   C. abruptly   D. disgracefully

12. … could not gainsay the irresistible conclusion; but, at the same time, some <u>paramount</u> consideration prevailed with him to reply as he did.

    A. prudent   B. reckless   C. predominant D. anxious

13. I closed the doors, and again advanced towards Bartleby. I felt additional <u>incentives</u> tempting me to my fate.

    A. motivations   B. initiation   C. commitment D. impulse

14. Strangely <u>huddled</u> at the base of the wall, his knees drawn up, and lying on his side, his head touching the cold stones, I saw the wasted Bartleby.

    A. pinched up   B. pulled up   C. curled up   D. sprung up

15. Yet here I hardly know whether I should <u>divulge</u> one little item of rumor, which came to my ear a few months after the scrivener's decease.

    A. dwell   B. dwindle   C. devote   D. disclose

Topics for Discussion

1. What information do you gain from the opening paragraph? How does it create an impression on you as a reader? What qualifications and disclaimers can be found in the language used?

2. What are the positive and negative aspects of Turkey, Nippers, and Ginger Nut that Melville presents? What similarities and differences can be found between them? How do they prepare the reader for the introduction of Bartleby?

3. How does the narrator's description of Bartleby expand as the story develops, and how does his initial characterization foreshadow Bartleby's end?

4. How does Bartleby's "passive resistance" impede the lawyer-narrator, and how do Bartleby's "preferences" affect the culture of the lawyer's office?

5. How does Bartleby's belief in "preferences" rather than "assumptions" differ from the legal profession's approach to precedents?

6. What is the significance of the subtitle "A Story of Wall Street" in terms of the literal walls that Melville describes in the office and in the Tombs?

7. Analyze how the narrator's responses to Bartleby change throughout the story, and consider how this affects his initial philosophy of "the easiest way of life is the best". Examine how his self-awareness develops or deteriorates, and interpret his statement, "In vain I persisted that Bartleby was nothing to me—no more than to any one else".

8. Can you identify any examples of humor in the story, and how do they contribute to characterization or commentary?

9. Is it plausible that Bartleby's rejection of life was caused by his work in the Dead Letter Office? How does this fit with the theme of the story that Herman Melville has created?

10. What is the relevance of "The Story of Wall Street" to our current opinion of Wall Street? How do our views on money and materialism shape the narrative of this story? Is the depiction of Wall Street as a cold and impersonal place still accurate in the 21st century?

Discussion Tips

Herman Melville's works are renowned for their deliberate ambiguity, a literary device that intentionally employs words, symbols, or plot constructions with multiple distinct meanings. While previously considered a stylistic flaw, ambiguity is now recognized as a powerful tool that adds depth and complexity to narratives. Melville, in particular, crafts stories with layers of potential meanings, challenging readers who seek a clear, definitive message. He often compels readers to consider his characters and events from multiple perspectives, creating a narrative open to diverse interpretations.

In "Bartleby the Scrivener", Melville employs an unreliable narrator, the lawyer, whose perspective adds a layer of complexity to the story. The lawyer's subjective interpretation of events makes it difficult for readers to fully trust his account. His biases and assumptions color his narration, leading to a distorted portrayal of the situations he describes. This is evident in his evasiveness regarding Turkey's behavior and his misguided self-congratulation on handling Bartleby's dismissal. The unreliable nature of the narrator further complicates the understanding of Bartleby's enigmatic behavior, prompting readers to carefully discern the accuracy of the lawyer's perceptions.

The story is also rich in symbolism, with two key symbols being walls and dead letters. The pervasive presence of walls in the narrative, particularly in the office located on Wall Street, and Bartleby's fixation on staring at them, symbolizes his psychological confinement and ultimate fate of dying in prison. The concept of being "walled off from society" is further underscored by the symbol of "dead letters", which the lawyer believes may have influenced Bartleby's state of mind. The notion of failed communication and missed opportunities for comfort and hope represented by the "dead letters" reflects Bartleby's profound sense of isolation and the inability of others to reach him. Moreover, Melville's exploration touches upon themes related to alienation and nihilism. Bartleby's passive resistance—his repeated refrain "I would prefer not to"—highlights existential questions about free will versus societal expectations. His detachment from work signifies not just personal withdrawal but also critiques modernity's dehumanizing effects on individuals within capitalist structures. As Bartleby becomes increasingly isolated behind metaphorical walls—both physical and emotional—he embodies a profound disconnection from life itself; this alienation culminates in an overwhelming sense of despair akin to nihilism. In this way, Melville invites readers not only to ponder individual meaning but also broader existential concerns surrounding identity and purpose in an indifferent world.

Unit 5
Charlotte Perkins Gilman: "The Yellow Wallpaper"

About the author

Charlotte Perkins Gilman (1860–1935)

Charlotte Perkins Gilman was an American author, feminist, and social reformer who lived from 1860 to 1935. She is best known for her writings that challenge gender norms and advocate for women's economic and social independence. Gilman's personal life and struggles with depression also heavily influenced her work. Gilman was born in Hartford, Connecticut and raised in poverty by her estranged mother. She briefly studied art before marrying her first husband, Charles Walter Stetson, and having a daughter. However, her marriage and motherhood were sources of great dissatisfaction and depression for Gilman. She eventually separated from her husband and began to focus on her writing and activism. In 1892, Gilman published her best-known work, "The Yellow Wallpaper", a short story that criticizes the way women were treated for mental and emotional disorders during her time. The story portrays the confinement and isolation experienced by the protagonist, who is prohibited from writing and forced to hide her thoughts due to her husband's expectations of her. Gilman's own experiences with postpartum depression and the controversial "rest cure" treatment inspired the story. In addition to her literary works, Gilman was a prominent feminist and social reformer. She founded the *Forerunner*, a feminist magazine that published both her own writings and those of other leading feminists of the time. Gilman advocated for women's reproductive rights, economic independence through work outside of the home, and the abolition of traditional gender roles. Gilman's beliefs and advocacy for gender equality made her a controversial figure during her time. However, her works and activism paved the way for future generations of feminists and helped to shape the modern understanding of women's rights. She died of breast cancer in 1935, but her work continued to inspire generations of feminists and remains a vital part of the feminist literary canon.

The Literary History

Charlotte Perkins Gilman and the Feminist Writing of the American Short Story

Feminist writing in the American short story during the turn of the 20th century centered around the conflict between traditional gender roles and the emergence of the "New Woman". Women writers of this time explored the potential freedom that the New Woman identity offered, challenging the constraints of the "True Woman" archetype which defined women as pure, pious, subservient, and silent.

Women writers of this era often gravitated towards exploring the concept of the New Woman and the potential freedom that this new identity could bring. They recognized that in the world they inhabited, language was primarily gendered as masculine and belonged to male and white speakers. This linguistic bias resulted in women being defined solely in relation to the male subject, depriving them of their own identity and voice.

One of the most influential texts for women short story writers during this period was Gilman's "The Yellow Wallpaper". This story exemplified the conflict between masculine and feminine modes of discourse. It depicted how male authority imposed limiting definitions on women, while women yearned for more expansive forms of self-definition. Gilman's story shed light on the struggle for women to break free from linguistic constraints and create their own narratives.

Nearly two decades later, Gilman wrote another short story called "An Honest Woman". This story highlighted that women are capable of learning to use language effectively. It also delved into how women could understand and manipulate the underlying processes of meaning creation and linguistic authority. Through her writing, Gilman demonstrated that women possess the power to navigate and challenge the biases ingrained in language, asserting their own agency and shaping their own stories.

In summary, Charlotte Perkins Gilman was a key figure in feminist writing during the turn of the 20th century. Her works, such as "The Yellow Wallpaper" and "An Honest Woman", explored the dichotomy between traditional gender roles and the potential for liberation. These stories illuminated the struggles women faced in a society where language favored men, but also showcased the potential for women to redefine their identities and reclaim their voices. Gilman's writings continue to be influential in feminist discourse and remain relevant in contemporary discussions on gender and language.

Literary Terms

Feminist Criticism

Feminist criticism emerged as a distinct and focused approach to literature in the late 1960s. Its main objective is to investigate the ways in which literature and other cultural productions either reinforce or challenge the economic, political, social, and psychological oppression of women. While individual feminist critics may have different perspectives on the issues they examine, they share certain assumptions and concepts that shape their analysis of sexual difference and privilege in literary works.

A foundational belief of feminist criticism is that women are subjected to various forms of oppression by patriarchy in economic, political, social, and psychological spheres. This oppression is perpetuated through patriarchal ideology, which objectifies and marginalizes women, defining them solely in relation to male norms and values. Moreover, feminist critics argue that Western civilization itself is deeply entrenched in patriarchal ideology, evident in the tendency of highly revered literary works to center around male protagonists while portraying female characters as peripheral and subordinate.

Another key tenet of feminist criticism is that while biological sex determines our male or female status, gender is a product of cultural influence rather than innate traits. Feminist critics contend that all behaviors associated with masculinity and femininity are learned and not biologically inherent. Thus, the promotion of gender equality is seen as the ultimate objective of feminist theory and literary criticism, aimed at bringing about positive social change.

Feminist critics recognize that gender issues permeate every aspect of human production and experience, including literature, whether we consciously acknowledge them or not. They raise crucial questions about literary texts, such as: How are women depicted in these works, and how do these portrayals reflect the gender issues of the time? What insights does the text offer regarding the intersection of gender with race, class, and other cultural factors in shaping women's experiences? Does the work suggest the potential for sisterhood to resist patriarchy and improve women's social, economic, political, or psychological circumstances? How does the history of the work's reception reveal the workings of patriarchy? What does the work signify about women's creativity? What role does the work play within women's literary history and tradition?

The Story

The Yellow Wallpaper[1]

It is very seldom that mere ordinary people like John and myself secure ancestral halls for the summer.

---

1   Charlotte Perkins Gilman, *The Yellow Wallpaper and Other Writings* (Dover Publications, 1997), pp. 1–24.

A colonial mansion, a hereditary estate, I would say a haunted house, and reach the height of romantic felicity but that would be asking too much of fate!

Still I will proudly declare that there is something queer about it.

Else, why should it be let so cheaply? And why have stood so long untenanted?

John laughs at me, of course, but one expects that in marriage.

John is practical in the extreme. He has no patience with faith, an intense horror of superstition, and he scoffs openly at any talk of things not to be felt and seen and put down in figures.

John is a physician, and—perhaps (I would not say it to a living soul, of course, but this is dead paper and a great relief to my mind) perhaps that is one reason I do not get well faster.

You see he does not believe I am sick!

And what can one do?

If a physician of high standing, and one's own husband, assures friends and relatives that there is really nothing the matter with one but temporary nervous depression—a slight hysterical tendency—what is one to do?

My brother is also a physician, and also of high standing, and he says the same thing.

So I take phosphates or phospites—whichever it is, and tonics, and journeys, and air, and exercise, and am absolutely forbidden to "work" until I am well again.

Personally, I disagree with their ideas.

Personally, I believe that congenial work, with excitement and change, would do me good. But what is one to do?

I did write for a while in spite of them; but it does exhaust me a good deal—having to be so sly about it, or else meet with heavy opposition.

I sometimes fancy that in my condition if I had less opposition and more society and stimulus—but John says the very worst thing I can do is to think about my condition, and I confess it always makes me feel bad.

So I will let it alone and talk about the house.

The most beautiful place! It is quite alone, standing well back from the road, quite three miles from the village. It makes me think of English places that you read about, for there are hedges and walls and gates that lock, and lots of separate little houses for the gardeners and people.

There is a delicious garden! I never saw such a garden large and shady, full of box-bordered paths, and lined with long grape-covered arbors with seats under them.

There were greenhouses, too, but they are all broken now.

There was some legal trouble, I believe, something about the heirs and coheirs; anyhow, the place has been empty for years.

That spoils my ghostliness, I am afraid, but I don't care—there is something strange about the house—I can feel it.

I even said so to John one moonlight evening, but he said what I felt was a draught, and shut the window.

I get unreasonably angry with John sometimes. I'm sure I never used to be so sensitive. I think it is due to this nervous condition.

But John says if I feel so, I shall neglect proper self-control; so I take pains to control myself—before him, at least, and that makes me very tired.

I don't like our room a bit. I wanted one downstairs that opened on the piazza and had roses all over the window, and such pretty old-fashioned chintz hangings! but John would not hear of it.

He said there was only one window and not room for two beds, and no near room for him if he took another.

He is very careful and loving, and hardly lets me stir without special direction.

I have a schedule prescription for each hour in the day; he takes all care from me, and so I feel basely ungrateful not to value it more.

He said we came here solely on my account, that I was to have perfect rest and all the air I could get. "Your exercise depends on your strength, my dear," said he, "and your food somewhat on your appetite; but air you can absorb all the time." So we took the nursery at the top of the house.

It is a big, airy room, the whole floor nearly, with windows that look all ways, and air and sunshine galore. It was nursery first and then playroom and gymnasium, I should judge; for the windows are barred for little children, and there are rings and things in the walls.

The paint and paper look as if a boys' school had used it. It is stripped off—the paper—in great patches all around the head of my bed, about as far as I can reach, and in a great place on the other side of the room low down. I never saw a worse paper in my life.

One of those sprawling flamboyant patterns committing every artistic sin.

It is dull enough to confuse the eye in following pronounced enough to constantly irritate and provoke study, and when you follow the lame uncertain curves for a little distance they suddenly commit suicide—plunge off at outrageous angles, destroy themselves in unheard of contradictions.

The color is repellent, almost revolting; a smouldering unclean yellow, strangely faded by the slow-turning sunlight.

It is a dull yet lurid orange in some places, a sickly sulphur tint in others.

No wonder the children hated it! I should hate it myself if I had to live in this room long.

There comes John, and I must put this away, —he hates to have me write a word.

We have been here two weeks, and I haven't felt like writing before, since that first day.

I am sitting by the window now, up in this atrocious nursery, and there is nothing to hinder my writing as much as I please, save lack of strength.

John is away all day, and even some nights when his cases are serious.

I am glad my case is not serious!

But these nervous troubles are dreadfully depressing.

John does not know how much I really suffer. He knows there is no reason to suffer, and that satisfies him.

Of course it is only nervousness. It does weigh on me so not to do my duty in any way!

I meant to be such a help to John, such a real rest and comfort, and here I am a comparative burden already!

Nobody would believe what an effort it is to do what little I am able, —to dress and entertain, and order things.

It is fortunate Mary is so good with the baby. Such a dear baby!

And yet I cannot be with him, it makes me so nervous.

I suppose John never was nervous in his life. He laughs at me so about this wall-paper!

At first he meant to repaper the room, but afterwards he said that I was letting it get the better of me, and that nothing was worse for a nervous patient than to give way to such fancies.

He said that after the wall-paper was changed it would be the heavy bedstead, and then the barred windows, and then that gate at the head of the stairs, and so on.

"You know the place is doing you good," he said, "and really, dear, I don't care to renovate the house just for a three months' rental."

"Then do let us go downstairs," I said, "there are such pretty rooms there."

Then he took me in his arms and called me a blessed little goose, and said he would go down to the cellar, if I wished, and have it whitewashed into the bargain.

But he is right enough about the beds and windows and things.

It is an airy and comfortable room as any one need wish, and, of course, I would not be so silly as to make him uncomfortable just for a whim.

I'm really getting quite fond of the big room, all but that horrid paper.

Out of one window I can see the garden, those mysterious deep shaded arbors, the riotous old fashioned flowers, and bushes and gnarly trees.

Out of another I get a lovely view of the bay and a little private wharf belonging to the estate. There is a beautiful shaded lane that runs down there from the house. I always fancy I see people walking in these numerous paths and arbors, but John has cautioned me not to g ve way to fancy in the least. He says that with my imaginative power and habit of story-making, a nervous weakness like mine is sure to lead to all manner of excited fancies, and that I ought to use my will and good sense to check the tendency. So I try.

I think sometimes that if I were only well enough to write a little it would relieve the press of ideas and rest me.

But I find I get pretty tired when I try.

It is so discouraging not to have any advice and companionship about my work. When I get really well, John says we will ask Cousin Henry and Julia down for a long visit; but he says he would as soon put fireworks in my pillow case as to let me have those stimulating people about now.

I wish I could get well faster.

But I must not think about that. This paper looks to me as if it knew what a vicious influence it had!

There is a recurrent spot where the pattern lolls like a broken neck and two bulbous eyes stare at you upside down.

I get positively angry with the impertinence of it and the everlastingness. Up and down and sideways they crawl, and those absurd, unblinking eyes are everywhere. There is one place where two breaths didn't match, and the eyes go all up and down the line, one a little higher than the other.

I never saw so much expression in an inanimate thing before, and we all know how much expression they have! I used to lie awake as a child and get more entertainment and terror out of blank walls and plain furniture than most children could find in a toy-store.

I remember what a kindly wink the knobs of our big, old bureau used to have, and there was one chair that always seemed like a strong friend

I used to feel that if any of the other thing' looked too fierce I could always hop into that chair and be safe.

The furniture in this room is no worse than inharmonious, however, for we had to bring it all from downstairs. I suppose when this was used as a playroom they had to take the nursery things out, and no wonder! I never saw such ravages as the children have made here.

The wall-paper, as I said before, is torn off in spots, and it sticketh closer than a brother—they must have had perseverance as well as hatred.

Then the floor is scratched and gouged and splintered, the plaster itself is dug out here and there, and this great heavy bed which is all we found in the room, looks as if it had been through the wars.

But I don't mind it a bit—only the paper.

There comes John's sister. Such a dear girl as she is, and so careful of me! I must not let her find me writing.

She is a perfect and enthusiastic housekeeper, and hopes for no better profession. I verily believe she thinks it is the writing which made me sick!

But I can write when she is out, and see her a long way off from these windows.

There is one that commands the road, a lovely shaded winding road, and one that just looks off over the country. A lovely country, too, full of great elms and velvet meadows.

This wall-paper has a kind of sub-pattern in a different shade, a particularly irritating one, for you can only see it in certain lights, and not clearly then.

But in the places where it isn't faded and where the sun is just so I can see a strange, provoking, formless sort of figure, that seems to skulk about behind that silly and conspicuous front design.

There's sister on the stairs!

Well, the Fourth of July is over! The people are all gone and I am tired out. John thought it might do me good to see a little company, so we just had mother and Nellie and the children down for a week.

Of course I didn't do a thing. Jennie sees to everything now.

But it tired me all the same.

John says if I don't pick up faster he shall send me to Weir Mitchell in the fall.

But I don't want to go there at all. I had a friend who was in his hands once, and she says he is just like John and my brother, only more so!

Besides, it is such an undertaking to go so far.

I don't feel as if it was worth while to turn my hand over for anything, and I'm getting dreadfully fretful and querulous.

I cry at nothing, and cry most of the time.

Of course I don't when John is here, or anybody else, but when I am alone.

And I am alone a good deal just now. John is kept in town very often by serious cases, and Jennie is good and lets me alone when I want her to.

So I walk a little in the garden or down that lovely lane, sit on the porch under the roses, and lie down up here a good deal.

I'm getting really fond of the room in spite of the wall-paper. Perhaps because of the wall-paper.

It dwells in my mind so!

I lie here on this great immovable bed—it is nailed down, I believe—and follow that pattern about by the hour. It is as good as gymnastics, I assure you. I start, we'll say, at the bottom, down in the corner over there where it has not been touched, and I determine for the thousandth time that I will follow that pointless pattern to some sort of a conclusion.

I know a little of the principle of design, and I know this thing was not arranged on any laws of I radiation, or alternation, or repetition, or symmetry, or anything else that I ever heard of.

It is repeated, of course, by the breadths, but not otherwise.

Looked at in one way each breadth stands alone, the bloated curves and flourishes— a kind of "debased Romanesque" with delirium tremens—go waddling up and down in isolated columns of fatuity.

But, on the other hand, they connect diagonally, and the sprawling outlines run off in great slanting waves of optic horror, like a lot of wallowing seaweeds in full chase.

The whole thing goes horizontally, too, at least it seems so, and I exhaust myself in trying to distinguish the order of its going in that direction.

They have used a horizontal breadth for a frieze, and that adds wonderfully to the confusion.

There is one end of the room where it is almost intact, and there, when the crosslights fade and the low sun shines directly upon it, I can almost fancy radiation after all, — the interminable grotesques seem to form around a common centre and rush off in headlong plunges of equal distraction.

It makes me tired to follow it. I will take a nap I guess.

I don't know why I should write this.

I don't want to.

I don't feel able.

And I know John would think it absurd. But must say what I feel and think in some way—it is such a relief!

But the effort is getting to be greater than the relief.

Half the time now I am awfully lazy, and lie down ever so much.

John says I mustn't lose my strength, and has me take cod liver oil and lots of tonics and things, to say nothing of ale and wine and rare meat.

Dear John! He loves me very dearly, and hates to have me sick. I tried to have a real earnest reasonable talk with him the other day, and tell him how I wish he would let me go and make a visit to Cousin Henry and Julia.

But he said I wasn't able to go, nor able to stand it after I got there; and I did not make out a very good case for myself, for I was crying before I had finished.

It is getting to be a great effort for me to think straight. Just this nervous weakness I suppose.

And dear John gathered me up in his arms, and just carried me upstairs and laid me on the bed, and sat by me and read to me till it tired my head.

He said I was his darling and his comfort and all he had, and that I must take care of myself for his sake, and keep well.

He says no one but myself can help me out of it, that I must use my will and self-control and not let any silly fancies run away with me.

There's one comfort, the baby is well and happy, and does not have to occupy this nursery with the horrid wall-paper.

If we had not used it, that blessed child would have! What a fortunate escape! Why, I wouldn't have a child of mine, an impressionable little thing, live in such a room for worlds.

I never thought of it before, but it is lucky that John kept me here after all, I can stand it so much easier than a baby, you see.

Of course I never mention it to them any more—I am too wise, —but I keep watch of it all the same.

There are things in that paper that nobody knows but me, or ever will.

Behind that outside pattern the dim shapes get clearer every day.

It is always the same shape, only very numerous.

And it is like a woman stooping down and creeping about behind that pattern. I don't like it a bit. I wonder—I begin to think—I wish John would take me away from here!

It is so hard to talk with John about my case, because he is so wise, and because he loves me so.

But I tried it last night.

It was moonlight. The moon shines in all around just as the sun does.

I hate to see it sometimes, it creeps so slowly, and always comes in by one window or another.

John was asleep and I hated to waken him, so I kept still and watched the moonlight on that undulating wall-paper till I felt creepy.

The faint figure behind seemed to shake the pattern, just as if she wanted to get out.

I got up softly and went to feel and see if the paper did move, and when I came back John was awake.

"What is it, little girl?" he said. "Don't go walking about like that—you'll get cold."

I thought it was a good time to talk, so I told him that I really was not gaining here, and that I wished he would take me away.

"Why darling!" said he, "our lease will be up in three weeks, and I can't see how to leave before.

"The repairs are not done at home, and I cannot possibly leave town just now. Of course if you were in any danger, I could and would, but you really are better, dear, whether you can see it or not. I am a doctor, dear, and I know. You are gaining flesh and color, your appetite is better, I feel really much easier about you."

"I don't weigh a bit more," said I, "nor as much; and my appetite may be better in the evening when you are here, but it is worse in the morning when you are away!"

"Bless her little heart!" said he with a big hug, "she shall be as sick as she pleases! But now let's improve the shining hours by going to sleep, and talk about it in the morning!"

"And you won't go away?" I asked gloomily.

"Why, how can I, dear? It is only three weeks more and then we will take a nice little trip of a few days while Jennie is getting the house ready. Really dear you are better! "

"Better in body perhaps—" I began, and stopped short, for he sat up straight and looked at me with such a stern, reproachful look that I could not say another word.

"My darling," said he, "I beg of you, for my sake and for our child's sake, as well as for your own, that you will never for one instant let that idea enter your mind! There is nothing so dangerous, so fascinating, to a temperament like yours. It is a false and foolish fancy. Can you not trust me as a physician when I tell you so?"

So of course I said no more on that score, and we went to sleep before long. He thought I was asleep first, but I wasn't, and lay there for hours trying to decide whether that front pattern and the back pattern really did move together or separately.

On a pattern like this, by daylight, there is a lack of sequence, a defiance of law, that is a constant irritant to a normal mind.

The color is hideous enough, and unreliable enough, and infuriating enough, but the pattern is torturing.

You think you have mastered it, but just as you get well underway in following, it turns a back somersault and there you are. It slaps you in the face, knocks you down, and tramples upon you. It is like a bad dream.

The outside pattern is a florid arabesque, reminding one of a fungus. If you can imagine a toadstool in joints, an interminable string of toadstools, budding and sprouting in endless convolutions—why, that is something like it.

That is, sometimes!

There is one marked peculiarity about this paper, a thing nobody seems to notice but myself and that is that it changes as the light changes.

When the sun shoots in through the east window—I always watch for that first long, straight ray—it changes so quickly that I never can quite believe it.

That is why I watch it always.

By moonlight—the moon shines in all night when there is a moon—I wouldn't know it was the same paper.

At night in any kind of light, in twilight, candle light, lamplight, and worst of all by moonlight, it becomes bars! The outside pattern I mean, and the woman behind it is as plain as can be.

I didn't realize for a long time what the thing was that showed behind, that dim sub-pattern, but l now I am quite sure it is a woman.

By daylight she is subdued, quiet. I fancy it is the pattern that keeps her so still. It is so puzzling. It keeps me quiet by the hour.

I lie down ever so much now. John says it is good for me, and to sleep all I can.

Indeed he started the habit by making me lie down for an hour after each meal.

It is a very bad habit I am convinced, for you see I don't sleep.

And that cultivates deceit, for I don't tell them I'm awake—O no!

The fact is I am getting a little afraid of John.

He seems very queer sometimes, and even Jennie has an inexplicable look.

It strikes me occasionally, just as a scientific hypothesis, —that perhaps it is the paper!

I have watched John when he did not know I was looking, and come into the room suddenly on the most innocent excuses, and I've caught him several times looking at the paper! And Jennie too. I caught Jennie with her hand on it once.

She didn't know I was in the room, and when I asked her in a quiet, a very quiet voice, with the most restrained manner possible, what she was doing with the paper— she turned around as if she had been caught stealing, and looked quite angry—asked me why I should frighten her so!

Then she said that the paper stained everything it touched, that she had found yellow smooches on all my clothes and John's, and she wished we would be more careful!

Did not that sound innocent? But I know she was studying that pattern, and I am determined that nobody shall find it out but myself!

Life is very much more exciting now than it used to be. You see I have something more to expect, to look forward to, to watch. I really do eat better, and am more quiet than I was.

John is so pleased to see me improve! He laughed a little the other day, and said I seemed to be flourishing in spite of my wall-paper.

I turned it off with a laugh. I had no intention of telling him it was because of the wall-paper—he would make fun of me. He might even want to take me away.

I don't want to leave now until I have found it out. There is a week more, and I think that will be enough.

I'm feeling ever so much better! I don't sleep much at night, for it is so interesting to watch developments; but I sleep a good deal in the daytime.

In the daytime it is tiresome and perplexing.

There are always new shoots on the fungus, and new shades of yellow all over it. I cannot keep count of them, though I have tried conscientiously.

It is the strangest yellow, that wall-paper! It makes me think of all the yellow things I ever saw--not beautiful ones like buttercups, but old foul, bad yellow things.

But there is something else about that paper—the smell! I noticed it the moment we came into the room, but with so much air and sun it was not bad. Now we have had a week of fog and rain, and whether the windows are open or not, the smell is here.

It creeps all over the house.

I find it hovering in the dining-room, skulking in the parlor, hiding in the hall, lying in wait for me on the stairs.

It gets into my hair.

Even when I go to ride, if I turn my head suddenly and surprise it—there is that smell!

Such a peculiar odor, too! I have spent hours in trying to analyze it, to find what it smelled like.

It is not bad—at first, and very gentle, but quite the subtlest, most enduring odor I ever met.

In this damp weather it is awful, I wake up in the night and find it hanging over me.

It used to disturb me at first. I thought seriously of burning the house—to reach the smell.

But now I am used to it. The only thing I can think of that it is like is the color of the paper! A yellow smell.

There is a very funny mark on this wall, low down, near the mopboard. A streak that runs round the room. It goes behind every piece of furniture, except the bed, a long, straight, even smooch, as if it had been rubbed over and over.

I wonder how it was done and who did it, and what they did it for. Round and round and round—round and round and round—it makes me dizzy!

I really have discovered something at last.

Through watching so much at night, when it changes so, I have finally found out.

The front pattern does move—and no wonder! The woman behind shakes it!

Sometimes I think there are a great many women behind, and sometimes only one, and she crawls around fast, and her crawling shakes it all over.

Then in the very bright spots she keeps still, and in the very shady spots she just takes hold of the bars and shakes them hard.

And she is all the time trying to climb through. But nobody could climb through that pattern—it strangles so; I think that is why it has so many heads.

They get through, and then the pattern strangles them off and turns them upside down, and makes their eyes white!

If those heads were covered or taken off it would not be half so bad.

I think that woman gets out in the daytime!

And I'll tell you why—privately—I've seen her!

I can see her out of every one of my windows!

It is the same woman, I know, for she is always creeping, and most women do not creep by daylight.

I see her on that long road under the trees, creeping along, and when a carriage comes she hides under the blackberry vines.

I don't blame her a bit. It must be very humiliating to be caught creeping by daylight!

I always lock the door when I creep by daylight. I can't do it at night, for I know John would suspect something at once.

And John is so queer now, that I don't want to irritate him. I wish he would take another room! Besides, I don't want anybody to get that woman out at night but myself.

I often wonder if I could see her out of all the windows at once.

But, turn as fast as I can, I can only see out of one at one time.

And though I always see her, she may be able to creep faster than I can turn!

I have watched her sometimes away off in the open country, creeping as fast as a cloud shadow in a high wind.

If only that top pattern could be gotten off from the under one! I mean to try it, little by little.

I have found out another funny thing, but I shan't tell it this time! It does not do to trust people too much.

There are only two more days to get this paper off, and I believe John is beginning to notice. I don't like the look in his eyes.

And I heard him ask Jennie a lot of professional questions about me. She had a very good report to give.

She said I slept a good deal in the daytime.

John knows I don't sleep very well at night, for all I'm so quiet!

He asked me all sorts of questions, too, and pretended to be very loving and kind.

As if I couldn't see through him!

Still, I don't wonder he acts so, sleeping under this paper for three months.

It only interests me, but I feel sure John and Jennie are secretly affected by it.

Hurrah! This is the last day, but it is enough. John to stay in town overnight, and won't be out until this evening.

Jennie wanted to sleep with me—the sly thing! but I told her I should undoubtedly rest better for a night all alone.

That was clever, for really I wasn't alone a bit! As soon as it was moonlight and that poor thing began to crawl and shake the pattern, I got up and ran to help her.

I pulled and she shook, I shook and she pulled, and before morning we had peeled off yards of that paper.

A strip about as high as my head and half around the room.

And then when the sun came and that awful pattern began to laugh at me, I declared I would finish it to-day!

We go away to-morrow, and they are moving all my furniture down again to leave things as they were before.

Jennie looked at the wall in amazement, but I told her merrily that I did it out of pure spite at the vicious thing.

She laughed and said she wouldn't mind doing it herself, but I must not get tired.

How she betrayed herself that time!

But I am here, and no person touches this but me, —not alive!

She tried to get me out of the room—it was too patent! But I said it was so quiet and empty and clean now that I believed I would lie down again and sleep all I could; and not to wake me even for dinner—I would call when I woke.

So now she is gone, and the servants are gone, and the things are gone, and there is nothing left but that great bedstead nailed down, with the canvas mattress we found on it.

We shall sleep downstairs to-night, and take the boat home to-morrow.

I quite enjoy the room, now it is bare again.

How those children did tear about here!

This bedstead is fairly gnawed!

But I must get to work.

I have locked the door and thrown the key down into the front path.

I don't want to go out, and I don't want to have anybody come in, till John comes.

I want to astonish him.

I've got a rope up here that even Jennie did not find. If that woman does get out, and tries to get away, I can tie her!

But I forgot I could not reach far without anything to stand on!

This bed will not move!

I tried to lift and push it until I was lame, and then I got so angry I bit off a little piece at one corner—but it hurt my teeth.

Then I peeled off all the paper I could reach standing on the floor. It sticks horribly and the pattern just enjoys it! All those strangled heads and bulbous eyes and waddling fungus growths just shriek with derision!

I am getting angry enough to do something desperate. To jump out of the window would be admirable exercise, but the bars are too strong even to try.

Besides I wouldn't do it. Of course not. I know well enough that a step like that is improper and might be misconstrued.

I don't like to look out of the windows even—there are so many of those creeping women, and they creep so fast.

I wonder if they all come out of that wall-paper as I did?

But I am securely fastened now by my well-hidden rope—you don't get me out in the road there!

I suppose I shall have to get back behind the pattern when it comes night, and that is hard!

It is so pleasant to be out in this great room and creep around as I please!

I don't want to go outside. I won't, even if Jennie asks me to.

For outside you have to creep on the ground, and everything is green instead of yellow.

But here I can creep smoothly on the floor, and my shoulder just fits in that long smooch around the wall, so I cannot lose my way.

Why there's John at the door!

It is no use, young man, you can't open it!

How he does call and pound!

Now he's crying for an axe.

It would be a shame to break down that beautiful door!

"John dear!" said I in the gentlest voice, "the key is down by the front steps, under a plantain leaf! "

That silenced him for a few moments.

Then he said very quietly indeed, "Open the door, my darling!"

"I can't," said I. "The key is down by the front door under a plantain leaf!"

And then I said it again, several times, very gently and slowly, and said it so often that he had to go and see, and he got it of course, and came in. He stopped short by the door.

"What is the matter?" he cried. "For God's sake, what are you doing!"

I kept on creeping just the same, but I looked at him over my shoulder.

"I've got out at last," said I, "in spite of you and Jane. And I've pulled off most of the paper, so you can't put me back! "

118

Now why should that man have fainted? But he did, and right across my path by the wall, so that I had to creep over him every time!

Plot Summary

The story begins with the woman and her husband, John, moving into a colonial mansion for the summer. John is a physician and believes that rest and quiet are the best cures for his wife's mental illness. He forbids her from writing or engaging in any stimulating activities, and instead encourages her to rest and take walks in the garden. The woman soon becomes obsessed with the yellow wallpaper in her room. She begins to see a figure in the wallpaper, and her mental state deteriorates. She becomes increasingly paranoid and believes that the figure in the wallpaper is a woman trying to escape from the room. She also believes that the wallpaper is alive and is trying to control her. John is frustrated with his wife's behavior and believes that she is simply imagining things. He continues to encourage her to rest and take walks, but her mental state continues to deteriorate. Eventually, she becomes so obsessed with the wallpaper that she tears it off the walls in an attempt to free the woman she believes is trapped inside. The story ends with the woman's husband finding her in a state of exhaustion and hysteria. The story is a powerful critique of the medical profession's treatment of mental illness in the 19th century. It also serves as a warning against the dangers of confining women to restrictive roles.

Language Exercises

Choose the item that best replaces or explains the underlined part of the sentence.

1. Personally, I believe that <u>congenial</u> work, with excitement and change, would do me good.
   A. critical   B. original   C. suitable   D. rational
2. The color is <u>repellent</u>, almost revolting; a smouldering unclean yellow, strangely faded by the slow-turning sunlight.
   A. pleasant   B. pungent   C. poignant   D. disgusting
3. I am sitting by the window now, up in this <u>atrocious</u> nursery, and there is nothing to hinder my writing as much as I please, save lack of strength.
   A. favorable   B. attractive   C. glamorous   D. unpleasant
4. Then the floor is scratched and gouged and <u>splintered</u>, the plaster itself is dug out here and there, and this great heavy bed which is all we found in the room, looks as if it had been through the wars.
   A. broken   B. exhausted   C. indulged   D. overwhelmed

119

5. But in the places where it isn't faded and where the sun is just so I can see a strange, provoking, formless sort of figure, that seems to skulk about behind that silly and <u>conspicuous</u> front design.
    A. auspicious   B. eye-catching   C. suspicious   D. vicious

6. I don't feel as if it was worth while to turn my hand over for anything, and I'm getting dreadfully <u>fretful</u> and querulous.
    A. detached   B. distracted   C. distanced   D. distressed

7. But, on the other hand, they connect diagonally, and the sprawling outlines run off in great slanting waves of optic horror, like a lot of <u>wallowing</u> seaweeds in full chase.
    A. surging   B. soaring   C. rolling   D. hovering

8. There is one end of the room where it is almost intact, and there, when the cross lights fade and the low sun shines directly upon it, I can almost fancy radiation after all, —the <u>interminable</u> grotesques seem to form around a common center and rush off in headlong plunges of equal distraction.
    A. endless   B. temperate   C. tangible   D. habitual

9. The color is <u>hideous</u> enough, and unreliable enough, and infuriating enough, but the pattern is torturing.
    A. dim   B. ugly   C. vague   D. invisible

10. They get through, and then the pattern <u>strangles</u> them off and turns them upside down, and makes their eyes white!
    A. hurls   B. howls   C. hauls   D. hides

11. I don't blame her a bit. It must be very <u>humiliating</u> to be caught creeping by daylight!
    A. frustrating   B. depressing   C. embarrassing D. insulting

12. And John is so <u>queer</u> now, that I don't want to irritate him.
    A. abnormal   B. hysterical   C. snobbish   D. stubborn

13. Jennie looked at the wall in amazement, but I told her merrily that I did it out of pure spite at the <u>vicious</u> thing.
    A. virtuous   B. evil   C. corrupt   D. rotten

14. She tried to get me out of the room—it was too <u>patent</u>! But I said it was so quiet and empty and clean now that I believed I would lie down again and sleep all I could; and not to wake me even for dinner—I would call when I woke.
    A. obvious   B. abrupt   C. exotic   D. erratic

15. All those strangled heads and bulbous eyes and waddling fungus growths just shriek with <u>derision</u>!
    A. compliment   B. complacence   C. complex   D. contempt

Topics for Discussion

1. What role does John feel a woman should play in society? How might a contemporary feminist view John? What are the attitudes toward acceptable roles for women today?

2. The most important symbol in the story is the yellow wallpaper. Comment on the symbolic meaning of the yellow wallpaper.

3. "The Yellow Wallpaper" was written and published in 1892. Research the historical context of the story and analyze the theme of the story.

4. Read Oilman's autobiography *The Living of Charlotte Perkins* (1935) and compare her real-life experience with depression to that of the protagonist in "The Yellow Wallpaper".

5. "The Yellow Wallpaper" is an example of a first-person narrative because it is told exclusively from the viewpoint of the unnamed protagonist, what are the advantages of such point of view?

6. "The Yellow Wallpaper" takes place in a country house that is located about three miles from the nearest village. Commet on the setting of the story.

7. The story is considered an example of psychological realism because it attempts to accurately portray the mental deterioration of the narrator. Discuss the elements of realism in the story.

8. Oilman utilizes numerous conventions of Gothic fiction in "The Yellow Wallpaper". What are they? Give some examples in the text to illustrate this point.

9. Research literature on hysteria and other "women's problems" published at the end of the 1800s and relate them to "The Yellow Wall".

10. "The Yellow Wallpaper" examines the role of women in nineteenth-century American society. How do the characters in the story represent the nineteenth-century view of the role of women?

Discussion Tips

"The Yellow Wallpaper", originally published in 1892 in the New England Magazine, stands as Charlotte Perkins Gilman's most acclaimed work of short fiction. Rooted in Gilman's personal encounter with postpartum depression, the narrative unfolds as a first-person portrayal of a young mother's mental unraveling. Mirroring the prevailing medical theories of the time, the protagonist is prescribed absolute physical and intellectual inactivity, forbidden to engage in reading, writing, or even seeing her newborn. To enforce these measures, the woman's husband relocates her to a rural dwelling with a room adorned in yellow wallpaper.

The narrative delves into the societal roles of women in nineteenth-century America, exploring dynamics within marital relationships, the economic and social reliance of women on men, and the stifling of female individuality and sexuality. The Victorian Age's influence on societal values, emphasizing women's confinement within the domestic sphere, is evident. Struggling with postpartum depression, the protagonist is instructed to observe complete bed rest by her husband and brother, disregarding her desire for intellectual pursuits. Despite clandestinely maintaining a journal, her agency is subjugated to her husband's decisions, portraying her as a charming wife and capable mother. The husband's paternalistic treatment, referring to her as his "little girl" and "blessed little goose", further underscores her subordinate role.

The psychological dimension of "The Yellow Wallpaper" positions it as a work of psychological fiction. Gilman skillfully addresses themes of madness, depression, despair, and self-worth by providing a vivid and startling account of the stages of mental deterioration. The narrator, devoid of meaningful occupation and agency in her treatment, projects her suppressed emotions onto the yellow wallpaper, culminating in her conviction that a woman is trapped within its pattern—a poignant symbol of her emotional and intellectual confinement. Hindered in expressing her feelings or seeking liberation, the narrator succumbs to insanity.

The narrative also critiques the late nineteenth-century perspectives on mental illness, particularly the views of renowned neurologist S. Weir Mitchell. During this era, psychologists often dismissed severe conditions like depression as mere hysteria or "nerves", advocating complete bed rest while deeming intellectual activity detrimental to women's mental well-being. Gilman clarified the narrative's intent in her autobiography in 1935, highlighting her aim to challenge Dr. Mitchell's approach. Reports suggest that Mitchell, influenced by "The Yellow Wallpaper", altered his treatment of nervous prostration, validating Gilman's conviction that her work had a meaningful impact.

Part II

Realism and the American Short Story

Unit 6
Sarah Orne Jewett: "A White Heron"

Sarah Orne Jewett (1849–1909)

Sarah Orne Jewett was an influential American writer from the late 19th century known for her distinctive regionalist writing style. Born in South Berwick, Maine in 1849, Jewett's writing often focused on the rural life and traditions of the New England area. She is best known for her collection of short stories, including *The Country of the Pointed Firs*, which is considered her masterpiece. Jewett's writing often depicted the everyday lives of ordinary people in rural communities, and she captured the essence of the New England landscape with vivid and detailed descriptions. Her work reflected a deep appreciation for the natural world and an understanding of the importance of preserving local traditions and customs. Jewett's writing style is characterized by its realistic and detailed portrayal of rural life, as well as its use of local dialect and idiom. Her keen observations and keen sense of place earned her a reputation as a prominent regionalist writer. Throughout her career, Jewett became a prominent figure in American literary circles, and her work continues to be celebrated for its rich depiction of the New England landscape and its insight into the lives of its people.

The Literary History

The Transition into the New Century

At the turn of the 20th century, American short story writing underwent a period of transition and innovation, influenced by social, cultural, and technological advancements. This era witnessed the rise of renowned short story writers who contributed significantly to the development of the genre.

Mark Twain, known for his pioneering work in American literature, made substantial contributions to the short story form during this period. His witty and satirical writing style, as exemplified in works such as "The Celebrated Jumping Frog of Calaveras County" and "The Man That Corrupted Hadleyburg", captured the essence of American life and human nature, reflecting the changing social and political landscape of the era.

Sarah Orne Jewett also emerged as a prominent figure in American short story writing during this period. Her stories depicted the rural life and traditions of New England, capturing the essence of local communities and characters. Jewett's writing style was characterized by its realistic portrayal of everyday life and its keen observation of human behavior, offering insight into the complexities of human relationships and the transformations occurring in American society at the time.

Furthermore, the transition into the new century saw the emergence of writers such as O. Henry, whose distinctive use of surprise endings and clever plot twists became hallmarks of his short stories. O. Henry's skilled portrayal of diverse characters and his ability to capture the essence of urban life in works like "The Gift of the Magi" and "The Ransom of Red Chief" reflected the changing dynamics of American society and the human experience during this period.

These writers, among others, played pivotal roles in shaping the development of American short stories at the turn of the century, using their unique voices and storytelling techniques to encapsulate the essence of the changing times. Their contributions not only enriched the genre but also provided valuable insights into the social, cultural, and technological transformations that characterized the transition into the new century.

Literary Terms

American realism

American realism was a literary and artistic movement that emerged in the late 19th century as a response to the rapid changes occurring in American society. It sought to depict everyday life in a realistic and objective manner, often focusing on ordinary people and their struggles. One of the key figures associated with American Realism is Mark Twain, whose novels such as *The Adventures of Huckleberry Finn* and *The Adventures of Tom Sawyer* captured the essence of life along the Mississippi River. Twain's works were known for their satirical wit and sharp social commentary, exposing the racial and social injustices of the time. Another prominent writer of this movement was Henry James, who explored the complexities of human relationships and psychological intricacies in his novels. James' works, such as *The Portrait of a Lady* and *The Turn of the Screw*, delved into the inner lives of his characters, providing a nuanced portrayal of human nature. American Realism also found expression in the visual arts. The Ashcan School, led by painters such as George Bellows and Edward Hopper, depicted urban life in New York City. They focused on the grittier aspects of society, painting scenes of tenements, factories, and crowded streets, capturing the raw energy and diversity of the city. While American Realism celebrated the mundane and ordinary, it also confronted social and political issues of the time. Upton Sinclair's novel *The Jungle* exposed the appalling conditions of the meatpacking industry and sparked significant food safety reforms. Similarly, Edith Wharton's novel *The House of Mirth* critiqued the restrictive social expectations placed on women. American Realism reflected a growing interest in understanding and depicting the realities of everyday life. It offered a departure from previous romanticized notions of literature and embraced a more objective and truthful approach. Through its literary and artistic works, American Realism captured the essence of a rapidly changing nation and laid the foundation for modern American literature and art.

Local colorism

Local colorism was devoted to capturing the unique customs, manners, speech, folklore, and any other qualities of a particular regional community, usually in humorous short stories. Local colorists concerned themselves with presenting and interpreting the local character of their regions. They tended to idealize and embellish their stories, but they never forgot to keep an eye on the truthful color of local life. Socially, the different regions of the United States felt the need to assert their cultural identity, seeking understanding and recognition by showing their local character. Intellectually, the frontier tall-tale tradition paves the way for the flourishing of local colorism. American influences upon those authors known as local-color writers may be found in Down East humor and in the frontier tradition of tall tales. General features of local colorism include a tendency of embellishment and idealization, a nostalgic feeling for the past, minutely accurate descriptions of the life of the regions, and truthful depiction of the common people.

Tall tale

Tall tale referred to the type of American frontier anecdote characterized by exaggeration or violent understatement, with realistic details of character or local customs that work toward a cumulative effect of the grotesque, romantic, or humorous. Tall tales depend for their humor partly upon the incongruity between the realism in which the scene and narrator are portrayed and the fantastically comic world of the enclosed narrative. Frontier storytellers created the oral tradition of the tall tale. Later, the anecdotes began to be printed, and the tall tale became a distinct literary genre, which delightfully pictures the social life of the frontier. Among the most famous literary examples are Longstreet's *Georgia Scenes*, and many passages in the works of Mark Twain.

Ecocriticism

Ecocriticism is a literary and cultural theory that examines the representation and treatment of nature in literature, as well as the broader interconnectedness of human society and the environment. It emerged in response to the growing environmental concerns and aims to explore the ways in which literature and culture shape and reflect our attitudes towards nature. Ecocriticism draws from a range of disciplines including literary studies, environmental studies, sociology, anthropology, and philosophy. It delves into topics such as environmental ethics, sustainability, biodiversity, and eco-activism. Ecocriticism encourages a deeper understanding of our relationship with the natural world and the impact of human activities on the environment, offering new insights into the ways literature and culture can address and respond to environmental challenges.

Bildungsroman

Bildungsroman, a German term meaning "novel of formation" or "novel of education", refers to a genre of literature that focuses on the psychological, moral, and intellectual growth of the protagonist from childhood to adulthood. Originating in the late 18th and early 19th centuries, this genre gained prominence in German literature before spreading to other cultures and languages. At the core of a Bildungsroman is the protagonist's coming-of-age journey, typically portrayed against the backdrop of social, cultural, and historical changes. The narrative often unfolds in a chronological sequence, tracing the protagonist's evolution through various experiences, challenges, and self-discoveries. These experiences may include education, initiation into society, romantic relationships, and encounters with mentors or influential figures. Central to the Bildungsroman is the theme of self-realization, as the protagonist grapples with identity formation, societal expectations, and personal aspirations. This introspective exploration often leads to a deeper understanding of the self and the world, as the protagonist navigates moral dilemmas, confronts obstacles, and matures emotionally and intellectually. Notable examples of Bildungsroman include Johann Wolfgang von Goethe's *Wilhelm Meister's Apprenticeship*, Charles Dickens' *Great Expectations*, and Harper Lee's *To Kill a Mockingbird*. This genre continues to captivate readers by capturing the profound and transformative journey from youth to maturity, resonating with the universal quest for self-discovery and personal fulfillment.

The Story

A White Heron[1]

I.

The woods were already filled with shadows one June evening, just before eight o'clock, though a bright sunset still glimmered faintly among the trunks of the trees.

---

1   Sarah Orne Jewett, *The Country of the Pointed Firs and Other Stories* (Penguin Classics, 1997), pp. 67–83.

A little girl was driving home her cow, a plodding, dilatory, provoking creature in her behavior, but a valued companion for all that. They were going away from whatever light there was, and striking deep into the woods, but their feet were familiar with the path, and it was no matter whether their eyes could see it or not.

There was hardly a night the summer through when the old cow could be found waiting at the pasture bars; on the contrary, it was her greatest pleasure to hide herself away among the huckleberry bushes, and though she wore a loud bell she had made the discovery that if one stood perfectly still it would not ring. So Sylvia had to hunt for her until she found her, and call Co' ! Co' ! with never an answering Moo, until her childish patience was quite spent. If the creature had not given good milk and plenty of it, the case would have seemed very different to her owners. Besides, Sylvia had all the time there was, and very little use to make of it. Sometimes in pleasant weather it was a consolation to look upon the cow's pranks as an intelligent attempt to play hide and seek, and as the child had no playmates she lent herself to this amusement with a good deal of zest. Though this chase had been so long that the wary animal herself had given an unusual signal of her whereabouts, Sylvia had only laughed when she came upon Mistress Moolly at the swamp-side, and urged her affectionately homeward with a twig of birch leaves. The old cow was not inclined to wander farther, she even turned in the right direction for once as they left the pasture, and stepped along the road at a good pace. She was quite ready to be milked now, and seldom stopped to browse. Sylvia wondered what her grandmother would say because they were so late. It was a great while since she had left home at half-past five o'clock, but everybody knew the difficulty of making this errand a short one. Mrs. Tilley had chased the hornéd torment too many summer evenings herself to blame any one else for lingering, and was only thankful as she waited that she had Sylvia, nowadays, to give such valuable assistance. The good woman suspected that Sylvia loitered occasionally on her own account; there never was such a child for straying about out-of-doors since the world was made! Everybody said that it was a good change for a little maid who had tried to grow for eight years in a crowded manufacturing town, but, as for Sylvia herself, it seemed as if she never had been alive at all before she came to live at the farm. She thought often with wistful compassion of a wretched geranium that belonged to a town neighbor.

"Afraid of folks," old Mrs. Tilley said to herself, with a smile, after she had made the unlikely choice of Sylvia from her daughter's houseful of children, and was returning to the farm. "Afraid of folks," they said! "I guess she won't be troubled no great with'em up to the old place!" When they reached the door of the lonely house and stopped to unlock it, and the cat came to purr loudly, and rub against them, a deserted pussy, indeed, but fat with young robins, Sylvia whispered that this was a beautiful place to live in, and she never should wish to go home.

The companions followed the shady wood-road, the cow taking slow steps and the child very fast ones. The cow stopped long at the brook to drink, as if the pasture were not half a swamp, and Sylvia stood still and waited, letting her bare feet cool themselves in the shoal water, while the great twilight moths struck softly against her. She waded on through the brook as the cow moved away, and listened to the thrushes with a heart that beat fast with pleasure. There was a stirring in the great boughs overhead. They were full of little birds and beasts that seemed to be wide awake, and going about their world, or else saying good-night to each other in sleepy twitters. Sylvia herself felt sleepy as she walked along. However, it was not much farther to the house, and the air was soft and sweet. She was not often in the woods so late as this, and it made her feel as if she were a part of the gray shadows and the moving leaves. She was just thinking how long it seemed since she first came to the farm a year ago, and wondering if everything went on in the noisy town just the same as when she was there, the thought of the great red-faced boy who used to chase and frighten her made her hurry along the path to escape from the shadow of the trees.

Suddenly this little woods-girl is horror-stricken to hear a clear whistle not very far away. Not a bird's-whistle, which would have a sort of friendliness, but a boy's whistle, determined, and somewhat aggressive. Sylvia left the cow to whatever sad fate might await her, and stepped discreetly aside into the bushes, but she was just too late. The enemy had discovered her, and called out in a very cheerful and persuasive tone, "Halloa, little girl, how far is it to the road?" and trembling Sylvia answered almost inaudibly, "A good ways."

She did not dare to look boldly at the tall young man, who carried a gun over his shoulder, but she came out of her bush and again followed the cow, while he walked alongside.

"I have been hunting for some birds," the stranger said kindly, "and I have lost my way, and need a friend very much. Don't be afraid," he added gallantly. "Speak up and tell me what your name is, and whether you think I can spend the night at your house, and go out gunning early in the morning."

Sylvia was more alarmed than before. Would not her grandmother consider her much to blame? But who could have foreseen such an accident as this? It did not seem to be her fault, and she hung her head as if the stem of it were broken, but managed to answer "Sylvy," with much effort when her companion again asked her name.

Mrs. Tilley was standing in the doorway when the trio came into view. The cow gave a loud moo by way of explanation.

"Yes, you'd better speak up for yourself, you old trial! Where'd she tucked herself away this time, Sylvy?" But Sylvia kept an awed silence; she knew by instinct that her grandmother did not comprehend the gravity of the situation. She must be mistaking the stranger for one of the farmer-lads of the region.

The young man stood his gun beside the door, and dropped a lumpy game-bag beside it; then he bade Mrs. Tilley good-evening, and repeated his wayfarer's story, and asked if he could have a night's lodging.

"Put me anywhere you like," he said. "I must be off early in the morning, before day; but I am very hungry, indeed. You can give me some milk at any rate, that's plain."

"Dear sakes, yes," responded the hostess, whose long slumbering hospitality seemed to be easily awakened. "You might fare better if you went out to the main road a mile or so, but you're welcome to what we've got. I'll milk right off, and you make yourself at home. You can sleep on husks or feathers," she proffered graciously. "I raised them all myself. There's good pasturing for geese just below here towards the ma'sh. Now step round and set a plate for the gentleman, Sylvy!" And Sylvia promptly stepped. She was glad to have something to do, and she was hungry herself.

It was a surprise to find so clean and comfortable a little dwelling in this New England wilderness. The young man had known the horrors of its most primitive housekeeping, and the dreary squalor of that level of society which does not rebel at the companionship of hens. This was the best thrift of an old-fashioned farmstead, though on such a small scale that it seemed like a hermitage. He listened eagerly to the old woman's quaint talk, he watched Sylvia's paleface and shining gray eyes with ever growing enthusiasm, and insisted that this was the best supper he had eaten for a month, and afterward the new-made friends sat down in the door-way together while the moon came up.

Soon it would be berry-time, and Sylvia was a great help at picking. The cow was a good milker, though a plaguy thing to keep track of, the hostess gossiped frankly, adding presently that she had buried four children, so Sylvia's mother, and a son (who might be dead) in California were all the children she had left. "Dan, my boy, was a great hand to go gunning," she explained sadly. "I never wanted for pa'tridges or gray squer'ls while he was to home. He's been a great wand'rer, I expect, and he's no hand to write letters. There, I don't blame him, I'd ha' seen the world myself if it had been so I could."

"Sylvy takes after him," the grandmother continued affectionately, after a minute's pause. "There ain't a foot o'ground she don't know her way over, and the wild creaturs counts her one o' themselves. Squer'ls she'll tame to come an'feed right out o'her hands, and all sorts o'birds. Last winter she got the jay-birds to bangeing here, and I believe she'd 'a' scanted herself of her own meals to have plenty to throw out amongst 'em, if I hadn't kep'watch. Anything but crows, I tell her, I'm willin' to help support— though Dan he had a tamed one o'them that did seem to have reason same as folks. It was round here a good spell after he went away. Dan an'his father they didn't hitch, — but he never held up his head ag'in after Dan had dared him an' gone off."

The guest did not notice this hint of family sorrows in his eager interest in something else.

"So Sylvy knows all about birds, does she?" he exclaimed, as he looked round at the little girl who sat, very demure but increasingly sleepy, in the moonlight. "I am making a collection of birds myself. I have been at it ever since I was a boy." (Mrs. Tilley

131

smiled.) "There are two or three very rare ones I have been hunting for these five years. I mean to get them on my own ground if they can be found."

"Do you cage 'em up?" asked Mrs. Tilley doubtfully, in response to this enthusiastic announcement.

"Oh no, they're stuffed and preserved, dozens and dozens of them," said the ornithologist, "and I have shot or snared every one myself. I caught a glimpse of a white heron a few miles from here on Saturday, and I have followed it in this direction. They have never been found in this district at all. The little white heron, it is," and he turned again to look at Sylvia with the hope of discovering that the rare bird was one of her acquaintances.

But Sylvia was watching a hop-toad in the narrow footpath.

"You would know the heron if you saw it," the stranger continued eagerly. "A queer tall white bird with soft feathers and long thin legs. And it would have a nest perhaps in the top of a high tree, made of sticks, something like a hawk's nest."

Sylvia's heart gave a wild beat; she knew that strange white bird, and had once stolen softly near where it stood in some bright green swamp grass, away over at the other side of the woods. There was an open place where the sunshine always seemed strangely yellow and hot, where tall, nodding rushes grew, and her grandmother had warned her that she might sink in the soft black mud underneath and never be heard of more. Not far beyond were the salt marshes just this side the sea itself, which Sylvia wondered and dreamed much about, but never had seen, whose great voice could sometimes be heard above the noise of the woods on stormy nights.

"I can't think of anything I should like so much as to find that heron's nest," the handsome stranger was saying. "I would give ten dollars to anybody who could show it to me," he added desperately, "and I mean to spend my whole vacation hunting for it if need be. Perhaps it was only migrating, or had been chased out of its own region by some bird of prey."

Mrs. Tilley gave amazed attention to all this, but Sylvia still watched the toad, not divining, as she might have done at some calmer time, that the creature wished to get to its hole under the door-step, and was much hindered by the unusual spectators at that hour of the evening. No amount of thought, that night, could decide how many wished-for treasures the ten dollars, so lightly spoken of, would buy.

The next day the young sportsman hovered about the woods, and Sylvia kept him company, having lost her first fear of the friendly lad, who proved to be most kind and sympathetic. He told her many things about the birds and what they knew and where they lived and what they did with themselves. And he gave her a jack-knife, which she thought as great a treasure as if she were a desert-islander. All day long he did not once make her troubled or afraid except when he brought down some unsuspecting singing creature from its bough. Sylvia would have liked him vastly better without his gun; she could not understand why he killed the very birds he seemed to like so much. But as the day waned, Sylvia still watched the young man with loving admiration. She had never seen anybody so charming and delightful; the woman's heart, asleep in the child, was vaguely thrilled by a dream of love. Some premonition of that great power stirred and swayed these young creatures who traversed the solemn woodlands with soft-footed silent care. They stopped to listen to a bird's song; they pressed forward again eagerly, parting the branches—speaking to each other rarely and in whispers; the young man going first and Sylvia following, fascinated, a few steps behind, with her gray eyes dark with excitement.

She grieved because the longed-for white heron was elusive, but she did not lead the guest, she only followed, and there was no such thing as speaking first. The sound of her own unquestioned voice would have terrified her—it was hard enough to answer yes or no when there was need of that. At last evening began to fall, and they drove the cow home together, and Sylvia smiled with pleasure when they came to the place where she heard the whistle and was afraid only the night before.

II.

Half a mile from home, at the farther edge of the woods, where the land was highest, a great pine-tree stood, the last of its generation. Whether it was left for a boundary mark, or for what reason, no one could say; the woodchoppers who had felled its mates were dead and gone long ago, and a whole forest of sturdy trees, pines and oaks and maples, had grown again. But the stately head of this old pine towered above them all and made a landmark for sea and shore miles and miles away. Sylvia knew it well. She had always believed that whoever climbed to the top of it could see the ocean; and the little girl had often laid her hand on the great rough trunk and looked up wistfully at those dark boughs that the wind always stirred, no matter how hot and still the air might be below. Now she thought of the tree with a new excitement, for why, if one climbed it at break of day, could not one see all the world, and easily discover from whence the white heron flew, and mark the place, and find the hidden nest?

What a spirit of adventure, what wild ambition! What fancied triumph and delight and glory for the later morning when she could make known the secret! It was almost too real and too great for the childish heart to bear.

All night the door of the little house stood open and the whippoorwills came and sang upon the very step. The young sportsman and his old hostess were sound asleep, but Sylvia's great design kept her broad awake and watching. She forgot to think of sleep. The short summer night seemed as long as the winter darkness, and at last when the whippoorwills ceased, and she was afraid the morning would after all come too soon, she stole out of the house and followed the pasture path through the woods, hastening toward the open ground beyond, listening with a sense of comfort and companionship to the drowsy twitter of a half-awakened bird, whose perch she had jarred in passing. Alas, if the great wave of human interest which flooded for the first time this dull little life should sweep away the satisfactions of an existence heart to heart with nature and the dumb life of the forest!

There was the huge tree asleep yet in the paling moonlight, and small and silly Sylvia began with utmost bravery to mount to the top of it, with tingling, eager blood coursing the channels of her whole frame, with her bare feet and fingers, that pinched and held like bird's claws to the monstrous ladder reaching up, up, almost to the sky itself. First she must mount the white oak tree that grew alongside, where she was almost lost among the dark branches and the green leaves heavy and wet with dew; a bird fluttered off its nest, and a red squirrel ran to and fro and scolded pettishly at the harmless housebreaker. Sylvia felt her way easily. She had often climbed there, and knew that higher still one of the oak's upper branches chafed against the pine trunk, just where its lower boughs were set close together. There, when she made the dangerous pass from one tree to the other, the great enterprise would really begin.

She crept out along the swaying oak limb at last, and took the daring step across into the old pine-tree. The way was harder than she thought; she must reach far and hold fast, the sharp dry twigs caught and held her and scratched her like angry talons, the pitch made her thin little fingers clumsy and stiff as she went round and round the tree's great stem, higher and higher upward. The sparrows and robins in the woods below were beginning to wake and twitter to the dawn, yet it seemed much lighter there aloft in the pine-tree, and the child knew she must hurry if her project were to be of any use.

The tree seemed to lengthen itself out as she went up, and to reach farther and farther upward. It was like a great main-mast to the voyaging earth; it must truly have been amazed that morning through all its ponderous frame as it felt this determined spark of human spirit wending its way from higher branch to branch. Who know show steadily the least twigs held themselves to advantage this light, weak creature on her way! The old pine must have loved his new dependent. More than all the hawks, and bats, and moths, and even the sweet voiced thrushes, was the brave, beating heart of the solitary gray-eyed child. And the tree stood still and frowned away the winds that June morning while the dawn grew bright in the east.

Sylvia's face was like a pale star, if one had seen it from the ground, when the last thorny bough was past, and she stood trembling and tired but wholly triumphant, high in the tree-top. Yes, there was the sea with the dawning sun making a golden dazzle over it, and toward that glorious east flew two hawks with slow-moving pinions. How low they looked in the air from that height when one had only seen them before far up, and dark against the blue sky. Their gray feathers were as soft as moths; they seemed only a little way from the tree, and Sylvia felt as if she too could go flying away among the clouds. Westward, the woodlands and farms reached miles and miles into the distance; here and there were church steeples, and white villages, truly it was a vast and awesome world

The birds sang louder and louder. At last the sun came up bewilderingly bright.

Sylvia could see the white sails of ships out at sea, and the clouds that were purple and rose-colored and yellow at first began to fade away. Where was the white heron's nest in the sea of green branches, and was this wonderful sight and pageant of the world the only reward for having climbed to such a giddy height? Now look down again, Sylvia, where the green marsh is set among the shining birches and dark hemlocks; there where you saw the white heron once you will see him again; look, look! a white spot of him like a single floating feather comes up from the dead hemlock and grows larger, and rises, and comes close at last, and goes by the landmark pine with steady sweep of wing and outstretched slender neck and crested head. And wait! wait! do not move a foot or a finger, little girl, do not send an arrow of light and consciousness from your two eager eyes, for the heron has perched on a pine bough not far beyond yours, and cries back to his mate on the nest and plumes his feathers for the new day!

The child gives a long sigh a minute later when a company of shouting cat-birds comes also to the tree, and vexed by their fluttering and lawlessness the solemn heron goes away. She knows his secret now, the wild, light, slender bird that floats and wavers, and goes back like an arrow presently to his home in the green world beneath. Then Sylvia, well satisfied, makes her perilous way down again, not daring to look far below the branch she stands on, ready to cry sometimes because her fingers ache and her lamed feet slip. Wondering over and over again what the stranger would say to her, and what he would think when she told him how to find his way straight to the heron's nest.

"Sylvy, Sylvy!" called the busy old grandmother again and again, but nobody answered, and the small husk bed was empty and Sylvia had disappeared.

The guest waked from a dream, and remembering his day's pleasure hurried to dress himself that it might sooner begin. He was sure from the way the shy little girl looked once or twice yesterday that she had at least seen the white heron, and now she must really be made to tell. Here she comes now, paler than ever, and her worn old frock is torn and tattered, and smeared with pine pitch. The grandmother and the sportsman stand in the door together and question her, and the splendid moment has come to speak of the dead hemlock-tree by the green marsh.

But Sylvia does not speak after all, though the old grandmother fretfully rebukes her, and the young man's kind, appealing eyes are looking straight in her own. He can make them rich with money; he has promised it, and they are poor now. He is so well worth making happy, and he waits to hear the story she can tell.

No, she must keep silence! What is it that suddenly forbids her and makes her dumb? Has she been nine years growing and now, when the great world for the first time puts out a hand to her, must she thrust it aside for a bird's sake? The murmur of the pine's green branches is in her ears, she remembers how the white heron came flying through the golden air and how they watched the sea and the morning together, and Sylvia cannot speak; she cannot tell the heron's secret and give its life away.

Dear loyalty, that suffered a sharp pang as the guest went away disappointed later in the day, that could have served and followed him and loved him as a dog loves! Many a night Sylvia heard the echo of his whistle haunting the pasture path as she came home with the loitering cow. She forgot even her sorrow at the sharp report of his gun and the sight of thrushes and sparrows dropping silent to the ground, their songs hushed and their pretty feathers stained and wet with blood. Were the birds better friends than their hunter might have been, —who can tell? Whatever treasures were lost to her, woodlands and summer-time, remember! Bring your gifts and graces and tell your secrets to this lonely country child!

Plot Summary

"A White Heron" by Sarah Orne Jewett is a captivating short story that follows the journey of a young girl, Sylvia, who lives in a rural farmhouse with her grandmother. Through Sylvia's eyes, the readers are immersed in the tranquil and picturesque countryside setting, where she encounters a young hunter, who has come to their area in search of a rare white heron. The story unfolds as Sylvia befriends the hunter, providing him with shelter and hospitality, whilst also wrestling with her own conflicted emotions. As Sylvia gets to know the hunter, she becomes captivated by his charming demeanor, yet she also feels torn by her loyalty to the birds that inhabit the nearby forest. Sylvia's internal conflict is drawn out by the offer of a reward if she can reveal the whereabouts of the elusive white heron, which forces her to reassess her allegiances and her connection to nature. Ultimately, Sylvia finds herself torn between the temptation of the reward and her deep appreciation for the natural world. As the story reaches its poignant climax, the narrative takes a surprising turn that presents Sylvia with a moral dilemma. In the end, Sylvia's deep affinity for the beauty and sanctity of nature triumphs, as she makes a decision that aligns with her values and demonstrates her profound connection to the natural world. "A White Heron" masterfully captures the tension between human desires and the preservation of nature, expertly weaving together themes of innocence, ethical choices, and the intrinsic value of the natural world. Jewett's evocative storytelling and vivid descriptions lay bare the beauty of the countryside and the complexities of human relationships, leaving a lasting impression on readers long after the story's conclusion.

Language Exercises

Choose the item that best replaces or explains the underlined part of the sentence.
1.   A little girl was driving home her cow, a plodding, <u>dilatory</u>, provoking creature in

her behavior, but a valued companion for all that.

    A. placid   B. saucy   C. slow   D. elegant

2. Sometimes in pleasant weather it was a <u>consolation</u> to look upon the cow's pranks as an intelligent attempt to play hide and seek, and…

    A. anxiety   B. solace   C. tranquility   D. torment

3. Sylvia left the cow to whatever sad fate might await her, and stepped <u>discreetly</u> aside into the bushes, but she was just too late.

    A. boldly   B. recklessly   C. sensibly   D. prudently

4. "I have been hunting for some birds," the stranger said kindly, "and I have lost my way, and need a friend very much. Don't be afraid," he added <u>gallantly</u>.

    A. chivalrously   B. timidly   C. cowardly   D. conspicuously

5. "Dear sakes, yes," responded the hostess, whose long <u>slumbering</u> hospitality seemed to be easily awakened.

    A. alert   B. dormant   C. poignant   D. bleak

6. He listened eagerly to the old woman's <u>quaint</u> talk, he watched Sylvia's paleface and shining gray eyes with ever growing enthusiasm, …

    A. ordinary   B. queer   C. old-fashioned   D. controversial

7. "So Sylvy knows all about birds, does she?" he exclaimed, as he looked round at the little girl who sat, very <u>demure</u> but increasingly sleepy, in the moonlight.

    A. reserved   B. assertive   C. passionate   D. melancholy

8. The next day the young sportsman <u>hovered</u> about the woods, and Sylvia kept him company, having lost her first fear of the friendly lad, who proved to be most kind and sympathetic.

    A. departed   B. loitered   C. wafted   D. lingered

9. She grieved because the longed-for white heron was <u>elusive</u>, but she did not lead the guest, she only followed, and there was no such thing as speaking first.

    A. graceful   B. eligible   C. mystical   D. accessible

10. … it must truly have been amazed that morning through all its <u>ponderous</u> frame as it felt this determined spark of human spirit wending its way from higher branch to branch.

    A. bulky   B. slender   C. tedious   D. subtle

11. The child gives a long sigh a minute later when a company of shouting cat-birds comes also to the tree, and vexed by their <u>fluttering</u> and lawlessness the solemn heron goes away.

    A. stillness   B. flattering   C. sobriety   D. flapping

12. Then Sylvia, well satisfied, makes her <u>perilous</u> way down again, not daring to look far below the branch she stands on, ready to cry sometimes because her fingers ache and her lamed feet slip.

    A. prudent   B. cautious   C. rugged   D. risky

13. Here she comes now, paler than ever, and her worn old frock is torn and tattered,

and <u>smeared</u> with pine pitch.

    A. indulged   B. daubed   C. dodged   D. immersed

14. But Sylvia does not speak after all, though the old grandmother <u>fretfully</u> rebukes her, and the young man's kind, appealing eyes are looking straight in her own.

    A. serenely   B. fervently   C. anxiously   D. viciously

15. Has she been nine years growing and now, when the great world for the first time puts out a hand to her, must she <u>thrust</u> it aside for a bird's sake?

    A. retract   B. shove   C. withdraw   D. shiver

Topics for Discussion

1. How does Sylvia's discovery and connection with the white heron impact her internal struggle in the story?
2. What specific elements of the setting help to build the atmosphere and mood of the story?
3. How does the character of the hunter serve as a foil to Sylvia?
4. What specific techniques does the author use to establish Sylvia's deep connection to nature?
5. In what ways does Sylvia navigate the conflict between her loyalty to nature and her growing fondness for the hunter?
6. What role does the theme of innocence and loss of innocence play in the story?
7. How does the imagery of the white heron symbolize different meanings throughout the story?
8. How does the author use foreshadowing to hint at the story's outcome?
9. What is the significance of the decision Sylvia makes at the climax of the story?
10. How does the resolution of "A White Heron" reflect Sylvia's character development and the overall themes of the story?

Discussion Tips

    When "A White Heron" debuted in 1886 as the title story in Sarah Orne Jewett's collection *A White Heron and Other Stories*, the author had already established herself as one of the most accomplished local color writers in the United States. Throughout the past century, critics have delved into various themes present in "A White Heron", including the contrasts between good and evil, spirit and flesh, nature and civilization, feminine and masculine perspectives, and innocence and experience. In the story, Sylvia's progression towards her decision follows the typical pattern of a hero's journey or Bildungsroman. Before Sylvia can transition from innocence to maturity, or from an ordinary individual to a hero, she must undergo a ritual test to demonstrate her worthiness and strength. While Sylvia feels a deep connection to the forest and is reluctant to leave, her relationship with nature has never been challenged. Accordingly, her test takes the form of a literal ascent to a higher vantage point, from which she can gain a broader perspective of the world. As she approaches the tallest tree, she is filled with uncertainty about what she will do. Despite her prior thoughts of potentially seeing the ocean from the tree's summit, she has never dared to attempt the climb. Jewett portrays Sylvia's ascent in the language of the hero's myth, highlighting her spirit of adventure, ambition, and the perceived triumph and glory. As Sylvia bravely climbs, she encounters resistance from the birds, squirrels, and the natural elements, yet the great tree itself seems to assist her in her endeavor. Ultimately, she reaches the top, trembling and fatigued, yet wholly triumphant. However, the test is not yet complete. Sylvia initially believes that her achievement is for the benefit of the hunter, expecting to return to him to claim the reward and his affection. To her surprise, and the reader's expectation, she ultimately decides not to disclose the heron's nesting place. Through this decision, she emerges from the test as a stronger, wiser, and more mature individual. Like a typical young hero, she has undergone the rites of passage, although she may not yet fully comprehend the extent of her own power.

Unit 7
Jack London: "To Build a Fire"

About the Author

Jack London (1876–1916)

Jack London was an American writer, journalist, and social activist known for his powerful storytelling and vivid portrayals of life in the late 19th and early 20th centuries. Born in San Francisco, California, London's own experiences as a laborer, sailor, and adventurer heavily influenced his writing. London's most renowned works include *The Call of the Wild* (1903) and *White Fang* (1906), which are set in the harsh landscapes of the Yukon and explore the struggle for survival in the wilderness. These novels, along with many of his other stories, reflect his deep fascination with nature and his belief in the power of the individual to triumph over adversity. London's protagonists often grapple with existential questions, challenging societal norms and searching for their true identities. London was heavily influenced by the social and political climate of his time, which witnessed rapid industrialization, urbanization, and widening economic disparities. His writings often critiqued the detrimental effects of capitalism, focusing on themes of social inequality, exploitation, and the plight of the working class. London's own experiences as a sailor and his exposure to the harsh conditions faced by workers during the Gilded Age informed his passionate advocacy for labor rights and socialist ideologies. Beyond his fiction, London was a committed activist and wrote extensively on social and political issues, including his critique of imperialism in "The Iron Heel" (1908) and his travel memoir "The People of the Abyss" (1903), which exposed the poverty and squalor of the working-class neighborhoods in London. Jack London's literary contributions and his commitment to social justice continue to resonate with readers around the world. His works remain celebrated for their vivid descriptions, compelling characters, and insightful commentary on the human condition, making him one of the most enduring and influential American authors of his time.

The Literary History

Jack London and American Naturalistic Writing

American naturalism, which emerged in the late 19th century, aimed to present a bleak and deterministic view of human existence. Influenced by the theories of Charles Darwin and the social theories of thinkers like Herbert Spencer, naturalist writers sought to depict the forces of nature and society as powerful and unforgiving, shaping human lives in ways that were beyond individual control. Jack London, as one of America's most well-known authors of the early 20th century, his short story "To Build a Fire" exemplifies many of the key characteristics of this literary style.

"To Build a Fire" is set in the harsh and unforgiving Yukon Territory during the Klondike Gold Rush, highlighting the brutal conditions that characters face in the extreme wilderness. The story follows an unnamed protagonist, a newcomer to the territory, who disregards the advice of more experienced locals and sets out on a journey through the freezing cold. As the man faces one obstacle after another, including falling through the ice and getting wet, his survival becomes increasingly uncertain.

London's portrayal of nature in "To Build a Fire" is unforgiving and indifferent to human life. The frigid temperatures, the biting wind, and the vast, unending landscape create a sense of isolation and vulnerability for the protagonist. Nature is depicted as an unfeeling and merciless force that offers little chance for survival. This aligns with the naturalistic belief that humans are at the mercy of their environment, unable to escape the grip of fate.

The protagonist's struggle for survival also reflects the naturalistic theme of the individual's powerlessness against larger social and natural forces. The man's lack of experience and arrogance in disregarding the advice of wiser, more seasoned individuals ultimately leads to his downfall. This emphasizes the naturalistic view that human actions are subject to the determinism of the environment and social circumstances.

"To Build a Fire" stands as a prime example of London's mastery of vivid and descriptive storytelling. His detailed descriptions of the protagonist's physical sensations—the numbing cold, the freezing moisture, and the desperation for heat—create a palpable sense of harshness and struggle. The stark realism with which London presents the story's events allows readers to experience the protagonist's increasing desperation as he fights against the elements.

Jack London's "To Build a Fire" showcases his skill in portraying the harsh realities of the natural world and the fragility of human existence. Through its themes of determinism, powerlessness, and the conflict between man and nature, the story exemplifies the main principles of American naturalism. It remains a significant contribution to American literature and continues to captivate readers with its portrayal of the uncompromising human struggle for survival in a hostile environment.

Literary Terms

Naturalism

Naturalism is a style of fiction that emerged from a group of writers who adhered to a specific philosophical view. This perspective was born from the biological theories of the post-Darwinian era and posited that humans are solely products of the natural world and lack a soul or any connection to a spiritual plane beyond it. Thus, humans are seen as advanced animals who are entirely shaped by their hereditary traits and environment. Social and economic factors such as familial background, class, and surroundings have a significant impact on an individual. Typical characteristics of naturalistic literature include:

1. Stress the importance of realism and objectivity, avoiding the use of hyperbole and refraining from criticism.
2. Prioritize the experiences of those from lower socioeconomic backgrounds and the general public.
3. Show concern for how social surroundings impact individuals, believing them to be at the mercy of both genetic and environmental forces.
4. Interpret human actions and society through biological principles, with an emphasis on the role of animal instincts and heredity in human behavior.
5. Incorporate scientific experimentation into writing, exploring how individuals respond in various environments.
6. Possess a highly negative attitude toward society, often leaning towards determinism.

Some prominent American writers associated with Naturalism include:

Stephen Crane: Known for works like *The Red Badge of Courage*, which explores the psychological and physical effects of war.

Frank Norris: His novels, such as *McTeague* and *The Octopus*, depict the harsh realities of life and the influence of environment and heredity on human behavior.

Theodore Dreiser: Renowned for his novels like *Sister Carrie* and *An American Tragedy*, which examine social conditions and moral dilemmas faced by individuals.

Jack London: Famous for stories like *The Call of the Wild* and *White Fang*, focusing on survival, nature, and the struggle against environmental forces.

These authors contributed significantly to the Naturalist movement by portraying characters whose lives are shaped by their environments, social conditions, and biological factors.

Historical context

In literature, historical context refers to the social, cultural, political, and economic conditions that existed during a specific time period in which a literary work is set or written. It encompasses the prevailing ideas, values, and events that influenced the author and shaped their perspective. Understanding the historical context of a literary work helps readers analyze and interpret its themes, characters, and plot. It provides insights into the motivations and beliefs of the author, enabling readers to appreciate the work in its intended context. Historical context can also illuminate the social issues and struggles depicted in the literature, offering a deeper understanding of the human condition and the world in which the characters exist. By considering the historical context, readers can better grasp the nuances, symbols, and metaphors employed by the author, gaining a richer and more comprehensive understanding of the literary work as a whole.

The Story

To Build a Fire[1]

Day had broken cold and gray, exceedingly cold and gray, when the man turned aside from the main Yukon trail and climbed the high earth-bank, where a dim and little traveled trail led eastward through the fat spruce timberland. It was a steep bank, and he paused for breath at the top, excusing the act to himself by looking at his watch. It was nine o'clock. There was no sun nor hint of sun, though there was not a cloud in the sky. It was a clear day, and yet there seemed an intangible pall over the face of things, a subtle gloom that made the day dark, and that was due to the absence of sun. This fact did not worry the man. He was used to the lack of sun. It had been days since he had seen the sun, and he knew that a few more-days must pass before that cheerful orb, due south, would just peep above the sky-line and dip immediately from view.

The man flung a look back along the way he had come. The Yukon lay a mile wide and hidden under three feet of ice. On top of this ice were as many feet of snow. It was all pure white, rolling in gentle, undulations where the ice jams of the freeze-up had formed. North and south, as far as his eye could see, it was unbroken white, save for a dark hairline that curved and twisted from around the spruce-covered island to the south, and that curved and twisted away into the north, where it disappeared behind another spruce-covered island. This dark hair-line was the trail—the main trail—that led south five hundred miles to the Chilcoot Pass, Dyea, and salt water; and that led north seventy miles to Dawson, and still on to the north a thousand miles to Nulato, and finally to St. Michael on Bering Sea, a thousand miles and half a thousand more.

---

1 Jack London, *The Son of the Wolf* (Dover Publications, 1990), pp. 1–10.

But all this—the mysterious, far-reaching hair-line trail, the absence of sun from the sky, the tremendous cold, and the strangeness and weirdness of it all—made no impression on the man. It was not because he was long used to it. He was a newcomer in the land, a chechaquo, and this was his first winter. The trouble with him was that he was without imagination. He was quick and alert in the things of life, but only in the things, and not in the significances. Fifty degrees below zero meant eighty-odd degrees of frost. Such fact impressed him as being cold and uncomfortable, and that was all. It did not lead him to meditate upon his frailty as a creature of temperature, and upon man's frailty in general, able only to live within certain narrow limits of heat and cold; and from there on it did not lead him to the conjectural field of immortality and man's place in the universe. Fifty degrees below zero stood forte bite of frost that hurt and that must be guarded against by the use of mittens, ear-flaps, warm moccasins, and thick socks. Fifty degrees below zero was to him just precisely fifty degrees below zero. That there should be anything more to it than that was a thought that never entered his head.

As he turned to go on, he spat speculatively. There was a sharp, explosive crackle that startled him. He spat again. And again, in the air, before it could fall to the snow, the spittle crackled. He knew that at fifty below spittle crackled on the snow, but this spittle had crackled in the air. Undoubtedly it was colder than fifty below--how much colder he did not know. But the temperature did not matter. He was bound for the old claim on the left fork of Henderson Creek, where the boys were already. They had come over across the divide from the Indian Creek country, while he had come the roundabout way to take a look at the possibilities of getting out logs in the spring from the islands in the Yukon. He would be in to camp by six o'clock; a bit after dark, it was true, but the boys would be there, a fire would be going, and a hot supper would be ready. As for lunch, he pressed his hand against the protruding bundle under his jacket. It was also under his shirt, wrapped up in a handkerchief and lying against the naked skin. It was the only way to keep the biscuits from freezing. He smiled agreeably to himself as he thought of those biscuits, each cut open and sopped in bacon grease, and each enclosing a generous slice of fried bacon.

He plunged in among the big spruce trees. The trail was faint. A foot of snow had fallen since the last sled had passed over, and he was glad he was without a sled, traveling light. In fact, he carried nothing but the lunch wrapped in the handkerchief. He was surprised, however, at the cold. It certainly was cold, he concluded, as he rubbed his numb nose and cheek-bones with his mittened hand. He was a warm-whiskered man, but the hair on his face did not protect the high cheek-bones and the eager nose that thrust itself aggressively into the frosty air.

At the man's heels trotted a dog, a big native husky, the proper wolfdog, gray-coated and without any visible or temperamental difference from its brother, the wild wolf. The animal was depressed by the tremendous cold. It knew that it was no time for traveling. Its instinct told it a truer tale than was told to the man by the man's judgment.

In reality, it was not merely colder than fifty below zero; it was colder than sixty below, than seventy below. It was seventy-five below zero. Since the freezing point is thirty-two above zero, it meant that one hundred and seven degrees of frost obtained. The dog did not know anything about thermometers. Possibly in its brain there was no sharp consciousness of a condition of very cold such as was in the man's brain. But the brute had its instinct. It experienced a vague but menacing apprehension that subdued it and made it slink along at the man's heels, and that made it question eagerly every unwonted movement of the man as if expecting him to go into camp or to seek shelter somewhere and build a fire. The dog had learned fire, and it wanted fire, or else to burrow under the snow and cuddle its warmth away from the air.

The frozen moisture of its breathing had settled on its fur in a fine powder of frost, and especially were its jowls, muzzle, and eyelashes whitened by its crystalled breath. The man's red beard and mustache were likewise frosted, but more solidly, the deposit taking the form of ice and increasing with every warm, moist breath he exhaled. Also, the man was chewing tobacco, and the muzzle of ice held his lips so rigidly that he was unable to clear his chin when he expelled the juice. The result was that a crystal beard of the color and solidity of amber was increasing its length on his chin. If he fell down it would shatter itself, like glass, into brittle fragments. But he did not mind the appendage. It was the penalty all tobacco-chewers paid in that country, and he had been out before in two cold snaps. They had not been so cold as this, he knew, but by the spirit thermometer at Sixty Mile he knew they had been registered at fifty below and at fifty-five.

He held on through the level stretch of woods for several miles, crossed a wide flat of nigger-heads, and dropped down a bank to the frozen bed of a small stream. This was Henderson Creek, and he knew he was ten miles from the forks. He looked at his watch. It was ten o'clock. He was making four miles an hour, and he calculated that he would arrive at the forks at half-past twelve. He decided to celebrate that event by eating his lunch there.

The dog dropped in again at his heels, with a tail drooping discouragement, as the man swung along the creek-bed. The furrow of the old sled-trail was plainly visible, but a dozen inches of snow covered the marks of the last runners. In a month no man had come up or down that silent creek. The man held steadily on. He was not much given to thinking, and just then particularly he had nothing to think about save that he would eat lunch at the forks and that at six o'clock he would be in camp with the boys. There was nobody to talk to and, had there been, speech would have been impossible because of the ice-muzzle on his mouth. So he continued monotonously to chew tobacco and to increase the length of his amber beard.

Once in a while the thought reiterated itself that it was very cold and that he had never experienced such cold. As he walked along he rubbed his cheek-bones and nose with the back of his mittened hand. He did this automatically, now and again changing hands. But rub as he would, the instant he stopped his cheek-bones went numb, and the following instant the end of his nose went numb. He was sure to frost his cheeks; he knew that, and experienced a pang of regret that he had not devised a nose-strap of the sort Bud wore in cold snaps. Such a strap passed across the cheeks, as well, and saved them. But it didn't matter much, after all. What were frosted cheeks? A bit painful, that was all; they were never serious.

Empty as the man's mind was of thoughts, he was keenly observant, and he noticed the changes in the creek, the curves and bends and timber jams, and always he sharply noted where he placed his feet. Once coming around a bend, he shied abruptly, like a startled horse, curved away from the place where he had been walking, and retreated several paces back along the trail. The creek he knew was frozen clear to the bottom, —no creek could contain water in that arctic winter, —but he knew also that there were springs that bubbled out from the hillsides and ran along under the snow and on top the ice of the creek. He knew that the coldest snaps never froze these springs, and he knew likewise their danger. They were traps. They hid pools of water under the snow that might be three inches deep, or three feet. Sometimes a skin of ice half an inch thick covered them, and in turn was covered by the snow Sometimes there were alternate layers of water and ice-skin, so that when one broke through he kept on breaking through for a while, sometimes wetting himself to the waist.

That was why he had shied in such panic. He had felt the give under his feet and heard the crackle of a snow-hidden ice-skin. And to get his feet wet in such a temperature meant trouble and danger. At the very least it meant delay, for he would be forced to stop and build a fire, and under its protection to bare his feet while he dried his socks and moccasins. He stood and studied the creek-bed and its banks, and decided that the flow of water came from the right. He reflected a while, rubbing his nose and cheeks, then skirted to the left, stepping gingerly and testing the footing for each step. Once clear of the danger, he took a fresh chew of tobacco and swung along at his four-mile gait.

In the course of the next two hours he came upon several similar traps. Usually the snow above the hidden pools had a sunken, candied appearance that advertised the danger. Once again, however, he had a close call; and once, suspecting danger, he compelled the dog to go on in front. The dog did not want to go. It hung back until the man shoved it forward, and then it went quickly across the white, unbroken surface. Suddenly it broke through, floundered to one side, and got away to firmer footing. It had wet its forefeet and legs, and almost immediately the water that clung to it turned to ice. It made quick efforts to lick the ice off its legs, then dropped down in the snow and began to bite out the ice that had formed between the toes. This was a matter of instinct. To permit the ice to remain would mean sore feet. It did not know this. It merely obeyed the mysterious prompting that arose from the deep crypts of its being. But the man knew, having achieved a judgment on the subject, and he removed the mitten from

146

his right hand and helped tear out the ice-particles. He did not expose his fingers more than a minute, and was astonished at the swift numbness that smote them. It certainly was cold. He pulled on the mitten hastily, and beat the hand savagely across his chest.

At twelve o'clock the day was at its brightest. Yet the sun was too far south on its winter journey to clear the horizon. The bulge of the earth intervened between it and Henderson Creek, where the man walked under a clear sky at noon and cast no shadow. At half-past twelve, to the minute, he arrived at the forks of the creek. He was pleased at the speed he had made. If he kept it up, he would certainly be with the boys by six. He unbuttoned his jacket and shirt and drew forth his lunch. The action consumed no more than a quarter of a minute, yet in that brief moment the numbness laid hold of the exposed fingers. He did not put the mitten on, but, instead struck the fingers a dozen sharp smashes against his leg. Then he sat down on a snow-covered log to eat. The sting that followed upon the striking of his fingers against his leg ceased so quickly that he was startled. He had had no chance to take a bite of biscuit. He struck the fingers repeatedly and returned them to the mitten, baring the other hand for the purpose of eating. He tried to take a mouthful, but the ice-muzzle prevented. He had forgotten to build a fire and thaw out. He chuckled at his foolishness, and as he chuckled he noted the numbness creeping into the exposed fingers. Also, he noted that the stinging which had first come to his toes when he sat down was already passing away. He wondered whether the toes were warm or numb. He moved them inside the moccasins and decided that they were numb.

He pulled the mitten on hurriedly and stood up. He was a bit frightened. He stamped up and down until the stinging returned into the feet. It certainly was cold, was his thought. That man from Sulphur Creek had spoken the truth when telling how cold it sometimes got in the country. And he had laughed at him at the time! That showed one must not be too sure of things. There was no mistake about it, it was cold. He strode up and down, stamping his feet and threshing his arms, until reassured by the returning warmth. Then he got out matches and proceeded to make a fire. From the undergrowth, where high water of the previous spring had lodged a supply of seasoned twigs, he got his firewood. Working carefully from a small beginning, he soon had a roaring fire, over which he thawed the ice from his face and in the protection of which he ate his biscuits. For the moment the cold of space was outwitted. The dog took satisfaction in the fire, stretching out close enough for warmth and far enough away to escape being singed.

When the man had finished, he filled his pipe and took his comfortable time over a smoke. Then he pulled on his mittens, settled the ear-flaps of his cap firmly about his ears, and took the creek trail up the left fork. The dog was disappointed and yearned back toward the fire. This man did not know cold. Possibly all the generations of his ancestry had been ignorant of cold, of real cold, of cold one hundred and seven degrees below freezing point. But the dog knew; all its ancestry knew, and it had inherited the knowledge. And it knew that it was not good to walk abroad in such fearful cold. It was the time to lie snug in a hole in the snow and wait for a curtain of cloud to be drawn across the face of outer space whence this cold came. On the other hand, there was no keen intimacy between the dog and the man. The one was the toil-slave of the other, and the only caresses it had ever received were the caresses of the whiplash and of harsh and menacing throat-sounds that threatened the whiplash. So, the dog made no effort to communicate its apprehension to the man. It was not concerned in the welfare of the man; it was for its own sake that it yearned back toward the fire. But the man whistled, and spoke to it with the sound of whiplashes and the dog swung in at the man's heels and followed after.

The man took a chew of tobacco and proceeded to start a new amber beard. Also, his moist breath quickly powdered with white his mustache, eyebrows, and lashes. There did not seem to be so many springs on the left fork of the Henderson, and for half an hour the man saw no signs of any. And then it happened. At a place where there were no signs, where the soft, unbroken snow seemed to advertise solidity beneath, the man broke through. It was not deep. He wet himself halfway to the knees before he floundered out to the firm crust.

He was angry, and cursed his luck aloud. He had hoped to get into camp with the boys at six o'clock, and this would delay him an hour, for he would have to build a fire and dry out his footgear. This was imperative at that low temperature—he knew that much; and he turned aside to the bank, which he climbed. On top, tangled in the underbrush about the trunks of several small spruce trees, was a high-water deposit of dry firewood—sticks and twigs principally, but also larger portions of seasoned branches and fine, dry, last-year's grasses. He threw down several large pieces on top of the snow. This served for a foundation and prevented the young flame from drowning itself in the snow it otherwise would melt. The flame he got by touching a match to a small shred of birch bark that he took from his pocket. This burned even more readily than paper. Placing it on the foundation, he fed the young flame with wisps of dry grass and with the tiniest dry twigs.

He worked slowly and carefully, keenly aware of his danger. Gradually, as the flame grew stronger, he increased the size of the twigs with which he fed it. He squatted in the snow, pulling the twigs out from their entanglement in the brush and feeding directly to the flame. He knew there must be no failure. When it is seventy-five below zero, a man must not fail in his first attempt to build a fire—that is, if his feet are wet. If his feet are dry, and he fails, he can run along the trail for half a mile and restore his circulation. But the circulation of wet and freezing feet cannot be restored by running when it is seventy-five below. No matter how fast he runs, the wet feet will freeze the harder.

All this the man knew. The old-timer on Sulphur Creek had told him about it the previous fall, and now he was appreciating the advice. Already all sensation had gone out of his feet. To build the fire he had been forced to remove his mittens, and the fingers had quickly gone numb. His pace of four miles an hour had kept his heart pumping blood to the surface of his body and to all the extremities. But the instant he stopped, the action of the pump eased down. The cold of space smote the unprotected tip of the planet, and he, being on that unprotected tip, received the full force of the blow. The blood of his body recoiled before it. The blood was alive, like the dog, and like the dog it wanted to hide away and cover itself up from the fearful cold. So long as he walked four miles an hour, he pumped that blood, willy-nilly, to the surface; but now it ebbed away and sank down into the recesses of his body. The extremities were the first to feel its absence. His wet feet froze the faster, and his exposed fingers numbed the faster, though they had not yet begun to freeze. Nose and cheeks were already freezing, while the skin of all his body chilled as it lost its blood.

But he was safe. Toes and nose and cheeks would be only touched by the frost, for the fire was beginning to burn with strength. He was feeding it with twigs the size of his finger. In another minute he would be able to feed it with branches the size of his wrist, and then he could remove his wet foot-gear, and, while it dried, he could keep his naked feet warm by the fire, rubbing them at first, of course, with snow. The fire was a success. He was safe. He remembered the advice of the old-timer on Sulphur Creek, and smiled. The old-timer had been very serious in laying down the law that no man must travel alone in the Klondike after fifty below. Well, here he was; he had had the accident; he was alone; and he had saved himself. Those old-timers were rather womanish, some of them, he thought. All a man had to do was to keep his head, and he was all right. Any man who was a man could travel alone. But it was surprising, the rapidity with which his cheeks and nose were freezing. And he had not thought his fingers could go lifeless in so short a time. Lifeless they were, for he could scarcely make them move together to grip a twig, and they seemed remote from his body and from him. When he touched a twig, he had to look and see whether or not he had hold of it. The wires were pretty well down between him and his finger-ends.

All of which counted for little. There was the fire, snapping and crackling and promising life with every dancing flame. He started to untie his moccasins. They were coated with ice; the thick German socks were like sheaths of iron halfway to the knees; and the moccasin strings were like rods of steel all twisted and knotted as by some conflagration. For a moment he tugged with his numb fingers, then, realizing the folly of it, he drew his sheath-knife.

But before he could cut the strings, it happened. It was his own fault or, rather, his mistake. He should not have built the fire under the spruce tree. He should have built it in the open. But it had been easier to pull the twigs from the brush and drop them directly on the fire. Now the tree under which he had done this carried a weight of snow on its boughs. No wind had blown for weeks, and each bough was fully freighted. Each time he had pulled a twig he had communicated a slight agitation to the tree— an imperceptible agitation, so far as he was concerned, but an agitation sufficient to bring about the disaster. High up in the tree one bough capsized its load of snow. This fell on the boughs beneath, capsizing them. This process continued, spreading out and involving the whole tree. It grew like an avalanche, and it descended without warning upon the man and the fire, and the fire was blotted out! Where it had burned was a mantle of fresh and disordered snow.

The man was shocked. It was as though he had just heard his own sentence of death. For a moment he sat and stared at the spot where the fire had been. Then he grew very calm. Perhaps the old-timer on Sulphur Creek was right. If he had only had a trail-mate he would have been in no danger now. The trail-mate could have built the fire. Well, it was up to him to build the fire over again, and this second time there must be no failure. Even if he succeeded, he would most likely lose some toes. His feet must be badly frozen by now, and there would be some time before the second fire was ready.

Such were his thoughts, but he did not sit and think them. He was busy all the time they were passing through his mind. He made a new foundation for a fire, this time in the open, where no treacherous tree could blot it out. Next, he gathered dry grasses and tiny twigs from the high-water flotsam. He could not bring his fingers together to pull them out, but he was able to gather them by the handful. In this way he got many rotten twigs and bits of green moss that were undesirable, but it was the best he could do. He worked methodically, even collecting an armful of the larger branches to be used later when the fire gathered strength. And all the while the dog sat and watched him, a certain yearning wistfulness in its eyes, for it looked upon him as the fire-provider, and the fire was slow in coming.

When all was ready, the man reached in his pocket for a second piece of birch bark. He knew the bark was there, and, though he could not feel it with his fingers, he could hear its crisp rustling as he fumbled for it. Try as he would, he could not clutch hold of it. And all the time, in his consciousness, was the knowledge that each instant his feet were freezing. This thought tended to put him in a panic, but he fought against it and kept calm. He pulled on his mittens with his teeth, and threshed his arms back and forth, beating his hands with all his might against his sides. He did this sitting down, and he stood up to do it; and all the while the dog sat in the snow, its wolf-brush of a tail curled around warmly over its forefeet, its sharp wolf-ears pricked forward intently as it watched the man. And the man, as he beat and threshed with his arms and hands, felt a great surge of envy as he regarded the creature that was warm ant secure in its natural covering.

After a time he was aware of the first far-away signals of sensation in his beaten fingers. The faint tingling grew stronger till it evolved into a stinging ache that was excruciating, but which the man hailed with satisfaction. He stripped the mitten from his right hand and fetched forth the birch bark. The exposed fingers were quickly going numb again. Next he brought out his bunch of sulphur matches. But the tremendous cold had already driven the life out of his fingers. In his effort to separate one match from the others, the whole bunch fell in the snow. He tried to pick it out of the snow, but failed. The dead fingers could neither touch nor clutch. He was very careful. He drove the thought of his freezing feet, and nose, and cheeks, out of his mind, devoting his whole soul to the matches. He watched, using the sense of vision in place of that of touch, and when he saw his fingers on each side the bunch, he closed them—that is, he willed to close them, for the wires were drawn, and the fingers did not obey. He pulled the mitten on the right hand and beat it fiercely against his knee. Then, with both mittened hands, he scooped the bunch of matches, along with much snow, into his lap. Yet he was no better off.

After some manipulation he managed to get the bunch between the heels of his mittened hands. In this fashion he carried it to his mouth. The ice crackled and snapped when by a violent effort he opened his mouth. He drew the lower jaw in, curled the upper lip out of the way, and scraped the bunch with his upper teeth in order to separate a match. He succeeded in getting one, which he dropped on his lap. He was no better off. He could not pick it up. Then he devised a way. He picked it up in his teeth and scratched it on his leg. Twenty times he scratched before he succeeded in lighting it. As it flamed he held it with his teeth to the birch bark. But the burning brimstone went up his nostrils and into his lungs, causing him to cough spasmodically. The match fell into the snow and went out.

The old-timer on Sulphur Creek was right, he thought in the moment of controlled despair that ensued: after fifty below, a man should travel with a partner. He beat his hands, but failed in exciting any sensation. Suddenly he bared both hands, removing the mittens with his teeth. He caught the whole bunch between the heels of his hands. His arm muscles not being frozen enabled him to press the hand-heels tightly against the matches. Then he scratched the bunch along his leg. It flared into flame, seventy sulphur matches at once! There was no wind to blow them out. He kept his head to one side to escape the strangling fumes, and held the blazing bunch to the birth bark. As he so held it, he became aware of sensation in his hand. His flesh was burning. He could smell it. Deep down below the surface he could feel it. The sensation developed into pain that grew acute. And still he endured, it holding the flame of the matches clumsily to the bark that would not light readily because his own burning hands were in the way, absorbing most of the flame.

At last, when he could endure no more, he jerked his hands apart. The blazing matches fell sizzling into the snow, but the birch bark was alight. He began laying dry grasses and the tiniest twigs on the flame. He could not pick and choose, for he had to lift the fuel between the heels of his hands. Small pieces of rotten wood and green moss clung to the twigs, and he bit them off as well as he could with his teeth. He cherished the flame carefully and awkwardly. It meant life, and it must not perish. The withdrawal of blood from the surface of his body now made him begin to shiver, and he grew more awkward. A large piece of green moss fell squarely on the little fire. He

151

tried to poke it out with his fingers, but his shivering frame made him poke too far, and he disrupted the nucleus of the little fire, the burning grasses and tiny twigs separating and scattering. He tried to poke them together again, but in spite of the tenseness of the effort, his shivering got away with him, and the twigs were hopelessly scattered. Each twig gushed a puff of smoke and went out. The fire-provider had failed. As he looked apathetically about him, his eyes chanced on the dog, sitting across the ruins of the fire from him, in the snow, making restless, hunching movements, slightly lifting one forefoot and then the other, shifting its weight back and forth on them with wistful eagerness.

The sight of the dog put a wild idea into his head. He remembered the tale of the man, caught in a blizzard, who killed a steer and crawled inside the carcass, and so was saved. He would kill the dog and bury his hands in the warm body until the numbness went out of them. Then he could build another fire. He spoke to the dog, calling it to him; but in his voice was a strange note of fear that frightened the animal, who had never known the man to speak in such way before. Something was the matter, and its suspicious nature sensed danger—it knew not what danger, but somewhere, somehow, in its brain arose an apprehension of the man. It flattened its ears down at the sound of the man's voice, and its restless, hunching movements and the liftings and shiftings of its forefeet became more pronounced; but it would not come to the man. He got on his hands and knees and crawled toward the dog. This unusual posture again excited suspicion, and the animal sidled mincingly away.

The man sat up in the snow for a moment and struggled for calmness. Then he pulled on his mittens, by means of his teeth, and got upon his feet. He glanced down at first in order to assure himself that he was really standing up, for the absence of sensation in his feet left him unrelated to the earth. His erect position in itself started to drive the webs of suspicion from the dog's mind; and when he spoke peremptorily, with the sound of whiplashes in his voice, the dog rendered its customary allegiance and came to him. As it came within reaching distance, the man lost his control. His arms flashed out to the dog, and he experienced genuine surprise when he discovered that his hands could not clutch, that there was neither bend nor feeling in the fingers. He had forgotten for the moment that they were frozen and that they were freezing more and more. All this happened quickly, and before the animal could get away, he encircled its body with his arms. He sat down in the snow, and in this fashion held the dog, while it snarled and whined and struggled.

But it was all he could do, hold its body encircled in his arms and sit there. He realized that he could not kill the dog. There was no way to do it. With his helpless hands he could neither draw nor hold his sheath knife nor throttle the animal. He released it, and it plunged wildly away, with tail between its legs, and still snarling. It halted forty feet away and surveyed him curiously, with ears sharply pricked forward. The man looked down at his hands in order to locate them, and found them hanging on the ends of his arms. It struck him as curious that one should have to use his eyes in order to find out where his hands were. He began threshing his arms back and forth, beating the mittened hands against his sides. He did this for five minutes, violently, and his heart pumped enough blood up to the surface to put a stop to his shivering. But no sensation was aroused in the hands. He had an impression that they hung like weights on the ends of his arms, but when he tried to run the impression down, he could not find it.

A certain fear of death, dull and oppressive, came to him. This fear quickly became poignant as he realized that it was no longer a mere matter of freezing his fingers and toes, or of losing his hands and feet, but that it was a matter of life and death with the chances against him. This threw him into a panic, and he turned and ran up the creekbed along the old, dim trail. The dog joined in behind and kept up with him. He ran blindly, without intention, in fear such as he had never known in his life. Slowly, as he plowed and floundered through the snow, he began to see things again, the banks of the creek, the old timber-jams, the leafless aspens, and the sky. The running made him feel better. He did not shiver. Maybe, if he ran on, his feet would thaw out; and, anyway, if he ran far enough, he would reach camp and the boys. Without doubt he would lose some fingers and toes and some of his face; but the boys would take care of him, and save the rest of him when he got there. And at the same time there was another thought in his mind that said he would never get to the camp and the boys; that it was too many miles away, that the freezing had too great a start on him, and that he would soon be stiff and dead. This thought he kept in the background and refused to consider. Sometimes it pushed itself forward and demanded to be heard, but he thrust it back and strove to think of other things.

It struck him as curious that he could run at all on feet so frozen that he could not feel them when they struck the earth and took the weigh of his body. He seemed to himself to skim along above the surface, and to have no connection with the earth. Somewhere he had once seen a winged Mercury, and he wondered if Mercury felt as he felt when skimming over the earth.

His theory of running until he reached camp and the boys had one flaw in it: he lacked the endurance. Several times he stumbled, and finally he tottered, crumpled up, and fell. When he tried to rise, he failed. He must sit and rest, he decided, and next time he would merely walk and keep on going. As he sat and regained his breath, he noted that he was feeling quite warm and comfortable. He was not shivering, and it even seemed that a warm glow had come to his chest and trunk. And yet, when he touched his nose or cheeks, there was no sensation. Running would not thaw them out. Nor would it thaw out his hands and feet. Then the thought came to him that the frozen portions of his body must be extending. He tried to keep this thought down, to forget it, to think of something else; he was aware of the panicky feeling that it caused, and he was afraid of the panic. But the thought asserted itself, and persisted, until it produced a vision of his body totally frozen. This was too much, and he made another wild run along the trail. Once he slowed down to a walk, but the thought of the freezing extending itself made him run again.

And all the time the dog ran with him, at his heels. When he fell down a second time, it curled its tail over its forefeet and sat in front of him, facing him, curiously eager and intent. The warmth and security of the animal angered him, and he cursed it till it flattened down its ears appealingly. This time the shivering came more quickly upon the man. He was losing in his battle with the frost. It was creeping into his body from all sides. The thought of it drove him on, but he ran no more than a hundred feet, when he staggered and pitched headlong. It was his last panic. When he had recovered his breath and control, he sat up and entertained in his mind the conception of meeting death with dignity. However, the conception did not come to him in such terms. His idea of it was that he had been making a fool of himself, running around like a chicken with its head cut off—such was the simile that occurred to him. Well, he was bound to freeze anyway, and he might as well take it decently. With this new-found peace of mind came the first glimmerings of drowsiness. A good idea, he thought, to sleep off to death. It was like taking an anaesthetic. Freezing was not so bad as people thought. There were lots worse ways to die.

He pictured the boys finding his body next day. Suddenly he found himself with them, coming along the trail and looking for himself. And, still with them, he came around a turn in the trail and found himself lying in the snow. He did not belong with himself any more, for even then he was out of himself, standing with the boys and looking at himself in the snow. It certainly was cold, was his thought. When he got back to the States he could tell the folks what real cold was. He drifted on from this to a vision of the old-timer on Sulphur Creek. He could see him quite clearly, warm and comfortable, and smoking a pipe.

"You were right, old hoss; you were right," the man mumbled to the old-timer of Sulphur Creek.

Then the man drowsed off into what seemed to him the most comfortable and satisfying sleep he had ever known. The dog sat facing him and waiting. The brief day drew to a close in a long, slow twilight. There were no signs of a fire to be made, and, besides, never in the dog's experience had it known a man to sit like that in the snow and make no fire. As the twilight drew on, its eager yearning for the fire mastered it, and with a great lifting and shifting of forefeet, it whined softly, then flattened its ears down in anticipation of being chidden by the man. But the man remained silent. Later, the dog whined loudly. And still later it crept close to the man and caught the scent of death. This made the animal bristle and back away. A little longer it delayed, howling under the stars that leaped and danced and shone brightly in the cold sky. Then it turned and trotted up the trail in the direction of the camp it knew, where were the other food-providers and fire-providers.

Plot Summary

"To Build a Fire" is a gripping, naturalistic short story by Jack London that follows an unnamed protagonist through the unforgiving, frozen Yukon. The man, accompanied only by his dog, is on a journey to meet his companions at a remote mining camp. Despite being cautioned about the extreme cold, he is determined to make the journey alone in temperatures as low as fifty degrees below zero. As the man and his dog navigate through the harsh terrain, the tension builds as the reader witnesses the protagonist's struggle against nature's indifference. The man's overconfidence and underestimation of the dangers he faces lead to a series of errors, ultimately resulting in a life-threatening situation. He struggles to keep himself warm and faces several obstacles, including falling through the ice and his inability to start a fire due to the extreme cold. Ultimately, the protagonist succumbs to the brutal elements, highlighting the story's central theme of man's helplessness in the face of nature's power. The dog, by instinctively understanding the dangers and listening to its instincts, survives while the man perishes, leaving a stark and haunting portrayal of the indifferent and formidable force of nature.

Language Exercises

Choose the item that best replaces or explains the underlined part of the sentence.

1. It was a clear day, and yet there seemed an <u>intangible</u> pall over the face of things, a subtle gloom that made the day dark, and that was due to the absence of sun.
   A. ineluctable   B. inseparable C. incurable   D. impalpable

2. He was a warm-whiskered man, but the hair on his face did not protect the high cheek-bones and the eager nose that thrust itself <u>aggressively</u> into the frosty air.
   A. timidly   B. assertively C. furtively   D. vigilantly

3. The dog had learned fire, and it wanted fire, or else to burrow under the snow and <u>cuddle</u> its warmth away from the air.
   A. stutter   B. stunt   C. strive   D. snuggle

4. It was the <u>penalty</u> all tobacco-chewers paid in that country, and he had been out before in two cold snaps.
   A. incentive   B. punishment C. ammunition D. symmetry

5. The <u>furrow</u> of the old sled-trail was plainly visible, but a dozen inches of snow covered the marks of the last runners.
   A. track   B. stain   C. frown   D. pack

6. Once in a while the thought <u>reiterated</u> itself that it was very cold and that he had never experienced such cold.
   A. simulated   B. sneezed   C. repeated   D. rehearsed

155

7. This was <u>imperative</u> at that low temperature—he knew that much; and he turned aside to the bank, which he climbed.

    A. optional   B. crucial   C. vibrant   D. transient

8. He squatted in the snow, pulling the twigs out from their <u>entanglement</u> in the brush and feeding directly to the flame.

    A. clarity   B. venue   C. thorn   D. tangle

9. The cold of space <u>smote</u> the unprotected tip of the planet, and he, being on that unprotected tip, received the full force of the blow.

    A. struck   B. shielded   C. embraced   D. avoided

10. It grew like an <u>avalanche</u>, and it descended without warning upon the man and the fire, and the fire was blotted out!

    A. a sudden and rapid increase

    B. a large mass of snow, ice, and rocks falling rapidly down a mountainside

    C. a powerful force or overwhelming quantity

    D. a type of natural disaster involving falling debris and rocks

11. He made a new foundation for a fire, this time in the open, where no <u>treacherous</u> tree could blot it out.

    A. unreliable   B. harmful and deceitful

    C. secure and trustworthy   D. unpredictable

12. The faint tingling grew stronger till it evolved into a stinging ache that was <u>excruciating</u>, but which the man hailed with satisfaction.

    A. pleasant   B. mild discomfort

    C. intense and unbearable pain   D. satisfactory

13. But the burning brimstone went up his nostrils and into his lungs, causing him to cough <u>spasmodically</u>.

    A. smoothly   B. suddenly and violently   C. regularly   D. steadily

14. As he looked <u>apathetically</u> about him, his eyes chanced on the dog, sitting across the ruins of the fire from him, in the snow, making restless, hunching movements, slightly lifting one forefoot and then the other, shifting its weight back and forth on them with wistful eagerness.

    A. emotionally   B. indifferently   C. excitedly   D. passionately

15. This fear quickly became <u>poignant</u> as he realized that it was no longer a mere matter of freezing his fingers and toes, or of losing his hands and feet, but that it was a matter of life and death with the chances against him.

    A. strong   B. insignificant   C. tranquil   D. indignant

Topics for Discussion

1. What is the significance of the man's insistence on traveling alone despite warnings

about the extreme cold in "To Build a Fire"?

2. What role does the setting play in creating the atmosphere of isolation and peril in the story?

3. How does the author use the character of the dog to emphasize the man's lack of preparation and understanding of the harsh environment?

4. What are the main obstacles the man faces as he attempts to build a fire?

5. What is the symbolic meaning of the man's failure to heed the advice of others and his neglect of the warning signs in the environment?

6. How does the man's lack of experience and understanding of the Yukon territory contribute to his downfall?

7. In what ways does the author use the man's thoughts and actions to illustrate the themes of arrogance and hubris?

8. What is the thematic significance of the man's progression from confidence to desperation as he struggles to survive?

9. In what ways does the author use the landscape and weather to create a sense of impending doom in the story?

10. How does the author use the man's ultimate demise to convey a message about the unforgiving and relentless nature of the wilderness?

Discussion Tips

Jack London had already solidified his reputation as a popular writer when his gripping story, "To Build a Fire", made its debut in the Century Magazine in 1908. This tale, depicting an unnamed man's harrowing journey across the unforgiving Yukon Territory near Alaska, resonated deeply with readers and literary critics of the time. London drew inspiration for the story from his own arduous travels through the harsh, frozen landscapes of Alaska and Canada during the Klondike gold rush of 1897–98. Additionally, he is said to have drawn from the firsthand accounts detailed in Jeremiah Lynch's book, *Three Years in the Klondike*. Critics lauded London's narrative for its vivid portrayal of the Klondike territory, particularly emphasizing his masterful use of repetition and precise description to underscore the brutal coldness and merciless terrain of the Northland. Set against this backdrop, the inexperienced protagonist, accompanied only by a dog, valiantly struggles but ultimately fails to save himself from succumbing to the freezing temperatures after a series of mishaps. The themes of fear, death, and the individual versus nature are intricately woven throughout the narrative, positioning "To Build a Fire" as a naturalistic work of fiction. In this genre, London depicts human beings as inherently subject to the laws of nature and profoundly influenced by their environment and physical constitution. London's use of short, matter-of-fact sentences in "To Build a Fire" not only serves to drive the narrative forward but also encapsulates the essence of his best literary work. This writing style, characterized by its succinctness and clarity, left a lasting impact on subsequent writers, notably influencing the prose of Ernest Hemingway and others who sought to capture the raw, unadorned realities of human existence in their own literary endeavors. In essence, "To Build a Fire" stands as a testament to London's ability to craft a narrative that transcends time, resonating with readers across generations and leaving an indelible mark on the literary landscape.

Part III
Modernism and the American Short Story

Part III

Modernism and the American Short Story

Unit 8
Willliam Faulkner: "A Rose for Emily"

About the Author

Willliam Faulkner (1897–1962)

William Faulkner was an American novelist and poet born in Mississippi in 1897. He is regarded as one of the most influential and celebrated writers of the 20th century, and his works are well-known for their intricate, nonlinear narratives, distinctive use of language, and exploration of the South's history and culture. Faulkner began his writing career in the 1920s, publishing his first novel, *Soldiers' Pay* in 1926. It was followed by other novels such as *Sartoris*, *The Sound and the Fury*, *As I Lay Dying*, and *Light in August*, which remain popular and widely read to this day. Faulkner's work is characterized by its exploration of themes such as family, race, class, gender, and sexuality. He often used his writing to challenge the social norms and values of his day and to give a voice to the marginalized. His novels are also known for their complex and experimental narrative structure. He often used non-linear narratives, shifting points of view, and stream-of-consciousness techniques, to create rich and layered stories that explored the psychology and inner workings of his characters. One of Faulkner's most famous works is *The Sound and the Fury*, a novel that tells the story of a Southern family's decline and dissolution from the perspectives of four different characters, including the mentally disabled Benjy. Faulkner's use of stream-of-consciousness and shifting points of view in this novel is considered groundbreaking and continues to inspire writers to this day. Another hallmark of Faulkner's writing is his distinctive use of language. He often used difficult and sometimes obscure vocabulary, as well as sentence fragments and unconventional punctuation, to create a sense of the South's rich, complex, and often troubled history. Faulkner was awarded the Nobel Prize in Literature in 1949 for his contributions to the literary world. He died in 1962 at the age of 64. His legacy continues to inspire writers and readers around the world.

The Literary History

William Faulkner's Short Stories

William Faulkner is one of the most distinguished American writers of the twentieth century. His short stories, in particular, are praised for their exploration of the complexities of human nature, their poetic language, and their vivid depiction of the Southern United States in the early 1900s.

Faulkner's short stories often feature recurring themes, such as the decline of an aristocratic South, the legacy of slavery, and the impact of time on the human psyche. His characters are usually drawn from the middle and lower classes of Southern society, and their struggles with identity, race, and class are central to many of his narratives.

One of Faulkner's most famous short stories is "A Rose for Emily", which tells the story of a woman who is ostracized by her community and lives a reclusive life. The story explores themes of psychology, gender roles, and the psychological effects of isolation. In the story, Emily's father keeps her from marrying, and after his death, she becomes increasingly isolated from the community. Eventually, she kills her lover and keeps his body in her house. The story has been interpreted as a critique of Southern aristocracy and an examination of the South's historical legacy of repression.

Other notable short stories by Faulkner include "Barn Burning", which explores the relationship between a father and son and their struggle with poverty, "Dry September", which examines the mob mentality of a Southern town and the consequences of racism, and "The Bear", which depicts the adventures of a group of hunters in the woods of Mississippi and explores the idea of the hunter as a heroic figure.

Faulkner's writing style is characterized by his use of stream-of-consciousness narration, which captures the inner thoughts and emotions of his characters. He also employs florid and poetic language, often using metaphors and symbolism to convey deeper meanings. His stories are known for their complex structure and non-linear timelines, which can make them challenging to read but also add to their richness and depth.

Overall, William Faulkner's short stories are powerful and evocative works of literature that explore the human condition and delve into the complexities of Southern society. They are a must-read for anyone interested in exploring the legacy of the South and the human experience.

Literary Terms

Modernism

Modernism is a cultural, artistic, and literary movement that emerged in the late

19th and early 20th centuries, marked by a rejection of traditional forms and a focus on experimentation, individualism, and the complexities of modern life. It challenged conventional norms and sought to capture the fragmented, chaotic, and uncertain nature of the modern world. Modernist literature, such as the works of Virginia Woolf, James Joyce, and T.S. Eliot, often employed innovative narrative techniques, including stream-of-consciousness, non-linear storytelling, and a focus on the inner worlds of characters. These techniques reflected the disorienting and tumultuous experiences of individuals in the rapidly changing world of the early 20th century. Modernist literature also grappled with themes of existential angst, alienation, and the search for meaning in a world marked by upheaval and disillusionment. Overall, modernism sought to break free from the constraints of traditional forms and explore the complexities and uncertainties of the modern age.

Stream-of-consciousness

Stream-of-consciousness is a narrative technique that seeks to capture the flow of a character's thoughts and feelings in an uninterrupted and unfiltered manner. This literary style often dispenses with traditional grammar and structure, instead presenting a continuous and sometimes fragmented stream of inner monologue. Writers such as James Joyce, Virginia Woolf, and William Faulkner are known for pioneering this technique in their works. Stream-of-consciousness allows for the exploration of a character's subconscious and inner world, often delving into the complexities of human thought and emotion. It can create a sense of immediacy and intimacy, immersing the reader in the character's mind and providing insight into their motivations, fears, and desires. By capturing the spontaneous and wandering nature of thoughts, stream-of-consciousness can mirror the chaotic and non-linear aspects of human cognition, offering a unique and introspective literary experience.

Reader-response criticism

Reader-response criticism is a literary theory that emphasizes the reader's role in interpreting and creating meaning from a text. It suggests that the reader's individual experiences, beliefs, and emotions play a significant role in shaping their understanding of a literary work. This approach focuses on the reader's personal response to the text rather than solely on the author's intention or the text's inherent meaning. Reader-response critics argue that each reader brings a unique perspective and background to their reading, leading to a variety of interpretations and responses to the same text. This theory highlights the active engagement of the reader in shaping the meaning of a literary work and emphasizes the subjectivity of interpretation. Reader-response criticism encourages a recognition of the diversity of responses to literature and the importance of considering the reader's role in the process of meaning-making.

The Story

A Rose for Emily[1]

I

When Miss Emily Grierson died, our whole town went to her funeral: the men through a sort of respectful affection for a fallen monument, the women mostly out of curiosity to see the inside of her house, which no one save an old man-servant—a combined gardener and cook—had seen in at least ten years.

It was a big, squarish frame house that had once been white, decorated with cupolas and spires and scrolled balconies in the heavily lightsome style of the seventies, set on what had once been our most select street. But garages and cotton gins had encroached and obliterated even the august names of that neighborhood; only Miss Emily's house was left, lifting its stubborn and coquettish decay above the cotton wagons and the gasoline pumps—an eyesore among eyesores. And now Miss Emily had gone to join the representatives of those august names where they lay in the cedar-bemused cemetery among the ranked and anonymous graves of Union and Confederate soldiers who fell at the battle of Jefferson.

Alive, Miss Emily had been a tradition, a duty, and a care; a sort of hereditary obligation upon the town, dating from that day in 1894 when Colonel Sartoris, the mayor—he who fathered the edict that no Negro woman should appear on the streets without an apron—remitted her taxes, the dispensation dating from the death of her father on into perpetuity. Not that Miss Emily would have accepted charity. Colonel Sartoris invented an involved tale to the effect that Miss Emily's father had loaned money to the town, which the town, as a matter of business, preferred this way of repaying. Only a man of Colonel Sartoris' generation and thought could have invented it, and only a woman could have believed it.

When the next generation, with its more modern ideas, became mayors and aldermen, this arrangement created some little dissatisfaction. On the first of the year they mailed her a tax notice. February came, and there was no reply. They wrote her a formal letter, asking her to call at the sheriff's office at her convenience. A week later the mayor wrote her himself, offering to call or to send his car for her, and received in reply a note on paper of an archaic shape, in a thin, flowing calligraphy in faded ink, to the effect that she no longer went out at all. The tax notice was also enclosed, without comment.

They called a special meeting of the Board of Aldermen. A deputation waited upon her, knocked at the door through which no visitor had passed since she ceased giving china-painting lessons eight or ten years earlier. They were admitted by the old Negro

---

1   William Faulkner, *Collected Stories of William Faulkner* (Vintage, 1995), pp. 119–130.

into a dim hall from which a stairway mounted into still more shadow. It smelled of dust and disuse—a close, dank smell. The Negro led them into the parlor. It was furnished in heavy, leather-covered furniture. When the Negro opened the blinds of one window, they could see that the leather was cracked; and when they sat down, a faint dust rose sluggishly about their thighs, spinning with slow motes in the single sun-ray. On a tarnished gilt easel before the fireplace stood a crayon portrait of Miss Emily's father.

They rose when she entered—a small, fat woman in black, with a thin gold chain descending to her waist and vanishing into her belt, leaning on an ebony cane with a tarnished gold head. Her skeleton was small and spare; perhaps that was why what would have been merely plumpness in another was obesity in her. She looked bloated, like a body long submerged in motionless water, and of that pallid hue. Her eyes, lost in the fatty ridges of her face, looked like two small pieces of coal pressed into a lump of dough as they moved from one face to another while the visitors stated their errand.

She did not ask them to sit. She just stood in the door and listened quietly until the spokesman came to a stumbling halt. Then they could hear the invisible watch ticking at the end of the gold chain.

Her voice was dry and cold. "I have no taxes in Jefferson. Colonel Sartoris explained it to me. Perhaps one of you can gain access to the city records and satisfy yourselves."

"But we have. We are the city authorities, Miss Emily. Didn't you get a notice from the sheriff, signed by him?"

"I received a paper, yes," Miss Emily said. "Perhaps he considers himself the sheriff... I have no taxes in Jefferson."

"But there is nothing on the books to show that, you see. We must go by the—"

"See Colonel Sartoris. I have no taxes in Jefferson."

"But, Miss Emily—"

"See Colonel Sartoris." (Colonel Sartoris had been dead almost ten years.) "I have no taxes in Jefferson. Tobe!" The Negro appeared. "Show these gentlemen out."

II

So she vanquished them, horse and foot, just as she had vanquished their fathers thirty years before about the smell. That was two years after her father's death and a short time after her sweetheart—the one we believed would marry her—had deserted her. After her father's death she went out very little; after her sweetheart went away, people hardly saw her at all. A few of the ladies had the temerity to call, but were not received, and the only sign of life about the place was the Negro man—a young man then—going in and out with a market basket.

"Just as if a man—any man—could keep a kitchen properly," the ladies said; so they were not surprised when the smell developed. It was another link between the gross, teeming world and the high and mighty Griersons.

165

A neighbor, a woman, complained to the mayor, Judge Stevens, eighty years old.

"But what will you have me do about it, madam?" he said.

"Why, send her word to stop it," the woman said. "Isn't there a law?"

"I'm sure that won't be necessary," Judge Stevens said. "It's probably just a snake or a rat that nigger of hers killed in the yard. I'll speak to him about it."

The next day he received two more complaints, one from a man who came in diffident deprecation. "We really must do something about it, Judge. I'd be the last one in the world to bother Miss Emily, but we've got to do something." That night the Board of Aldermen met—three graybeards and one younger man, a member of the rising generation.

"It's simple enough," he said. "Send her word to have her place cleaned up. Give her a certain time to do it in, and if she don't..."

"Dammit, sir," Judge Stevens said, "will you accuse a lady to her face of smelling bad?"

So the next night, after midnight, four men crossed Miss Emily's lawn and slunk about the house like burglars, sniffing along the base of the brickwork and at the cellar openings while one of them performed a regular sowing motion with his hand out of a sack slung from his shoulder. They broke open the cellar door and sprinkled lime there, and in all the outbuildings. As they recrossed the lawn, a window that had been dark was lighted and Miss Emily sat in it, the light behind her, and her upright torso motionless as that of an idol. They crept quietly across the lawn and into the shadow of the locusts that lined the street. After a week or two the smell went away.

That was when people had begun to feel really sorry for her. People in our town, remembering how old lady Wyatt, her great-aunt, had gone completely crazy at last, believed that the Griersons held themselves a little too high for what they really were. None of the young men were quite good enough for Miss Emily and such. We had long thought of them as a tableau, Miss Emily a slender figure in white in the background, her father a spraddled silhouette in the foreground, his back to her and clutching a horsewhip, the two of them framed by the back-flung front door. So when she got to be thirty and was still single, we were not pleased exactly, but vindicated; even with insanity in the family she wouldn't have turned down all of her chances if they had really materialized.

When her father died, it got about that the house was all that was left to her; and in a way, people were glad. At last they could pity Miss Emily. Being left alone, and a pauper, she had become humanized. Now she too would know the old thrill and the old despair of a penny more or less.

The day after his death all the ladies prepared to call at the house and offer condolence and aid, as is our custom. Miss Emily met them at the door, dressed as usual and with no trace of grief on her face. She told them that her father was not dead. She did that for three days, with the ministers calling on her, and the doctors, trying to persuade her to let them dispose of the body. Just as they were about to resort to law and force, she broke down, and they buried her father quickly.

We did not say she was crazy then. We believed she had to do that. We remembered all the young men her father had driven away, and we knew that with nothing left, she would have to cling to that which had robbed her, as people will.

III

She was sick for a long time. When we saw her again, her hair was cut short, making her look like a girl, with a vague resemblance to those angels in colored church windows—sort of tragic and serene.

The town had just let the contracts for paving the sidewalks, and in the summer after her father's death they began the work. The construction company came with riggers and mules and machinery, and a foreman named Homer Barron, a Yankee—a big, dark, ready man, with a big voice and eyes lighter than his face. The little boys would follow in groups to hear him cuss the riggers, and the riggers singing in time to the rise and fall of picks. Pretty soon he knew everybody in town. Whenever you heard a lot of laughing anywhere about the square, Homer Barron would be in the center of the group. Presently we began to see him and Miss Emily on Sunday afternoons driving in the yellow-wheeled buggy and the matched team of bays from the livery stable.

At first we were glad that Miss Emily would have an interest, because the ladies all said, "Of course a Grierson would not think seriously of a Northerner, a day laborer." But there were still others, older people, who said that even grief could not cause a real lady to forget noblesse oblige—without calling it noblesse oblige. They just said, "Poor Emily. Her kinsfolk should come to her." She had some kin in Alabama; but years ago her father had fallen out with them over the estate of old lady Wyatt, the crazy woman, and there was no communication between the two families. They had not even been represented at the funeral.

And as soon as the old people said, "Poor Emily," the whispering began. "Do you suppose it's really so?" they said to one another. "Of course it is. What else could..." This behind their hands; rustling of craned silk and satin behind jalousies closed upon the sun of Sunday afternoon as the thin, swift clop-clop-clop of the matched team passed: "Poor Emily."

She carried her head high enough—even when we believed that she was fallen. It was as if she demanded more than ever the recognition of her dignity as the last Grierson; as if it had wanted that touch of earthiness to reaffirm her imperviousness. Like when she bought the rat poison, the arsenic. That was over a year after they had begun to say "Poor Emily," and while the two female cousins were visiting her.

"I want some poison," she said to the druggist. She was over thirty then, still a slight woman, though thinner than usual, with cold, haughty black eyes in a face the flesh of which was strained across the temples and about the eye-sockets as you imagine a lighthouse-keeper's face ought to look. "I want some poison," she said.

"Yes, Miss Emily. What kind? For rats and such? I'd recom—"

"I want the best you have. I don't care what kind."

The druggist named several. "They'll kill anything up to an elephant. But what you want is—"

"Arsenic," Miss Emily said. "Is that a good one?"

"Is . . . arsenic? Yes, ma'am. But what you want—"

"I want arsenic."

The druggist looked down at her. She looked back at him, erect, her face like a strained flag. "Why, of course," the druggist said. "If that's what you want. But the law requires you to tell what you are going to use it for."

Miss Emily just stared at him, her head tilted back in order to look him eye for eye, until he looked away and went and got the arsenic and wrapped it up. The Negro delivery boy brought her the package; the druggist didn't come back. When she opened the package at home there was written on the box, under the skull and bones: "For rats."

IV

So the next day we all said, "She will kill herself"; and we said it would be the best thing. When she had first begun to be seen with Homer Barron, we had said, "She will marry him." Then we said, "She will persuade him yet," because Homer himself had remarked—he liked men, and it was known that he drank with the younger men in the Elks' Club—that he was not a marrying man. Later we said, "Poor Emily" behind the jalousies as they passed on Sunday afternoon in the glittering buggy, Miss Emily with her head high and Homer Barron with his hat cocked and a cigar in his teeth, reins and whip in a yellow glove.

Then some of the ladies began to say that it was a disgrace to the town and a bad example to the young people. The men did not want to interfere, but at last the ladies forced the Baptist minister—Miss Emily's people were Episcopal—to call upon her. He would never divulge what happened during that interview, but he refused to go back again. The next Sunday they again drove about the streets, and the following day the minister's wife wrote to Miss Emily's relations in Alabama.

So she had blood-kin under her roof again and we sat back to watch developments. At first nothing happened. Then we were sure that they were to be married. We learned that Miss Emily had been to the jeweler's and ordered a man's toilet set in silver, with the letters H. B. on each piece. Two days later we learned that she had bought a complete outfit of men's clothing, including a nightshirt, and we said, "They are married." We were really glad. We were glad because the two female cousins were even more Grierson than Miss Emily had ever been.

So we were not surprised when Homer Barron—the streets had been finished some time since—was gone. We were a little disappointed that there was not a public blowing-off, but we believed that he had gone on to prepare for Miss Emily's coming, or to give her a chance to get rid of the cousins. (By that time it was a cabal, and we were all Miss Emily's allies to help circumvent the cousins.) Sure enough, after another week they departed. And, as we had expected all along, within three days Homer Barron was back in town. A neighbor saw the Negro man admit him at the kitchen door at dusk one evening.

And that was the last we saw of Homer Barron. And of Miss Emily for some time. The Negro man went in and out with the market basket, but the front door remained closed. Now and then we would see her at a window for a moment, as the men did that night when they sprinkled the lime, but for almost six months she did not appear on the streets. Then we knew that this was to be expected too; as if that quality of her father which had thwarted her woman's life so many times had been too virulent and too furious to die.

When we next saw Miss Emily, she had grown fat and her hair was turning gray. During the next few years it grew grayer and grayer until it attained an even pepper-and-salt iron-gray, when it ceased turning. Up to the day of her death at seventy-four it was still that vigorous iron-gray, like the hair of an active man.

From that time on her front door remained closed, save for a period of six or seven years, when she was about forty, during which she gave lessons in china-painting. She fitted up a studio in one of the downstairs rooms, where the daughters and granddaughters of Colonel Sartoris' contemporaries were sent to her with the same regularity and in the same spirit that they were sent to church on Sundays with a twenty-five-cent piece for the collection plate. Meanwhile her taxes had been remitted.

Then the newer generation became the backbone and the spirit of the town, and the painting pupils grew up and fell away and did not send their children to her with boxes of color and tedious brushes and pictures cut from the ladies' magazines. The front door closed upon the last one and remained closed for good. When the town got free postal delivery, Miss Emily alone refused to let them fasten the metal numbers above her door and attach a mailbox to it. She would not listen to them.

Daily, monthly, yearly we watched the Negro grow grayer and more stooped, going in and out with the market basket. Each December we sent her a tax notice, which would be returned by the post office a week later, unclaimed. Now and then we would see her in one of the downstairs windows—she had evidently shut up the top floor of the house—like the carven torso of an idol in a niche, looking or not looking at us, we could never tell which. Thus she passed from generation to generation—dear, inescapable, impervious, tranquil, and perverse.

And so she died. Fell ill in the house filled with dust and shadows, with only a doddering Negro man to wait on her. We did not even know she was sick; we had long since given up trying to get any information from the Negro. He talked to no one, probably not even to her, for his voice had grown harsh and rusty, as if from disuse.

She died in one of the downstairs rooms, in a heavy walnut bed with a curtain, her gray head propped on a pillow yellow and moldy with age and lack of sunlight.

V

The Negro met the first of the ladies at the front door and let them in, with their hushed, sibilant voices and their quick, curious glances, and then he disappeared. He walked right through the house and out the back and was not seen again.

The two female cousins came at once. They held the funeral on the second day, with the town coming to look at Miss Emily beneath a mass of bought flowers, with the crayon face of her father musing profoundly above the bier and the ladies sibilant and macabre; and the very old men—some in their brushed Confederate uniforms—on the porch and the lawn, talking of Miss Emily as if she had been a contemporary of theirs, believing that they had danced with her and courted her perhaps, confusing time with its mathematical progression, as the old do, to whom all the past is not a diminishing road but, instead, a huge meadow which no winter ever quite touches, divided from them now by the narrow bottle-neck of the most recent decade of years.

Already we knew that there was one room in that region above stairs which no one had seen in forty years, and which would have to be forced. They waited until Miss Emily was decently in the ground before they opened it.

The violence of breaking down the door seemed to fill this room with pervading dust. A thin, acrid pall as of the tomb seemed to lie everywhere upon this room decked and furnished as for a bridal: upon the valance curtains of faded rose color, upon the rose-shaded lights, upon the dressing table, upon the delicate array of crystal and the man's toilet things backed with tarnished silver, silver so tarnished that the monogram was obscured. Among them lay a collar and tie, as if they had just been removed, which, lifted, left upon the surface a pale crescent in the dust. Upon a chair hung the suit, carefully folded; beneath it the two mute shoes and the discarded socks.

The man himself lay in the bed.

For a long while we just stood there, looking down at the profound and fleshless grin. The body had apparently once lain in the attitude of an embrace, but now the long sleep that outlasts love, that conquers even the grimace of love, had cuckolded him. What was left of him, rotted beneath what was left of the nightshirt, had become inextricable from the bed in which he lay; and upon him and upon the pillow beside him lay that even coating of the patient and biding dust.

Then we noticed that in the second pillow was the indentation of a head. One of us lifted something from it, and leaning forward, that faint and invisible dust dry and acrid in the nostrils, we saw a long strand of iron-gray hair.

170

Plot Summary

"A Rose for Emily" is a short story written by William Faulkner that tells the story of a southern woman named Emily Grierson and her mysterious life in the town of Jefferson. The story is told from the perspective of the town's collective memory, with flashbacks to important events in the life of Emily Grierson. The town is fascinated by Emily's life and her family history, which involves her father's past wealth and status in the community, and her reclusive life following his death. The events of the story begin with the death of Emily Grierson at the age of 74. The townspeople gather to attend her funeral, and their memories of Emily's life start to come to the surface. The townspeople recall that Emily had been living alone in her decaying mansion for many years, and that she was rarely seen in public. As the story progresses, it becomes clear that Emily had been deeply affected by the loss of her father, and her reclusion was a result of her inability to cope with his death. The townspeople also recall a scandal involving Emily in which she was rumored to be dating a northerner, which was considered disgraceful at the time. As the town prepares to bury Emily, the narrator reveals a shocking discovery inside her home. In a locked upstairs room, the townspeople discovered the preserved corpse of Homer Barron, a laborer and former suitor of Emily's. It is revealed that Emily had been romantically involved with Homer Barron, and had even gone so far as to purchase arsenic to kill him and preserve his body. The townspeople had suspected that Homer had left town and assumed he had abandoned Emily, but it is revealed that Emily had murdered him out of fear of abandonment. The conclusion of the story brings a sense of closure to the long-standing mystery surrounding Emily's past. The townspeople realize that Emily had been living her life in a state of delusion, and that her mental state had been slowly deteriorating over the years. In the end, "A Rose for Emily" explores themes of isolation, mental illness, and the consequences of clinging to the past. Faulkner's evocative prose and complex characterizations make this story a haunting and unforgettable exploration of the human psyche.

Language Exercises

Choose the item that best replaces or explains the underlined part of the sentence.

1. It was a big, squarish frame house that had once been white, decorated with cupolas and spires and scrolled balconies in the heavily lightsome style of the seventies, set on what had once been our most select street.
    A. strolled   B. curved   C. sculptured   D. unadorned

2. ... only Miss Emily's house was left, lifting its stubborn and coquettish decay above the cotton wagons and the gasoline pumps—an eyesore among eyesores.
    A. flirtatious   B. demure   C. arrogant   D. humble

3.   … and when they sat down, a faint dust rose <u>sluggishly</u> about their thighs, spinning with slow motes in the single sun-ray.

    A. mournfully   B. briskly   C. nostalgically D. languidly

4.   They rose when she entered—a small, fat woman in black, with a thin gold chain descending to her waist and vanishing into her belt, leaning on an ebony cane with a <u>tarnished</u> gold head.

    A. gleaming   B. stained   C. discolored   D. lustrous

5.   She looked bloated, like a body long submerged in motionless water, and of that <u>pallid</u> hue.

    A. vibrant   B. delicate   C. robust   D. pale

6.   So she <u>vanquished</u> them, horse and foot, just as she had vanquished their fathers thirty years before about the smell.

    A. submitted   B. yielded   C. defeated   D. sufficed

7.   They broke open the cellar door and <u>sprinkled</u> lime there, and in all the outbuildings.

    A. spurted   B. scattered   C. spilled   D. sprayed

8.   We had long thought of them as a tableau, Miss Emily a slender figure in white in the background, her father a <u>spraddled</u> silhouette in the foreground, …

    A. clustered   B. splayed   C. slung   D. darkened

9.   The day after his death all the ladies prepared to call at the house and offer <u>condolence</u> and aid, as is our custom.

    A. indifference   B. consultation C. detachment D. sympathy

10. It was as if she demanded more than ever the recognition of her dignity as the last Grierson; as if it had wanted that touch of earthiness to reaffirm her <u>imperviousness</u>.

    A. invulnerability B. compliancy C. immensity D. complacency

11. By that time it was a cabal, and we were all Miss Emily's allies to help <u>circumvent</u> the cousins.

    A. confront   B. endow   C. bypass   D. reckon

12. Then we knew that this was to be expected too; as if that quality of her father which had thwarted her woman's life so many times had been too <u>virulent</u> and too furious to die.

    A. cranky   B. filial   C. chaotic   D. venomous

13. Thus she passed from generation to generation—dear, inescapable, impervious, tranquil, and <u>perverse</u>.

    A. stoic   B. transient   C. obstinate   D. sacred

14. The Negro met the first of the ladies at the front door and let them in, with their hushed, <u>sibilant</u> voices and their quick, curious glances, and then he disappeared.

    A. hissing   B. mellifluous C. melodious   D. fanatic

15. What was left of him, rotted beneath what was left of the nightshirt, had become

<u>inextricable</u> from the bed in which he lay; and upon him and upon the pillow beside him lay that even coating of the patient and biding dust.

A. perceptible   B. conceivable   C. inseparable   D. tangible

Topics for Discussion

1. Discuss the significance of time and its impact on the theme of decay and change in the story.
2. Analyze the character of Colonel Sartoris and his relevance to the theme of societal expectations and authority.
3. How does Faulkner explore the theme of power and control through the character of Emily's father?
4. Discuss the theme of love and its distorted nature in the story, focusing on Emily's relationship with Homer Barron.
5. How does Faulkner's use of foreshadowing contribute to the theme of inevitability and tragedy in the story?
6. Discuss the role of the narrator in "A Rose for Emily" and its impact on our understanding of the story.
7. How does Faulkner use symbolism in the story, particularly in relation to Emily's house and the physical aspects of her life?
8. How does Faulkner explore the theme of denial and its consequences in the story, particularly in relation to Emily's actions and decisions?
9. Find evidence to certify that Miss Emily is both conservative and unconventional.
10. Why is Emily pitiable? What facts have justified this statement?

Discussion Tips

William Faulkner, born in New Albany, Mississippi, hailed from a once-affluent family of former plantation owners whose fortunes were diminished by the aftermath of the Civil War. His creation of the mythical Yoknapatawpha County, Mississippi, provided him with an abundant wellspring of vibrant characters and narratives, serving as the backdrop for many of his greatest novels and short stories, including "A Rose for Emily," set in the town of Jefferson within this fictional county. Faulkner's upbringing in a family with aristocratic roots and connections to similar households acquainted him with the haughtiness exhibited by figures like the Griersons. These individuals, despite the loss of their wealth, continued to carry themselves as if they were still privileged plantation owners. Born into a Southern family with a rich heritage, Faulkner's understanding of the American South's tragic history of rise and decline became an integral part of his imaginative and creative endeavors, imbuing his works with a profound exploration of the impact of social change on individuals, evoking both nostalgia and a sense of impending doom in modern readers.

The majority of Faulkner's works are anchored in the fictional town of Jefferson, situated in the South. The protagonist of "A Rose for Emily", Miss Emily, epitomizes the pride, self-importance, and obstinacy characteristic of the Griersons. As a woman from such a family, she enjoyed a lofty yet antiquated social standing, placed on a pedestal for others to admire as a paragon of perfection. Under constant scrutiny by the community, she was expected to bring honor to the town and serve as a role model for the younger generation, representing the Southern tradition as an "idol in the niche". Constrained by her father's dominance, Miss Emily was deprived of the opportunity for a fulfilling marriage and a conventional woman's life. Her courtship with Homer Barron, a Northern laborer, provoked accusations of disgracing the town and setting a negative example for the youth. Subjected to patriarchal and societal pressures, her character became distorted as she endeavored to cling to a past symbolizing privilege and glory. Retreating from the evolving world, she chose complete self-isolation. Over time, Miss Emily underwent a transformation from a subservient young lady under her domineering father's control to a middle-aged woman courting a laborer against the community's censure, ultimately evolving into a murderer who not only ended her lover's life but also preserved his corpse. This progression reflects the profound impact of tradition, societal expectations, and personal isolation on an individual's psyche, intricately woven into the fabric of Faulkner's narrative.

Unit 9
F. Scott Fitzgerald: "Babylon Revisited"

About the Author

F. Scott Fitzgerald (1896–1940)

F. Scott Fitzgerald, a native of St. Paul, Minnesota, and an alumnus of Princeton University, is celebrated for his portrayal of the Jazz Age and incisive social commentary. His literary journey began with the writing of his debut novel, *This Side of Paradise*, crafted during his time in army boot camp. During the zenith of his career, Fitzgerald encountered personal and financial hardships, compounded by his wife Zelda's struggles with mental health and his own health issues. Seeking to alleviate his financial woes, he ventured into Hollywood as a screenwriter, albeit without much success. He penned his most renowned works, *The Great Gatsby* during this tumultuous period, and *The Last Tycoon*, which was published posthumously following his passing at the age of forty-four. The initial reception of *The Great Gatsby* was tepid, with lukewarm reviews and modest sales. However, it was only after his death that the book garnered widespread acclaim and positive critiques. The republication of the novel propelled it to become one of the most beloved American literary works of the century. Fitzgerald's enduring legacy as a literary luminary lies in his adept portrayal of the complexities of the human condition, the allure and decadence of the Jazz Age, and the timeless themes of love, loss, and the pursuit of the American Dream. His works continue to captivate readers and scholars alike, offering profound insights into the societal mores and individual aspirations of his era, cementing his status as a pivotal figure in American literature.

Literary History

The Short Stories of F. Scott Fitzgerald: Structure, Narrative Technique, Style

F. Scott Fitzgerald, an iconic American writer of the 20th century, is well-known for his novels like *The Great Gatsby*, but his short stories are equally captivating and showcase his exceptional storytelling abilities.

Fitzgerald's short stories are characterized by their carefully crafted structures, reflecting his unique narrative approach. His stories often employ circular or non-linear structures, which heighten suspense and intrigue, captivating readers from the very beginning. This structural choice enables Fitzgerald to weave complex threads of plot and theme, ultimately delivering a powerful and memorable story. One notable example is "The Curious Case of Benjamin Button", a tale that unfolds in reverse chronological order. This unconventional structure reinforces the story's exploration of time, aging, and the fragility of human existence. By structuring the narrative in this way, Fitzgerald challenges the traditional linear concept of time and crafts a thought-provoking reading experience.

Fitzgerald's mastery of narrative technique is another defining aspect of his short stories. One technique he frequently employs is the use of a first-person narrator, which allows readers to intimately engage with the protagonist's thoughts, emotions, and struggles. This technique is evident in stories like "Winter Dreams" and "Babylon Revisited", where the first-person perspective enhances the reader's connection to the central character's desires and conflicts. Furthermore, Fitzgerald expertly employs vivid imagery and descriptive language to immerse readers in his stories. Through his meticulous attention to detail, he creates a vibrant and evocative atmosphere that enriches the overall reading experience. This narrative technique is particularly prominent in stories like "The Diamond as Big as the Ritz" and "The Ice Palace", where Fitzgerald's vivid descriptions transport readers to lush settings, heightening the emotional impact of the stories.

Fitzgerald's unique writing style is characterized by a delicate blend of realism and idealism. Inspired by the Jazz Age and the Roaring Twenties, his prose reflects the decadence, excess, and disillusionment of the era. This style establishes a poignant atmosphere, exploring themes such as love, ambition, and the pursuit of the American Dream.

One notable stylistic aspect of Fitzgerald's stories is his use of lyrical and poetic language. Through his beautiful and melodic prose, he creates a sense of enchantment that resonates with readers long after they finish the stories. This enchanting style can be observed in his masterpiece, *The Great Gatsby*, where Fitzgerald's poetic descriptions evoke both the unattainable beauty of Daisy Buchanan and the tragedy of Jay Gatsby's unrequited love.

Additionally, Fitzgerald's portrayal of social class and the divide between the wealthy elite and the struggling middle class is a recurring theme in his stories. Through his distinct style, he explores the complexities and tensions arising from these class divisions, shedding light on the social and cultural dynamics of the time.

In Conclusion, F. Scott Fitzgerald's short stories are not only a testament to his literary prowess but also reveal his mastery of structure, narrative technique, and style. By embracing circular or non-linear structures, employing first-person narrators, and utilizing poetic language, Fitzgerald creates immersive narratives that strike a chord with readers. Furthermore, his unique style captures the essence of the Jazz Age, exploring timeless themes that continue to resonate with audiences today. The structural choices, narrative techniques, and stylistic elements employed by Fitzgerald make his short stories enduring literary treasures, deserving of ongoing appreciation and analysis.

Literary Terms

Jazz Age

The Jazz Age was a period in American history during the 1920s, characterized by a significant cultural shift marked by a spirit of rebellion, innovation, and societal change. The term "Jazz Age" was popularized by F. Scott Fitzgerald in his writings, particularly in *The Great Gatsby*, where he captured the essence of the era. Jazz music, with its lively and improvisational nature, became a symbol of the era, representing the break from traditional values and the embrace of modernity. The Jazz Age was also associated with a newfound sense of freedom, particularly for women, who began to challenge traditional gender roles and embrace more liberated lifestyles. This period saw the rise of flappers, speakeasies, and a general sense of exuberance, excess, and hedonism. However, the Jazz Age was also marked by underlying tensions, including racial and social inequalities, economic disparities, and the looming shadow of Prohibition. Despite its vibrant and glamorous facade, the Jazz Age ultimately came to an end with the onset of the Great Depression, which brought an abrupt halt to the carefree and extravagant lifestyle that had defined the era.

Lost Generation

The Lost Generation refers to the disillusioned and disenchanted group of writers and artists who came of age during World War I and the post-war years. Coined by Gertrude Stein and popularized by Ernest Hemingway, the term encapsulates the sense of aimlessness, disillusionment, and moral questioning that characterized the generation. Many young men who had experienced the horrors of war returned home profoundly affected, leading to a collective feeling of alienation and a loss of faith in traditional values and institutions. F. Scott Fitzgerald, along with other prominent writers such as Ernest Hemingway and T.S. Eliot, is often associated with the Lost Generation, as their works grappled with themes of existential angst, moral ambiguity, and a search for meaning in a world that seemed to have lost its bearings. The Lost Generation's literary output reflected a sense of fragmentation, uncertainty, and a rejection of the status quo, capturing the collective disillusionment of a generation that had witnessed the devastation of war and struggled to find its place in a rapidly changing world.

The Story

Babylon Revisited[1]

I

"And where's Mr. Campbell?" Charlie asked.

"Gone to Switzerland. Mr. Campbell's a pretty sick man, Mr. Wales."

"I'm sorry to hear that. And George Hardt?" Charlie inquired.

"Back in America, gone to work."

"And where is the Snow Bird?"

"He was in here last week. Anyway, his friend, Mr. Schaeffer, is in Paris."

Two familiar names from the long list of a year and a half ago. Charlie scribbled an address in his notebook and tore out the page.

"If you see Mr. Schaeffer, give him this," he said. "It's my brother-in-law's address. I haven't settled on a hotel yet."

He was not really disappointed to find Paris was so empty. But the stillness in the bar was strange, almost portentous. It was not an American bar any more—he felt polite in it, and not as if he owned it. It had gone back into France. He felt the stillness from the moment he got out of the taxi and saw the doorman, usually in a frenzy of activity at this hour, gossiping with a *chasseur* by the servants' entrance.

Passing through the corridor, he heard only a single, bored voice in the once-clamorous women's room. When he turned into the bar he traveled the twenty feet of green carpet with his eyes fixed straight ahead by old habit; and then, with his foot firmly on the rail, he turned and surveyed the room, encountering only a single pair of eyes that fluttered up from a newspaper in the corner. Charlie asked for the head barman, Paul, who in the latter days of the bull market had come to work in his own custom-built car—disembarking, however, with due nicety at the nearest corner. But Paul was at his country house today and Alix giving him information.

"No, no more," Charlie said, "I'm going slow these days."

Alix congratulated him: "You were going pretty strong a couple of years ago."

"I'll stick to it all right," Charlie assured him. "I've stuck to it for over a year and a half now."

"How do you find conditions in America?"

"I haven't been to America for months. I'm in business in Prague, representing a couple of concerns there. They don't know about me down there."

Alix smiled. "Remember the night of George Hardt's bachelor dinner here?" said Charlie. "By the way, what's become of Claude Fessenden?"

Alix lowered his voice confidentially: "He's in Paris, but he doesn't come here

---

1   F. Scott Fitzgerald, *Tales of the Jazz Age* (Scribner, 2004), pp. 69–90.

anymore. Paul doesn't allow it. He ran up a bill of thirty thousand francs, charging all his drinks and his lunches, and usually his dinner, for more than a year. And when Paul finally told him he had to pay, he gave him a bad check."

Alix shook his head sadly.

"I don't understand it, such a dandy fellow. Now he's all bloated up——" He made a plump apple of his hands.

Charlie watched a group of strident queens installing themselves in a corner.

"Nothing affects them," he thought. "Stocks rise and fall, people loaf or work, but they go on forever." The place oppressed him. He called for the dice and shook with Alix for the drink.

"Here for long, Mr. Wales?"

"I'm here for four or five days to see my little girl."

"Oh-h! You have a little girl?"

Outside, the fire-red, gas-blue, ghost-green signs shone smokily through the tranquil rain. It was late afternoon and the streets were in movement; the *bistros* gleamed. At the corner of the Boulevard des Capucines he took a taxi. The Place de la Concorde moved by in pink majesty; they crossed the logical Seine, and Charlie felt the sudden provincial quality of the Left Bank.

Charlie directed his taxi to the Avenue de l'Opéra, which was out of his way. But he wanted to see the blue hour spread over the magnificent façade, and imagine that the cab horns, playing endlessly the first few bars of 'Le Plus que Lent', were the trumpets of the Second Empire. They were closing the iron grill in front of Brentano's Bookstore, and people were already at dinner behind the trim little bourgeois hedge of Duval's. He had never eaten at a really cheap restaurant in Paris. Five-course dinner, four francs fifty, eighteen cents, wine included. For some odd reason he wished that he had.

As they rolled on to the Left Bank and he felt its sudden provincialism, he thought, "I spoiled this city for myself. I didn't realize it, but the days came along one after another, and then two years were gone, and everything was gone, and I was gone."

He was thirty-five, and good to look at. The Irish mobility of his face was sobered by a deep wrinkle between his eyes. As he rang his brother-in-law's bell in the Rue Palatine, the wrinkle deepened till it pulled down his brows; he felt a cramping sensation in his belly. From behind the maid who opened the door darted a lovely little girl of nine who shrieked "Daddy!" and flew up, struggling like a fish, into his arms. She pulled his head around by one ear and set her cheek against his.

"My old pie," he said.

"Oh, daddy, daddy, daddy, daddy, dads, dads, dads!"

She drew him into the salon, where the family waited, a boy and girl his daughter's age, his sister-in-law and her husband. He greeted Marion with his voice pitched carefully to avoid either feigned enthusiasm or dislike, but her response was more frankly tepid, and she minimized her expression of unalterable distrust by directing her regard toward his child. The two men clasped hands in a friendly way and Lincoln Peters rested his for a moment on Charlie's shoulder.

The room was warm and comfortably American. The three children moved intimately about, playing through the yellow oblongs that led to other rooms; the cheer of six o'clock spoke in the eager smacks of the fire and the sounds of French activity in the kitchen. But Charlie did not relax; his heart sat up rigidly in his body and he drew confidence from his daughter, who from time to time came close to him, holding in her arms the doll he had brought.

"Really extremely well," he declared in answer to Lincoln's question. "There's a lot of business there that isn't moving at all, but we're doing even better than ever. In fact, damn well. I'm bringing my sister over from America next month to keep house for me. My income last year was bigger than it was when I had money. You see, the Czechs—"

His boasting was for a specific purpose; but after a moment, seeing a faint restiveness in Lincoln's eye, he changed the subject:

"Those are fine children of yours, well brought up, good manners."

"We think Honoria's a great little girl too."

Marion Peters came from the kitchen. She was a tall woman with worried eyes, who had once possessed a fresh American loveliness. Charlie had never been sensitive to it and was always surprised when people spoke of how pretty she had been. From the first there had been an instinctive antipathy between them.

"Well, how do you find Honoria?" she asked.

"Wonderful. I was astonished how much she's grown in ten months. All the children are looking well."

"We haven't had a doctor for a year. How do you like being back in Paris?"

"It seems very funny to see so few Americans around."

"I'm delighted," Marion said vehemently. "Now at least you can go into a store without their assuming you're a millionaire. We've suffered like everybody, but on the whole it's a good deal pleasanter."

"But it was nice while it lasted," Charlie said. "We were a sort of royalty, almost infallible, with a sort of magic around us. In the bar this afternoon"—he stumbled, seeing his mistake—"there wasn't a man I knew."

She looked at him keenly. "I should think you'd have had enough of bars."

"I only stayed a minute. I take one drink every afternoon, and no more."

"Don't you want a cocktail before dinner?" Lincoln asked.

"I take only one drink every afternoon, and I've had that."

"I hope you keep to it," said Marion.

Her dislike was evident in the coldness with which she spoke, but Charlie only smiled; he had larger plans. Her very aggressiveness gave him an advantage, and he knew enough to wait. He wanted them to initiate the discussion of what they knew had brought him to Paris.

At dinner he couldn't decide whether Honoria was most like him or her mother. Fortunate if she didn't combine the traits of both that had brought them to disaster. A great wave of protectiveness went over him. He thought he knew what to do for her. He believed in character; he wanted to jump back a whole generation and trust in character again as the eternally valuable element. Everything else wore out.

He left soon after dinner, but not to go home. He was curious to see Paris by night with clearer and more judicious eyes than those of other days. He bought a *strapontin* for the Casino and watched Josephine Baker go through her chocolate arabesques.

After an hour he left and strolled toward Montmartre, up the Rue Pigalle into the Place Blanche. The rain had stopped and there were a few people in evening clothes disembarking from taxis in front of cabarets, and *cocottes* prowling singly or in pairs, and many Negroes. He passed a lighted door from which issued music, and stopped with the sense of familiarity; it was Bricktop's, where he had parted with so many hours and so much money. A few doors farther on he found another ancient rendezvous and incautiously put his head inside. Immediately an eager orchestra burst into sound, a pair of professional dancers leaped to their feet and a maître d'hôtel swooped toward him, crying, "Crowd just arriving, sir!" But he withdrew quickly.

"You have to be damn drunk," he thought.

Zelli's was closed, the bleak and sinister cheap hotels surrounding it were dark; up in the Rue Blanche there was more light and a local, colloquial French crowd. The Poet's Cave had disappeared, but the two great mouths of the Café of Heaven and the Café of Hell still yawned—even devoured, as he watched, the meager contents of a tourist bus—a German, a Japanese, and an American couple who glanced at him with frightened eyes.

So much for the effort and ingenuity of Montmartre. All the catering to vice and waste was on an utterly childish scale, and he suddenly realized the meaning of the word "dissipate"—to dissipate into thin air; to make nothing out of something. In the little hours of the night every move from place to place was an enormous human jump, an increase of paying for the privilege of slower and slower motion.

He remembered thousand-franc notes given to an orchestra for playing a single number, hundred-franc notes tossed to a doorman for calling a cab.

But it hadn't been given for nothing.

It had been given, even the most wildly squandered sum, as an offering to destiny that he might not remember the things most worth remembering, the things that now he would always remember—his child taken from his control, his wife escaped to a grave in Vermont.

In the glare of a *brasserie* a woman spoke to him. He bought her some eggs and coffee, and then, eluding her encouraging stare, gave her a twenty-franc note and took a taxi to his hotel.

181

II

He woke upon a fine fall day—football weather. The depression of yesterday was gone and he liked the people on the streets. At noon he sat opposite Honoria at Le Grand Vatel, the only restaurant he could think of not reminiscent of champagne dinners and long luncheons that began at two and ended in a blurred and vague twilight.

"Now, how about vegetables? Oughtn't you to have some vegetables?"

"Well, yes."

"Here's *épinards* and *chou-fleur* and carrots and *haricots*."

"I'd like choux-fleurs."

"Wouldn't you like to have two vegetables?"

"I usually only have one at lunch."

The waiter was pretending to be inordinately fond of children. "*Qu'elle est mignonne la petite? Elle parle exactement comme une française.*"

"How about dessert? Shall we wait and see?"

The waiter disappeared. Honoria looked at her father expectantly.

"What are we going to do?"

"First, we're going to that toy store in the Rue Saint-Honoré and buy you anything you like. And then we're going to the vaudeville at the Empire."

She hesitated. "I like it about the vaudeville, but not the toy store."

"Why not?"

"Well, you brought me this doll." She had it with her. "And I've got lots of things. And we're not rich any more, are we?"

"We never were. But to-day you are to have anything you want."

"All right," she agreed resignedly.

When there had been her mother and a French nurse he had been inclined to be strict; now he extended himself, reached out for a new tolerance; he must be both parents to her and not shut any of her out of communication.

"I want to get to know you," he said gravely. "First let me introduce myself. My name is Charles J. Wales, of Prague."

"Oh, daddy!" her voice cracked with laughter.

"And who are you, please?" he persisted, and she accepted a rôle immediately: "Honoria Wales, Rue Palatine, Paris."

"Married or single?"

"No, not married. Single."

He indicated the doll. "But I see you have a child, madame."

Unwilling to disinherit it, she took it to her heart and thought quickly: "Yes, I've been married, but I'm not married now. My husband is dead."

He went on quickly, "And the child's name?"

"Simone. That's after my best friend at school."

"I'm very pleased that you're doing so well at school."

"I'm third this month," she boasted. "Elsie"—that was her cousin—"is only about eighteenth, and Richard is about at the bottom."

"You like Richard and Elsie, don't you?"

"Oh, yes. I like Richard quite well and I like her all right."

Cautiously and casually he asked: "And Aunt Marion and Uncle Lincoln—which do you like best?"

"Oh, Uncle Lincoln, I guess."

He was increasingly aware of her presence. As they came in, a murmur of "...adorable" followed them, and now the people at the next table bent all their silences upon her, staring as if she were something no more conscious than a flower.

"Why don't I live with you?" she asked suddenly. "Because mamma's dead?"

"You must stay here and learn more French. It would have been hard for daddy to take care of you so well."

"I don't really need much taking care of any more. I do everything for myself."

Going out of the restaurant, a man and a woman unexpectedly hailed him.

"Well, the old Wales!"

"Hello there, Lorraine... Dunc."

Sudden ghosts out of the past: Duncan Schaeffer, a friend from college. Lorraine Quarrles, a lovely, pale blond of thirty; one of a crowd who had helped them make months into days in the lavish times of three years ago.

"My husband couldn't come this year," she said, in answer to his question. "We're poor as hell. So he gave me two hundred a month and told me I could do my worst on that... This your little girl?"

"What about coming back and sitting down?" Duncan asked.

"Can't do it." He was glad for an excuse. As always, he felt Lorraine's passionate, provocative attraction, but his own rhythm was different now.

"Well, how about dinner?" she asked.

"I'm not free. Give me your address and let me call you."

"Charlie, I believe you're sober," she said judicially. "I honestly believe he's sober, Dunc. Pinch him and see if he's sober."

Charlie indicated Honoria with his head. They both laughed.

"What's your address?" said Duncan skeptically.

He hesitated, unwilling to give the name of his hotel.

"I'm not settled yet. I'd better call you. We're going to see the vaudeville at the Empire."

"There! That's what I want to do," Lorraine said. "I want to see some clowns and acrobats and jugglers. That's just what we'll do, Dunc."

"We've got to do an errand first," said Charlie. "Perhaps we'll see you there."

"All right, you snob... Good-by, beautiful little girl."

"Good-by."

Honoria bobbed politely.

Somehow, an unwelcome encounter, Charlie thought. They liked him because he was functioning, because he was serious; they wanted to see him, because he was stronger than they were now, because they wanted to draw a certain sustenance from his strength.

At the Empire, Honoria proudly refused to sit upon her father's folded coat. She was already an individual with a code of her own, and Charlie was more and more absorbed by the desire of putting a little of himself into her before she crystallized utterly. It was hopeless to try to know her in so short a time.

Between the acts they came upon Duncan and Lorraine in the lobby where the band was playing.

"Have a drink?"

"All right, but not up at the bar. We'll take a table."

"The perfect father."

Listening abstractedly to Lorraine, Charlie watched Honoria's eyes leave their table, and he followed them wistfully about the room, wondering what they saw. He met her glance and she smiled.

"I liked that lemonade," she said.

What had she said? What had he expected? Going home in a taxi afterward, he pulled her over until her head rested against his chest.

"Darling, do you ever think about your mother?"

"Yes, sometimes," she answered vaguely.

"I don't want you to forget her. Have you got a picture of her?"

"Yes, I think so. Anyhow, Aunt Marion has. Why don't you want me to forget her?"

"She loved you very much."

"I loved her too."

They were silent for a moment.

"Daddy, I want to come and live with you," she said suddenly.

His heart leaped; he had wanted it to come like this.

"Aren't you perfectly happy?"

"Yes, but I love you better than anybody. And you love me better than anybody, don't you, now that mummy's dead?"

"Of course I do. But you won't always like me best, honey. You'll grow up and meet somebody your own age and go marry him and forget you ever had a daddy."

"Yes, that's true," she agreed tranquilly.

He didn't go in. He was coming back at nine o'clock and he wanted to keep himself fresh and new for the thing he must say then.

"When you're safe inside, just show yourself in that window."

"All right. Good-by, dads, dads, dads, dads."

184

He waited in the dark street until she appeared, all warm and glowing, in the window above and kissed her fingers out into the night.

III

They were waiting. Marion sat behind the coffee service in a dignified black dinner dress that just faintly suggested mourning. Lincoln was walking up and down with the animation of one who had already been talking. They were as anxious as he was to get into the question. He opened it almost immediately:

"I suppose you know what I want to see you about—why I really came to Paris."

Marion played with the black stars on her necklace and frowned.

"I'm awfully anxious to have a home," he continued. "And I'm awfully anxious to have Honoria in it. I appreciate your taking in Honoria for her mother's sake, but things have changed now"—he hesitated and then continued more forcibly—"changed radically with me, and I want to ask you to reconsider the matter. It would be silly for me to deny that about two years ago I was acting badly—"

Marion looked up at him with hard eyes.

"—but all that's over. As I told you, I haven't had more than a drink a day for over a year, and I take that drink deliberately, so that the idea of alcohol won't get too big in my imagination. You see the idea?"

"No," said Marion succinctly.

"It's a sort of stunt I set myself. It keeps the matter in proportion."

"I get you," said Lincoln. "You don't want to admit it's got any attraction for you."

"Something like that. Sometimes I forget and don't take it. But I try to take it. Anyhow, I couldn't afford to drink in my position. The people I represent are more than satisfied with what I've done, and I'm bringing my sister over from Burlington to keep house for me, and I want awfully to have Honoria too. You know that even when her mother and I weren't getting along well I never let anything that happened touch Honoria. I know she's fond of me and I know I'm able to take care of her and—well, there you are. How do you feel about it?"

He knew that now he would have to take a beating. It would last an hour or two hours, and it would be difficult, but if he modulated his inevitable resentment to the chastened attitude of the reformed sinner, he might win his point in the end.

Keep your temper, he told himself. You don't want to be justified. You want Honoria.

Lincoln spoke first: "We've been talking it over ever since we got your letter last month. We're happy to have Honoria here. She's a dear little thing, and we're glad to be able to help her, but of course that isn't the question—"

Marion interrupted suddenly. "How long are you going to stay sober, Charlie?" she asked.

"Permanently, I hope."

"How can anybody count on that?"

185

"You know I never did drink heavily until I gave up business and came over here with nothing to do. Then Helen and I began to run around with—"

"Please leave Helen out of it. I can't bear to hear you talk about her like that."

He stared at her grimly; he had never been certain how fond of each other the sisters were in life.

"My drinking only lasted about a year and a half—from the time we came over until I—collapsed."

"It was time enough."

"It was time enough," he agreed.

"My duty is entirely to Helen," she said. "I try to think what she would have wanted me to do. Frankly, from the night you did that terrible thing you haven't really existed for me. I can't help that. She was my sister."

"Yes."

"When she was dying she asked me to look out for Honoria. If you hadn't been in a sanitarium then, it might have helped matters."

He had no answer.

"I'll never in my life be able to forget the morning when Helen knocked at my door, soaked to the skin and shivering, and said you'd locked her out."

Charlie gripped the sides of the chair. This was more difficult than he expected; he wanted to launch out into a long expostulation and explanation, but he only said: "The night I locked her out—" and she interrupted, "I don't feel up to going over that again."

After a moment's silence Lincoln said: "We're getting off the subject. You want Marion to set aside her legal guardianship and give you Honoria. I think the main point for her is whether she has confidence in you or not."

"I don't blame Marion," Charlie said slowly, "but I think she can have entire confidence in me. I had a good record up to three years ago. Of course, it's within human possibilities I might go wrong any time. But if we wait much longer I'll lose Honoria's childhood and my chance for a home." He shook his head, "I'll simply lose her, don't you see?"

"Yes, I see," said Lincoln.

"Why didn't you think of all this before?" Marion asked.

"I suppose I did, from time to time, but Helen and I were getting along badly. When I consented to the guardianship, I was flat on my back in a sanitarium and the market had cleaned me out. I knew I'd acted badly, and I thought if it would bring any peace to Helen, I'd agree to anything. But now it's different. I'm functioning, I'm behaving damn well, so far as—"

"Please don't swear at me," Marion said.

He looked at her, startled. With each remark the force of her dislike became more and more apparent. She had built up all her fear of life into one wall and faced it toward him. This trivial reproof was possibly the result of some trouble with the cook several hours before. Charlie became increasingly alarmed at leaving Honoria in this atmosphere of hostility against himself; sooner or later it would come out, in a word here, a shake of the head there, and some of that distrust would be irrevocably implanted in Honoria. But he pulled his temper down out of his face and shut it up inside him; he had won a point, for Lincoln realized the absurdity of Marion's remark and asked her lightly since when she had objected to the word "damn."

"Another thing," Charlie said: "I'm able to give her certain advantages now. I'm going to take a French governess to Prague with me. I've got a lease on a new apartment—"

He stopped, realizing that he was blundering. They couldn't be expected to accept with equanimity the fact that his income was again twice as large as their own.

"I suppose you can give her more luxuries than we can," said Marion. "When you were throwing away money we were living along watching every ten francs... I suppose you'll start doing it again."

"Oh, no," he said. "I've learned. I worked hard for ten years, you know—until I got lucky in the market, like so many people. Terribly lucky. It won't happen again."

There was a long silence. All of them felt their nerves straining, and for the first time in a year Charlie wanted a drink. He was sure now that Lincoln Peters wanted him to have his child.

Marion shuddered suddenly; part of her saw that Charlie's feet were planted on the earth now, and her own maternal feeling recognized the naturalness of his desire; but she had lived for a long time with a prejudice—a prejudice founded on a curious disbelief in her sister's happiness, and which, in the shock of one terrible night, had turned to hatred for him. It had all happened at a point in her life where the discouragement of ill-health and adverse circumstances made it necessary for her to believe in tangible villainy and a tangible villain.

"I can't help what I think!" she cried out suddenly. "How much you were responsible for Helen's death, I don't know. It's something you'll have to square with your own conscience."

An electric current of agony surged through him; for a moment he was almost on his feet, an unuttered sound echoing in his throat. He hung on to himself for a moment, another moment.

"Hold on there," said Lincoln uncomfortably. "I never thought you were responsible for that."

"Helen died of heart trouble," Charlie said dully.

"Yes, heart trouble." Marion spoke as if the phrase had another meaning for her.

Then, in the flatness that followed her outburst, she saw him plainly and she knew he had somehow arrived at control over the situation. Glancing at her husband, she found no help from him, and as abruptly as if it were a matter of no importance, she threw up the sponge.

187

"Do what you like!" she cried, springing up from her chair. "She's your child. I'm not the person to stand in your way. I think if it were my child I'd rather see her—" She managed to check herself. "You two decide it. I can't stand this. I'm sick. I'm going to bed."

She hurried from the room; after a moment Lincoln said:

"This has been a hard day for her. You know how strongly she feels—" His voice was almost apologetic: "When a woman gets an idea in her head."

"Of course."

"It's going to be all right. I think she sees now that you—can provide for the child, and so we can't very well stand in your way or Honoria's way."

"Thank you, Lincoln."

"I'd better go along and see how she is."

"I'm going."

He was still trembling when he reached the street, but a walk down the Rue Bonaparte to the *quais* set him up, and as he crossed the Seine, fresh and new by the *quai* lamps, he felt exultant. But back in his room he couldn't sleep. The image of Helen haunted him. Helen whom he had loved so until they had senselessly begun to abuse each other's love, and tear it into shreds. On that terrible February night that Marion remembered so vividly, a slow quarrel that had gone on for hours. There was a scene at the Florida, and then he attempted to take her home, and then she kissed young webb at a table; after that there was what she had hysterically said. When he arrived home alone he turned the key in the lock in wild anger. How could he know she would arrive an hour later alone, that there would be a snowstorm in which she wandered about in slippers, too confused to find a taxi? Then the aftermath, her escaping pneumonia by a miracle, and all the attendant horror. They were "reconciled," but that was the beginning of the end, and Marion, who had seen with her own eyes and who imagined it to be one of many scenes from her sister's martyrdom, never forgot.

Going over it again brought Helen nearer, and in the white, soft light that steals upon half sleep near morning he found himself talking to her again. She said that he was perfectly right about Honoria and that she wanted Honoria to be with him. She said she was glad he was being good and doing better. She said a lot of other things—very friendly things—but she was in a swing in a white dress, and swinging faster and faster all the time, so that at the end he could not hear clearly all that she said.

IV

He woke up feeling happy. The door of the world was open again. He made plans, vistas, futures for Honoria and himself, but suddenly he grew sad, remembering all the plans he and Helen had made. She had not planned to die. The present was the thing—work to do and someone to love. But not to love too much, for he knew the injury that a father can do to a daughter or a mother to a son by attaching them too closely:

afterward, out in the world, the child would seek in the marriage partner the same blind tenderness and, failing probably to find it, turn against love and life.

It was another bright, crisp day. He called Lincoln Peters at the bank where he worked and asked if he could count on taking Honoria when he left for Prague. Lincoln agreed that there was no reason for delay. One thing—the legal guardianship. Marion wanted to retain that a while longer. She was upset by the whole matter, and it would oil things if she felt that the situation was still in her control for another year. Charlie agreed, wanting only the tangible, visible child.

Then the question of a governess. Charlie sat in a gloomy agency and talked to a cross Béarnaise and to a buxom Breton peasant, neither of whom he could have endured. There were others whom he could see tomorrow.

He lunched with Lincoln Peters at the Griffon, trying to keep down his exultation.

"There's nothing quite like your own child," Lincoln said. "But you understand how Marion feels too."

"She's forgotten how hard I worked for seven years there," Charlie said. "She just remembers one night."

"There's another thing." Lincoln hesitated. "While you and Helen were tearing around Europe throwing money away, we were just getting along. I didn't touch any of the prosperity because I never got ahead enough to carry anything but my insurance. I think Marion felt there was some kind of injustice in it—you not even working toward the end, and getting richer and richer."

"It went just as quick as it came," said Charlie.

"Yes, a lot of it stayed in the hands of *chasseurs* and saxophone players and maîtres d'hôtel—well, the big party's over now. I just said that to explain Marion's feeling about those crazy years. If you drop in about six o'clock tonight before Marion's too tired, we'll settle the details on the spot."

Back at his hotel, Charlie found a *pneumatique* that had been redirected from the Ritz bar where Charlie had left his address for the purpose of finding a certain man.

DEAR CHARLIE: You were so strange when we saw you the other day that I wondered if I did something to offend you. If so, I'm not conscious of it. In fact, I have thought about you too much for the last year, and it's always been in the back of my mind that I might see you if I came over here. We *did* have such good times that crazy spring, like the night you and I stole the butcher's tricycle, and the time we tried to call on the president and you had the old derby and the wire cane. Everybody seems so old lately, but I don't feel old a bit. Couldn't we get together some time today for old time's sake? I've got a vile hang-over for the moment, but will be feeling better this afternoon and will look for you about five in the sweet-shop at the Ritz.

Always devotedly,

LORRAINE.

His first feeling was one of awe that he had actually, in his mature years, stolen a tricycle and pedaled Lorraine all over the Étoile between the small hours and dawn. In retrospect it was a nightmare. Locking out Helen didn't fit in with any other act of his life, but the tricycle incident did—it was one of many. How many weeks or months of dissipation to arrive at that condition of utter irresponsibility?

He tried to picture how Lorraine had appeared to him then—very attractive; Helen was unhappy about it, thongh she said nothing. Yesterday, in the restaurant, Lorraine had seemed trite, blurred, worn away. He emphatically did not want to see her, and he was glad Alix had not given away his hotel address. It was a relief to think, instead, of Honoria, to think of Sundays spent with her and of saying good morning to her and of knowing she was there in his house at night, drawing her breath in the darkness.

At five he took a taxi and bought presents for all the Peters—a piquant cloth doll, a box of Roman soldiers, flowers for Marion, big linen handkerchiefs for Lincoln.

He saw, when he arrived in the apartment, that Marion had accepted the inevitable. She greeted him now as though he were a recalcitrant member of the family, rather than a menacing outsider. Honoria had been told she was going; Charlie was glad to see that her tact made her conceal her excessive happiness. Only on his lap did she whisper her delight and the question "When?" before she slipped away with the other children.

He and Marion were alone for a minute in the room, and on an impulse he spoke out boldly:

"Family quarrels are bitter things. They don't go according to my rules. They're not like aches or wounds; they're more like splits in the skin that won't heal because there's not enough material. I wish you and I could be on better terms."

"Some things are hard to forget," she answered. "It's a question of confidence." There was no answer to this and presently she asked, "When do you propose to take her?"

"As soon as I can get a governess. I hoped the day after tomorrow."

"That's impossible. I've got to get her things in shape. Not before Saturday."

He yielded. Coming back into the room, Lincoln offered him a drink.

"I'll take my daily whisky," he said.

It was warm here, it was a home, people together by a fire. The children felt very safe and important; the mother and father were serious, watchful. They had things to do for the children more important than his visit here. A spoonful of medicine was, after all, more important than the strained relations between Marion and himself. They were not dull people, but they were very much in the grip of life and circumstances. He wondered if he couldn't do something to get Lincoln out of his rut at the bank.

A long peal at the doorbell; the *bonne à tout faire* passed through and went down the corridor. The door opened upon another long ring, and then voices, and the three in the salon looked up expectantly; Richard moved to bring the corridor within his range of vision, and Marion rose. Then the maid came along the corridor, closely followed by the voices, which developed under the light into Duncan Schaeffer and Lorraine Quarrles.

They were gay, they were hilarious, they were roaring with laughter. For a moment Charlie was astounded; unable to understand how they ferreted out the peters' address.

"Ah-h-h!" Duncan wagged his finger roguishly at Charlie. "Ah-h-h!"

They both slid down another cascade of laughter. Anxious and at a loss, Charlie shook hands with them quickly and presented them to Lincoln and Marion. Marion nodded, scarcely speaking. She had drawn back a step toward the fire; her little girl stood beside her, and Marion put an arm about her shoulder.

With growing annoyance at the intrusion, Charlie waited for them to explain themselves. After some concentration Duncan said:

"We came to take you out to dinner. Lorraine and I insist that all this shi-shi, cagy business' bout your address got to stop."

Charlie came closer to them, as if to force them backward down the corridor.

"Sorry, but I can't. Tell me where you'll be and we'll call you in half an hour."

This made no impression. Lorraine sat down suddenly on the side of a chair, and focusing her eyes on Richard, cried, "Oh, what a nice little boy! Come here, little boy." Richard glanced at his mother, but did not move. With a perceptible shrug of her shoulders, Lorraine turned back to Charlie:

"Come and dine. Sure your cousins won' mine. See you so sel'om. Or solemn."

"How about a little drink?" said Duncan to the room at large.

"I can't," said Charlie sharply. "You two have dinner and I'll phone you."

Her voice became suddenly unpleasant. "All right, we'll go along. But I remember once when you hammered on my door at four A. M. I was enough of a good sport to give you a drink. Come on, Dunc."

Still in slow motion, with blurred, angry faces, with uncertain feet, they retired along the corridor.

"Good night," Charlie said.

"Good night!" responded Lorraine emphatically.

When he went back into the salon Marion had not moved, only now her son was standing in the circle of her other arm. Lincoln was still swinging Honoria back and forth like a pendulum from side to side.

"What an outrage!" Charlie broke out. "What an absolute outrage!"

Neither of them answered. Charlie dropped into an armchair, picked up his drink, set it down again and said:

"People I haven't seen for two years having the colossal nerve—"

He broke off. Marion had made the sound "Oh!" in one swift, furious breath, turned her body from him with a jerk and left the room.

Lincoln set down Honoria carefully.

"You children go in and start your soup," he said, and when they obeyed, he said to

Charlie:

"Marion's not well and she can't stand shocks. That kind of people make her really physically sick."

"I didn't tell them to come here. They wormed your name out of somebody. They deliberately—"

"Well, it's too bad. It doesn't help matters. Excuse me a minute."

Left alone, Charlie sat tense in his chair. In the next room he could hear the children eating, talking in monosyllables, already oblivious of the scene between their elders. He heard a murmur of conversation from a farther room and then the ticking bell of a telephone receiver picked up, and in a panic he moved to the other side of the room and out of earshot.

In a minute Lincoln came back. "Look here, Charlie. I think we'd better call off dinner for tonight. Marion's in bad shape."

"Is she angry with me?"

"Sort of," he said, almost roughly. "She's not strong and—"

"You mean she's changed her mind about Honoria?"

"She's pretty bitter right now. I don't know. You phone me at the bank tomorrow."

"I wish you'd explain to her I never dreamed these people would come here. I'm just as sore as you are."

"I couldn't explain anything to her now."

Charlie got up. He took his coat and hat and started down the corridor. Then he opened the door of the dining room and said in a strange voice, "Good night, children."

Honoria rose and ran around the table to hug him.

"Good night, sweetheart," he said vaguely, and then trying to make his voice more tender, trying to conciliate something, "Good night, dear children."

V

Charlie went directly to the Ritz bar with the furious idea of finding Lorraine and Duncan, but they were not there, and he realized that in any case there was nothing he could do. He had not touched his drink at the Peters', and now he ordered a whisky-and-soda. Paul came over to say hello.

"It's a great change," he said sadly. "We do about half the business we did. So many fellows I hear about back in the States lost everything, maybe not in the first crash, but then in the second. Your friend George Hardt lost every cent, I hear. Are you back in the States?"

"No, I'm in business in Prague."

"I heard that you lost a lot in the crash."

"I did," and he added grimly, "but I lost everything I wanted in the boom."

"Selling short."

"Something like that."

Again the memory of those days swept over him like a nightmare—the people they had met traveling; then people who couldn't add a row of figures or speak a coherent sentence. The little man Helen had consented to dance with at the ship's party, who had insulted her ten feet from the table; the women and girls carried something with drink or drugs out of public places.

The men who locked their wives out in the snow, because the snow of twenty-nine wasn't real snow. If you didn't want it to be snow, you just paid some money.

He went to the phone and called the Peters' apartment; Lincoln answered.

"I called up because this thing is on my mind. Has Marion said anything definite?"

"Marion's sick," Lincoln answered shortly. "I know this thing isn't altogether your fault, but I can't have her go to pieces about it. I'm afraid we'll have to let it slide for six months; I can't take the chance of working her up to this state again."

"I see."

"I'm sorry, Charlie."

He went back to his table. His whisky glass was empty, but he shook his head when Alix looked at it questioningly. There wasn't much he could do now except send Honoria some things; he would send her a lot of things tomorrow. He thought rather angrily that that was just money—he had given so many people money...

"No, no more," he said to another waiter. "What do I owe you?"

He would come back some day; they couldn't make him pay forever. But he wanted his child, and nothing was much good now, beside that fact. He wasn't young any more, with a lot of nice thoughts and dreams to have by himself. He was absolutely sure Helen wouldn't have wanted him to be so alone.

Plot Summary

"Babylon Revisited" is a short story by F. Scott Fitzgerald. It tells the story of Charlie Wales, a former playboy who is trying to regain custody of his daughter, Honoria, from his sister-in-law, Marion. At the beginning of the story, Charlie has returned to Paris, the city of his former wild lifestyle, to try to prove to Marion that he has changed and is now a responsible father. However, Marion is still skeptical of Charlie's reformation, as she cannot forget the night Charlie locked Helen, his wife, out in the snow, leading to her illness and eventual death. Meanwhile, Marion's husband, Lincoln, is more sympathetic to Charlie and tends to agree that Charlie take Honoria for a trial period. Charlie takes Honoria to Le Grand Vatel for lunch, the only restaurant he can think of that doesn't remind him of the decadence of the old days. While at lunch, Charlie runs into Duncan Schaeffer and Lorraine Quarrles, two of his old acquaintances whom he considers "sudden ghosts out of the past" and is now unwilling to deal with. Charlie feels deeply moved and delighted, as Honoria says she wants to move to Prague and live with him. When Charlie arrives at the Peters' later that evening, during a tense confrontation with Marion, he is desperate to convince her that he has abandoned his decadent ways, has given up drinking excessively, and is capable of providing a good life for his daughter. At the end of the story, Marion agrees to transfer custody of Honoria with a certain reluctance, swayed by Charlie's pleading and apparent stability, as well as her husband Lincoln's opinions. However, just when things are getting better for Charlie, Duncan and Lorraine arrive at the Peters' self-invitedly and drunkenly, asking Charlie to come to dinner with them. Although he declines their invitation, sends them out, and tries to smooth things over, the intrusion, which reminds Marion about Charlie's past mistakes, has disturbed Marion so thoroughly that she changes her mind about allowing Charlie to take Honoria back to Prague with him. Based on the historical background of the economic boom of the United States in the 1920s and the Great Depression that followed, "Babylon Revisited" tells a story of self-redemption, how the haunting past affects the present, and how the extravagant life corrupts people.

Language Exercises

Choose the item that best replaces or explains the underlined part of the sentence.

1. He felt the stillness from the moment he got out of the taxi and saw the doorman, usually in a _frenzy_ of activity at this hour, gossiping with a *chasseur* by the servants' entrance.
   A. a state of intense excitement or confusion   B. a feeling of deep nostalgia
   C. a tendency to resist authority   D. a trigger for strong emotions

2. His boasting was for a specific purpose; but after a moment, seeing a faint _restiveness_ in Lincoln's eye, he changed the subject...
   A. eagerness and enthusiasm   B. tension and resistance
   C. calmness and composure   D. indifference and apathy

3. At noon he sat opposite Honoria at Le Grand Vatel, the only restaurant he could think of not _reminiscent_ of champagne dinners and long luncheons that began at two and ended in a blurred and vague twilight.
   A. dissimilar   B. infinitive   C. stagnant   D. evocative

4. When there had been her mother and a French nurse he had been inclined to be strict; now he extended himself, reached out for a new _tolerance_; he must be both parents to her and not shut any of her out of communication.
   A. respect   B. patience   C. appreciation D. leniency

5. As always, he felt Lorraine's passionate, _provocative_ attraction, but his own rhythm was different now.
   A. soothing   B. pacifying   C. rippling   D. stimulating

6. It would last an hour or two hours, and it would be difficult, but if he _modulated_

his inevitable resentment to the chastened attitude of the reformed sinner, he might win his point in the end.

A. controlled and adjusted   B. increased and amplified

C. ignored and dismissed   D. expressed and vocalized

7. This was more difficult than he expected; he wanted to launch out into a long expostulation and explanation, but he only said: ...

A. silence and reservation   B. agreement and compliance

C. clarification and elaboration   D. disagreement and argument

8. He looked at her, startled. With each remark the force of her dislike became more and more apparent.

A. exotic   B. weird   C. absurd   D. obvious

9. They couldn't be expected to accept with equanimity the fact that his income was again twice as large as their own.

A. happiness   B. calmness   C. uneasiness   D. hostility

10. It had all happened at a point in her life where the discouragement of ill-health and adverse circumstances made it necessary for her to believe in tangible villainy and a tangible villain.

A. concrete   B. solid   C. real   D. visible

11. He was still trembling when he reached the street, but a walk down the Rue Bonaparte to the *quais* set him up, and as he crossed the Seine, fresh and new by the *quai* lamps, he felt exultant.

A. disappointed   B. joyful   C. indifferent   D. anxious

12. They were "reconciled," but that was the beginning of the end, and Marion, who had seen with her own eyes and who imagined it to be one of many scenes from her sister's martyrdom, never forgot.

A. consolation   B. indifference   C. affliction   D. indignation

13. He emphatically did not want to see her, and he was glad Alix had not given away his hotel address.

A. confidently   B. clearly   C. resolutely   D. reluctantly

14. She greeted him now as though he were a recalcitrant member of the family, rather than a menacing outsider.

A. friendly   B. threatening   C. cynical   D. hopeful

15. They were gay, they were hilarious, they were roaring with laughter.

A. serious   B. ridiculous   C. solemn   D. amusing

Topics for Discussion

1. Analyze the title "Babylon Revisited" and its connection to the story's themes and characters.

2. Discuss the main character, Charlie Wales, and his struggle with the past. How does he attempt to redeem himself?

3. Examine the role of Paris as a setting and its significance in the context of Charlie's past and present circumstances.

4. How does Fitzgerald depict the theme of wealth and its corrupting influence on characters in the story?

5. Discuss the portrayal of gender dynamics in "Babylon Revisited". How do female characters like Helen and Marion impact the story?

6. How does Fitzgerald use the motif of weather to enhance the story's atmosphere and reflect the internal conflicts of the characters?

7. How does Fitzgerald depict the Jazz Age and its aftermath in "Babylon Revisited"?

8. Analyze the character of Duncan Schaeffer and his significance in the story's plot and themes.

9. Discuss Fitzgerald's use of flashback and its impact on the narrative structure of "Babylon Revisited".

10. How does the story's ending contribute to its overall message and themes?

Discussion Tips

"Babylon Revisited" follows the journey of a recovering alcoholic who returns to Paris during the Depression in an attempt to regain custody of his daughter, portraying a man striving to rebuild his life after making regrettable choices in the aftermath of his wealth accumulation during the 1920s stock market boom. In the story, the protagonist, Charlie, grapples with the aftermath of his wife's passing, financial ruin in the 1929 stock market crash, and his own battle with alcoholism as he seeks to regain custody of his daughter. A central theme of the narrative revolves around Charlie's struggle to convince both himself and others that he has left behind the dissolute lifestyle he led prior to the crash. Through nuanced details, Fitzgerald depicts Charlie's substantial reformation while subtly hinting that his challenges may not be entirely resolved. Throughout the story, Charlie is confronted with temptations that threaten to lure him back to the irresponsible behavior of his past, which he must overcome to demonstrate his genuine understanding that personal integrity is an enduring and invaluable trait. His internal conflict is palpable as he grapples with guilt over his wife's death, the loss of custody of his daughter, and the squandering of his earlier successes in alcohol-fueled dissipation. In his pursuit to regain custody of his daughter, Charlie must convince his now-guardian sister-in-law that he has acknowledged his guilt and embraced a new way of life. Despite admitting his past transgressions, he expresses hope that his sobriety is enduring, while acknowledging the potential for future mistakes. However, his sister-in-law, Marion, interprets his words as confirmation of her suspicions about his character, refusing to perceive them as sincere reflections of self-awareness.

The story intertwines themes of change, transformation, guilt, and innocence, underscoring Charlie's profound capacity to self-punish and experience guilt, which is mirrored by Marion's own sentiments. Fitzgerald also introduces the theme of money, wealth, and envy, adding complexity to Charlie's sense of guilt. Not only does Charlie grapple with guilt over his wife's demise, his alcoholism, and the loss of custody, but he also wrestles with remorse over his financial prosperity during the prosperous years preceding the stock market crash. In "Babylon Revisited", money is depicted as a corrosive force, with virtually all characters preoccupied with it. However, Charlie comes to realize that when it comes to matters of the heart, money holds no value. This multifaceted exploration of guilt, wealth, and personal transformation underscores the depth and complexity of Fitzgerald's narrative, leaving readers to ponder the enduring themes long after the story's conclusion.

Unit 10
Saul Bellow: "Looking for Mr. Green"

Saul Bellow (1915–2005)

Saul Bellow is a renowned Canadian-American writer who is considered one of the twentieth century's most significant literary figures. He was born on June 10, 1915, in Lachine, Quebec, Canada, and died on April 5, 2005, in Brookline, Massachusetts, United States. Throughout his career, Bellow won numerous awards, including the Pulitzer Prize, the National Book Award, and the Nobel Prize in Literature. Bellow's parents were Jewish immigrants from Russia who moved to Canada before he was born. His family settled in Chicago after he was four years old, and Bellow spent most of his childhood in the city's Humboldt Park neighborhood. Bellow attended the University of Chicago, where he earned a bachelor's degree in anthropology and sociology. He then continued his education at Northwestern University, where he earned a Master of Arts degree in anthropology. Bellow's first novel, *Dangling Man*, was published in 1943, and since then, he wrote several other novels, including *The Adventures of Augie March* (1953), *Herzog* (1964), *Humboldt's Gift* (1975), and *The Dean's December* (1982). Bellow's works are known for their introspection, existentialism, and focus on identity and the individual's search for meaning. His writing often explores the relationship between intellect and emotion, as well as the complexities of human experience. While Bellow's early works were heavily influenced by the literary modernists, such as James Joyce and Virginia Woolf, his later works showcased a departure from modernism and a keen interest in realism. His recognition as a literary icon came from his novel, *Herzog*, which garnered him the Pulitzer Prize and National Book Award in 1964. In addition to writing novels, Bellow also wrote essays and reviews, and his work appeared in prominent publications such as *The New York Times* and *The New Yorker*. His non-fiction work includes *To Jerusalem and Back* (1976), in which he chronicles his journey to Jerusalem and his search for spiritual enlightenment, and *It All Adds Up: From the Dim Past to the Uncertain Future* (1994), a collection of essays on topics such as philosophy, politics, and aging. Overall, Saul Bellow is a literary giant whose contributions to modern literature cannot be understated. His unique style and themes of identity, the search for meaning, and the complexities of human experience made him a prominent figure in the literary world. Even today, his works remain influential and continue to inspire writers and readers alike, cementing his status as one of the most important writers of the twentieth century.

The Literary History

Saul Bellow and the American Short Story

Saul Bellow was a renowned American writer who won the Nobel Prize in Literature in 1976. Born in 1915 in Canada, Bellow moved to the United States at an early age and studied at Northwestern University in Chicago. Throughout his career as a writer, Bellow explored the struggles and experiences of urban life in America, often using humor and satire to illuminate the complexities of modern society. He is considered one of the most important writers of the mid-twentieth century, and his influence on American literature is still widely felt today.

Bellow's work is particularly significant within the context of the American short story, a genre that developed in the early nineteenth century and flourished in the post-World War II period. Within this genre, Bellow's stories stand out for their vivid portrayal of contemporary life in America, particularly in the fast-paced, vibrant urban centers of cities like New York and Chicago. His stories explore the experiences of ordinary people, from struggling artists and intellectuals to working-class immigrants and businessmen, and often delve into larger issues of identity, morality, and the human condition. In many cases, Bellow's stories reflect the social and cultural changes taking place in America in the mid-20th century, from the rise of consumer culture to the shifting roles of gender and ethnicity in society.

One of Bellow's most famous short stories is "A Silver Dish", which was first published in Partisan Review in 1948. The story tells the tale of an aging Jewish deli owner in Chicago, and his relationship with his son, a would-be poet struggling to find his place in the world. The story grapples with themes of family, tradition, and cultural identity, as well as the tension between artistic ambition and practical concerns. With its vivid characters and complex narrative structure, "A Silver Dish" is a poignant example of Bellow's ability to use the short story form to explore a wide range of human experiences and emotions.

Another notable story by Bellow is "The Old System", which was first published in The New Yorker in 1957. The story focuses on the relationship between a wealthy businessman and his former secretary, who has fallen on hard times and come to him for help. The story explores issues of class, power, and social hierarchy in mid-century America, as well as the ethical responsibilities of those who hold positions of wealth and authority. Like many of Bellow's stories, "The Old System" is notable for its complex and nuanced portrayal of human relationships and the moral dilemmas that arise from them.

Saul Bellow's contributions to the American short story are significant and enduring. His stories continue to offer insight into the complexities of modern life in America, and provide a rich portrait of the social, cultural, and emotional issues that define our shared human experience. Through his unique voice and perspective, Bellow helped to shape the American literary landscape in the mid-20th century, and his legacy continues to influence writers and readers today.

Literary Terms

Satire

Satire is a literary technique that employs humor, irony, ridicule, or exaggeration to criticize and mock societal norms, human behavior, institutions, or political figures. Through the use of satire, writers often aim to provoke thought, challenge prevailing attitudes, and highlight the absurdities or flaws within a particular aspect of society. Satirical works often employ wit and sarcasm to expose hypocrisy, social injustices, or moral shortcomings, using humor as a tool for social commentary and critique. Satire can take various forms, including written works, plays, or visual art, and is characterized by its subversive and critical nature. This literary technique allows authors to engage with serious subjects in a lighthearted and entertaining manner, inviting readers to reflect on the underlying issues being satirized.

Existentialism

Existentialism is a philosophical and literary movement that emphasizes the individual's experience of existence, freedom, and the search for meaning in an apparently indifferent or absurd world. In literature, existentialist themes often revolve around questions of human existence, personal responsibility, and the struggle to find purpose in a universe that may seem devoid of inherent meaning. Existentialist works frequently explore the complexities of human emotions, the individual's confrontation with mortality, and the challenges of navigating an uncertain and often chaotic reality. Characters in existentialist literature often grapple with feelings of alienation, anxiety, and the quest for authenticity, reflecting the movement's focus on the individual's subjective experience and the exploration of profound philosophical inquiries.

Urban Realism

Urban Realism is a literary movement that portrays the everyday lives, experiences, and social dynamics of urban environments with a focus on authenticity and detail. Works of urban realism often capture the bustling energy, diversity, and complexities of city life, offering vivid depictions of urban landscapes, neighborhoods, and the diverse array of characters that inhabit them. This literary approach seeks to provide a realistic and unvarnished portrayal of urban settings, addressing the challenges, opportunities, and social issues that arise within metropolitan areas. Urban realism often delves into the interactions between individuals from different backgrounds, the impact of urbanization on communities, and the portrayal of cityscapes as dynamic and multifaceted spaces. Through urban realism, authors aim to convey the richness and complexity of urban life, offering readers an immersive and authentic portrayal of the urban experience.

Psychological Realism

Psychological Realism is a literary approach that emphasizes the detailed and nuanced depiction of characters' inner thoughts, emotions, and motivations. Works of psychological realism delve into the complexities of human psychology, offering deep insights into the inner lives of characters and their subjective experiences. This literary technique often explores the intricacies of human relationships, the impact of personal histories on behavior, and the psychological dynamics at play within individuals and within interpersonal interactions. Psychological realist works often prioritize the portrayal of authentic and relatable human experiences, emphasizing the internal conflicts, desires, and emotional landscapes of the characters. Through psychological realism, authors seek to create multi-dimensional and psychologically rich portrayals of their characters, inviting readers to empathize with and understand the complexities of the human psyche.

The Story

Looking for Mr. Green[1]

Whatsoever thy hand findeth to do, do it with thy might....

Hard work? No, it wasn't really so hard. He wasn't used to walking and stair-climbing, but the physical difficulty of his new job was not what George Grebe felt most. He was delivering relief checks in the Negro district, and although he was a native Chicagoan this was not a part of the city he knew much about—it needed a depression to introduce him to it. No, it wasn't literally hard work, not as reckoned in foot-pounds, but yet he was beginning to feel the strain of it, to grow aware of its peculiar difficulty. He could find the streets and numbers, but the clients were not where they were supposed to be, and he felt like a hunter inexperienced in the camouflage

---

1   Saul Bellow, *Him with His Foot in His Mouth and Other Stories* (Penguin Classics, 2004), pp. 3–26.

of his game. It was an unfavorable day, too—fall, and cold, dark weather, windy. But, anyway, instead of shells in his deep trench-coat pocket he had the cardboard of checks, punctured for the spindles of the file, the holes reminding him of the holes in player-piano paper. And he didn't look much like a hunter, either; his was a city figure entirely, belted up in this Irish conspirator's coat. He was slender without being tall, stiff in the back, his legs looking shabby in a pair of old tweed pants gone through and fringy at the cuffs. With this stiffness, he kept his head forward, so that his face was red from the sharpness of the weather; and it was an indoors sort of face with gray eyes that persisted in some kind of thought and yet seemed to avoid definiteness or conclusion. He wore sideburns that surprised you somewhat by the tough curl of the blond hair and the effect of assertion in their length. He was not so mild as he looked, nor so youthful; and nevertheless there was no effort on his part to seem what he was not. He was an educated man; he was a bachelor; he was in some ways simple; without lushing, he liked a drink; his luck had not been good. Nothing was deliberately hidden.

He felt that his luck was better than usual today. When he had reported for work that morning he had expected to be shut up in the relief office at a clerk's job, for he had been hired downtown as a clerk, and he was glad to have, instead, the freedom of the streets and welcomed, at least at first, the vigor of the cold and even the blowing of the hard wind. But on the other hand he was not getting on with the distribution of the checks. It was true that it was a city job; nobody expected you to push too hard at a city job. His supervisor, that young Mr. Raynor, had practically told him that. Still, he wanted to do well at it. For one thing, when he knew how quickly he could deliver a batch of checks, he would know also how much time he could expect to clip for himself. And then, too, the clients would be waiting for their money. That was not the most important consideration, though it certainly mattered to him. No, but he wanted to do well, simply for doing-well's sake, to acquit himself decently of a job because he so rarely had a job to do that required just this sort of energy. Of this peculiar energy he now had a superabundance; once it had started to flow, it flowed all too heavily. And, for the time being anyway, he was balked. He could not find Mr. Green.

So he stood in his big-skirted trench coat with a large envelope in his hand and papers showing from his pocket, wondering why people should be so hard to locate who were too feeble or sick to come to the station to collect their own checks. But Raynor had told him that tracking them down was not easy at first and had offered him some advice on how to proceed. "If you can see the postman, he's your first man to ask, and your best bet. If you can't connect with him, try the stores and tradespeople around. Then the janitor and the neighbors. But you'll find the closer you come to your man the less people will tell you. They don't want to tell you anything."

"Because I'm a stranger."

"Because you're white. We ought to have a Negro doing this, but we don't at the moment, and of course you've got to eat, too, and this is public employment. Jobs have to be made. Oh, that holds for me too. Mind you, I'm not letting myself out. I've got three years of seniority on you, that's all. And a law degree. Otherwise, you might be back of the desk and I might be going out into the field this cold day. The same dough pays us both and for the same, exact, identical reason. What's my law degree got to do with it? But you have to pass out these checks, Mr. Grebe, and it'll help if you're stubborn, so I hope you are."

"Yes, I'm fairly stubborn."

Raynor sketched hard with an eraser in the old dirt of his desk, left-handed, and said, "Sure, what else can you answer to such a question. Anyhow, the trouble you're going to have is that they don't like to give information about anybody. They think you're a plainclothes dick or an installment collector, or summons-server or something like that. Till you've been seen around the neighborhood for a few months and people know you're only from the relief."

It was dark, ground-freezing, pre-Thanksgiving weather; the wind played hob with the smoke, rushing it down, and Grebe missed his gloves, which he had left in Raynor's office. And no one would admit knowing Green. It was past three o'clock and the postman had made his last delivery. The nearest grocer, himself a Negro, had never heard the name Tulliver Green, or said he hadn't. Grebe was inclined to think that it was true, that he had in the end convinced the man that he wanted only to deliver a check. But he wasn't sure. He needed experience in interpreting looks and signs and, even more, the will not to be put off or denied and even the force to bully if need be. If the grocer did know, he had got rid of him easily. But since most of his trade was with reliefers, why should he prevent the delivery of a check? Maybe Green, or Mrs. Green, if there was a Mrs. Green, patronized another grocer. And was there a Mrs. Green? It was one of Grebe's great handicaps that he hadn't looked at any of the case records. Raynor should have let him read files for a few hours. But he apparently saw no need for that, probably considering the job unimportant. Why prepare systematically to deliver a few checks?

But now it was time to look for the janitor. Grebe took in the building in the wind and gloom of the late November day—trampled, frost-hardened lots on one side; on the other, an automobile junk yard and then the infinite work of Elevated frames, weak-looking, gaping with rubbish fires; two sets of leaning brick porches three stories high and a flight of cement stairs to the cellar. Descending, he entered the underground passage, where he tried the doors until one opened and he found himself in the furnace room. There someone rose toward him and approached, scraping on the coal grit and bending under the canvas-jacketed pipes.

"Are you the janitor?"

"What do you want?"

"I'm looking for a man who's supposed to be living here. Green."

"What Green?"

"Oh, you maybe have more than one Green?" said Grebe with new, pleasant hope. "This is Tulliver Green."

"I don't think I c'n help you, mister. I don't know any."

"A crippled man."

The janitor stood bent before him. Could it be that he was crippled? Oh, God! what if he was. Grebe's gray eyes sought with excited difficulty to see. But no, he was only very short and stooped. A head awakened from meditation, a strong-haired beard, low, wide shoulders. A staleness of sweat and coal rose from his black shirt and the burlap sack he wore as an apron.

"Crippled how?"

Grebe thought and then answered with the light voice of unmixed candor, "I don't know. I've never seen him." This was damaging, but his only other choice was to make a lying guess, and he was not up to it. "I'm delivering checks for the relief to shut-in cases. If he weren't crippled he'd come to collect himself. That's why I said crippled. Bedridden, chair-ridden—is there anybody like that?"

This sort of frankness was one of Grebe's oldest talents, going back to childhood. But it gained him nothing here.

"No suh. I've got four buildin's same as this that I take care of. I don' know all the tenants, leave alone the tenants' tenants. The rooms turn over so fast, people movin' in and out every day. I can't tell you."

The janitor opened his grimy lips, but Grebe did not hear him in the piping of the valves and the consuming pull of air to flame in the body of the furnace. He knew, however, what he had said.

"Well, all the same, thanks. Sorry I bothered you. I'll prowl around upstairs again and see if I can turn up someone who knows him."

Once more in the cold air and early darkness he made the short circle from the cellarway to the entrance crowded between the brickwork pillars and began to climb to the third floor. Pieces of plaster ground under his feet; strips of brass tape from which the carpeting had been torn away marked old boundaries at the sides. In the passage, the cold reached him worse than in the street; it touched him to the bone. The hall toilets ran like springs. He thought grimly as he heard the wind burning around the building with a sound like that of the furnace, that this was a great piece of constructed shelter. Then he struck a match in the gloom and searched for names and numbers among the writings and scribbles on the walls. He saw WHOODY-DOODY GO TO JESUS, and zigzags, caricatures, sexual scrawls, and curses. So the sealed rooms of pyramids were also decorated, and the caves of human dawn.

The information on his card was, TULLIVER GREEN—APT 3D. There were no names, however, and no numbers. His shoulders drawn up, tears of cold in his eyes, breathing vapor, he went the length of the corridor and told himself that if he had been lucky enough to have the temperament for it he would bang on one of the doors and bawl out "Tulliver Green!" until he got results. But it wasn't in him to make an uproar and he continued to burn matches, passing the light over the walls. At the rear, in a corner off the hall, he discovered a door he had not seen before and he thought it best to investigate. It sounded empty when he knocked, but a young Negress answered, hardly more than a girl. She opened only a bit, to guard the warmth of the room.

"Yes suh?"

"I'm from the district relief station on Prairie Avenue. I'm looking for a man named Tulliver Green to give him his check. Do you know him?"

No, she didn't; but he thought she had not understood anything of what he had said. She had a dream-bound, dream-blind face, very soft and black, shut off. She wore a man's jacket and pulled the ends together at her throat. Her hair was parted in three directions, at the sides and transversely, standing up at the front in a dull puff.

"Is there somebody around here who might know?"

"I jus' taken this room las' week."

He observed that she shivered, but even her shiver was somnambulistic and there was no sharp consciousness of cold in the big smooth eyes of her handsome face.

"All right, miss, thank you. Thanks," he said, and went to try another place. Here he was admitted. He was grateful, for the room was warm. It was full of people, and they were silent as he entered—ten people, or a dozen, perhaps more, sitting on benches like a parliament. There was no light, properly speaking, but a tempered darkness that the window gave, and everyone seemed to him enormous, the men padded out in heavy work clothes and winter coats, and the women huge, too, in their sweaters, hats, and old furs. And, besides, bed and bedding, a black cooking range, a piano piled towering to the ceiling with papers, a dining-room table of the old style of prosperous Chicago. Among these people Grebe, with his cold-heightened fresh color and his smaller stature, entered like a schoolboy. Even though he was met with smiles and goodwill, he knew, before a single word was spoken, that all the currents ran against him and that he would make no headway. Nevertheless he began. "Does anybody here know how I can deliver a check to Mr. Tulliver Green?"

"Green?" It was the man that had let him in who answered. He was in short sleeves, in a checkered shirt, and had a queer, high head, profusely overgrown and long as a shako; the veins entered it strongly from his forehead. "I never heard mention of him. Is this where he live?"

"This is the address they gave me at the station. He's a sick man, and he'll need his check. Can't anybody tell me where to find him?"

He stood his ground and waited for a reply, his crimson wool scarf wound about his neck and drooping outside his trench coat, pockets weighted with the block of checks and official forms. They must have realized that he was not a college boy employed afternoons by a bill collector, trying foxily to pass for a relief clerk, recognized that he was an older man who knew himself what need was, who had had more than an average seasoning in hardship. It was evident enough if you looked at the marks under his eyes and at the sides of his mouth. "Anybody know this sick man?"

"No suh." On all sides he saw heads shaken and smiles of denial. No one knew. And maybe it was true, he considered, standing silent in the earthen, musky human gloom of the place as the rumble continued. But he could never really be sure.

"What's the matter with this man?" said shako-head.

"I've never seen him. All I can tell you is that he can't come in person for his money. It's my first day in this district."

"Maybe they given you the wrong number?"

"I don't believe so. But where else can I ask about him?" He felt that this persistence amused them deeply, and in a way he shared their amusement that he should stand up so tenaciously to them. Though smaller, though slight, he was his own man, he retracted nothing about himself, and he looked back at them, gray-eyed, with amusement and also with a sort of courage. On the bench some man spoke in his throat, the words impossible to catch, and a woman answered with a wild, shrieking laugh, which was quickly cut off.

"Well, so nobody will tell me?"

"Ain't nobody who knows."

"At least, if he lives here, he pays rent to someone. Who manages the building?"

"Greatham Company. That's on Thirty-ninth Street."

Grebe wrote it in his pad. But, in the street again, a sheet of wind-driven paper clinging to his leg while he deliberated what direction to take next, it seemed a feeble lead to follow. Probably this Green didn't rent a flat, but a room. Sometimes there were as many as twenty people in an apartment; the real estate agent would know only the lessee. And not even the agent could tell you who the renters were. In some places the beds were even used in shifts, watchmen or jitney drivers or short-order cooks in night joints turning out after a day's sleep and surrendering their beds to a sister, a nephew, or perhaps a stranger, just off the bus. There were large numbers of newcomers in this terrific, blight-bitten portion of the city between Cottage Grove and Ashland, wandering from house to house and room to room. When you saw them, how could you know them? They didn't carry bundles on their backs or look picturesque. You only saw a man, a Negro, walking in the street or riding in the car, like everyone else, with his thumb closed on a transfer. And therefore how were you supposed to tell? Grebe thought the Greatham agent would only laugh at his question.

But how much it would have simplified the job to be able to say that Green was old, or blind, or consumptive. An hour in the files, taking a few notes, and he needn't have been at such a disadvantage. When Raynor gave him the block of checks Grebe asked, "How much should I know about these people?" Then Raynor had looked as though Grebe were preparing to accuse him of trying to make the job more important than it was. Grebe smiled, because by then they were on fine terms, but nevertheless he had

206

been getting ready to say something like that when the confusion began in the station over Staika and her children.

Grebe had waited a long time for this job. It came to him through the pull of an old schoolmate in the Corporation Counsel's office, never a close friend, but suddenly sympathetic and interested—pleased to show, moreover, how well he had done, how strongly he was coming on even in these miserable times. Well, he was coming through strongly, along with the Democratic administration itself. Grebe had gone to see him in City Hall, and they had had a counter lunch or beers at least once a month for a year, and finally it had been possible to swing the job. He didn't mind being assigned the lowest clerical grade, nor even being a messenger, though Raynor thought he did.

This Raynor was an original sort of guy and Grebe had taken to him immediately. As was proper on the first day, Grebe had come early, but he waited long, for Raynor was late. At last he darted into his cubicle of an office as though he had just jumped from one of those hurtling huge red Indian Avenue cars. His thin, rough face was wind-stung and he was grinning and saying something breathlessly to himself. In his hat, a small fedora, and his coat, the velvet collar a neat fit about his neck, and his silk muffler that set off the nervous twist of his chin, he swayed and turned himself in his swivel chair, feet leaving the ground, so that he pranced a little as he sat. Meanwhile he took Grebe's measure out of his eyes, eyes of an unusual vertical length and slightly sardonic. So the two men sat for a while, saying nothing, while the supervisor raised his hat from his miscombed hair and put it in his lap. His cold-darkened hands were not clean. A steel beam passed through the little makeshift room, from which machine belts once had hung. The building was an old factory.

"I'm younger than you; I hope you won't find it hard taking orders from me," said Raynor. "But I don't make them up, either. You're how old, about?"

"Thirty-five."

"And you thought you'd be inside doing paperwork. But it so happens I have to send you out."

"I don't mind."

"And it's mostly a Negro load we have in this district."

"So I thought it would be."

"Fine. You'll get along. *C'est un bon boulot.* Do you know French?"

"Some."

"I thought you'd be a university man."

"Have you been in France?" said Grebe.

"No, that's the French of the Berlitz School. I've been at it for more than a year, just as I'm sure people have been, all over the world, office boys in China and braves in Tanganyika. In fact, I damn well know it. Such is the attractive power of civilization. It's overrated, but what do you want? *Que voulez-vous?* I get *Le Rire* and all the spicy papers, just like in Tanganyika. It must be mystifying, out there. But my reason is that

I'm aiming at the diplomatic service. I have a cousin who's a courier, and the way he describes it is awfully attractive. He rides in the *wagon-lits* and reads books. While we—What did you do before?"

"I sold."

"Where?"

"Canned meat at Stop and Shop. In the basement."

"And before that?"

"Window shades, at Goldblatt's."

"Steady work?"

"No, Thursdays and Saturdays. I also sold shoes."

"You've been a shoe-dog too. Well. And prior to that? Here it is in your folder." He opened the record. "Saint Olafs College, instructor in classical languages. Fellow, University of Chicago, 1926–27. I've had Latin, too. Let's trade quotations—'*Dum spiro spew*.'"

" '*De dextram misero.*' "

" '*Alea jacta est.*' "

" '*Excelsior.*' "

Raynor shouted with laughter, and other workers came to look at him over the partition. Grebe also laughed, feeling pleased and easy. The luxury of fun on a nervous morning.

When they were done and no one was watching or listening, Raynor said rather seriously, "What made you study Latin in the first place? Was it for the priesthood?"

"No."

"Just for the hell of it? For the culture? Oh, the things people think they can pull!" He made his cry hilarious and tragic. "I ran my pants off so I could study for the bar, and I've passed the bar, so I get twelve dollars a week more than you as a bonus for having seen life straight and whole. I'll tell you, as a man of culture, that even though nothing looks to be real, and everything stands for something else, and that thing for another thing, and that thing for a still further one—there ain't any comparison between twenty-five and thirty-seven dollars a week, regardless of the last reality. Don't you think that was clear to your Greeks? They were a thoughtful people, but they didn't part with their slaves."

This was a great deal more than Grebe had looked for in his first interview with his supervisor. He was too shy to show all the astonishment he felt. He laughed a little, aroused, and brushed at the sunbeam that covered his head with its dust. "Do you think my mistake was so terrible?"

"Damn right it was terrible, and you know it now that you've had the whip of hard times laid on your back. You should have been preparing yourself for trouble. Your people must have been well-off to send you to the university. Stop me, if I'm stepping on your toes. Did your mother pamper you? Did your father give in to you? Were you brought up tenderly, with permission to go and find out what were the last things that everything else stands for while everybody else labored in the fallen world of appearances?"

"Well, no, it wasn't exactly like that." Grebe smiled. *The fallen world of appearances!* no less. But now it was his turn to deliver a surprise. "We weren't rich. My father was the last genuine English butler in Chicago—"

"Are you kidding?"

"Why should I be?"

"In a livery?"

"In livery. Up on the Gold Coast."

"And he wanted you to be educated like a gentleman?"

"He did not. He sent me to the Armour Institute to study chemical engineering. But when he died I changed schools."

He stopped himself, and considered how quickly Raynor had reached him. In no time he had your valise on the table and all your stuff unpacked. And afterward, in the streets, he was still reviewing how far he might have gone, and how much he might have been led to tell if they had not been interrupted by Mrs. Staika's great noise.

But just then a young woman, one of Raynor's workers, ran into the cubicle exclaiming, "Haven't you heard all the fuss?"

"We haven't heard anything."

"It's Staika, giving out with all her might. The reporters are coming. She said she phoned the papers, and you know she did."

"But what is she up to?" said Raynor.

"She brought her wash and she's ironing it here, with our current, because the relief won't pay her electric bill. She has her ironing board set up by the admitting desk, and her kids are with her, all six. They never are in school more than once a week. She's always dragging them around with her because of her reputation."

"I don't want to miss any of this," said Raynor, jumping up. Grebe, as he followed with the secretary, said, "Who is this Staika?"

"They call her the 'Blood Mother of Federal Street.' She's a professional donor at the hospitals. I think they pay ten dollars a pint. Of course it's no joke, but she makes a very big thing out of it and she and the kids are in the papers all the time."

A small crowd, staff and clients divided by a plywood barrier, stood in the narrow space of the entrance, and Staika was shouting in a gruff, mannish voice, plunging the iron on the board and slamming it on the metal rest.

"My father and mother came in a steerage, and I was born in our house, Robey by Huron. I'm no dirty immigrant. I'm a U. S. citizen. My husband is a gassed veteran from France with lungs weaker'n paper, that hardly can he go to the toilet by himself. These six children of mine, I have to buy the shoes for their feet with my own blood. Even a lousy little white Communion necktie, that's a couple of drops of blood; a little piece of mosquito veil for my Vadja so she won't be ashamed in church for the other girls, they take my blood for it by Goldblatt. That's how I keep goin'. A fine thing if I had to depend on the relief. And there's plenty of people on the rolls—fakes! There's nothin' *they* can't get, that can go and wrap bacon at Swift and Armour anytime. They're lookin' for them by the Yards. They never have to be out of work. Only they rather lay in their lousy beds and eat the public's money." She was not afraid, in a predominantly Negro station, to shout this way about Negroes.

Grebe and Raynor worked themselves forward to get a closer view of the woman. She was flaming with anger and with pleasure at herself, broad and huge, a golden-headed woman who wore a cotton cap laced with pink ribbon. She was barelegged and had on black gym shoes, her Hoover apron was open and her great breasts, not much restrained by a man's undershirt, hampered her arms as she worked at the kid's dress on the ironing board. And the children, silent and white, with a kind of locked obstinacy, in sheepskins and lumber-jackets, stood behind her. She had captured the station, and the pleasure this gave her was enormous. Yet her grievances were true grievances. She was telling the truth. But she behaved like a liar. The look of her small eyes was hidden, and while she raged she also seemed to be spinning and planning.

"They send me out college caseworkers in silk pants to talk me out of what I got comin'. Are they better'n me? Who told them? Fire them. Let 'em go and get married, and then you won't have to cut electric from people's budget."

The chief supervisor, Mr. Ewing, couldn't silence her and he stood with folded arms at the head of his staff, bald-bald-headed, saying to his subordinates like the ex-school principal he was, "Pretty soon she'll be tired and go."

"No she won't," said Raynor to Grebe. "She'll get what she wants. She knows more about the relief even than Ewing. She's been on the rolls for years, and she always gets what she wants because she puts on a noisy show. Ewing knows it. He'll give in soon. He's only saving face. If he gets bad publicity, the commissioner'll have him on the carpet, downtown. She's got him submerged; she'll submerge everybody in time, and that includes nations and governments."

Grebe replied with his characteristic smile, disagreeing completely. Who would take Staika's orders, and what changes could her yelling ever bring about?

No, what Grebe saw in her, the power that made people listen, was that her cry expressed the war of flesh and blood, perhaps turned a little crazy and certainly ugly, on this place and this condition. And at first, when he went out, the spirit of Staika somehow presided over the whole district for him, and it took color from her; he saw her color, in the spotty curb fires, and the fires under the El, the straight alley of flamey gloom. Later, too, when he went into a tavern for a shot of rye, the sweat of beer, association with West Side Polish streets, made him think of her again.

He wiped the corners of his mouth with his muffler, his handkerchief being inconvenient to reach for, and went out again to get on with the delivery of his checks.

The air bit cold and hard and a few flakes of snow formed near him. A train struck by and left a quiver in the frames and a bristling icy hiss over the rails.

Crossing the street, he descended a flight of board steps into a basement grocery, setting off a little bell. It was a dark, long store and it caught you with its stinks of smoked meat, soap, dried peaches, and fish. There was a fire wrinkling and flapping in the little stove, and the proprietor was waiting, an Italian with a long, hollow face and stubborn bristles. He kept his hands warm under his apron.

No, he didn't know Green. You knew people but not names. The same man might not have the same name twice. The police didn't know, either, and mostly didn't care. When somebody was shot or knifed they took the body away and didn't look for the murderer. In the first place, nobody would tell them anything. So they made up a name for the coroner and called it quits. And in the second place, they didn't give a goddamn anyhow. But they couldn't get to the bottom of a thing even if they wanted to. Nobody would get to know even a tenth of what went on among these people. They stabbed and stole, they did every crime and abomination you ever heard of, men and men, women and women, parents and children, worse than the animals. They carried on their own way, and the horrors passed off like a smoke. There was never anything like it in the history of the whole world.

It was a long speech, deepening with every word in its fantasy and passion and becoming increasingly senseless and terrible: a swarm amassed by suggestion and invention, a huge, hugging, despairing knot, a human wheel of heads, legs, bellies, arms, rolling through his shop.

Grebe felt that he must interrupt him. He said sharply, "What are you talking about! All I asked was whether you knew this man."

"That isn't even the half of it. I been here six years. You probably don't want to believe this. But suppose it's true?"

"All the same," said Grebe, "there must be a way to find a person."

The Italian's close-spaced eyes had been queerly concentrated, as were his muscles, while he leaned across the counter trying to convince Grebe. Now he gave up the effort and sat down on his stool. "Oh—I suppose. Once in a while. But I been telling you, even the cops don't get anywhere."

"They're always after somebody. It's not the same thing."

"Well, keep trying if you want. I can't help you."

But he didn't keep trying. He had no more time to spend on Green. He slipped Green's check to the back of the block. The next name on the list was FIELD, WINSTON.

He found the backyard bungalow without the least trouble; it shared a lot with another house, a few feet of yard between. Grebe knew these two-shack arrangements. They had been built in vast numbers in the days before the swamps were filled and the streets raised, and they were all the same—a boardwalk along the fence, well under

211

street level, three or four ball-headed posts for clotheslines, greening wood, dead shingles, and a long, long flight of stairs to the rear door.

A twelve-year-old boy let him into the kitchen, and there the old man was, sitting by the table in a wheelchair.

"Oh, it's d' Government man," he said to the boy when Grebe drew out his checks. "Go bring me my box of papers." He cleared a space on the table.

"Oh, you don't have to go to all that trouble," said Grebe. But Field laid out his papers: Social Security card, relief certification, letters from the state hospital in Manteno, and a naval discharge dated San Diego, 1920.

"That's plenty," Grebe said. "Just sign."

"You got to know who I am," the old man said. "You're from the Government. It's not your check, it's a Government check and you got no business to hand it over till everything is proved."

He loved the ceremony of it, and Grebe made no more objections. Field emptied his box and finished out the circle of cards and letters.

"There's everything I done and been. Just the death certificate and they can close book on me." He said this with a certain happy pride and magnificence. Still he did not sign; he merely held the little pen upright on the golden-green corduroy of his thigh. Grebe did not hurry him. He felt the old man's hunger for conversation.

"I got to get better coal," he said. "I send my little gran'son to the yard with my order and they fill his wagon with screening. The stove ain't made for it. It fall through the grate. The order says Franklin County egg-size coal."

"I'll report it and see what can be done."

"Nothing can be done, I expect. You know and I know. There ain't no little ways to make things better, and the only big thing is money. That's the only sunbeams, money. Nothing is black where it shines, and the only place you see black is where it ain't shining. What we colored have to have is our own rich. There ain't no other way."

Grebe sat, his reddened forehead bridged levelly by his close-cut hair and his cheeks lowered in the wings of his collar—the caked fire shone hard within the isinglass-and-iron frames but the room was not comfortable—sat and listened while the old man unfolded his scheme. This was to create one Negro millionaire a month by subscription. One clever, good-hearted young fellow elected every month would sign a contract to use the money to start a business employing Negroes. This would be advertised by chain letters and word of mouth, and every Negro wage earner would contribute a dollar a month. Within five years there would be sixty millionaires.

"That'll fetch respect," he said with a throat-stopped sound that came out like a foreign syllable. "You got to take and organize all the money that gets thrown away on the policy wheel and horse race. As long as they can take it away from you, they got no respect for you. Money, that's d' sun of humankind!" Field was a Negro of mixed blood, perhaps Cherokee, or Natchez; his skin was reddish. And he sounded, speaking

212

about a golden sun in this dark room, and looked—shaggy and slab-headed—with the mingled blood of his face and broad lips, and with the little pen still upright in his hand, like one of the underground kings of mythology, old judge Minos himself.

And now he accepted the check and signed. Not to soil the slip, he held it down with his knuckles. The table budged and creaked, the center of the gloomy, heathen midden of the kitchen covered with bread, meat, and cans, and the scramble of papers.

"Don't you think my scheme'd work?"

"It's worth thinking about. Something ought to be done, I agree."

"It'll work if people will do it. That's all. That's the only thing, anytime. When they understand it in the same way, all of them."

"That's true," said Grebe, rising. His glance met the old man's.

"I know you got to go," he said. "Well, God bless you, boy, you ain't been sly with me. I can tell it in a minute."

He went back through the buried yard. Someone nursed a candle in a shed, where a man unloaded kindling wood from a sprawl-wheeled baby buggy and two voices carried on a high conversation. As he came up the sheltered passage he heard the hard boost of the wind in the branches and against the house fronts, and then, reaching the sidewalk, he saw the needle-eye red of cable towers in the open icy height hundreds of feet above the river and the factories—those keen points. From here, his view was obstructed all the way to the South Branch and its timber banks, and the cranes beside the water. Rebuilt after the Great Fire, this part of the city was, not fifty years later, in ruins again, factories boarded up, buildings deserted or fallen, gaps of prairie between. But it wasn't desolation that this made you feel, but rather a faltering of organization that set free a huge energy, an escaped, unattached, unregulated power from the giant raw place. Not only must people feel it but, it seemed to Grebe, they were compelled to match it. In their very bodies. He no less than others, he realized. Say that his parents had been servants in their time, whereas he was supposed not to be one. He thought that they had never done any service like this, which no one visible asked for, and probably flesh and blood could not even perform. Nor could anyone show why it should be performed; or see where the performance would lead. That did not mean that he wanted to be released from it, he realized with a grimly pensive face. On the contrary. He had something to do. To be compelled to feel this energy and yet have no task to do—that was horrible; that was suffering; he knew what that was. It was now quitting time. Six o'clock. He could go home if he liked, to his room, that is, to wash in hot water, to pour a drink, lie down on his quilt, read the paper, eat some liver paste on crackers before going out to dinner. But to think of this actually made him feel a little sick, as though he had swallowed hard air. He had six checks left, and he was determined to deliver at least one of these: Mr. Green's check.

So he started again. He had four or five dark blocks to go, past open lots, condemned houses, old foundations, closed schools, black churches, mounds, and he reflected that there must be many people alive who had once seen the neighborhood rebuilt and new. Now there was a second layer of ruins; centuries of history accomplished through human massing. Numbers had given the place forced growth; enormous numbers had also broken it down. Objects once so new, so concrete that it could never have occurred to anyone they stood for other things, had crumbled. Therefore, reflected Grebe, the secret of them was out. It was that they stood for themselves by agreement, and were natural and not unnatural by agreement, and when the things themselves collapsed the agreement became visible. What was it, otherwise, that kept cities from looking peculiar? Rome, that was almost permanent, did not give rise to thoughts like these. And was it abidingly real? But in Chicago, where the cycles were so fast and the familiar died out, and again rose changed, and died again in thirty years, you saw the common agreement or covenant, and you were forced to think about appearances and realities. (He remembered Raynor and he smiled. Raynor was a clever boy.) Once you had grasped this, a great many things became intelligible. For instance, why Mr. Field should conceive such a scheme. Of course, if people were to agree to create a millionaire, a real millionaire would come into existence. And if you wanted to know how Mr. Field was inspired to think of this, why, he had within sight of his kitchen window the chart, the very bones of a successful scheme—the El with its blue and green confetti of signals. People consented to pay dimes and ride the crash-box cars, and so it was a success. Yet how absurd it looked; how little reality there was to start with. And yet Yerkes, the great financier who built it, had known that he could get people to agree to do it. Viewed as itself, what a scheme of a scheme it seemed, how close to an appearance. Then why wonder at Mr. Field's idea? He had grasped a principle. And then Grebe remembered, too, that Mr. Yerkes had established the Yerkes Observatory and endowed it with millions. Now how did the notion come to him in his New York Museum of a palace or his Aegean-bound yacht to give money to astronomers? Was he awed by the success of his bizarre enterprise and therefore ready to spend money to find out where in the universe being and seeming were identical? Yes, he wanted to know what abides; and whether flesh is Bible grass; and he offered money to be burned in the fire of suns. Okay, then, Grebe thought further, these things exist because people consent to exist with them—we have got so far—and also there is a reality which doesn't depend on consent but within which consent is a game. But what about need, the need that keeps so many vast thousands in position? You tell me that, you *private* little gentleman and *decent* soul—he used these words against himself scornfully. Why is the consent given to misery? And why so painfully ugly? Because there is *something* that is dismal and permanently ugly? Here he sighed and gave it up, and thought it was enough for the present moment that he had a real check in his pocket for a Mr. Green who must be real beyond question. If only his neighbors didn't think they had to conceal him.

This time he stopped at the second floor. He struck a match and found a door.

Presently a man answered his knock and Grebe had the check ready and showed it even before he began. "Does Tulliver Green live here? I'm from the relief."

The man narrowed the opening and spoke to someone at his back. "Does he live here?"

"Uh-uh. No."

"Or anywhere in this building? He's a sick man and he can't come for his dough." He exhibited the check in the light, which was smoky—the air smelled of charred lard—and the man held off the brim of his cap to study it. "Uh-uh. Never seen the name."

"There's nobody around here that uses crutches?"

He seemed to think, but it was Grebe's impression that he was simply waiting for a decent interval to pass. "No, suh. Nobody I ever see."

"I've been looking for this man all afternoon"—Grebe spoke out with sudden force—"and I'm going to have to carry this check back to the station. It seems strange not to be able to find a person to *give* him something when you're looking for him for a good reason. I suppose if I had bad news for him I'd find him quick enough."

There was a responsive motion in the other man's face. "That's right, I reckon."

"It almost doesn't do any good to have a name if you can't be found by it. It doesn't stand for anything. He might as well not have any," he went on, smiling. It was as much of a concession as he could make to his desire to laugh.

"Well, now, there's a little old knot-back man I see once in a while. He might be the one you lookin' for. Downstairs."

"Where? Right side or left? Which door?"

"I don't know which. Thin-face little knot-back with a stick." But no one answered at any of the doors on the first floor. He went to the end of the corridor, searching by matchlight, and found only a stairless exit to the yard, a drop of about six feet. But there was a bungalow near the alley, an old house like Mr. Field's. To jump was unsafe. He ran from the front door, through the underground passage and into the yard. The place was occupied. There was a light through the curtains, upstairs. The name on the ticket under the broken, scoop-shaped mailbox was Green! He exultantly rang the bell and pressed against the locked door. Then the lock clicked faintly and a long staircase opened before him. Someone was slowly coming down—a woman. He had the impression in the weak light that she was shaping her hair as she came, making herself presentable, for he saw her arms raised. But it was for support that they were raised; she was feeling her way downward, down the wall, stumbling. Next he wondered about the pressure of her feet on the treads; she did not seem to be wearing shoes. And it was a freezing stairway. His ring had got her out of bed, perhaps, and she had forgotten to put them on. And then he saw that she was not only shoeless but naked; she was entirely naked, climbing down while she talked to herself, a heavy woman, naked and drunk. She blundered into him. The contact of her breasts, though they touched only his coat, made him go back against the door with a blind shock. See what he had tracked down,

215

in his hunting game!

The woman was saying to herself, furious with insult, "So I cain't fuck, huh? I'll show that son of a bitch kin I, cain't I."

What should he do now? Grebe asked himself. Why, he should go. He should turn away and go. He couldn't talk to this woman. He couldn't keep her standing naked in the cold. But when he tried he found himself unable to turn away.

He said, "Is this where Mr. Green lives?"

But she was still talking to herself and did not hear him.

"Is this Mr. Green's house?"

At last she turned her furious drunken glance on him. "What do you want?"

Again her eyes wandered from him; there was a dot of blood in their enraged brilliance. He wondered why she didn't feel the cold.

"I'm from the relief."

"Awright, what?"

"I've got a check for Tulliver Green."

This time she heard him and put out her hand.

"No, no, for *Mr.* Green. He's got to sign," he said. How was he going to get Green's signature tonight!

"I'll take it. He cain't."

He desperately shook his head, thinking of Mr. Field's precautions about identification. "I can't let you have it. It's for him. Are you Mrs. Green?"

"Maybe I is, and maybe I ain't. Who want to know?"

"Is he upstairs?"

"Awright. Take it up yourself, you goddamn fool."

Sure, he was a goddamn fool. Of course he could not go up because Green would probably be drunk and naked, too. And perhaps he would appear on the landing soon. He looked eagerly upward. Under the light was a high narrow brown wall. Empty! It remained empty!

"Hell with you, then!" he heard her cry. To deliver a check for coal and clothes, he was keeping her in the cold. She did not feel it, but his face was burning with frost and self-ridicule. He backed away from her.

"I'll come tomorrow, tell him."

"Ah, hell with you. Don't never come. What you doin' here in the nighttime? Don' come back." She yelled so that he saw the breadth of her tongue. She stood astride in the long cold box of the hall and held on to the banister and the wall. The bungalow itself was shaped something like a box, a clumsy, high box pointing into the freezing air with its sharp, wintry lights.

"If you are Mrs. Green, I'll give you the check," he said, changing his mind.

"Give here, then." She took it, took the pen offered with it in her left hand, and tried to sign the receipt on the wall. He looked around, almost as though to see whether his madness was being observed, and came near to believing that someone was standing on a mountain of used tires in the auto-junking shop next door.

"But are you Mrs. Green?" he now thought to ask. But she was already climbing the stairs with the check, and it was too late, if he had made an error, if he was now in trouble, to undo the thing. But he wasn't going to worry about it. Though she might not be Mrs. Green, he was convinced that Mr. Green was upstairs. Whoever she was, the woman stood for Green, whom he was not to see this time. Well, you silly bastard, he said to himself, so you think you found him. So what? Maybe you really did find him—what of it? But it was important that there was a real Mr. Green whom they could not keep him from reaching because he seemed to come as an emissary from hostile appearances. And though the self-ridicule was slow to diminish, and his face still blazed with it, he had, nevertheless, a feeling of elation, too. "For after all," he said, "he *could* be found!"

Plot Summary

"Looking for Mr. Green" by Saul Bellow takes place in Chicago during the Great Depression, around Thanksgiving. In the inciting incident, George Grebe is tasked by his brand-new employer, Mr. Raynor, to deliver relief checks to the Black community. Grebe, an instructor of classical languages who has been working menial tasks since the Depression hit, wants to do his job well, even though it is not expected by Mr. Raynor. The story then leaves the flashback and returns to the search. Grebe asks an Italian grocer if he knows a Mr. Green, but he is answered with a rant about the crime rate in that part of Chicago. Referring to Black people of all ages and genders, he says, "They did every crime and abomination you ever heard of." Growing frustrated, Grebe decides to look for Winston Field instead of Mr. Green. He finds him easily and spends some time going through the "ceremony" of checking Mr. Field's identification because Field insists that his identity be satisfactorily proved before he takes the check. Grebe has the feeling that Field just wants the company, and it does seem to be the case, because Field talks quite a bit during their interaction. He tells Grebe his "scheme" for making sixty Black millionaires. His plan involves better organization of system and horse racing money, as well as job creation for the Black community and small donations by those employees. After leaving Field home, Grebe contemplates the "disorganization" of that "unregulated" part of the city, which is dilapidated and full of shut-down factories. As if that part of the city is a microcosm of the economic system during the Great Depression, where some are very wealthy and most are very poor, he also thinks about the nonsensical nature of economic systems. In his mind, he compares Field nonsensical scheme to other successful schemes that seem to make just as little sense but that have been effective. He also contemplates the plight that the poor have

217

accepted. After six o'clock rolls around, the stubborn Grebe continues to search for Mr. Green. In the climax, he talks to a man on the second floor of an apartment building and convinces him to give him information about Mr. Green's whereabouts by complaining about the difficulty of finding someone to give them a relief check. He asks the man what good a name is to a man if it cannot function to identify him. The comment seems to reach the man, and he tells Grebe that Green is on the first floor. Finding Mr. Green's place, or at least a place with his name on it, Grebe gives the check to a naked, drunk woman. He fears he has made a mistake in handing the check to someone who may or may not be Mr. Green's wife, but he did not want to go inside in case he would find Mr. Green drunk and naked in the bedroom. The woman takes the check without assuring him that she is Mr. Green's wife, and Grebe consoles himself that at least he has been able to find the man by his name.

Language Exercises

Choose the item that best replaces or explains the underlined part of the sentence.

1. He could find the streets and numbers, but the clients were not where they were supposed to be, and he felt like a hunter inexperienced in the camouflage of his game.
   A. disguise   B. concealment   C. deception   D. intrigue

2. He was slender without being tall, stiff in the back, his legs looking shabby in a pair of old tweed pants gone through and fringy at the cuffs.
   A. flannelled   B. embroidered   C. elaborated   D. frayed

3. The janitor opened his grimy lips, but Grebe did not hear him in the piping of the valves and the consuming pull of air to flame in the body of the furnace.
   A. plump   B. chapped   C. dirty   D. thin

4. He felt that this persistence amused them deeply, and in a way he shared their amusement that he should stand up so tenaciously to them.
   A. half-heartedly   B. hesitantly   C. ferociously   D. steadfastly

5. But how much it would have simplified the job to be able to say that Green was old, or blind, or consumptive.
   A. healthy   B. tubercular   C. crippled   D. handicapped

6. At last he darted into his cubicle of an office as though he had just jumped from one of those hurtling huge red Indian Avenue cars.
   A. dynamic   B. static   C. stationary   D. speeding

7. A small crowd, staff and clients divided by a plywood barrier, stood in the narrow space of the entrance, and Staika was shouting in a gruff, mannish voice, plunging the iron on the board and slamming it on the metal rest.
   A. amiable   B. filthy   C. rough   D. gentle

8. And the children, silent and white, with a kind of locked <u>obstinacy</u>, in sheepskins and lumber-jackets, stood behind her.
   A. stubbornness   B. flexibility   C. tolerance   D. resilience

9. From here, his view was <u>obstructed</u> all the way to the South Branch and its timber banks, and the cranes beside the water.
   A. blocked   B. cleared   C. diverted   D. confused

10. But it wasn't desolation that this made you feel, but rather a <u>faltering</u> of organization that set free a huge energy, an escaped, unattached, unregulated power from the giant raw place.
    A. filtering   B. restricting   C. wavering   D. stabilizing

11. To be <u>compelled</u> to feel this energy and yet have no task to do—that was horrible; that was suffering; he knew what that was.
    A. implored   B. encouraged   C. forced   D. permitted

12. Objects once so new, so concrete that it could never have occurred to anyone they stood for other things, had <u>crumbled</u>.
    A. strengthened   B. expanded   C. disintegrated   D. melted

13. The bungalow itself was shaped something like a box, a <u>clumsy</u>, high box pointing into the freezing air with its sharp, wintry lights.
    A. elegantly designed   B. lacking in coordination
    C. efficiently constructed   D. delicately crafted

14. But it was important that there was a real Mr. Green whom they could not keep him from reaching because he seemed to come as an <u>emissary</u> from hostile appearances.
    A. messenger   B. ambassador   C. governor   D. therapist

15. And though the self-ridicule was slow to <u>diminish</u>, and his face still blazed with it, he had, nevertheless, a feeling of elation, too.
    A. expand   B. weaken   C. enhance   D. amplify

Topics for Discussion

1. How does the protagonist's search for Mr. Green reflect the broader themes in the story?

2. Who is Mrs. Staika in the short story "Looking for Mr. Green"?

3. How does Bellow use language and imagery to create a sense of atmosphere in the story?

4. What can be inferred about the protagonist's internal struggle based on his interactions with Mr. Green?

5. What do you think the title "Looking for Mr. Green" represents in the context of the story?

6. How does Bellow use symbolism in "Looking for Mr. Green" to convey deeper meaning?

7. How does the relationship between the protagonist and Mr. Green evolve throughout the story?

8. What are some of the key turning points in the story, and how do they contribute to the overall narrative?

9. What is the central theme of "Looking for Mr. Green"?

10. In what ways does "Looking for Mr. Green" reflect Bellow's larger body of work and literary style?

Discussion Tips

"Looking for Mr. Green" is a profound testament to Saul Bellow's literary genius, capturing the essence of post-war America through the eyes of George Grebe, a character navigating the bleak landscapes of the Great Depression. Against the backdrop of 1930s economic turmoil, Bellow skillfully unravels the complexities of societal upheaval, providing insight into the struggles of individuals grappling with poverty and destitution. At its core, the narrative serves as a poignant exploration of existential themes, prompting readers to ponder the meaning of existence in the face of adversity. Through George Grebe's quest to find recipients of social relief in the slums, Bellow weaves a story that transcends mere storytelling, delving into the depths of human experience with profound sensitivity. Bellow's prose, marked by precision and restraint, stands in contrast to the sprawling epics of his peers. Each word is meticulously chosen, imbued with layers of meaning that invite readers to uncover hidden depths. From moments of solemn reflection to instances of uproarious humor, Bellow traverses the spectrum of human emotion, creating a narrative that resonates on a visceral level. Attempting to confine Bellow's work within rigid labels proves futile. His writing defies categorization, evading traditional literary constraints with ease, pulsating with a vitality that eludes explanation. Central to the novel's thematic exploration is the enigmatic figure of Mr. Green—a symbol of the intangible desires propelling humanity forward. Though elusive, Mr. Green embodies human aspiration, serving as a beacon of hope in a bleak landscape. His presence challenges readers to confront their existential quandaries and grapple with the complexities of the human condition. In conclusion, "Looking for Mr. Green" stands as a timeless masterpiece, cementing Saul Bellow's legacy as a preeminent literary voice of the 20th century. Through its rich tapestry of characters and themes, the novel offers a profound meditation on existence, leaving an indelible mark on all who dare to explore its pages.

Part IV

Postmodernism and the American Short Story

Unit 11
Donald Barthelme: "The Glass Mountain"

About the Author

Donald Barthelme (1931–1989)

Donald Barthelme remains a significant and influential figure in American literature, renowned for his trailblazing and experimental approach that defied traditional literary norms. As a prominent contributor to the postmodern literary movement, Barthelme's impact is felt through his daring use of fragmented narratives, metafiction, and a fusion of high and low culture references. His innovative style challenged conventional storytelling, inviting readers to engage with literature in new and thought-provoking ways. Barthelme's stories, notably "Snow White" and "The Balloon", stand as testaments to his deconstruction of traditional storytelling conventions. Through these works, he delved into themes such as communication, identity, and the absurdity of contemporary life, offering readers a fresh perspective on the complexities of human experience. His narratives often navigated the blurred lines between reality and fiction, inviting readers to question and explore the nature of storytelling itself. What sets Barthelme's writing apart is his distinctive and playful tone, which often veers into the surreal. This unique approach has continued to captivate audiences and inspire new generations of writers, as his work challenges the boundaries of literary expression. By infusing his stories with humor, irony, and a touch of absurdity, Barthelme crafted a literary legacy that remains as relevant and thought-provoking today as it was during his lifetime. Donald Barthelme's contributions to American literature have left an indelible mark, solidifying his position as a key figure in the evolution of literary form and content. His legacy continues to influence and shape the landscape of contemporary literature, inviting readers and writers to embrace the boundless possibilities of storytelling.

The Literary History

Donald Barthelme and the Postmodernist Writing in American Short Story

Donald Barthelme was a central figure in the development of postmodernist writing in American short stories. His work exemplifies postmodernist principles such as deconstruction, intertextuality, and self-reflexivity, pushing the boundaries of traditional narrative forms and inviting readers to engage with complex and contradictory themes.

One of Barthelme's notable contributions to postmodernist writing is his use of deconstruction, a method that challenges the stability of meaning and truth. In stories like "The Balloon" and "The School", Barthelme disrupts conventional narrative structures and language to dismantle traditional storytelling conventions. By fragmenting and reassembling narrative elements, Barthelme prompts readers to question the coherence and significance of the stories they encounter, reflecting the postmodernist skepticism towards metanarratives and absolute truths.

Barthelme's embrace of intertextuality is another hallmark of his postmodernist writing. In his story "The Indian Uprising", he weaves together elements from diverse sources, including historical accounts, popular culture references, and literary allusions. These intertextual layers create a rich tapestry of meaning, blurring the boundaries between high and low culture and challenging the notion of originality in storytelling. By incorporating multiple voices and references, Barthelme's work reflects the postmodernist belief in the interconnectedness of texts and the impossibility of creating purely autonomous works.

Furthermore, Barthelme's self-reflexive approach to storytelling is evident in stories like "The Glass Mountain" and "Concerning the Bodyguard". These narratives often draw attention to their own artifice, inviting readers to reflect on the nature of storytelling and the construction of meaning. By foregrounding the act of storytelling and the conventions of fiction, Barthelme prompts readers to consider the role of the author, the reader, and the text itself in shaping the narrative experience. This self-awareness underscores Barthelme's engagement with postmodernist concerns about the nature of representation and the instability of language.

In conclusion, Donald Barthelme's contribution to postmodernist writing in American short stories is characterized by his relentless deconstruction of narrative structures, his embrace of intertextuality, and his self-reflexive approach to storytelling. Through stories that challenge traditional forms and language, Barthelme invites readers to grapple with the complexities and contradictions of the postmodern condition, leaving a lasting impact on the evolution of literature.

Literary Terms

Postmodernism

Postmodernism is a philosophical and cultural movement that emerged in the mid-20th century, characterized by skepticism towards grand narratives, absolute truths, and traditional forms of authority. It challenges established norms and conventions in various fields, including literature, art, architecture, and philosophy. In literature, postmodernism is marked by a departure from traditional storytelling techniques, nonlinear narratives, intertextuality, and self-reflexivity. Postmodern writers often experiment with narrative structure and language, blurring the boundaries between fiction and reality. They frequently incorporate pastiche, irony, and metafictional elements to comment on the nature of storytelling and the complexities of human experience. Postmodernism also embraces diversity and fragmentation, reflecting the multifaceted nature of contemporary society. It questions binary oppositions and embraces the idea of hybridity, embracing the coexistence of conflicting perspectives and ideologies. In essence, postmodernism seeks to deconstruct established norms and challenge the idea of a singular, objective truth. Instead, it celebrates the plurality of voices and narratives, often embracing ambiguity and complexity. This approach encourages readers to critically engage with texts and interpret meaning in a more subjective and open-ended manner, reflecting the diverse and ever-changing nature of the postmodern world.

Intertextuality

Intertextuality is a key aspect of postmodernist writing, and Donald Barthelme's short stories are rich examples of this technique. Intertextuality refers to the way a text refers to, borrows from, or is influenced by other texts, creating layers of meaning and connections between different works. Barthelme frequently employed intertextuality in his stories, incorporating references to popular culture, art, literature, and philosophy. For example, in his story "The School", he juxtaposes mundane events with references to historical figures and literary works, creating a surreal and thought-provoking narrative. Furthermore, his use of intertextuality serves to challenge the notion of originality and authorial authority, inviting readers to engage with the web of references and reinterpretations. By blurring the boundaries between different texts and sources, Barthelme's intertextual approach underscores the fragmented and multi-layered nature of the postmodern world, while also inviting readers to critically examine the relationship between texts and their broader cultural context.

Pastiche

Pastiche is a writing technique that involves imitating or mimicking the style, themes, or form of another artist or work. It is a form of homage or parody that combines different elements from various sources to create a new, original piece. Pastiche can involve incorporating the writing styles, characters, settings, and even plot elements from other works into a new narrative. The purpose of pastiche can range from celebrating and paying tribute to a particular style or artist to critiquing or satirizing the original work. Through pastiche, writers can showcase their versatility and skill by seamlessly blending multiple influences into a cohesive and unique creative expression.

It often requires a deep understanding of the source material and a careful balancing act between imitation and innovation to create a compelling and engaging piece.

Parody

Parody is a literary or artistic technique that involves imitating a specific work, style, or genre for comedic or satirical effect. It often involves exaggerating and distorting the characteristics of the original, creating a humorous or critical commentary on the source material. Parody can target various aspects of the original work, including its themes, characters, writing style, or visual elements, to create a new work that both mimics and mocks the original. In literature, parody can take the form of a text that closely imitates the structure and style of a well-known work while infusing it with humorous or critical elements. Parodic elements can also be found in other art forms such as music, film, and visual arts. Parody requires a keen understanding of the source material and a skillful manipulation of its elements to deliver the desired comedic or satirical effect. It often serves as a means of cultural commentary, allowing creators to engage with and subvert familiar tropes, characters, and narratives in a playful or critical manner. Overall, parody is a valuable tool for both entertainment and social critique.

The Story

The Glass Mountain[1]

1. I was trying to climb the glass mountain.
2. The glass mountain stands at the corner of Thirteenth Street and Eighth Avenue.
3. I had attained the lower slope.
4. People were looking up at me.
5. I was new in the neighborhood.
6. Nevertheless I had acquaintances.
7. I had strapped climbing irons to my feet and each hand grasped sturdy plumber's friend.
8. I was 200 feet up.
9. The wind was bitter.
10. My acquaintances had gathered at the bottom of the mountain to offer encouragement.
11. "Shithead."
12. "Asshole."
13. Everyone in the city knows about the glass mountain.
14. People who live here tell stories about it.

---

1   Donald Barthelme, *Sixty Stories* (Penguin Books, 1997), pp. 203–208.

15. It is pointed out to visitors.
16. Touching the side of the mountain, one feels coolness.
17. Peering into the mountain, one sees sparkling blue-white depths.
18. The mountain towers over that part of Eighth Avenue like some splendid, immense office building.
19. The top of the mountain vanishes into the clouds, or on cloudless days, into the sun.
20. I unstuck the righthand plumber's friend leaving the lefthand one in place.
21. Then I stretched out and reattached the righthand one a little higher up, after which I inched my legs into new positions.
22. The gain was minimal, not an arm's length.
23. My acquaintances continued to comment.
24. "Dumb motherfucker."
25. I was new in the neighborhood.
26. In the streets were many people with disturbed eyes.
27. Look for yourself.
28. In the streets were hundreds of young people shooting up in doorways, behind parked cars.
29. Older people walked dogs.
30. The sidewalks were full of dogshit in brilliant colors: ocher, umber, Mars yellow, sienna, viridian, ivory black, rose madder.
31. And someone had been apprehended cutting down trees, a row of elms broken-backed among the VWs and Valiants.
32. Done with a power saw, beyond a doubt.
33. I was new in the neighborhood yet I had accumulated acquaintances.
34. My acquaintances passed a brown bottle from hand to hand.
35. "Better than a kick in the crotch."
36. "Better than a poke in the eye with a sharp stick."
37. "Better than a slap in the belly with a wet fish."
38. "Better than a thump on the back with a stone."
39. "Won't he make a splash when he falls, now?"
40. "I hope to be here to see it. Dip my handkerchief in the blood."
41. "Fart-faced fool."
42. I unstuck the lefthand plumber's friend leawing the rightand one in place.
43. And reached out.
44. To climb the glass mountain, one first requires a good reason.
45. No one has ever climbed the mountain on behalf of science, or in search of celebrity, or because the mountain was a challenge.
46. Those are not good reasons.
47. But good reasons exist.

48. At the top of the mountain there is a castle of pure gold, and in a room in the castle tower sits...

49. My acquaintances were shouting at me.

50. "Ten bucks you bust your ass in the next four minutes!"

51. ...a beautiful enchanted symbol.

52. I unstuck the righthand plumber's friend leaving the lefthand one in place.

53. And reached out.

54. It was cold there at 206 feet and when I looked down I was not encouraged.

55. A heap of corpses both of horses and riders ringed the bottom of the mountain, many dying men groaning there.

56. "A weakening of the libidinous interest in reality has recently come to a close." (Anton Ehrenzweig)

57. A few questions thronged into my mind.

58. Does one climb a glass mountain, at considerable personal discomfort, simply to disenchant a symbol?

59. Do today's stronger egos still need symbols?

60. I decided that the answer to these questions was "yes."

61. Otherwise what was I doing there, 206 feet above the power-sawed elms, whose white meat I could see from my height?

62. The best way to fail to climb the mountain is to be a knight in full armor—one whose horse's hoofs strike fiery sparks from the sides of the mountain.

63. The following-named knights had failed to climb the mountain and were groaning in the heap: Sir Giles Guilford, Sir Henry Lovell, Sir Albert Denny, Sir Nicholas Vaux, Sir Patrick Grifford, Sir Gisbourne Gower, Sir Thomas Grey, Sir Peter Coleville, Sir John Blunt, Sir Richard Vernon, Sir Walter Willoughby, Sir Stephen Spear, Sir Roger Faulconbridge, Sir Clarence Vaughan, Sir Hubert Ratcliffe, Sir james Tyrrel, Sir Walter Herbert, Sir Robert Brakenbury, Sir Lionel Beaufort, and many others.

64. My acquaintances moved among the fallen knights.

65. My acquaintances moved among the fallen knights, collecting rings, wallets, pocket watches, ladies' favors.

66. "Calm reigns in the country, thanks to the confident wisdom of everyone."(M. Pompidou)

67. The golden castle is guarded by a lean-headed eagle with blazing rubies for eyes.

68. I unstuck the lefthand plumber's friend, wondering if—

69. My acquaintances were prising out the gold teeth of not-yet dead knights.

70. In the streets were people concealing their calm behind a façade of vague dread.

71. "The conventional symbol (such as the nightingale, often associated with melancholy), even though it is recognized only through agreement, is not a sign (like the traffic light) because, again, it presumably arouses deep feelings and is

regarded as possessing properties beyond what the eye alone sees." (*A Dictionary of Literary Terms*)

72. A number of nightingales with traffic lights tied to their legs flew past me.
73. A knight in pale pink armor appeared above me.
74. He sank, his armor making tiny shrieking sounds against the glass.
75. He gave me a sideways glance as he passed me.
76. He uttered the word "Muerte" as he passed me.
77. I unstuck the righthand plumber's friend.
78. My acquaintances were debating the question, which of them would get my apartment?
79. I reviewed the conventional means of attaining the castle.
80. The conventional means of attaining the castle are as follows: "The eagle dug its sharp claws into the tender flesh of the youth, but he bore the pain without a sound, and seized the bird's two feet with his hands. The creature in terror lifted him high up into the air and began to circle the castle. The youth held on bravely. He saw the glittering palace, which by the pale rays of the moon looked like a dim lamp; and he saw the windows and balconies of the castle tower. Drawing a small knife from his belt, he cut off both the eagle's feet. The bird rose up in the air with a yelp, and the youth dropped lightly onto a broad balcony. At the same moment a door opened, and he saw a courtyard filled with flowers and trees, and there, the beautiful enchanted princess." (*The Yellow Fairy Book*)
81. I was afraid.
82. I had forgotten the Bandaids.
83. When the eagle dug its sharp claws into my tender flesh—
84. Should I go back for the Bandaids?
85. But if I went back for the Bandaids I would have to endure the contempt of my acquaintances.
86. I resolved to proceed without the Bandaids.
87. "In some centuries, his [man's] imagination has made life an intense practice of all the lovelier energies." (John Masefield)
88. The eagle dug its sharp claws into my tender flesh.
89. But I bore the pain without a sound, and seized the bird's two feet with my hands.
90. The plumber's friends remained in place, standing at right angles to the side of the mountain.
91. The creature in terror lifted me high in the air and began to circle the castle.
92. I held on bravely.
93. I saw the glittering palace, which by the pale rays of the moon looked like a dim lamp; and I saw the windows and balconies of the castle tower.
94. Drawing a small knife from my belt, I cut off both the eagle's feet.
95. The bird rose up in the air with a yelp, and I dropped lightly onto a broad balcony.

96. At the same moment a door opened, and I saw a courtyard filled with flowers and trees, and there, the beautiful enchanted symbol.

97. I approached the symbol, with its layers of meaning, but when I touched it, it changed into only a beautiful princess.

98. I threw the beautiful princess headfirst down the mountain to my acquaintances.

99. Who could be relied upon to deal with her.

100. Nor are eagles plausible, not at all, not for a moment.

Plot Summary

"The Glass Mountain" by Donald Barthelme is a short story that follows the protagonist, as he attempts to climb a glass mountain to find "the symbol". The story is a modern retelling of traditional fairy tales, incorporating elements of absurdity and existentialism. As he ascends the treacherous slope, he faces various challenges and obstacles, including a giant eagle and an array of strange and surreal landscapes. Ultimately, the protagonist reaches the summit of the glass mountain, only to find that the enchanted symbol he sought changed into a princess after his touch, and then he throws the princess off the glass mountain. Throughout the story, Barthelme uses the glass mountain as a symbol of the insurmountable challenges and illusions that individuals face in their lives. The characters' journey becomes a reflection of the human condition, addressing themes of existentialism, absurdity, and the search for meaning. Ultimately, the story does not conclude with a traditional resolution, leaving the fate of the characters and the outcome of their quest open to interpretation. "The Glass Mountain" challenges traditional narrative structures and explores the complexities of human existence through its unconventional and thought-provoking plot.

Language Exercises

Complete the following sentences, using the words listed below with proper forms.

> vanish; sturdy; umber; enchant; glittering; contempt; splendid; façade; libidinous; plausible

1. The _____ oak tree stood tall and unyielding in the face of the storm, its roots firmly anchored in the earth.

2. The magician's performance was so _____ that the entire audience was captivated by his spellbinding illusions.

3. The novel's protagonist was consumed by _____ desires, unable to resist the temptations that surrounded him.

4. Behind the _____ of wealth and success, she hid a deep sense of insecurity and self-doubt.

5. The city skyline was a _____ spectacle of lights, a testament to human ingenuity and creativity.

6. He couldn't conceal his _____ for the dishonesty and corruption that plagued the political system.

7. The detective presented a _____ theory about the crime, but there were still many unanswered questions.

8. The ballroom was adorned with _____ chandeliers and luxurious decorations, creating an atmosphere of opulence and grandeur.

9. As the sun set behind the mountains, the vibrant colors of the sky began to _____ into the darkness of night.

10. The artist used _____ tones to create a sense of warmth and depth in his landscape paintings, adding a rich and earthy quality to his work.

Topics for Discussion

1. What is the central theme or message conveyed in "The Glass Mountain"?
2. What role do the surreal and absurdist elements play in the narrative?
3. In what ways does the story subvert or challenge traditional fairy tale conventions?
4. How does the glass mountain function as a symbol within the story?
5. What is the significance of the encounters with the various characters the protagonist meets on his journey?
6. What is the role of ambiguity and open-endedness in the conclusion of the story?
7. How does Barthelme's writing style contribute to the overall tone and atmosphere of the narrative?
8. What commentary, if any, does the story offer on the human condition or the nature of reality?
9. How does the story utilize humor and irony to convey its themes or ideas?
10. How does the setting of the glass mountain contribute to the overall mood and atmosphere of the narrative?

Discussion Tips

Donald Barthelme is widely recognized as one of the most influential American postmodernist writers, celebrated for his unique ability to infuse his works with distinct postmodernist characteristics. Among his notable pieces, the short story "The Glass

Mountain" stands as a compelling example of Barthelme's penchant for parodying classic fairy tales while delving into the complexities of modern existence.

In "The Glass Mountain", Barthelme skillfully crafts a narrative that serves as a satirical reflection of contemporary society. Through the portrayal of indifferent interpersonal relationships, the story sheds light on the pervasive sense of detachment and alienation that permeates the modern human experience. The characters' interactions are marked by a sense of disconnection, emphasizing the breakdown of meaningful communication and genuine emotional connection in a world fraught with societal and environmental challenges.

Furthermore, Barthelme uses the deteriorating social and ecological environment depicted in "The Glass Mountain" to underscore the disquieting realities of the contemporary world. The narrative serves as a poignant commentary on the detrimental impact of human actions on the natural world, highlighting the consequences of unchecked industrialization, urbanization, and environmental degradation. By intertwining these themes with the protagonist's struggles, Barthelme invites readers to contemplate the profound implications of societal and environmental decay on individual lives.

At the heart of the story lie the protagonist's reasons for failure, which serve as a microcosm of the broader societal disillusionment and existential angst prevalent in the postmodern era. Through the protagonist's experiences, Barthelme illuminates the futility of individual efforts in a world fraught with absurdity and unpredictability. The narrative subtly underscores the challenges and limitations faced by individuals striving for meaning and fulfillment in a world characterized by uncertainty and disillusionment.

Barthelme's construction of a fictional world within "The Glass Mountain" serves as a deliberate artistic choice aimed at reflecting the absurdity of the real world. By blurring the lines between reality and fantasy, the author invites readers to question the very nature of existence and the validity of individual agency in a world rife with paradoxes and incongruities.

In essence, "The Glass Mountain" stands as a thought-provoking exploration of the postmodern condition, offering a compelling critique of contemporary society while challenging readers to confront the inherent complexities and contradictions of the modern human experience. Barthelme's astute portrayal of interpersonal dynamics, societal decay, and individual struggle coalesces into a narrative that resonates with enduring relevance, inviting readers to ponder the profound implications of living in a world where individual efforts often seem futile in the face of overwhelming absurdity.

Unit 12
Raymond Carver: "Will You Please Be Quiet, Please?"

About the Author

Raymond Carver (1938–1988)

Raymond Carver, born in Oregon and raised in Yakima, Washington, was a celebrated American author. His father worked in a sawmill and his mother was a waitress and retail clerk. Carver attended a creative writing course taught by John Gardner, a highly influential figure in his literary works. He later enrolled at the Iowa Writers' Workshop. His first story to be featured in *The Best American Short Stories* was "Will You Please Be Quiet, Please?" and he achieved further success in 1982 with "Cathedral" being selected for the same publication. The publication of *Beginners*, the original version of *What We Talk About When We Talk About Love*, has sparked a discussion and correction of Carver's impression of the term "minimalist", which he has described as having "smallness of vision and execution" that he does not like. Raymond Carver was an acclaimed author and poet who was nominated for the National Book Award, the National Book Critics Circle Award, and the Pulitzer Prize. He wrote five collections of stories and six books of poems, which were published posthumously in *All of Us*, his collected poems. Carver was the recipient of the Mildred and Harold Strauss Living Award in 1983, and in 1988 was inducted into the American Academy and Institute of Arts and Letters. He also received two NEA grants, a Guggenheim Fellowship, and an honorary doctor of letters degree from the University of Hartford. After a ten-year relationship, Carver and the writer Tess Gallagher celebrated their marriage in July 1988. Sadly, Carver passed away from lung cancer on August 2, 1988, at the age of fifty.

Literary History

The American Short Story in the Twenty-First Century

Raymond Carver, often hailed as a master of the short story, has had a profound influence on contemporary American literature. His minimalist style and focus

233

on everyday life resonate deeply with readers and writers alike. As we navigate through the twenty-first century, it becomes increasingly clear that Carver's themes, techniques, and narrative structures continue to shape the landscape of American short fiction.

Carver's writing is characterized by its simplicity and emotional depth. He employs sparse language to capture complex human emotions, focusing on moments of epiphany in ordinary lives. This approach has inspired a new generation of writers who seek to convey profound truths through brevity. In an era where attention spans are shorter than ever, Carver's concise storytelling offers a model for crafting impactful narratives that engage readers quickly while still allowing for deep reflection.

One significant aspect of Carver's work is his exploration of human relationships—particularly the struggles within them. His stories often depict characters at pivotal moments in their lives, grappling with issues such as love, loss, addiction, and existential despair. These themes remain relevant today as they reflect ongoing societal challenges. In the twenty-first century, authors like George Saunders and Lydia Davis have embraced similar explorations of interpersonal dynamics but often infuse them with contemporary contexts such as technology's impact on communication or shifting social norms.

Moreover, Carver's use of ambiguity allows readers to draw their own conclusions about character motivations and outcomes. This open-endedness invites multiple interpretations and engages readers in active participation in the storytelling process. Contemporary writers have adopted this technique to reflect the complexities of modern life—where answers are not always clear-cut—and encourage readers to ponder their interpretations long after finishing a story.

In addition to thematic influences, Carver's narrative structure has also left an indelible mark on twenty-first-century short fiction. His preference for fragmented storytelling mirrors today's fast-paced world where information is consumed rapidly. Writers now frequently employ non-linear narratives or juxtaposed vignettes that challenge traditional storytelling conventions. This shift reflects not only changing reader expectations but also an acknowledgment of life's inherent chaos—a hallmark of Carver's oeuvre.

Furthermore, diversity in voices has become more pronounced in recent years compared to Carver's time when white male perspectives dominated literary discourse. However, many contemporary authors build upon Carver's foundation by incorporating varied cultural backgrounds into their narratives while maintaining his emphasis on authenticity and emotional resonance. Writers like Sandra Cisneros and Yiyun Li echo his commitment to depicting ordinary lives while exploring broader societal issues through unique cultural lenses.

Ultimately, Raymond Carver's legacy endures in the twenty-first-century American short story through both stylistic choices and thematic concerns. His ability to distill complex emotions into succinct narratives resonates powerfully with today's writers who strive for clarity amid life's noise. As new voices emerge in literature—each adding layers to the rich tapestry of American storytelling—they do so against a backdrop established by pioneers like Carver, whose influence remains vital.

In conclusion, Carver's work remains foundational for contemporary writers navigating personal experiences within an evolving societal context. By embracing minimalism while addressing multifaceted human experiences, both past and present authors pay homage to a master who transformed our understanding of what short fiction can achieve.

Literary Terms

Minimalism

In the context of Raymond Carver's literary style, minimalism refers to a writing approach characterized by spare prose, economy of language, and a focus on the essential elements of a narrative. Carver's minimalist approach often involves the use of concise, unadorned language to convey profound emotional and psychological depth. This style eschews elaborate descriptions and ornate language in favor of a stripped-down, unembellished portrayal of characters and their experiences. In Carver's work, minimalism is evident in the economy of his storytelling, the understated nature of his dialogue, and the deliberate omission of extraneous details, allowing readers to engage actively in the construction of meaning and interpretation. The minimalist approach in Carver's writing often serves to underscore the raw and unvarnished realities of his characters' lives, emphasizing the power of understatement and the impact of what is left unsaid.

Dirty Realism

The term "dirty realism" is often used to describe a literary movement associated with writers like Raymond Carver, Ann Beattie, and Tobias Wolff, among others. Dirty realism is characterized by its unromanticized portrayal of everyday life, particularly the struggles and hardships faced by working-class individuals and those on the fringes of society. In Carver's work, dirty realism manifests in the depiction of ordinary characters navigating mundane settings, often grappling with themes of alienation, economic hardship, and the complexities of human relationships. This literary style eschews sentimentality and idealization, opting instead for a gritty, unvarnished portrayal of the human condition, emphasizing the harsh realities and emotional depth of ordinary existence. Dirty realism captures the often-overlooked aspects of life, presenting them with unflinching honesty and authenticity.

Hemingwayesque

The term "Hemingwayesque" is used to describe writing that shares stylistic and thematic similarities with the work of American author Ernest Hemingway. In the context of Raymond Carver's literary influence, Hemingwayesque elements are evident in Carver's spare prose, understated dialogue, and focus on the subtleties of human behavior. Like Hemingway, Carver's writing often features concise, direct language, a focus on the unsaid, and a portrayal of characters grappling with existential themes and the complexities of interpersonal relationships. The Hemingwayesque influence on Carver's work is reflected in the emphasis on understatement, the use of subtext to convey meaning, and the unadorned portrayal of characters' inner lives and emotional landscapes.

The Story

Will You Please Be Quiet, Please?[1]

1

When he was eighteen and was leaving home for the first time, Ralph Wyman was counseled by his father, principal of Jefferson Elementary School and trumpet soloist in the Weaverville Elks Club Auxiliary Band, that life was a very serious matter, an enterprise insisting on strength and purpose in a young person just setting out, an arduous undertaking, everyone knew that, but nevertheless a rewarding one, Ralph Wyman's father believed and said.

But in college Ralph's goals were hazy. He thought he wanted to be a doctor and he thought he wanted to be a lawyer, and he took pre-medical courses and courses in the history of jurisprudence and business law before he decided he had neither the emotional detachment necessary for medicine nor the ability for sustained reading required in law, especially as such reading might concern property and inheritance. Though he continued to take classes here and there in the sciences and in business, Ralph also took some classes in philosophy and literature and felt himself on the brink of some kind of huge discovery about himself. But it never came. It was during this time—his lowest ebb, as he referred to it later—that Ralph believed he almost had a breakdown; he was in a fraternity and he got drunk every night. He drank so much that he acquired a reputation and was called "Jackson," after the bartender at The Keg.

Then, in his third year, Ralph came under the influence of a particularly persuasive teacher. Dr. Maxwell was his name; Ralph would never forget him. He was a handsome, graceful man in his early forties, with exquisite manners and with just the trace of the South in his voice. He had been educated at Vanderbilt, had studied in Europe, and had later had something to do with one or two literary magazines back

---

1   Raymond Carver, *Will You Please Be Quiet, Please?* (Knopf, 1976), pp. 1–22.

East. Almost overnight, Ralph would later say, he decided on teaching as a career. He stopped drinking quite so much, began to bear down on his studies, and within a year was elected to Omega Psi, the national journalism fraternity; he became a member of the English Club; was invited to come with his cello, which he hadn't played in three years, and join in a student chamber-music group just forming; and he even ran successfully for secretary of the senior class. It was then that he met Marian Ross—a handsomely pale and slender girl who took a seat beside him in a Chaucer class.

Marian Ross wore her hair long and favored high-necked sweaters and always went around with a leather purse on a long strap swinging from her shoulder. Her eyes were large and seemed to take in everything at a glance. Ralph liked going out with Marian Ross. They went to The Keg and to a few other spots where everyone went, but they never let their going together or their subsequent engagement the next summer interfere with their studies. They were solemn students, and both sets of parents eventually gave approval to the match. Ralph and Marian did their student teaching at the same high school in Chico in the spring and went through graduation exercises together in June. They married in St. James Episcopal Church two weeks later.

They had held hands the night before their wedding and pledged to preserve forever the excitement and the mystery of marriage.

For their honeymoon they drove to Guadalajara, and while they both enjoyed visiting the decayed churches and the poorly lighted museums and the afternoons they spent shopping and exploring in the marketplace, Ralph was secretly appalled by the squalor and open lust he saw and was anxious to return to the safety of California. But the one vision he would always remember and which disturbed him most of all had nothing to do with Mexico. It was late afternoon, almost evening, and Marian was leaning motionless on her arms over the ironwork balustrade of their rented casita as Ralph came up the dusty road below. Her hair was long and hung down in front over her shoulders, and she was looking away from him, staring at something in the distance. She wore a white blouse with a bright red scarf at her throat, and he could see her breasts pushing against the white cloth. He had a bottle of dark, unlabeled wine under his arm, and the whole incident put Ralph in mind of something from a film, an intensely dramatic moment into which Marian could be fitted but he could not.

Before they left for their honeymoon they had accepted positions at a high school in Eureka, a town in the lumbering region in the northern part of the state. After a year, when they were sure the school and the town were exactly what they wanted to settle down to, they made a payment on a house in the Fire Hill district. Ralph felt, without really thinking about it, that he and Marian understood each other perfectly—as well, at least, as any two people might. Moreover, Ralph felt he understood himself—what he could do, what he could not do, and where he was headed with the prudent measure of himself that he made.

Their two children, Dorothea and Robert, were now five and four years old. A few months after Robert was born, Marian was offered a post as a French and English instructor at the junior college at the edge of town, and Ralph had stayed on at the high school. They considered themselves a happy couple, with only a single injury to their marriage, and that was well in the past, two years ago this winter. It was something they had never talked about since. But Ralph thought about it sometimes—indeed, he was willing to admit he thought about it more and more. Increasingly, ghastly images would be projected on his eyes, certain unthinkable particularities. For he had taken it into his head that his wife had once betrayed him with a man named Mitchell Anderson.

But now it was a Sunday night in November and the children were asleep and Ralph was sleepy and he sat on the couch grading papers and could hear the radio playing softly in the kitchen, where Marian was ironing, and he felt enormously happy. He stared a while longer at the papers in front of him, then gathered them all up and turned off the lamp.

"Finished, love?" Marian said with a smile when he appeared in the doorway. She was sitting on a tall stool, and she stood the iron up on its end as if she had been waiting for him.

"Damn it, no," he said with an exaggerated grimace, tossing the papers on the kitchen table.

She laughed—bright, pleasant—and held up her face to be kissed, and he gave her a little peck on the cheek. He pulled out a chair from the table and sat down, leaned back on the legs and looked at her. She smiled again and then lowered her eyes.

"I'm already half asleep," he said.

"Coffee?" she said, reaching over and laying the back of her hand against the percolator.

He shook his head.

She took up the cigaret she had burning in the ashtray, smoked it while she stared at the floor, and then put it back in the ashtray. She looked at him, and a warm expression moved across her face. She was tall and limber, with a good bust, narrow hips, and wide wonderful eyes.

"Do you ever think about that party?" she asked, still looking at him.

He was stunned and shifted in the chair, and he said, "Which party? You mean the one two or three years ago?"

She nodded.

He waited, and when she offered no further comment, he said, "What about it? Now that you brought it up, what about it?" Then: "He kissed you, after all, that night, didn't he? I mean, I knew he did. He did try to kiss you, or didn't he?"

"I was just thinking out it and I asked you, that's all," she said. "Sometimes I think about it," she said.

"Well, he did, didn't he? Come on, Marian," he said.

"Do you ever think about that night?" she said.

238

He said, "Not really. It was a long time ago, wasn't it? Three or four years ago. You can tell me now," he said. "This is still old Jackson you're talking to, remember?" And they both laughed abruptly together and abruptly she said, "Yes." She said, "He did kiss me a few times." She smiled.

He knew he should try to match her smile, but he could not. He said, "You told me before he didn't. You said he only put his arm around you while he was driving. So which is it?"

"What did you do that for?" she was saying dreamily. "Where were you all night?" he was screaming, standing over her, legs watery, fist drawn back to hit again. Then she said, "I didn't do anything. Why did you hit me?" she said.

"How did we ever get onto this?" she said.

"You brought it up," he said.

She shook her head. "I don't know what made me think of it." She pulled in her upper lip and stared at the floor. Then she straightened her shoulders and looked up. "If you'll move this ironing board for me, love, I'll make us a hot drink. A buttered rum. How does that sound?"

"Good," he said.

She went into the living room and turned on the lamp and bent to pick up a magazine from the floor. He watched her hips under the plaid woolen skirt. She moved in front of the window and stood looking out at the streetlight. She smoothed her palm down over her skirt, then began tucking in her blouse. He wondered if she wondered if he were watching her.

After he stood the ironing board in its alcove on the porch, he sat down again and, when she came into the kitchen, he said, "Well, what else went on between you and Mitchell Anderson that night?"

"Nothing," she said. "I was thinking about something else."

"What?"

"About the children, the dress I want Dorothea to have for next Easter. And about the class I'm going to have tomorrow. I was thinking of seeing how they'd go for a little Rimbaud," and she laughed. "I didn't mean to rhyme—really, Ralph, and really, nothing else happened. I'm sorry I ever said anything about it."

"Okay," he said.

He stood up and leaned against the wall by the refrigerator and watched her as she spooned out sugar into two cups and then stirred in the rum. The water was beginning to boil.

"Look, honey, it *has* been brought up now," he said, "and it *was* four years ago, so there's no reason at all I can think of that we *can't* talk about it now if we *want* to. Is there?"

She said, "There's really nothing to talk about."

He said, "I'd like to know."

239

She said, "Know what?"

"Whatever else he did besides kiss you. We're adults. We haven't seen the Andersons in literally years and we'll probably never see them again and it happened a *long* time ago, so what reason could there possibly be that we can't talk about it?" He was a little surprised at the reasoning quality in his voice. He sat down and looked at the tablecloth and then looked up at her again. "Well?" he said.

"Well," she said, with an impish grin, tilting her head to one side girlishly, remembering. "No, Ralph, really. I'd really just rather not."

"For Christ's sake, Marian! Now I mean it," he said, and he suddenly understood that he did.

She turned off the gas under the water and put her hand out on the stool; then she sat down again, hooking her heels over the bottom step. She sat forward, resting her arms across her knees, her breasts pushing at her blouse. She picked at something on her skirt and then looked up.

"You remember Emily'd already gone home with the Beattys, and for some reason Mitchell had stayed on. He looked a little out of sorts that night, to begin with. I don't know, maybe they weren't getting along, Emily and him, but I don't know that. And there were you and I, the Franklins, and Mitchell Anderson still there. All of us a little drunk. I'm not sure how it happened, Ralph, but Mitchell and I just happened to find ourselves alone together in the kitchen for a minute, and there was no whiskey left, only a part of a bottle of that white wine we had. It must've been close to one o'clock, because Mitchell said, 'If we ride on giant wings we can make it before the liquor store closes. You know how he could be so theatrical when he wanted? Soft-shoe stuff, facial expressions? Anyway, he was very witty about it all. At least it seemed that way at the time. And very drunk, too, I might add. So was I, for that matter. It was an impulse, Ralph. I don't know why I did it, don't ask me, but when he said let's go—I agreed. We went out the back, where his car was parked. We went just as… we were… didn't even get our coats out of the closet, thought we'd just be gone a few minutes. I don't know what we thought, I thought. I don't know *why* I went, Ralph. It was an impulse, that's all I can say. It was the wrong impulse." She paused. "It was my fault that night, Ralph, and I'm sorry. I shouldn't have done anything like that—I *know* that."

"Christ!" The word leaped out of him. "But you've always been that way, Marian!" And he knew at once that he had uttered a new and profound truth.

His mind filled with a swarm of accusations, and he tried to focus on one in particular. He looked down at his hands and noticed they had the same lifeless feeling they had had when he had seen her on the balcony. He picked up the red grading pencil lying on the table and then he put it down again.

"I'm listening," he said.

"Listening to what?" she said. "You're swearing and getting upset, Ralph. For nothing—nothing, honey!… there's nothing *else*," she said.

"Go on," he said.

She said, "*What* is the matter with us, anyway? Do you know how this started? Because I don't know how this started."

He said, "Go on, Marian."

"That's *all*, Ralph," she said. "I've told you. We went for a ride. We talked. He kissed me. I still don't see how we could've been gone three hours—or whatever it was you said we were."

"Tell me, Marian," he said, and he knew there was more and knew he had always known. He felt a fluttering in his stomach, and then he said, "No. If you don't want to tell me, that's all right. Actually, I guess I'd just as soon leave it at that," he said. He thought fleetingly that he would be someplace else tonight doing something else, that it would be silent somewhere if he had not married.

"Ralph," she said, "you won't be angry, will you? Ralph? We're just talking. You won't, will you?" She had moved over to a chair at the table.

He said, "I won't."

She said, "Promise?"

He said, "Promise."

She lit a cigaret. He had suddenly a great desire to see the children, to get them up and out of bed, heavy and turning in their sleep, and to hold each of them on a knee, to jog them until they woke up. He moved all his attention into one of the tiny black coaches in the tablecloth. Four tiny white prancing horses pulled each of the black coaches and the figure driving the horses had his arms up and wore a tall hat, and suitcases were strapped down atop the coach, and what looked like a kerosene lamp hung from the side, and if he were listening at all it was from inside the black coach.

"…We went straight to the liquor store, and I waited in the car until he came out. He had a sack in one hand and one of those plastic bags of ice in the other. He weaved a little getting into the car. I hadn't realized he was so drunk until we started driving again. I noticed the way he was driving. It was terribly slow. He was all hunched over the wheel. His eyes staring. We were talking about a lot of things that didn't make sense. I can't remember. We were talking about Nietzsche. Strindberg. He was directing *Miss Julie* second semester. And then something about Norman Mailer stabbing his wife in the breast. And then he stopped for a minute in the middle of the road. And we each took a drink out of the bottle. He said he'd hate to think of me being stabbed in the breast. He said he'd like to kiss my breast. He drove the car off the road. He put his head on my lap.…"

She hurried on, and he sat with his hands folded on the table and watched her lips. His eyes skipped around the kitchen—stove, napkin-holder, stove, cupboards, toaster, back to her lips, back to the coach in the tablecloth. He felt a peculiar desire for her flicker through his groin, and then he felt the steady rocking of the coach and he wanted to call stop and then he heard her say, "He said shall we have a go at it?" And then she was saying, "I'm to blame. I'm the one to blame. He said he'd leave it all up to me, I could do whatever I want."

He shut his eyes. He shook his head, tried to create possibilities, other conclusions. He actually wondered if he could restore that night two years ago and imagined himself coming into the kitchen just as they were at the door, heard himself telling her in a hearty voice, oh no, no, you're not going out for anything with that Mitchell Anderson! The fellow is drunk and he's a bad driver to boot and you have to go to bed now and get up with little Robert and Dorothea in the morning and stop! Thou shalt stop!

He opened his eyes. She had a hand up over her face and was crying noisily.

"Why did you, Marian?" he asked.

She shook her head without looking up.

Then suddenly he knew! His mind buckled. For a minute he could only stare dumbly at his hands. He knew! His mind roared with the knowing.

"Christ! No! Marian! *Jesus Christ*!" he said, springing back from the table. "Christ! *No*, Marian!"

"No, no," she said, throwing her head back.

"You let him!" he screamed.

"No, no," she pleaded.

"You let him! A go at it! Didn't you? Didn't you? A *go* at it! Is that what he said? Answer me!" he screamed. "Did he come in you? Did you let him come in you when you were having your go at it?

"Listen, listen to me, Ralph," she whimpered, "I swear to you he didn't. He didn't come. He didn't come in me." She rocked from side to side in the chair.

"Oh God! God *damn* you!" he shrieked.

"God!" she said, getting up, holding out her hands, "Are we crazy, Ralph? Have we lost our minds? Ralph? Forgive me, Ralph. Forgive—"

"Don't touch me! Get away from me!" he screamed. He was screaming.

She began to pant in her fright. She tried to head him off. But he took her by the shoulder and pushed her out of the way.

"Forgive me, Ralph! *Please*. Ralph!" she screamed.

2

He had to stop and lean against a car before going on. Two couples in evening clothes were coming down the sidewalk toward him, and one of the men was telling a story in a loud voice. The others were already laughing. Ralph pushed off from the car and crossed the street. In a few minutes he came to Blake's where he stopped some afternoons for a beer with Dick Koenig before picking up the children from nursery school.

It was dark inside. Candles flamed in long-necked bottles at the tables along one wall. Ralph glimpsed shadowy figures of men and women talking, their heads close together.

One of the couples, near the door, stopped talking and looked up at him. A boxlike fixture in the ceiling revolved overhead, throwing out pins of light. Two men sat at the end of the bar, and a dark cutout of a man leaned over the jukebox in the corner, his hands splayed on each side of the glass. That man is going to play something, Ralph thought as if making a momentous discovery, and he stood in the center of the floor, watching the man.

"Ralph! Mr. Wyman, sir!"

He looked around. It was David Parks calling to him from behind the bar. Ralph walked over, leaned heavily against the bar before sliding onto a stool.

"Should I draw one, Mr. Wyman?" Parks held a glass in his hand, smiling. Ralph nodded, watched Parks fill the glass, watched Parks hold the glass at an angle under the tap, smoothly straighten the glass as it filled.

"How's it going, Mr. Wyman?" Parks put his foot up on a shelf under the bar. "Who's going to win the game next week, Mr. Wyman?" Ralph shook his head, brought the beer to his lips. Parks coughed faintly. "I'll buy you one, Mr. Wyman. This one's on me." He put his leg down, nodded assurance, and reached under his apron into his pocket. "Here. I have it right here," Ralph said and pulled out some change, examined it in his hand. A quarter, nickel, two dimes, two pennies. He counted as if there were a code to be uncovered. He laid down the quarter and stood up, pushing the change back into his pocket. The man was still in front of the jukebox, his hands still out to its sides.

Outside, Ralph turned around, trying to decide what to do. His heart was jumping as if he'd been running. The door opened behind him and a man and woman came out. Ralph stepped out of the way and they got into a car parked at the curb and Ralph saw the woman toss her hair as she got into the car: He had never seen anything so frightening.

He walked to the end of the block, crossed the street, and walked another block before he decided to head downtown. He walked hurriedly, his hands balled into his pockets, his shoes smacking the pavement. He kept blinking his eyes and thought it incredible that this was where he lived. He shook his head. He would have liked to sit someplace for a while and think about it, but he knew he could not sit, could not think about it. He remembered a man he saw once sitting on a curb in Arcata, an old man with a growth of beard and a brown wool cap who just sat there with his arms between his legs. And then Ralph thought: Marian! Dorothea! Robert! It was impossible. He tried to imagine how all this would seem twenty years from now. But he could not imagine anything. And then he imagined snatching up a note being passed among his students and it said *Shall we have a go at it?* Then he could not think. Then he felt profoundly indifferent. Then he thought of Marian. He thought of Marian as he had seen her a little while ago, face crumpled. Then Marian on the floor, blood on her teeth: "Why did you hit me?" Then Marian reaching under her dress to unfasten her garter belt! Then Marian lifting her dress as she arched back! Then Marian ablaze, Marian crying out, *Go! Go! Go!*

He stopped. He believed he was going to vomit. He moved to the curb. He kept swallowing, looked up as a car of yelling teenagers went by and gave him a long blast on their musical horn. Yes, there was a great evil pushing at the world, he thought, and it only needed a little slipway, a little opening.

He came to Second Street, the part of town people called "Two Street." It started here at Shelton, under the streetlight where the old roominghouses ended, and ran for four or five blocks on down to the pier, where fishing boats tied up. He had been down here once, six years ago, to a secondhand shop to finger through the dusty shelves of old books. There was a liquor store across the street, and he could see a man standing just inside the glass door, looking at a newspaper.

A bell over the door tinkled. Ralph almost wept from the sound of it. He bought some cigarets and went out again, continuing along the street, looking in windows, some with signs taped up: a dance, the Shrine circus that had come and gone last summer, an election—*Fred C. Walters for Councilman*. One of the windows he looked through had sinks and pipe joints scattered around on a table, and this too brought tears to his eyes. He came to a Vic Tanney gym where he could see light sneaking under the curtains pulled across a big window and could hear water splashing in the pool inside and the echo of exhilarated voices calling across water. There was more light now, coming from bars and cafés on both sides of the street, and more people, groups of three or four, but now and then a man by himself or a woman in bright slacks walking rapidly. He stopped in front of a window and watched some Negroes shooting pool, smoke drifting in the light burning above the table. One of the men, chalking his cue, hat on, cigaret in his mouth, said something to another man and both men grinned, and then the first man looked intently at the balls and lowered himself over the table.

Ralph stopped in front of Jim's Oyster House. He had never been here before, had never been to any of these places before. Above the door the name was spelled out in yellow lightbulbs: JIM'S OYSTER HOUSE. Above this, fixed to an iron grill, there was a huge neon-lighted clam shell with a man's legs sticking out. The torso was hidden in the shell and the legs flashed red, on and off, up and down, so that they seemed to be kicking. Ralph lit another cigaret from the one he had and pushed the door open.

It was crowded, people bunched on the dance floor, their arms laced around each other, waiting in positions for the band to begin again. Ralph pushed his way to the bar, and once a drunken woman took hold of his coat. There were no stools and he had to stand at the end of the bar between a Coast Guardsman and a shriveled man in denims. In the mirror he could see the men in the band getting up from the table where they had been sitting. They wore white shirts and dark slacks with little red string ties around their necks. There was a fireplace with gas flames behind a stack of metal logs, and the band platform was to the side of this. One of the musicians plucked the strings of his electric guitar, said something to the others with a knowing grin. The band began to play.

Ralph raised his glass and drained it. Down the bar he could hear a woman say angrily, "Well, there's going to be trouble, that's all I've got to say." The musicians came to the end of their number and started another. One of the men, the bass player, moved to the microphone and began to sing. But Ralph could not understand the words. When the band took another break, Ralph looked around for the toilet. He could make out doors opening and closing at the far end of the bar and headed in that direction. He staggered a little and knew he was drunk now. Over one of the doors was a rack of antlers. He saw a man go in and he saw another man catch the door and come out. Inside, in line behind three other men, he found himself staring at opened thighs and vulva drawn on the wall over a pocket-comb machine. Beneath was scrawled EAT ME, and lower down someone had added *Betty M. Eats It–RA 52275*. The man ahead moved up, and Ralph took a step forward, his heart squeezed in the weight of Betty. Finally, he moved to the bowl and urinated. It was a bolt of lightning cracking. He sighed, leaned forward, and let his head rest against the wall. Oh, Betty, he thought. His life had changed, he was willing to understand. Were there other men, he wondered drunkenly, who could look at one event in their lives and perceive in it the tiny makings of the catastrophe that thereafter set their lives on a different course? He stood there a while longer, and then he looked down: he had urinated on his fingers. He moved to the wash basin, ran water over his hands after deciding against the dirty bar of soap. As he was unrolling the towel, he put his face up close to the pitted mirror and looked into his eyes. A face: nothing out of the ordinary. He touched the glass, and then he moved away as a man tried to get past him to the sink.

When he came out the door, he noticed another door at the other end of the corridor. He went to it and looked through the glass panel in the door at four card players around a green felt table. It seemed to Ralph immensely still and restful inside, the silent movements of the men languorous and heavy with meaning. He leaned against the glass and watched until he felt the men watching him.

Back at the bar there was a flourish of guitars and people began whistling and clapping. A fat middle-aged woman in a white evening dress was being helped onto the platform. She kept trying to pull back but Ralph could see that it was a mock effort, and finally she accepted the mike and made a little curtsy. The people whistled and stamped their feet. Suddenly he knew that nothing could save him but to be in the same room with the card players, watching. He took out his wallet, keeping his hands up over the sides as he looked to see how much he had. Behind him the woman began to sing in a low drowsy voice.

The man dealing looked up.

"Decided to join us?" he said, sweeping Ralph with his eyes and checking the table again. The others raised their eyes for an instant and then looked back at the cards skimming around the table. The men picked up their cards, and the man sitting with his back to Ralph breathed impressively out his nose, turned around in his chair and glared.

"Benny, bring another chair!" the dealer called to an old man sweeping under a table that had chairs turned up on the top. The dealer was a large man; he wore a white shirt, open at the collar, the sleeves rolled back once to expose forearms thick with black curling hair. Ralph drew a long breath.

"Want anything to drink?" Benny asked, carrying a chair to the table.

Ralph gave the old man a dollar and pulled out of his coat. The old man took the coat and hung it up by the door as he went out. Two of the men moved their chairs and Ralph sat down across from the dealer.

"How's it going?" the dealer said to Ralph, not looking up.

"All right," Ralph said.

The dealer said gently, still not looking up, "Low ball or five card. Table stakes, five-dollar limit on raises."

Ralph nodded, and when the hand was finished he bought fifteen dollars' worth of chips. He watched the cards as they flashed around the table, picked up his as he had seen his father do, sliding one card under the corner of another as each card fell in front of him. He raised his eyes once and looked at the faces of the others. He wondered if it had ever happened to any of them.

In half an hour he had won two hands, and, without counting the small pile of chips in front of him, he thought he must still have fifteen or even twenty dollars. He paid for another drink with a chip and was suddenly aware that he had come a long way that evening, a long way in his life. *Jackson*, he thought. He could be Jackson.

"You in or out?" one man asked. "Clyde, what's the bid, for Christ's sake?" the man said to the dealer.

"Three dollars," the dealer said.

"In," Ralph said. "I'm in." He put three chips into the pot.

The dealer looked up and then back at his cards. "You really want some action, we can go to my place when we finish here," the dealer said.

"No, that's all right," Ralph said. "Enough action tonight. I just found out tonight. My wife played around with another guy two years ago. I found out tonight." He cleared his throat.

One man laid down his cards and lit his cigar. He stared at Ralph as he puffed, then shook out the match and picked up his cards again. The dealer looked up, resting his open hands on the table, the black hair very crisp on his dark hands.

"You work here in town?" he said to Ralph.

"I live here," Ralph said. He felt drained, splendidly empty.

"We playing or not?" a man said. "Clyde?"

"Hold your water," the dealer said.

"For Christ's sake," the man said quietly.

"What did you find out tonight?" the dealer said.

"My wife," Ralph said. "I found out."

In the alley, he took out his wallet again, let his fingers number the bills he had left: two dollars—and he thought there was some change in his pocket. Enough for something to eat. But he was not hungry, and he sagged against the building trying to think. A car turned into the alley, stopped, backed out again. He started walking. He went the way he'd come. He stayed close to the buildings, out of the path of the loud groups of men and women streaming up and down the sidewalk. He heard a woman in a long coat say to the man she was with, "It isn't that way at all, Bruce. You don't understand."

He stopped when he came to the liquor store. Inside he moved up to the counter and studied the long orderly rows of bottles. He bought a half pint of rum and some more cigarets. The palm trees on the label of the bottle, the large drooping fronds with the lagoon in the background, had caught his eye, and then he realized *rum*! And he thought he would faint. The clerk, a thin bald man wearing suspenders, put the bottle in a paper sack and rang up the sale and winked. "Got you a little something tonight?" he said.

Outside, Ralph started toward the pier; he thought he'd like to see the water with the lights reflected on it. He thought how Dr. Maxwell would handle a thing like this, and he reached into the sack as he walked, broke the seal on the little bottle and stopped in a doorway to take a long drink and thought Dr. Maxwell would sit handsomely at the water's edge. He crossed some old streetcar tracks and turned onto another, darker, street. He could already hear the waves splashing under the pier, and then he heard someone move up behind him. A small Negro in a leather jacket stepped out in front of him and said, "Just a minute there, man." Ralph tried to move around. The man said, "Christ, baby, that's my feet you're steppin' on!" Before Ralph could run the Negro hit him hard in the stomach, and when Ralph groaned and tried to fall, the man hit him in the nose with his open hand, knocking him back against the wall, where he sat down with one leg turned under him and was learning how to raise himself up when the Negro slapped him on the cheek and knocked him sprawling onto the pavement.

3

He kept his eyes fixed in one place and saw them, dozens of them, wheeling and darting just under the overcast, seabirds, birds that came in off the ocean this time of morning. The street was black with the mist that was still falling, and he had to be careful not to step on the snails that trailed across the wet sidewalk. A car with its lights on slowed as it went past. Another car passed. Then another. He looked: mill workers, he whispered to himself. It was Monday morning. He turned a corner, walked past Blake's: blinds pulled, empty bottles standing like sentinels beside the door. It was cold. He walked as fast as he could, crossing his arms now and then and rubbing his shoulders. He came at last to his house, porch light on, windows dark. He crossed the lawn and went around to the back. He turned the knob, and the door opened quietly and the house was quiet. There was the tall stool beside the draining board. There was the table where they had sat. He had gotten up from the couch, come into the kitchen, sat down. What more had he done? He had done nothing more. He looked at the clock over the stove. He could see into the dining room, the table with the lace cloth, the heavy glass centerpiece of red flamingos, their wings opened, the draperies beyond the table open. Had she stood at that window watching for him? He stepped onto the living-room carpet. Her coat was thrown over the couch, and in the pale light he could make out a large ashtray full of her cork cigaret ends. He noticed the phone directory open on the coffee table as he went by. He stopped at the partially open door to their bedroom. Everything seemed to him open. For an instant he resisted the wish to look in at her, and then with his finger he pushed the door open a little bit more. She was sleeping, her head off the pillow, turned toward the wall, her hair black against the sheet, the covers bunched around her shoulders, covers pulled up from the foot of the bed. She was on her side, her secret body angled at the hips. He stared. What, after all, should he do? Take his things and leave? Go to a hotel? Make certain arrangements? How should a man act, given these circumstances? He understood things had been done. He did not understand what things now were to be done. The house was very quiet.

In the kitchen he let his head down onto his arms as he sat at the table. He did not know what to do. Not just now, he thought, not just in this, not just about this, today and tomorrow, but every day on earth. Then he heard the children stirring. He sat up and tried to smile as they came into the kitchen.

"Daddy, Daddy," they said, running to him with their little bodies.

"Tell us a story, Daddy," his son said, getting onto his lap.

"He can't tell us a story," his daughter said. "It's too early for a story. Isn't it, Daddy?"

"What's that on your face, Daddy?" his son said, pointing.

"Let me see!" his daughter said. "Let me see, Daddy."

"Poor Daddy," his son said.

"What did you do to your face, Daddy?" his daughter said.

"It's nothing" Ralph said. "It's all right, sweetheart. Now get down now, Robert, I hear your mother."

Ralph stepped quickly into the bathroom and locked the door.

"Is your father here?" he heard Marian calling. "Where is he, in the bathroom? Ralph?"

"Mama, Mama!" his daughter cried. "Daddy's face is hurt!"

"Ralph!" She turned the knob. "Ralph, let me in, please, darling. Ralph? Please let me in, darling. I want to see you. Ralph? Please!"

He said, "Go away, Marian."

She said, "I can't go away. Please, Ralph, open the door for a minute, darling. I just want to see you. Ralph. Ralph? The children said you were hurt. What's wrong, darling? Ralph?"

He said, "Go away."

She said, "Ralph, open up, please."

He said, "Will you please be quiet, please?"

He heard her waiting at the door, he saw the knob turn again, and then he could hear her moving around the kitchen, getting the children breakfast, trying to answer their questions. He looked at himself in the mirror a long time. He made faces at himself. He tried many expressions. Then he gave it up. He turned away from the mirror and sat down on the edge of the bathtub, began unlacing his shoes. He sat there with a shoe in his hand and looked at the clipper ships making their way across the wide blue sea of the plastic shower curtain. He thought of the little black coaches in the tablecloth and almost cried out *Stop!* He unbuttoned his shirt, leaned over the bathtub with a sigh, and pressed the plug into the drain. He ran hot water, and presently steam rose.

He stood naked on the tiles before getting into the water. He gathered in his fingers the slack flesh over his ribs. He studied his face again in the clouded mirror. He started in fear when Marian called his name.

"Ralph. The children are in their room playing. I called Von Williams and said you wouldn't be in today, and I'm going to stay home." Then she said, "I have a nice breakfast on the stove for you, darling, when you're through with your bath. Ralph?"

"Just be quiet, please," he said.

He stayed in the bathroom until he heard her in the children's room. She was dressing them, asking didn't they want to play with Warren and Roy? He went through the house and into the bedroom, where he shut the door. He looked at the bed before he crawled in. He lay on his back and stared at the ceiling. He had gotten up from the couch, had come into the kitchen, had... *sat... down*. He snapped shut his eyes and turned onto his side as Marian came into the room. She took off her robe and sat down on the bed. She put her hand under the covers and began stroking the lower part of his back.

"Ralph," she said.

He tensed at her fingers, and then he let go a little. It was easier to let go a little. Her hand moved over his hip and over his stomach and she was pressing her body over his now and moving over him and back and forth over him. He held himself, he later considered, as long as he could. And then he turned to her. He turned and turned in what might have been a stupendous sleep, and he was still turning, marveling at the impossible changes he felt moving over him.

Plot Summary

In Raymond Carver's short story "Will You Please Be Quiet, Please?" the protagonist, Ralph Wyman, is a middle-aged man facing internal conflicts and relational struggles. The story revolves around Ralph's deteriorating marriage and his attempts to reconcile with his wife Marian. As the narrative unfolds, Ralph finds himself caught in a loop of mundane routines and strained conversations that mirror the underlying tensions in his life. The story explores Ralph's attempt to navigate through his personal anxieties and the disconnection in his marriage, capturing the profound sense of isolation and emotional turmoil that plagues him. Ralph's interactions with his wife, his inner thoughts, and his encounters with other characters in the story shed light on his deep sense of unease and disillusionment. Carver's minimalist style and sharply detailed observations bring out the stark and poignant realities of Ralph's life, delving into themes of loneliness, communication breakdown, and the struggle to find meaning in everyday existence.

Language Exercises

Choose the item that best replaces or explains the underlined part of the sentence.

1. He was a handsome, graceful man in his early forties, with exquisite manners and with just the trace of the South in his voice.

   A. rough   B. refined   C. unpleasant   D. ordinary

2. ... he was a casual, eccentric dresser and sometimes, Marian had told Ralph, laughing, he wore a green velvet smoking jacket to school.

   A. ambitious   B. boring   C.predictable   D. unconventional

3. He walked hurriedly, his hands balled into his pockets, his shoes smacking the pavement.

   A. hitting the pavement gracefully   B. hitting the pavement swiftly

   C. hitting the pavement loudly   D. hitting the pavement quietly

4. Yes, there was a great evil pushing at the world, he thought, and it only needed a little slipway, a little opening.

   A. walkway   B. slideway   C. runway   D. sideway

5. It seemeal to Ralph immensely still and restful inside, the silent movements of the men languorous and heavy with meaning.

   A. hysterical   B. lethargic   C. sarcastic   D. vigorous

6. She kept trying to pull back but Ralph could see that it was a mock effort, and finally she accepted the mike and made a little curtsy.

   A. futile   B. joint   C. poor   D. false

7. The others raised their eyes for an instant and then looked back at the cards skimming around the table.

   A. piling   B. sliding   C. lying   D. skipping

8. Then he gave it up. He turned away from the mirror and sat down on the edge of

the bathtub, began <u>unlacing</u> his shoes.

   A. untying   B. unbuckling   C. unpacking   D. unbinding

9. He turned and turned in what might have been a stupendous sleep, and he was still turning, <u>marveling</u> at the impossible changes he felt moving over him.

   A. worrying   B. freaking   C. wondering   D. rushing

10. Then suddenly, he knew! His mind <u>buckled</u>. For a minute he could only stare dumbly at his hands.

   A. strengthened   B. collapsed   C. fastened   D. released

Topics for Discussion

1. How does Carver's use of minimalism and understatement contribute to the portrayal of the characters' emotional turmoil in the story?

2. In what ways does the theme of failed communication and unfulfilled intimacy manifest in the relationships depicted in the story?

3. How does Carver's depiction of alcoholism and its consequences shed light on the characters' sense of powerlessness and alienation?

4. What is the significance of the recurring motif of stalled or broken vehicles in the story, and what does it reveal about the characters' predicaments?

5. What do the various instances of infidelity and betrayal in the story reveal about the characters' search for fulfillment and meaning in their lives?

6. How does the story's fragmented and non-linear narrative structure reflect the disjointed nature of the characters' experiences and emotions?

7. What insights can be gleaned from examining the influence of Carver's own life on the themes and characters in the story?

8. How do memory and nostalgia shape the characters' perceptions of their past and present circumstances, and what implications does this have for their actions?

9. What is the significance of the Pacific Northwest setting and its impact on the characters' sense of place, identity, and belonging?

10. What effect does the use of unreliable narration have on the reader's interpretation of the story, and how does it add to the layers of meaning and understanding?

Discussion Tips

   Raymond Carver, renowned for his minimalist style, achieved literary acclaim through his intimate depiction of ordinary life's struggles and complexities. Despite facing personal hardships and setbacks, such as unemployment, alcoholism, and marital breakdown, Carver's experiences profoundly influenced his writing, which resonates with authenticity and emotional depth. Carver's narrative technique, characterized by sparse yet evocative language, captures the essence of everyday existence with poignant precision. His stories delve into the lives of blue-collar individuals, exploring themes of failure, addiction, and the bleakness of dead ends. Through his stark and unadorned prose, Carver illuminates the human condition in all its rawness and vulnerability. While some may perceive Carver's work as commonplace or lacking in grandeur, his stories serve as a reflection of the subtle complexities of life that often go unnoticed. By focusing on the nuances of human interaction and unspoken emotions, Carver's writing resonates with readers seeking a deeper understanding of the human experience. In "Will You Please Be Quiet, Please?" Carver masterfully navigates the intricacies of family life and intimate relationships. Through a teasing and revealing dialogue between a husband and wife, Carver explores themes of trust, betrayal, and emotional turmoil. The gradual unraveling of past secrets and unspoken tensions underscores Carver's ability to convey profound emotional depth through minimalist storytelling. Carver's minimalism is not about withholding details, but rather about capturing the silent moments and unspoken truths that lie beneath the surface of everyday interactions. His focus on what remains unsaid, the nuances of dialogue, and the hidden depths of human emotion sets him apart as a master of his craft. Ultimately, Carver's work offers readers a glimpse into the quiet moments of life that carry profound meaning. Through his minimalist approach and keen observation of human behavior, Carver's stories invite readers to contemplate the complexities of existence and the universal struggles that unite us all.

Supplementary Reading with Critical Essay

The Chrysanthemums[1]

John Steinbeck (1902–1968)

The high gray-flannel fog of winter closed off the Salinas Valley from the sky and from all the rest of the world. On every side it sat like a lid on the mountains and made of the great valley a closed pot. On the broad, level land floor the gang plows bit deep and left the black earth shining like metal where the shares had cut. On the foothill ranches across the Salinas River, the yellow stubble fields seemed to be bathed in pale cold sunshine, but there was no sunshine in the valley now in December. The thick willow scrub along the river flamed with sharp and positive yellow leaves.

It was a time of quiet and of waiting. The air was cold and tender. A light wind blew up from the southwest so that the farmers were mildly hopeful of a good rain before long; but fog and rain did not go together.

Across the river, on Henry Allen's foothill ranch there was little work to be done, for the hay was cut and stored and the orchards were plowed up to receive the rain deeply when it should come. The cattle on the higher slopes were becoming shaggy and rough-coated.

Elisa Allen, working in her flower garden, looked down across the yard and saw Henry, her husband, talking to two men in business suits. The three of them stood by the tractor shed, each man with one foot on the side of the little Fordson. They smoked cigarettes and studied the machine as they talked.

Elisa watched them for a moment and then went back to her work. She was thirty-five. Her face was lean and strong and her eyes were as clear as water. Her figure looked blocked and heavy in her gardening costume, a man's black hat pulled low down over her eyes, clod-hopper shoes, a figured print dress almost completely covered by a big corduroy apron with four big pockets to hold the snips, the trowel and scratcher, the seeds and the knife she worked with. She wore heavy leather gloves to protect her hands while she worked.

She was cutting down the old year's chrysanthemum stalks with a pair of short and powerful scissors. She looked down toward the men by the tractor shed now and then. Her face was eager and mature and handsome; even her work with the scissors was over-eager, over-powerful. The chrysanthemum stems seemed too small and easy for

---

1   John Steinbeck, *The Long Valley* (Penguin Classics, 1995), pp. 175–194.

her energy.

She brushed a cloud of hair out of her eyes with the back of her glove, and left a smudge of earth on her cheek in doing it. Behind her stood the neat white farm house with red geraniums close-banked around it as high as the windows. It was a hard-swept looking little house, with hard-polished windows, and a clean mud-mat on the front steps.

Elisa cast another glance toward the tractor shed. The strangers were getting into their Ford coupe. She took off a glove and put her strong fingers down into the forest of new green chrysanthemum sprouts that were growing around the old roots. She spread the leaves and looked down among the close-growing stems. No aphids were there, no sowbugs or snails or cutworms. Her terrier fingers destroyed such pests before they could get started.

Elisa started at the sound of her husband's voice. He had come near quietly, and he leaned over the wire fence that protected her flower garden from cattle and dogs and chickens.

"At it again," he said. "You've got a strong new crop coming."

Elisa straightened her back and pulled on the gardening glove again. "Yes. They'll be strong this coming year." In her tone and on her face, there was a little smugness.

"You've got a gift with things," Henry observed. "Some of those yellow chrysanthemums you had this year were ten inches across. I wish you'd work out in the orchard and raise some apples that big."

Her eyes sharpened. "Maybe I could do it, too. I've a gift with things, all right. My mother had it. She could stick anything in the ground and make it grow. She said it was having planters' hands that knew how to do it."

"Well, it sure works with flowers," he said.

"Henry, who were those men you were talking to?"

"Why, sure, that's what I came to tell you. They were from the Western Meat Company. I sold those thirty head of three-year-old steers. Got nearly my own price, too."

"Good," she said. "Good for you."

"And I thought," he continued, "I thought how it's Saturday afternoon, and we might go into Salinas for dinner at a restaurant, and then to a picture show—to celebrate, you see."

"Good," she repeated. "Oh, yes. That will be good."

Henry put on his joking tone. "There's fights tonight. How'd you like to go to the fights?"

"Oh, no," she said breathlessly. "No, I wouldn't like fights."

"Just fooling, Elisa. We'll go to a movie. Let's see. It's two now. I'm going to take Scotty and bring down those steers from the hill. It'll take us maybe two hours. We'll go in town about five and have dinner at the Cominos Hotel. Like that?"

"Of course I'll like it. It's good to eat away from home."

"All right, then. I'll go get up a couple of horses."

She said, "I'll have plenty of time transplant some of these sets, I guess."

She heard her husband calling Scotty down by the barn. And a little later she saw the two men ride up the pale-yellow hillside in search of the steers.

There was a little square sandy bed kept for rooting the chrysanthemums. With her trowel she turned the soil over and over, and smoothed it and patted it firm. Then she dug ten parallel trenches to receive the sets. Back at the chrysanthemum bed she pulled out the little crisp shoots, trimmed off the leaves of each one with her scissors and laid it on a small orderly pile.

A squeak of wheels and plod of hoofs came from the road. Elisa looked up. The country road ran along the dense bank of willows and cotton-woods that bordered the river, and up this road came a curious vehicle, curiously drawn. It was an old spring-wagon, with a round canvas top on it like the cover of a prairie schooner. It was drawn by an old bay horse and a little grey-and-white burro. A big stubble-bearded man sat between the cover flaps and drove the crawling team. Underneath the wagon, between the hind wheels, a lean and rangy mongrel dog walked sedately. Words were painted on the canvas in clumsy, crooked letters. "Pots, pans, knives, scissors, lawn mores, Fixed." Two rows of articles, and the triumphantly definitive "Fixed" below. The black paint had run down in little sharp points beneath each letter.

Elisa, squatting on the ground, watched to see the crazy, loose-jointed wagon pass by. But it didn't pass. It turned into the farm road in front of her house, crooked old wheels skirling and squeaking. The rangy dog darted from between the wheels and ran ahead. Instantly the two ranch shepherds flew out at him. Then all three stopped, and with stiff and quivering tails, with taut straight legs, with ambassadorial dignity, they slowly circled, sniffing daintily. The caravan pulled up to Elisa's wire fence and stopped. Now the newcomer dog, feeling outnumbered, lowered his tail and retired under the wagon with raised hackles and bared teeth.

The man on the wagon seat called out, "That's a bad dog in a fight when he gets started."

Elisa laughed. "I see he is. How soon does he generally get started?"

The man caught up her laughter and echoed it heartily. "Sometimes not for weeks and weeks," he said. He climbed stiffly down, over the wheel. The horse and the donkey drooped like unwatered flowers.

Elisa saw that he was a very big man. Although his hair and beard were graying, he did not look old. His worn black suit was wrinkled and spotted with grease. The laughter had disappeared from his face and eyes the moment his laughing voice ceased. His eyes were dark, and they were full of the brooding that gets in the eyes of teamsters and of sailors. The calloused hands he rested on the wire fence were cracked, and every crack was a black line. He took off his battered hat.

"I'm off my general road, ma'am," he said. "Does this dirt road cut over across the river to the Los Angeles highway?"

Elisa stood up and shoved the thick scissors in her apron pocket. "Well, yes, it does, but it winds around and then fords the river. I don't think your team could pull through the sand."

He replied with some asperity, "It might surprise you what them beasts can pull through."

"When they get started?" she asked.

He smiled for a second. "Yes. When they get started."

"Well," said Elisa, "I think you'll save time if you go back to the Salinas road and pick up the highway there."

He drew a big finger down the chicken wire and made it sing. "I ain't in any hurry, ma' am. I go from Seattle to San Diego and back every year. Takes all my time. About six months each way. I aim to follow nice weather."

Elisa took off her gloves and stuffed them in the apron pocket with the scissors. She touched the under edge of her man's hat, searching for fugitive hairs. "That sounds like a nice kind of a way to live," she said.

He leaned confidentially over the fence. "Maybe you noticed the writing on my wagon. I mend pots and sharpen knives and scissors. You got any of them things to do?"

"Oh, no," she said quickly. "Nothing like that." Her eyes hardened with resistance.

"Scissors is the worst thing," he explained. "Most people just ruin scissors trying to sharpen' em, but I know how. I got a special tool. It's a little bobbit kind of thing, and patented. But it sure does the trick."

"No. My scissors are all sharp."

"All right, then. Take a pot," he continued earnestly, "a bent pot, or a pot with a hole. I can make it like new so you don't have to buy no new ones. That's a saving for you."

"No," she said shortly. "I tell you I have nothing like that for you to do."

His face fell to an exaggerated sadness. His voice took on a whining undertone. "I ain't had a thing to do today. Maybe I won't have no supper tonight. You see I'm off my regular road. I know folks on the highway clear from Seattle to San Diego. They save their things for me to sharpen up because they know I do it so good and save them money."

"I'm sorry," Elisa said irritably. "I haven't anything for you to do."

His eyes left her face and fell to searching the ground. They roamed about until they came to the chrysanthemum bed where she had been working. "What's them plants, ma'am?"

The irritation and resistance melted from Elisa's face. "Oh, those are chrysanthemums, giant whites and yellows. I raise them every year, bigger than anybody around here."

"Kind of a long-stemmed flower? Looks like a quick puff of colored smoke?" he asked.

"That's it. What a nice way to describe them."

"They smell kind of nasty till you get used to them," he said.

"It's a good bitter smell," she retorted, "not nasty at all."

He changed his tone quickly. "I like the smell myself."

"I had ten-inch blooms this year," she said.

The man leaned farther over the fence. "Look. I know a lady down the road a piece, has got the nicest garden you ever seen. Got nearly every kind of flower but no chrysanthemums. Last time I was mending a copper-bottom washtub for her (that's a hard job but I do it good), she said to me, 'If you ever run across some nice chrysanthemums, I wish you'd try to get me a few seeds.' That's what she told me."

Elisa's eyes grew alert and eager. "She couldn't have known much about chrysanthemums. You can raise them from seed, but it's much easier to root the little sprouts you see there."

"Oh," he said. "I s'pose I can't take none to her, then."

"Why yes you can," Elisa cried. "I can put some in damp sand, and you can carry them right along with you. They'll take root in the pot if you keep them damp. And then she can transplant them."

"She'd sure like to have some, ma'am. You say they're nice ones?"

"Beautiful," she said. "Oh, beautiful." Her eyes shone. She tore off the battered hat and shook out her dark pretty hair. "I'll put them in a flower pot, and you can take them right with you. Come into the yard."

While the man came through the picket fence Elisa ran excitedly along the geranium-bordered path to the back of the house. And she returned carrying a big red flower pot. The gloves were forgotten now. She kneeled on the ground by the starting bed and dug up the sandy soil with her fingers and scooped it into the bright new flower pot. Then she picked up the little pile of shoots she had prepared. With her strong fingers she pressed them into the sand and tamped around them with her knuckles. The man stood over her. "I'll tell you what to do," she said. "You remember so you can tell the lady."

"Yes, I'll try to remember."

"Well, look. These will take root in about a month. Then she must set them out, about a foot apart in good rich earth like this, see?" She lifted a handful of dark soil for him to look at. "They'll grow fast and tall. Now remember this. In July tell her to cut them down, about eight inches from the ground."

"Before they bloom?" he asked.

"Yes, before they bloom." Her face was tight with eagerness. "They'll grow right up again. About the last of September the buds will start."

She stopped and seemed perplexed. "It's the budding that takes the most care," she said hesitantly. "I don't know how to tell you." She looked deep into his eyes, searchingly. Her mouth opened a little, and she seemed to be listening. "I'll try to tell you," she said. "Did you ever hear of planting hands?"

"Can't say I have, ma' am.

"Well, I can only tell you what it feels like. It's when you're picking off the buds you don't want. Everything goes right down into your fingertips. You watch your fingers work. They do it themselves. You can feel how it is. They pick and pick the buds. They never make a mistake. They're with the plant. Do you see? Your fingers and the plant. You can feel that, right up your arm. They know. They never make a mistake. You can feel it. When you're like that you can't do anything wrong. Do you see that? Can you understand that?"

She was kneeling on the ground looking up at him. Her breast swelled passionately.

The man's eyes narrowed. He looked away self-consciously. "Maybe I know," he said. "Sometimes in the night in the wagon there—"

Elisa's voice grew husky. She broke in on him. "I've never lived as you do, but I know what you mean. When the night is dark—why, the stars are sharp-pointed, and there's quiet. Why, you rise up and up! Every pointed star gets driven into your body. It's like that. Hot and sharp and—lovely."

Kneeling there, her hand went out toward his legs in the greasy black trousers. Her hesitant fingers almost touched the cloth. Then her hand dropped to the ground. She crouched low like a fawning dog.

He said, "It's nice, just like you say. Only when you don't have no dinner, it ain't."

She stood up then, very straight, and her face was ashamed. She held the flower pot out to him and placed it gently in his arms. "Here. Put it in your wagon, on the seat, where you can watch it. Maybe I can find something for you to do."

At the back of the house she dug in the can pile and found two old and battered aluminum saucepans. She carried them back and gave them to him. "Here, maybe you can fix these."

His manner changed. He became professional. "Good as new I can fix them." At the back of his wagon he set a little anvil, and out of an oily tool box dug a small machine hammer. Elisa came through the gate to watch him while he pounded out the dents in the kettles. His mouth grew sure and knowing. At a difficult part of the work he sucked his under-lip.

"You sleep right in the wagon?" Elisa asked.

"Right in the wagon, ma'am. Rain or shine I'm dry as a cow in there."

It must be nice," she said. "It must be very nice. I wish women could do such things."

"It ain't the right kind of a life for a woman."

Her upper lip raised a little, showing her teeth. "How do you know? How can you tell?" she said.

"I don't know, ma'am," he protested. "Of course I don't know. Now here's your kettles, done. You don't have to buy no new ones.

"How much?"

"Oh, fifty cents'll do. I keep my prices down and my work good. That's why I have all them satisfied customers up and down the highway."

Elisa brought him a fifty-cent piece from the house and dropped it in his hand. "You might be surprised to have a rival some time. I can sharpen scissors, too. And I can beat the dents out of little pots. I could show you what a woman might do."

He put his hammer back in the oily box and shoved the little anvil out of sight. "It would be a lonely life for a woman, ma'am, and a scarey life, too, with animals creeping under the wagon all night." He climbed over the singletree, steadying himself with a hand on the burro's white rump. He settled himself in the seat, picked up the lines. "Thank you kindly, ma'am," he said. "I'll do like you told me; I'll go back and catch the Salinas road."

"Mind," she called, "if you're long in getting there, keep the sand damp."

"Sand, ma'am?... Sand? Oh, sure. You mean around the chrysanthemums. Sure I will." He clucked his tongue. The beasts leaned luxuriously into their collars. The mongrel dog took his place between the back wheels. The wagon turned and crawled out the entrance road and back the way it had come, along the river.

Elisa stood in front of her wire fence watching the slow progress of the caravan. Her shoulders were straight, her head thrown back, her eyes half-closed, so that the scene came vaguely into them. Her lips moved silently, forming the words "Good-bye— good-bye." Then she whispered, "That's a bright direction. There's a glowing there." The sound of her whisper startled her. She shook herself free and looked about to see whether anyone had been listening. Only the dogs had heard. They lifted their heads toward her from their sleeping in the dust, and then stretched out their chins and settled asleep again. Elisa turned and ran hurriedly into the house.

In the kitchen she reached behind the stove and felt the water tank. It was full of hot water from the noonday cooking. In the bathroom she tore off her soiled clothes and flung them into the corner. And then she scrubbed herself with a little block of pumice, legs and thighs, loins and chest and arms, until her skin was scratched and red. When she had dried herself she stood in front of a mirror in her bedroom and looked at her body. She tightened her stomach and threw out her chest. She turned and looked over her shoulder at her back.

After a while she began to dress, slowly. She put on her newest underclothing and her nicest stockings and the dress which was the symbol of her prettiness. She worked carefully on her hair, penciled her eyebrows and rouged her lips.

Before she was finished she heard the little thunder of hoofs and the shouts of Henry and his helper as they drove the red steers into the corral. She heard the gate bang shut and set herself for Henry's arrival.

His step sounded on the porch. He entered the house calling, "Elisa, where are you?"

"In my room, dressing. I'm not ready. There's hot water for your bath. Hurry up. It's getting late."

When she heard him splashing in the tub, Elisa laid his dark suit on the bed, and shirt and socks and tie beside it. She stood his polished shoes on the floor beside the bed. Then she went to the porch and sat primly and stiffly down. She looked toward the river road where the willow-line was still yellow with frosted leaves so that under the high grey fog they seemed a thin band of sunshine. This was the only color in the grey afternoon. She sat unmoving for a long time. Her eyes blinked rarely.

Henry came banging out of the door, shoving his tie inside his vest as he came. Elisa stiffened and her face grew tight. Henry stopped short and looked at her. "Why—why, Elisa. You look so nice!"

"Nice? You think I look nice? What do you mean by 'nice'?"

Henry blundered on. "I don't know. I mean you look different, strong and happy."

"I am strong? Yes, strong. What do you mean 'strong'?"

He looked bewildered. "You're playing some kind of a game," he said helplessly. "It's a kind of a play. You look strong enough to break a calf over your knee, happy enough to eat it like a watermelon."

For a second she lost her rigidity. "Henry! Don't talk like that. You didn't know what you said." She grew complete again. "I'm strong," she boasted. "I never knew before how strong."

Henry looked down toward the tractor shed, and when he brought his eyes back to her, they were his own again. "I'll get out the car. You can put on your coat while I'm starting."

Elisa went into the house. She heard him drive to the gate and idle down his motor, and then she took a long time to put on her hat. She pulled it here and pressed it there. When Henry turned the motor off she slipped into her coat and went out.

The little roadster bounced along on the dirt road by the river, raising the birds and driving the rabbits into the brush. Two cranes flapped heavily over the willow-line and dropped into the river-bed.

Far ahead on the road Elisa saw a dark speck. She knew.

She tried not to look as they passed it, but her eyes would not obey. She whispered to herself sadly, "He might have thrown them off the road. That wouldn't have been much trouble, not very much. But he kept the pot," she explained. "He had to keep the pot. That's why he couldn't get them off the road."

The roadster turned a bend and she saw the caravan ahead. She swung full around toward her husband so she could not see the little covered wagon and the mismatched team as the car passed them.

In a moment it was over. The thing was done. She did not look back.

She said loudly, to be heard above the motor, "It will be good, tonight, a good dinner."

"Now you're changed again," Henry complained. He took one hand from the wheel and patted her knee. "I ought to take you in to dinner oftener. It would be good for both of us. We get so heavy out on the ranch."

"Henry," she asked, "could we have wine at dinner?"

"Sure we could. Say! That will be fine."

She was silent for a while; then she said, "Henry, at those prize fights, do the men hurt each other very much?"

"Sometimes a little, not often. Why?"

"Well, I've read how they break noses, and blood runs down their chests. I've read how the fighting gloves get heavy and soggy with blood."

He looked around at her. "What's the matter, Elisa? I didn't know you read things like that." He brought the car to a stop, then turned to the right over the Salinas River bridge.

"Do any women ever go to the fights?" she asked.

"Oh, sure, some. What's the matter, Elisa? Do you want to go? I don't think you'd like it, but I'll take you if you really want to go."

She relaxed limply in the seat. "Oh, no. No. I don't want to go. I'm sure I don't." Her face was turned away from him. "It will be enough if we can have wine. It will be plenty." She turned up her coat collar so he could not see that she was crying weakly— like an old woman.

Critical Essay

"The Chrysanthemums": The Story Shaped by Its Setting

The setting of a story is crucial as it shapes the entire narrative and provides context for the action. It encompasses the physical and spiritual background against which the story unfolds, including the geographical location, historical time, and social circumstances. Setting not only creates a sense of realism, but also sets the atmosphere and reveals the characters' inner thoughts. It is an integral part of the story, often conveying symbolic suggestions and directly influencing the development of the characters and themes. The intricacies of the setting, whether it be a foggy valley or a bustling city, can profoundly impact the mood and tone of the story, as well as the decisions and emotions of the characters. Furthermore, the historical and social context embedded in the setting can provide insight into the characters' motivations and challenges, enriching the reader's understanding of the narrative. In essence, the setting serves as a multifaceted backdrop that not only grounds the story in a specific time and place but also serves as a dynamic force that propels the plot and shapes the characters' experiences.

The setting in John Steinbeck's "The Chrysanthemums" is ingeniously devised and immensely helpful in understanding the characters and the theme. An analysis of the story would be incomplete without mentioning the author's deft manipulation of the setting.

The first three paragraphs of the story serve as the setting.

The high gray-flannel fog of winter closed off the Salinas Valley from the sky and from all the rest of the world. On every side, it sat like a lid on the mountains and made of the great valley a closed pot. On the broad, level land floor, the gang plows bit deep and left the black earth shining like metal where the shares had cut. On the foothill ranches across the Salinas River, the yellow stubble fields seemed to be bathed in pale cold sunshine, but there was no sunshine in the valley now in December. The thick willow scrub along the river flamed with sharp and positive yellow leaves.

In the first paragraph, the description of the fog and the Salinas Valley portrays an isolated and separated environment, aligning with the story's theme. The color grey suggests a dull and colorless background, while the mention of flannel foreshadows male dominance. The phrase "closed off from the sky" insinuates the protagonist's limited dreams or aspirations.

The foggy weather and the setting of the Salinas Valley are introduced at the beginning of the story. The overwhelming fog disconnects the valley from the outside world, creating an oppressive atmosphere. The simile "like a lid" and the metaphor "a closed pot" reinforce the negative impact of the fog on the valley, adding a sense of gloominess and desperation to the atmosphere.

The word "stubble" figuratively indicates that the fields have been deserted and neglected. The simile "black earth shining like metal" describes the barren field, intensifying the gloomy atmosphere. The deliberate mention that there is no sunshine in the valley further emphasizes the desperate and gloomy setting.

It was a time of quiet and of waiting. The air was cold and tender. A light wind blew up from the southwest so that the farmers were mildly hopeful of a good rain before long; but fog and rain did not go together.

The first sentence of the second paragraph sets the tone for the entire story, hinting at the fate of the protagonist. The word "quiet" implies a state of forced silence and obedience, while "waiting" suggests the unattainability of hope. The mention of the farmers' hope for rain adds to the atmosphere of desperation.

Across the river, on Henry Allen's foothill ranch there was little work to be done, for the hay was cut and stored and the orchards were plowed up to receive the rain deeply when it should come. The cattle on the higher slopes were becoming shaggy and rough-

coated.

The mention that the orchards were plowed up to receive rain deeply indicates the valley's great need for water, highlighting the dry and sterile environment. The description of the cattle becoming shaggy and rough-coated further symbolizes the deteriorating environment.

The initial introduction of the characters is also an indispensable component of the setting. The protagonist is described as "blocked and heavy" with a "lean and strong" face. She wears masculine costumes and gives the impression of being tough. This contrasts with her fragile, delicate, and sensitive nature, eliciting sympathy from the reader.

The chrysanthemum and the fence are vital symbols in the story. The chrysanthemum symbolizes both nature and women, as it represents their shared disadvantaged positions, physical appearance, and relationship with the outside world. The fence, while meant to protect the chrysanthemum, metaphorically represents the suffocating suppression women in that society suffer from.

The story "The Chrysanthemums" is largely shaped by its setting, permeating throughout the narrative. The setting creates an atmosphere of gloominess and desperation, reflecting the protagonist's closed-off world on multiple levels. Through the setting, the theme of the story is presented clearly to the reader.

The Egg[1]

Sherwood Anderson (1876–1941)

My father was, I am sure, intended by nature to be a cheerful, kindly man. Until he was thirty-four years old he worked as a farmhand for a man named Thomas Butterworth whose place lay near the town of Bidwell, Ohio. He had then a horse of his own and on Saturday evenings drove into town to spend a few hours in social intercourse with other farmhands. In town he drank several glasses of beer and stood about in Ben Head's saloon—crowded on Saturday evenings with visiting farmhands. Songs were sung and glasses thumped on the bar. At ten o'clock father drove home along a lonely country road, made his horse comfortable for the night and himself went to bed, quite happy in his position in life. He had at that time no notion of trying to rise in the world.

It was in the spring of his thirty-fifth year that father married my mother, then a country schoolteacher, and in the following spring I came wriggling and crying into the world. Something happened to the two people. They became ambitious. The American passion for getting up in the world took possession of them.

It may have been that mother was responsible. Being a schoolteacher she had no doubt read books and magazines. She had, I presume, read of how Garfield, Lincoln, and other Americans rose from poverty to fame and greatness and as I lay beside her—in the days of her lying-in—she may have dreamed that I would someday rule men and cities. At any rate she induced father to give up his place as a farmhand, sell his horse and embark on an independent enterprise of his own. She was a tall silent woman with a long nose and troubled grey eyes. For herself she wanted nothing. For father and myself she was incurably ambitious.

The first venture into which the two people went turned out badly. They rented ten acres of poor stony land on Griggs's Road, eight miles from Bidwell, and launched into chicken raising. I grew into boyhood on the place and got my first impressions of life there. From the beginning they were impressions of disaster and if, in my turn, I am a gloomy man inclined to see the darker side of life, I attribute it to the fact that what should have been for me the happy joyous days of childhood were spent on a chicken farm.

---

1   Sherwood Anderson, *Winesburg, Ohio* (Dover Publications,1990), pp. 3–12.

One unversed in such matters can have no notion of the many and tragic things that can happen to a chicken. It is born out of an egg, lives for a few weeks as a tiny fluffy thing such as you will see pictured on Easter cards, then becomes hideously naked, eats quantities of corn and meal bought by the sweat of your father's brow, gets diseases called pip, cholera, and other names, stands looking with stupid eyes at the sun, becomes sick and dies. A few hens and now and then a rooster, intended to serve God's mysterious ends, struggle through to maturity. The hens lay eggs out of which come other chickens and the dreadful cycle is thus made complete. It is all unbelievably complex. Most philosophers must have been raised on chicken farms. One hopes for so much from a chicken and is so dreadfully disillusioned. Small chickens, just setting out on the journey of life, look so bright and alert and they are in fact so dreadfully stupid. If disease does not kill them they wait until your expectations are thoroughly aroused and then walk under the wheels of a wagon—to go squashed and dead back to their maker. Vermin infest their youth, and fortunes must be spent for curative powders. In later life I have seen how a literature has been built up on the subject of fortunes to be made out of the raising of chickens. It is intended to be read by the gods who have just eaten of the tree of the knowledge of good and evil. It is a hopeful literature and declares that much may be done by simple ambitious people who own a few hens. Do not be led astray by it. It was not written for you. Go hunt for gold on the frozen hills of Alaska, put your faith in the honesty of a politician, believe if you will that the world is daily growing better and that good will triumph over evil, but do not read and believe the literature that is written concerning the hen. It was not written for you.

I, however, digress. My tale does not primarily concern itself with the hen. If correctly told it will center on the egg. For ten years my father and mother struggled to make our chicken farm pay and then they gave up that struggle and began another. They moved into the town of Bidwell, Ohio and embarked in the restaurant business. After ten years of worry with incubators that did not hatch, and with tiny—and in their own way lovely—balls of fluff that passed on into semi-naked pullethood and from that into dead henhood, we threw all aside and packing our belongings on a wagon drove down Griggs's Road toward Bidwell, a tiny caravan of hope looking for a new place from which to start on our upward journey through life.

We must have been a sad looking lot, not, I fancy, unlike refugees fleeing from a battlefield. Mother and I walked in the road. The wagon that contained our goods had been borrowed for the day from Mr. Albert Griggs, a neighbor. Out of its sides stuck the legs of cheap chairs and at the back of the pile of beds, tables, and boxes filled with kitchen utensils was a crate of live chickens, and on top of that the baby carriage in which I had been wheeled about in my infancy. Why we stuck to the baby carriage I don't know. It was unlikely other children would be born and the wheels were broken. People who have few possessions cling tightly to those they have. That is one of the

267

facts that make life so discouraging.

Father rode on top of the wagon. He was then a bald-headed man of forty-five, a little fat and from long association with mother and the chickens he had become habitually silent and discouraged. All during our ten years on the chicken farm he had worked as a laborer on neighboring farms and most of the money he had earned had been spent for remedies to cure chicken diseases, on Wilmer's White Wonder Cholera Cure or Professor Bidlow's Egg Producer or some other preparations that mother found advertised in the poultry papers. There were two little patches of hair on father's head just above his ears. I remember that as a child I used to sit looking at him when he had gone to sleep in a chair before the stove on Sunday afternoons in the winter. I had at that time already begun to read books and have notions of my own and the bald path that led over the top of his head was, I fancied, something like a broad road, such a road as Caesar might have made on which to lead his legions out of Rome and into the wonders of an unknown world. The tufts of hair that grew above father's ears were, I thought, like forests. I fell into a half-sleeping, half-waking state and dreamed I was a tiny thing going along the road into a far beautiful place where there were no chicken farms and where life was a happy eggless affair.

One might write a book concerning our flight from the chicken farm into town. Mother and I walked the entire eight miles—she to be sure that nothing fell from the wagon and I to see the wonders of the world. On the seat of the wagon beside father was his greatest treasure. I will tell you of that.

On a chicken farm where hundreds and even thousands of chickens come out of eggs, surprising things sometimes happen. Grotesques are born out of eggs as out of people. The accident does not often occur—perhaps once in a thousand births. A chicken is, you see, born that has four legs, two pairs of wings, two heads or what not. The things do not live. They go quickly back to the hand of their maker that has for a moment trembled. The fact that the poor little things could not live was one of the tragedies of life to father. He had some sort of notion that if he could but bring into henhood or roosterhood a five-legged hen or a two-headed rooster his fortune would be made. He dreamed of taking the wonder about to county fairs and of growing rich by exhibiting it to other farmhands.

At any rate he saved all the little monstrous things that had been born on our chicken farm. They were preserved in alcohol and put each in its own glass bottle. These he had carefully put into a box and on our journey into town it was carried on the wagon seat beside him. He drove the horses with one hand and with the other clung to the box. When we got to our destination the box was taken down at once and the bottles removed. All during our days as keepers of a restaurant in the town of Bidwell, Ohio, the grotesques in their little glass bottles sat on a shelf back of the counter. Mother sometimes protested but father was a rock on the subject of his treasure. The grotesques were, he declared, valuable. People, he said, liked to look at strange and wonderful things.

Did I say that we embarked in the restaurant business in the town of Bidwell, Ohio? I exaggerated a little. The town itself lay at the foot of a low hill and on the shore of a small river. The railroad did not run through the town and the station was a mile away to the north at a place called Pickleville. There had been a cider mill and pickle factory at the station, but before the time of our coming they had both gone out of business. In the morning and in the evening busses came down to the station along a road called Turner's Pike from the hotel on the main street of Bidwell. Our going to the out-of-the-way place to embark in the restaurant business was mother's idea. She talked of it for a year and then one day went off and rented an empty store building opposite the railroad station. It was her idea that the restaurant would be profitable. Travelling men, she said, would be always waiting around to take trains out of town and town people would come to the station to await incoming trains. They would come to the restaurant to buy pieces of pie and drink coffee. Now that I am older I know that she had another motive in going. She was ambitious for me. She wanted me to rise in the world, to get into a town school and become a man of the towns.

At Pickleville father and mother worked hard as they always had done. At first there was the necessity of putting our place into shape to be a restaurant. That took a month. Father built a shelf on which he put tins of vegetables. He painted a sign on which he put his name in large red letters. Below his name was the sharp command—"EAT HERE"—that was so seldom obeyed. A showcase was bought and filled with cigars and tobacco. Mother scrubbed the floor and the walls of the room. I went to school in the town and was glad to be away from the farm and from the presence of the discouraged, sad-looking chickens. Still I was not very joyous. In the evening I walked home from school along Turner's Pike and remembered the children I had seen playing in the town school yard. A troop of little girls had gone hopping about and singing. I tried that. Down along the frozen road I went hopping solemnly on one leg. "Hippity Hop to the Barber Shop," I sang shrilly. Then I stopped and looked doubtfully about. I was afraid of being seen in my gay mood. It must have seemed to me that I was doing a thing that should not be done by one who, like myself, had been raised on a chicken farm where death was a daily visitor.

Mother decided that our restaurant should remain open at night. At ten in the evening a passenger train went north past our door followed by a local freight. The freight crew had switching to do in Pickleville and when the work was done they came to our restaurant for hot coffee and food. Sometimes one of them ordered a fried egg. In the morning at four they returned northbound and again visited us. A little trade began to grow up. Mother slept at night and during the day tended the restaurant and fed our boarders while father slept. He slept in the same bed mother had occupied during the night and I went off to the town of Bidwell and to school. During the long nights, while mother and I slept, father cooked meats that were to go into sandwiches for the lunch baskets of our boarders. Then an idea in regard to getting up in the world came into his head. The American spirit took hold of him. He also became ambitious.

In the long nights when there was little to do father had time to think. That was his undoing. He decided that he had in the past been an unsuccessful man because he had not been cheerful enough and that in the future he would adopt a cheerful outlook on life. In the early morning he came upstairs and got into bed with mother. She woke and the two talked. From my bed in the corner I listened.

It was father's idea that both he and mother should try to entertain the people who came to eat at our restaurant. I cannot now remember his words, but he gave the impression of one about to become in some obscure way a kind of public entertainer. When people, particularly young people from the town of Bidwell, came into our place, as on very rare occasions they did, bright entertaining conversation was to be made. From father's words I gathered that something of the jolly innkeeper effect was to be sought. Mother must have been doubtful from the first, but she said nothing discouraging. It was father's notion that a passion for the company of himself and mother would spring up in the breasts of the younger people of the town of Bidwell. In the evening bright happy groups would come singing down Turner's Pike. They would troop shouting with joy and laughter into our place. There would be song and festivity. I do not mean to give the impression that father spoke so elaborately of the matter. He was as I have said an uncommunicative man. "They want some place to go. I tell you they want some place to go," he said over and over. That was as far as he got. My own imagination has filled in the blanks.

For two or three weeks this notion of father's invaded our house. We did not talk much but in our daily lives tried earnestly to make smiles take the place of glum looks. Mother smiled at the boarders and I, catching the infection, smiled at our cat. Father became a little feverish in his anxiety to please. There was no doubt lurking somewhere in him a touch of the spirit of the showman. He did not waste much of his ammunition on the railroad men he served at night but seemed to be waiting for a young man or woman from Bidwell to come in to show what he could do. On the counter in the restaurant there was a wire basket kept always filled with eggs, and it must have been before his eyes when the idea of being entertaining was born in his brain. There was something pre-natal about the way eggs kept themselves connected with the development of his idea. At any rate an egg ruined his new impulse in life. Late one night I was awakened by a roar of anger coming from father's throat. Both mother and I sat upright in our beds. With trembling hands she lighted a lamp that stood on a table by her head. Downstairs the front door of our restaurant went shut with a bang and in a few minutes father tramped up the stairs. He held an egg in his hand and his hand trembled as though he were having a chill. There was a half insane light in his eyes. As he stood glaring at us I was sure he intended throwing the egg at either mother or me. Then he laid it gently on the table beside the lamp and dropped on his knees beside mother's bed. He began to cry like a boy and I, carried away by his grief, cried with him. The two of us filled the little upstairs room with our wailing voices. It is ridiculous, but of the picture we made I can remember only the fact that mother's hand continually stroked the bald path that ran across the top of his head. I have forgotten what mother said to him and how she induced him to tell her of what had happened downstairs. His explanation also has gone out of my mind. I remember only my own grief and fright and the shiny path over father's head glowing in the lamplight as he knelt by the bed.

As to what happened downstairs. For some unexplainable reason I know the story as well as though I had been a witness to my father's discomfiture. One in time gets to know many unexplainable things. On that evening young Joe Kane, son of a merchant of Bidwell, came to Pickleville to meet his father, who was expected on the ten o'clock evening train from the south. The train was three hours late and Joe came into our place to loaf about and to wait for its arrival. The local freight train came in and the freight crew were fed. Joe was left alone in the restaurant with father.

From the moment he came into our place the Bidwell young man must have been puzzled by my father's actions. It was his notion that father was angry at him for hanging around. He noticed that the restaurant keeper was apparently disturbed by his presence and he thought of going out. However, it began to rain and he did not fancy the long walk to town and back. He bought a five-cent cigar and ordered a cup of coffee. He had a newspaper in his pocket and took it out and began to read. "I'm waiting for the evening train. It's late," he said apologetically.

For a long time father, whom Joe Kane had never seen before, remained silently gazing at his visitor. He was no doubt suffering from an attack of stage fright. As so often happens in life he had thought so much and so often of the situation that now confronted him that he was somewhat nervous in its presence.

For one thing, he did not know what to do with his hands. He thrust one of them nervously over the counter and shook hands with Joe Kane. "How-de-do," he said. Joe Kane put his newspaper down and stared at him. Father's eye lighted on the basket of eggs that sat on the counter and he began to talk. "Well," he began hesitatingly, "well, you have heard of Christopher Columbus, eh?" He seemed to be angry. "That Christopher Columbus was a cheat," he declared emphatically. "He talked of making an egg stand on its end. He talked, he did, and then he went and broke the end of the egg."

My father seemed to his visitor to be beside himself at the duplicity of Christopher Columbus. He muttered and swore. He declared it was wrong to teach children that Christopher Columbus was a great man when, after all, he cheated at the critical moment. Grumbling at Columbus, father took an egg from the basket on the counter and began to walk up and down. He rolled the egg between the palms of his hands. He smiled genially. He began to mumble words regarding the effect to be produced on an egg by the electricity that comes out of the human body. He declared that without breaking its shell and by virtue of rolling it back and forth in his hands he could stand the egg on its end. He explained that the warmth of his hands and the gentle rolling movement he gave the egg created a new center of gravity, and Joe Kane was mildly interested. "I have handled thousands of eggs," father said. "No one knows more about eggs than I do."

He stood the egg on the counter and it fell on its side. He tried the trick again and again, each time rolling the egg between the palms of his hands and saying the words regarding the wonders of electricity and the laws of gravity. When after a half hour's effort he did succeed in making the egg stand for a moment, he looked up to find that his visitor was no longer watching. By the time he had succeeded in calling Joe Kane's attention to the success of his effort, the egg had again rolled over and lay on its side.

Afire with the showman's passion and at the same time a good deal disconcerted by the failure of his first effort, father now took the bottles containing the poultry monstrosities down from their place on the shelf and began to show them to his visitor. "How would you like to have seven legs and two heads like this fellow?" he asked, exhibiting the most remarkable of his treasures. A cheerful smile played over his face. He reached over the counter and tried to slap Joe Kane on the shoulder as he had seen men do in Ben Head's saloon when he was a young farmhand and drove to town on Saturday evenings. His visitor was made a little ill by the sight of the body of the terribly deformed bird floating in the alcohol in the bottle and got up to go. Coming from behind the counter, father took hold of the young man's arm and led him back to his seat. He grew a little angry and for a moment had to turn his face away and force himself to smile. Then he put the bottles back on the shelf. In an outburst of generosity he fairly compelled Joe Kane to have a fresh cup of coffee and another cigar at his expense. Then he took a pan and filling it with vinegar, taken from a jug that sat beneath the counter, he declared himself about to do a new trick. "I will heat this egg in this pan of vinegar," he said. "Then I will put it through the neck of a bottle without breaking the shell. When the egg is inside the bottle it will resume its normal shape and the shell will become hard again. Then I will give the bottle with the egg in it to you. You can take it about with you wherever you go. People will want to know how you got the egg in the bottle. Don't tell them. Keep them guessing. That is the way to have fun with this trick."

Father grinned and winked at his visitor. Joe Kane decided that the man who confronted him was mildly insane but harmless. He drank the cup of coffee that had been given him and began to read his paper again. When the egg had been heated in vinegar, father carried it on a spoon to the counter and going into a back room got an empty bottle. He was angry because his visitor did not watch him as he began to do his trick, but nevertheless went cheerfully to work. For a long time he struggled, trying to get the egg to go through the neck of the bottle. He put the pan of vinegar

272

back on the stove, intending to reheat the egg, then picked it up and burned his fingers. After a second bath in the hot vinegar, the shell of the egg had been softened a little but not enough for his purpose. He worked and worked and a spirit of desperate determination took possession of him. When he thought that at last the trick was about to be consummated, the delayed train came in at the station and Joe Kane started to go nonchalantly out at the door. Father made a last desperate effort to conquer the egg and make it do the thing that would establish his reputation as one who knew how to entertain guests who came into his restaurant. He worried the egg. He attempted to be somewhat rough with it. He swore and the sweat stood out on his forehead. The egg broke under his hand. When the contents spurted over his clothes, Joe Kane, who had stopped at the door, turned and laughed.

A roar of anger rose from my father's throat. He danced and shouted a string of inarticulate words. Grabbing another egg from the basket on the counter, he threw it, just missing the head of the young man as he dodged through the door and escaped.

Father came upstairs to mother and me with an egg in his hand. I do not know what he intended to do. I imagine he had some idea of destroying it, of destroying all eggs, and that he intended to let mother and me see him begin. When, however, he got into the presence of mother something happened to him. He laid the egg gently on the table and dropped on his knees by the bed as I have already explained. He later decided to close the restaurant for the night and to come upstairs and get into bed. When he did so he blew out the light and after much muttered conversation both he and mother went to sleep. I suppose I went to sleep also, but my sleep was troubled. I awoke at dawn and for a long time looked at the egg that lay on the table. I wondered why eggs had to be and why from the egg came the hen who again laid the egg. The question got into my blood. It has stayed there, I imagine, because I am the son of my father. At any rate, the problem remains unsolved in my mind. And that, I conclude, is but another evidence of the complete and final triumph of the egg—at least as far as my family is concerned.

Critical Essay

Zooming in and Zooming out: A Study of Point of View in the Short Story "The Egg"

Point of view is the way a story is told. It is the voice outside the action that reaches readers and shapes their attitudes towards the events being presented, and their attitudes will be controlled by the author through his technical management of point of view. In a large way, point of view is often highly suggestive of the themes.

Sherwood Anderson's short story "The Egg" was published in the 1920s, when optimism was prevailing and people believed in their American Dreams. The story states very clearly at the very beginning that "The American passion for getting up in the world took possession of them." However, just as many people were attracted by their American Dreams, many people were also greatly disappointed when they failed to fulfill their dreams. In the story "The Egg", Sherwood Anderson vividly narrated the disillusionment of the American Dream.

A large part of the story is narrated through the participant narrator "I". As a child, "I" witnessed my father, "by nature a cheerful and kindly" farmer who had been infected with the American passion for "success", embarked on a series of unpromising affairs.

If one reads carefully, one will easily discern two distinct voices in the narration. One is the "experiencing narrative voice" and the other "recalling narrative voice". The "experiencing narrative voice" refers to the voice of narrator "I" when he is a child, narrating what he is experiencing. The "recalling narrative voice" refers to the voice of the narrator "I" when he has grown up and makes comments on what he has experienced as a child.

The "experiencing narrative voice" which is naïve and innocent in the story helps readers immensely to gain a glimpse into the boy's inner world, bringing a focus on the character's mentality and psychology.

I went to school in the town and was glad to be away from the farm and from the presence of the discouraged, sad-looking chickens. Still I was not very joyous. In the evening I walked home from school along Turner's Pike and remembered the children I had seen playing in the town school yard. A troop of little girls had gone hopping about and singing. I tried that. Down along the frozen road I went hopping solemnly on one leg. "Hippity Hop to the Barber Shop," I sang shrilly. Then I stopped and looked doubtfully about. I was afraid of being seen in my gay mood.

Additionally, in such a voice, the author is enabled to record realistically what a boy can possibly see, hear, and think of his parents. It contributes greatly to the authenticity of the narration as the boy recounts in minute details his experience with his parents.

The wagon that contained our goods had been borrowed for the day from Mr. Albert Griggs, a neighbor. Out of its sides stuck the legs of cheap chairs and at the back of the pile of beds, tables, and boxes filled with kitchen utensils was a crate of live chickens, and on top of that the baby carriage in which I had been wheeled about in my infancy. Why we stuck to the baby carriage I don't know. It was unlikely other children would be born and the wheels were broken.

While the first-hand experience makes the story convincing and vivid, it also gives the story a touch of humor as can be verified by the boy's account of the chickens' tragic and dreadful cycle.

It is born out of an egg, lives for a few weeks as a tiny fluffy thing such as you will see pictured on Easter cards, then becomes hideously naked, eats quantities of corn and meal bought by the sweat of your father's brow, gets diseases called pip, cholera, and other names, stands looking with stupid eyes at the sun, becomes sick and dies. A few hens and now and then a rooster, intended to serve God's mysterious ends, struggle through to maturity. The hens lay eggs out of which come other chickens and the dreadful cycle is thus made complete. It is all unbelievably complex.

The chicken's tragedy is, in a way, a metaphor for their own tragedy, which is made very obvious in a context where the theme is stated explicitly as soon as the story opens. It is an ingenious deliberation on the author's part to make the boy comment on the chicken's tragedy, totally unaware of the connection between himself and the chicken. While readers most probably could not help shedding sympathetic tears for the boy and his family, they would find a voluntary smile irresistible as the boy, prematurely, philosophies on a chicken's life.

Such a voice is very much like the "zooming in" in the shooting of a film, which helps readers tremendously obtain a very close look at the family. Meanwhile, as the camera zooms in, it needs to zoom out, too. In the present story, the narration is alternatively interrupted by the "recalling narrative voice", which is, in contrast, calm, rational and philosophical. It is like stepping away from the character and perceiving people and events from a more objective perspective. It serves ideally to make comments on and evaluate the characters and what they do as well as, at times, express his personal views about human life in general. Soon after the boy stops singing shrilly and looks doubtfully about, "afraid of being seen in [his] gay mood", the "recalling narrative voice" immediately provides a footnote, saying that "It must have seemed to me that I was doing a thing that should not be done by one who, like myself, had been raised on a chicken farm where death was a daily visitor." After the boy's meticulous account of the family's move to Bidwell, "a tiny caravan of hope looking for a new place from which to start on our upward journey through life", a "recalling narrative voice" laments, "People who have few possessions cling tightly to those they have. That is one of the facts that make life so discouraging."

A more obvious example occurs when the boy makes an account of the chicken's dreadful cycle. The "experiencing narrative voice" melts into a "recalling narrative voice", as a boy's innocent and naïve account was replaced by an adult's contemplation and reflection in the form of lengthy comments on life in general.

In later life I have seen how a literature has been built up on the subject of fortunes to be made out of the raising of chickens. It is intended to be read by the gods who have just eaten of the tree of the knowledge of good and evil. It is a hopeful literature and declares that much may be done by simple ambitious people who own a few hens. Do not be led astray by it. It was not written for you. Go hunt for gold on the frozen hills of Alaska, put your faith in the honesty of a politician, believe if you will that the world is daily growing better and that good will triumph over evil, but do not read and believe the literature that is written concerning the hen. It was not written for you.

Such alternative voices render the narration of the story artistically dimensional, lending such depth and richness to the story that a more straightforward narration, or one single narrative voice, could not possibly achieve.

What is more innovative as far as point of view is concerned in the story is that, towards the end of the story, the author changed first-person point of view to third-person omniscient point of view. Such a change, though unconventional, does provide great freedom for the narrator to move at will in time and place, to shift from character to character, and to report their doings, emotions, and states of consciousness in the most convenient way for both the readers' and the author's utmost benefits.

Father grinned and winked at his visitor. Joe Kane decided that the man who confronted him was mildly insane but harmless. He drank the cup of coffee that had been given him and began to read his paper again. When the egg had been heated in vinegar, father carried it on a spoon to the counter and going into a back room got an empty bottle. He was angry because his visitor did not watch him as he began to do his trick, but nevertheless went cheerfully to work. For a long time he struggled, trying to get the egg to go through the neck of the bottle... Grabbing another egg from the basket on the counter, he threw it, just missing the head of the young man as he dodged through the door and escaped.

The third-person omniscient point of view is very much in keeping with the "recalling narrative voice" in that it is also like a camera zooming out, but this time at an even greater distance. Overall, Sherwood Anderson makes a deft use of "zooming in" and "zooming out" technique as he shifts from "experiencing narrative voice" to "recalling narrative voice", from the first-person point of view to the third-person omniscient point of view. A good story is always told in a slanting way because, as exemplified by the present story, such a slant provides space and time for both factual details and thoughtful comments, both superficial delightfulness and philosophical profoundness.

The Bigness of the World[1]

Lori Ostlund (1965–)

The year that Ilsa Maria Lumpkin took care of us, Martin was ten going on eleven and I, eleven going on twelve. We considered ourselves almost adults, on the cusp of no longer requiring supervision, but because our days were far more interesting with Ilsa in them, we did not force the issue. Her job was to be there waiting when we arrived home from school, to prepare snacks and help with homework and ask about our days, for our parents were deeply involved at that time with what they referred to as their "careers," both of them spending long hours engaged in activities that seemed to Martin and me nebulous at best. We understood, of course, that our mother did something at our grandfather's bank, but when our father overheard us describing her job in this way to Ilsa, he admonished us later, saying, "Your mother is vice president of the bank. That is not just *something.*"

Then, perhaps suspecting that his job seemed to us equally vague, he took out his wallet and handed Martin and me one of his business cards, on which was inscribed his name, Matthew Koeppe, and the words *PR Czar.* For several long seconds, Martin and I stared down at the card, and our father stared at us. I believe that he wanted to understand us, wanted to know, for example, how we viewed the world, what interested or frightened or perplexed us, but this required patience, something that our father lacked, for he simply did not have enough time at his disposal to be patient, to stand there and puzzle out what it was about his business card that we did not understand. Instead, he went quietly off to his study to make telephone calls, and the next day, I asked Ilsa what a *czar* was, spelling the word out because I could not imagine how to pronounce a *c* and *z* together, but she said that they were people who lived in Russia, royalty, which made no sense.

Ilsa often spent evenings with us as well, for our parents kept an intense social calendar, attending dinners that were, my mother explained, an extension of what she did all day long, but in more elegant clothing. Ilsa wore perfume when she came at night, and while neither Martin nor I liked the smell, we appreciated the gesture, the implication that she thought of being with us as an evening out. She also brought popsicles, which she hid in her purse because our parents did not approve of popsicles,

---

1   Lori Ostlund, *The Bigness of the World* (Scribner, 2010), pp. 1–24.

though often she forgot about them until long after they had melted, and when she finally did remember and pulled them out, the seams of the packages oozing blue or red, our two favorite flavors, she would look dismayed for just a moment before announcing, "Not to worry, my young charges. We shall pop them in the freezer, and they will be as good as new." Of course, they never were as good as new but were instead like popsicles that had melted and been refrozen—shapeless with a thick, gummy coating. We ate them anyway because we did not want to hurt Ilsa's feelings, which we thought of as more real, more fragile, than other people's feelings.

Most afternoons, the three of us visited the park near our house. Though it was only four blocks away, Ilsa inevitably began to cry at some point during the walk, her emotions stirred by any number of things, which she loosely identified as *death*, *beauty*, and *inhumanity*: the bugs caught in the grilles of the cars that we passed (death); two loose dogs humping on the sidewalk across our path (beauty); and the owners who finally caught up with them and forced them apart before they were finished (inhumanity). We were not used to adults who cried freely or openly, for this was Minnesota, where people guarded their emotions, a tradition in which Martin and I had been well schooled. Ilsa, while she was from here, was not, as my mother was fond of saying, *of* here, which meant that she did not become impatient or embarrassed when we occasionally cried as well. In fact, she encouraged it. Still, I was never comfortable when it happened and did not want attention paid me over it—unlike Ilsa, who sank to the ground and sobbed while Martin and I sat on either side of her, holding her hands or resting ours on her back.

We also liked Ilsa because she was afraid of things, though not the normal things that we expected adults to be afraid of and certainly not the kinds of things that Martin and I had been taught to fear—strangers, candy found on the ground, accidentally poking out an eye. We kept careful track of her fears and divided them into two categories, the first comprising things of which she claimed to be "absolutely petrified", her euphemism for those things that she deeply disliked, among them abbreviated language of any sort. Ilsa frequently professed her disdain for what she called "the American compulsion toward brevity". She did not use contractions and scolded us when we did, claiming that they brought down the level of the conversation. Furthermore, when referring to people, she employed their full names: the first name, what she called the "Christian" name although she was not, to my knowledge, actively religious; the middle name, which she once described as a person's essence; and the surname, the name that, for better or worse, bound them to their families.

Ilsa eschewed all acronyms and initialisms, even those so entrenched in our vocabularies that we could not recall what the initials stood for. She once left the following message on my parents' answering machine: "I am very sorry that I will be unavailable to stay with the children Saturday evening, October 24, as I have been invited by a dear friend to spend the weekend in Washington, District of Columbia."

My parents listened to this message repeatedly, always maintaining a breathless silence until the very end, at which point they exploded into laughter. I did not understand what was funny about the message, but when I asked my mother to explain, she gave one of her typically vague responses. "That Ilsa," she said. "She's just such a pistol." Something else must have occurred to her then, for a moment later she turned back to add, "We shouldn't mention this to Ilsa, Veronica. Sometimes families have their little jokes." Of course, I had no intention of telling Ilsa, a decision based not on family allegiance but on my growing sense that laughter was rarely a straightforward matter.

My mother and Ilsa first met at Weight Brigade, to which my mother had belonged for years, certainly as long as I could remember, though she had never been fat, not even plump. She was fond of saying that she had no "love relationship" with food, lingo that she had picked up at her meetings, sitting amidst women who had not just love relationships with food but desperate, passionate affairs on the side. My mother, who kept track of numbers for a living, liked that Weight Brigade promoted a strict policy of calorie counting and exercise, which she thought of in terms of debits and credits, though I suspect that what she liked most of all was the easy sense of achievement that she felt there among women who struggled terribly, and often unsuccessfully, with their weight.

She rarely missed the weekly meetings, but because she preferred to compartmentalize the various areas of her life, she disapproved greatly of Weight Brigade's phone-buddy system, under which she was paired with another member who might call her at any time, day or night, to discuss temptation. I once heard her tell my father that these conversations, mostly breathy descriptions of ice cream that only served to work her phone partner into a frenzy of desire, were akin to phone sex. After several minutes of listening to her phone buddy's chatter, she would hear the freezer door open and the rattle of a cutlery drawer, and then her phone buddy would bid her an unintelligible goodbye, speaking through, as my mother liked to put it, "a mouthful of shame".

Over the years, my mother was paired with numerous women (as well as one man), all of whom she alienated quickly, unable to sympathize with their constant cravings or the ease with which they capitulated. Furthermore, when they sobbed hysterically during weigh-ins, she dealt with them sternly, even harshly, explaining that they knew the consequences of gorging themselves on potato chips and cookies, which made their responses to the weight gain disingenuous as far as she was concerned. My mother was always very clear in her opinions; she said that in banking one had to be, that she needed to be able to size people up quickly and then carry through on her assessment without hesitation or regret, a policy that she applied at home as well, which meant that if I failed to unload the dishwasher within two hours after it finished running or lied about completing a school assignment, she moved swiftly into punishment mode and became indignant when I feigned surprise. Among the members of Weight Brigade, her approach won her no few enemies. Eventually, she was no longer assigned phone buddies, and by the time she met Ilsa, the other members were refusing even to sit near my mother at meetings, though she claimed to be unbothered by this, citing envy as their sole motivation.

Ilsa was plump when we knew her but had not always been. This we learned from photographs of her holding animals from the pound where she volunteered, a variety of cats and dogs and birds for which she had provided temporary care. She went to Weight Brigade only that one time, the time that she met my mother, and never went back because she said that she could not bear to listen to the vilification of butter and sugar, but Martin and I had seen the lists that our mother kept of her own daily caloric intake, and we suspected that Ilsa had simply been overwhelmed by the math that belonging to Weight Brigade involved, for math was another thing that "absolutely petrified" Ilsa. When my parents asked how much they owed her, she always replied, "I am sure that you must know far better than I, for I have not the remotest idea." And when Martin or I required help with our math homework, she answered in the high, quivery voice that she used when she sang opera: "Mathematics is an entirely useless subject, and we shall not waste our precious time on it." Perhaps we appeared skeptical, for she often added, "Really, my dear children, I cannot remember the last time that I used mathematics."

Ilsa's fear of math stemmed, I suspect, from the fact that she seemed unable to grasp even the basic tenets upon which math rested. Once, for example, after we had made a pizza together and taken it from the oven, she suggested that we cut it into very small pieces because she was ravenous and that way, she said, there would be more of it to go around.

"More pieces you mean?" we clarified tentatively.

"No, my silly billies. More pizza," she replied confidently, and though we tried to convince her of the impossibility of such a thing, explaining that the pizza *was* the size it was, she had laughed in a way that suggested that she was charmed by our ignorance.

Ilsa wore colorful, flowing dresses and large hats that she did not take off, even when she opened the oven door to slide a pizza inside or sat eating refrozen popsicles with us on the back deck. Her evening hats were more complicated than the daytime hats, involving not just bows but flowers and actual feathers and even, on the hat that Martin and I privately referred to as "Noah's Ark," a simple diorama of three-dimensional animals made of pressed felt. Martin and I considered Ilsa's hats extremely *tasteful*, a word that we had heard our parents use often enough to have developed a feel for. That is, she did not wear holiday-themed hats decked with Christmas tree balls or blinking Halloween pumpkins, although she did favor pastels at Easter. Still, Ilsa's hats really only seemed appropriate on the nights that she sang opera, belting out arias while we sat on the sofa and listened. Once, she performed Chinese opera for us, which was like nothing that we had ever heard before and which we both found startling and a little frightening.

Later, when we told our parents that Ilsa had sung Chinese opera for us, our mother looked perplexed and said, "I didn't know that Ilsa knew Chinese."

"She doesn't," we replied. "She just makes it up." And then Martin and I proceeded to demonstrate, imitating the sounds that Ilsa had made, high-pitched, nasally sounds that resembled the word *sure*. Our parents looked troubled by this and said that they did not want us making fun of Chinese opera, which they called an ancient and respected art form.

"But we aren't making fun of it," I replied. "We like it." This was true, but they explained that if we really liked it, we wouldn't feel compelled to imitate it, which Martin and I later agreed made no sense. We did not say so to my parents because about some things there was simply no arguing. We knew that they had spoken to Ilsa as well, for she did not sing Chinese opera again, sticking instead with Puccini and Wagner though she did not know Italian or German either.

My mother, in sartorial contrast to Ilsa, favored tailored trousers, blazers, and crisply ironed shirts, and when my father occasionally teased her about her wardrobe, pointing out that it was possible to look vice presidential without completely hiding her figure, my mother sternly reminded him that the only figures she wanted her clients thinking about were the ones that she calculated for their loans. My mother liked clothes well enough but shopped mainly by catalog in order to save time, which meant that the UPS driver visited our house frequently. His name was Bruce, and Martin and I had always known him as a sullen man who did not respond to questions about his well-being, the weather, or his day, which were the sorts of questions that our parents and the babysitters prior to Ilsa tended to ask. Ilsa, however, was not interested in such things. Rather, she offered him milk on overcast days and pomegranate juice, which my parents stocked for her, on sunny, and then, as Bruce stood on the front step drinking his milk or pomegranate juice, she asked him whether he had ever stolen a package (no) and whether he had ever opened a package out of curiosity (yes, one time, but the contents had disappointed him greatly).

Martin and I generally stood behind Ilsa during these conversations, peering around her and staring at Bruce, in awe of his transformation into a pleasant human being, but when we heard her soliciting tips on how to pack her hats so that they would not be damaged during shipping, we both stepped forward, alarmed. "Are you moving?" we asked, for we lived in fear of losing Ilsa, believing, I suppose, that we did not really deserve her.

"No, my dears. I'm simply gathering information." She clasped her hands in front of her as she did when she sang opera, the right one curled down over the left as though her fingers were engaged in a tug-of-war. "It is a very sad thing that nowadays there is so little useless information," she declaimed, affecting even more of a British accent than she normally did. "That is our beloved Oscar, of course," she added, referring to Oscar Wilde, whom she was fond of quoting.

When Bruce left, she first washed his glass and then phoned my mother at work to let her know of the package's arrival, despite the fact that packages were delivered almost daily. My mother, who was fond of prefacing comments with the words, "I'm a busy woman," rarely took these calls. Instead, Ilsa left messages with my mother's secretary, Kenneth Bloomquist, their conversation generally evolving as follows: "Hello, Mr. Bloomquist. This is Ilsa Maria Lumpkin. Would you be so kind as to let Mrs. Koeppe know that the United Parcel Service driver has left a package?" She ended each call with neither a *goodbye* nor a *thank you* but with a statement of the time. "It is precisely 4:17 post meridiem," she would say, for even when it came to time, abbreviations were unacceptable.

Then there were the things of which Ilsa truly was afraid, but they, too, were things that I had never known adults to be afraid of. One night, as Martin and I sat at the dining room table completing our homework while Ilsa prepared grilled cheese sandwiches with pickles, she began to scream from the kitchen, a loud, continuous ejection of sound not unlike the honking of a car horn. Martin and I leapt up as one and rushed to her, both of us, I suspect, secretly wanting to be the one to calm her, though in those days he and I were rarely competitive.

"What is it?" we cried out in unison, and she pointed mutely to the bread, but when Martin examined the loaf, he found nothing odd save for a bit of green mold that had formed along the top crust. Ilsa would not go near the bread and begged him to take it into the garage and dispose of it immediately. He did not, for we both knew that my parents would not approve of such wastefulness, not when the mold could be scraped off and the bread eaten. I do not mean to suggest that my parents were in any way stingy, for they were not. However, they did not want money to stand between us and common sense, did not want us growing up under what my father was fond of calling "the tutelage of wastefulness". They were no longer churchgoers, either one of them, but Martin and I were raised according to the tenets of their residual Protestantism.

Ilsa was also deeply afraid to ride in cars with power windows, which both of ours had and which meant that she would not accept a ride home, even at the end of a very late evening. "What would happen if you were to drive into a lake?" she asked my father each time he suggested it. "However would we escape?" When my father explained to her that there were no lakes, no bodies of water of any sort, along the twelve blocks that lay between our house and her apartment, which was actually a tiny guest cottage behind another house, she laughed at him the way that she had laughed at Martin and me when we tried to explain about the pizza.

Our neighborhood was quite safe, but my father still felt obligated to walk Ilsa home, and while he complained mightily about having to do so, he always returned disheveled and laughing, and eventually my mother suggested that she walk Ilsa home sometimes instead, not because she distrusted my father, for she did not, but because she too wanted to return humming and laughing, her clothing wrinkled and covered with twigs. Martin and I encouraged this as well because we were worried about our mother, who had become increasingly distracted and often yelled at us for small things, for counting too slowly when she asked us to check how many eggs were left in the carton or forgetting to throw both dirty socks into the hamper. Of course most people will hear "twigs" and "clothing wrinkled" and think sex, and while I cannot absolutely rule this out, I am fairly sure that these outings did not involve anything as mundane as sex in the park. My certainty is based not on the child's inability to imagine her parents engaged in such things; they were probably not swingers in the classic sense of the word, but they were products of the time and just conservative enough on the surface to suggest the possibility. No, my conviction lies entirely with Ilsa.

It was my fault that things with Ilsa came to an end. One evening, after my father returned from walking her home, he went into the bathroom to brush his teeth and noticed that his toothbrush was wet. "Has one of you been playing with my toothbrush?" he asked from the hallway outside our bedrooms.

"No, Ilsa used it," I said at last, but only after he had come into my bedroom and turned on the light. "We had carrots, and she needs to brush her teeth immediately after she eats colorful foods."

My father stared at me for a moment. "Does Ilsa always use my toothbrush?"

"No," I said patiently. "Only when we have colorful foods." This was true. She had not used it since we had radishes the week before.

The next morning behind closed doors, he and my mother discussed Ilsa while Martin and I attempted, unsuccessfully, to eavesdrop. In the end, neither of them wanted to confront Ilsa about the toothbrush because they found it embarrassing. Instead, they decided to tell Ilsa that Martin and I had become old enough to supervise ourselves. We protested, suggesting that we simply buy Ilsa her own toothbrush, but my father and mother said that it was more than the toothbrush and that we really were old enough to stay alone. We insisted that we were not, but the call to Ilsa was made.

Nonetheless, for the next several weeks, my father was there waiting for us when we returned from school each day. He told us that he had made some scheduling changes at work, called in some favors, but we did not know what this meant because we still did not understand what our father did. He spent most afternoons on the telephone, talking in a jovial voice that became louder when he wanted something and louder again when the other party agreed. He did not make snacks for us, so Martin and I usually peeled carrots and then sat on my bed eating them as we talked about Ilsa, primarily concerning ourselves with two questions: whether she missed us and how we might manage to see her again. The latter was answered soon enough, for during the third week of this new arrangement, my father announced that he and my mother needed to go somewhere the next afternoon and that we would be left alone in order to prove our maturity.

The next day, we watched our parents drive away. Once they were out of sight,

I began counting to two hundred and eighty, for that, Ilsa had once explained, was the amount of time that it took the average person to realize that he or she had left something behind. "Two hundred and eighty," I announced several minutes later, and since our parents had not reappeared, we went into our bedrooms and put on our dress clothes, Martin a suit and tie, which he loved having the opportunity to wear, and I, a pair of dress slacks and a sweater, which is what I generally wore for holidays and events that my parents deemed worthy of something beyond jeans. Then, because we did not have a key, we locked the door of the house from the inside and climbed out a side window, leaving it slightly ajar behind us. We knew where Ilsa lived, for our parents had pointed it out on numerous occasions, and we set off running toward her in our dress shoes, but when we were halfway there, Martin stopped suddenly.

"We don't have anything for her," he said. "We can't go without something. It wouldn't be right."

Martin was what some of the boys in his class called a *sissy* because he did not like games that involved pushing or hitting, preferring to jump rope during recess, and because he always considered the feelings of others. Though I wanted to think that I too considered the feelings of others, I often fell short, particularly when it was not convenient to do so or when my temper dictated otherwise. When it came to pushing and hitting, Martin and I fully parted ways, for I was fond of both activities. Thus, several months earlier, when I heard that three of Martin's classmates had called him a sissy, I waited for them after school and threatened to punch the next one who used the word. I should mention that while Martin had inherited my mother's slender build, I took after my father, a man who had once picked up our old refrigerator by himself and carried it out to the garage, and so the three boys had looked down at the ground for a moment and then, one by one, slunk away. When we got home, I told Ilsa what had happened, and Martin stood nearby, listening to me relate the story with a thoughtful expression on his face. He had a habit of standing erectly, like a dancer, and when I finished, she turned to him and said, "Why, it is a marvelous thing to be a sissy, Martin. You will enjoy your life much more than those boys. You will be able to cook and enjoy flowers and appreciate all sorts of music. I absolutely adore sissies."

Thus, when Martin insisted that we could not visit Ilsa without a gift, I did not argue, for I trusted Martin about such things. We turned and ran back home, re-entering through the window, and Martin went into the kitchen and put together a variety of spices—cloves, a stick of cinnamon, and a large nutmeg pit—which he wrapped in cheesecloth and tied carefully with a piece of ribbon. "That's not a gift," I said, but Martin explained to me patiently that it was, was, in fact, the sort of gift Ilsa would love.

Fifteen minutes later, we stood on the porch of Ilsa's cottage, waiting for her to answer the door. We had already knocked three times, and I knocked twice more before I finally turned to Martin and asked fretfully, "What if she's not home?" To be honest, it had never occurred to us that Ilsa might not be home, for we could only think of Ilsa in regard to ourselves, which meant that when she was not with us, she was here, at her cottage, because we were incapable of imagining her elsewhere—certainly not with another family, caring for children who were not us.

"She must be at the pound," I said suddenly and with great relief.

But Ilsa was home. As we were about to leave, she opened her door and stared at us for several distressing seconds before pulling us to her tightly. "My bunnies!" she cried out, and we thought that she meant us, but she pulled us inside and shut the door, saying, "Quickly now, before their simple little minds plot an escape," and we realized then that she truly meant rabbits.

"Martin," she said, looking him up and down, her voice low and unsteady, and then she turned and scrutinized me as well. Her hair was pulled back in a very loose French braid, and she was not wearing a hat, the first time that either of us had seen her without one. It felt strange to be standing there in her tiny cottage, stranger yet to be seeing her without a hat, intimate in a way that seemed almost unbearable.

"You're not wearing a hat," Martin said matter-of-factly.

"I was just taking a wee nap," she replied. I could see that this was true, for her face was flushed and deeply creased from the pillow, her eyes dull with slumber, as though she had been sleeping for some time.

"We brought you something," said Martin, holding up the knotted cheesecloth.

"How lovely," she exclaimed, clapping her hands together clumsily before taking the ball of spices and holding it to her nose with both hands. She closed her eyes and inhaled deeply, but the moment went on and on, becoming uncomfortable.

"Kikes!" screamed a voice from a corner of the room, and Ilsa's eyes snapped open. "Kikes and dykes!" screamed the voice again.

"Martin, I will not tolerate such language," Ilsa said firmly.

"It wasn't me," said Martin, horrified, for we both knew what the words meant.

"I think it was him," I said, pointing to the corner where a large cage hung, inside of which perched a shabby-looking green parrot. The bird regarded us for a moment, screeched, "Ass pirates and muff divers!" leaned over, and tossed a beakful of seeds into the air like confetti.

"Of course it was him," said Ilsa. "The foul-mouthed rascal. I saved his life, but he hardly seems grateful. His name is Martin."

"Martin?" said Martin happily. "Like me?"

"Yes, I named him after you, my dear, though it was wishful thinking on my part. I dare say you could teach him a thing or two about manners."

"Why does he say those things?" asked Martin.

"Martin ended up at the pound a few months ago after his former owner, a thoroughly odious man, died in a house fire—he fell asleep smoking a cigar. Martin escaped through a window, but it seems there is no undoing the former owner's work, which

285

made adoption terribly unlikely. They were going to put him down, so I have taken him instead." She sighed. "The bunnies—poor souls—are absolutely terrified of him."

Martin and I looked around Ilsa's living room, trying to spot the bunnies, but the only indication of them lay in the fact that Ilsa had covered her small sofa and arm chair with plastic wrap as though she were about to paint the walls. "Where are the bunnies?" I asked. I did not say so, but I was afraid of rabbits, for I had been bitten by one at an Easter event at the shopping mall several years earlier. In truth, it had been nothing more than a nibble, but it had startled me enough that I had dropped the rabbit and then been scolded by the teenage attendant for my carelessness.

"I should imagine that they are in the escritoire," she said, and Martin nodded as though he knew what the escritoire was.

"Come," said Ilsa. "Let us go into the kitchen, away from this bad-mannered fellow. We shall mull some cider using your extraordinarily thoughtful gift."

We huddled at a square yellow table inside her small, dreary kitchen, watching her pour cider from a jug into a saucepan, focusing as deeply on this task as someone charged with splitting a neutron. "How are you, Ilsa?" asked Martin, sounding strangely grown up. She dropped the spice ball into the pan, adjusted the flame, and only then turned to answer.

"I am positively exuberant," she replied. "Indeed, Martin, things could not be better here at 53 Ridgecrest Drive." She paused, as though considering what topic we might discuss next, and then she asked how we were and, after we had both answered that we were well, she asked about our parents. We were in the habit of answering Ilsa honestly, and so I told her that our parents seemed strange lately.

"Strange?" she said, her mouth curling up as though the word had a taste attached to it that she did not care for.

"Yes," I said. "For one thing, our father is home every day when we arrive from school"—Martin looked at me, for on the way over we had agreed that we would not tell Ilsa this, lest it hurt her feelings to know that our parents had lied, so I went on quickly—"and our mother is gone until very late most nights, and when she is home, she hardly speaks, even to our father."

"I see," said Ilsa, but not as though she really did, and then she stood and ladled up three cups of cider, which she placed on saucers and carried to the table, one cup at a time. She fished out the soggy bundle of spices and placed that on a fourth saucer, which she set in the middle of the table as though it were a centerpiece, something aesthetically pleasing for us to consider as we sipped our cider.

"I may presume that your parents are aware of your visit to me?" she said, and we both held our cups to our mouths and blew across the surface of the cider, watching as it rippled slightly, and finally Martin replied that they were not.

"Children," Ilsa said, "that will not do." This was the closest that Ilsa had ever come to actually scolding us, though her tone spoke more of exhaustion than disapproval, and we both looked up at her sadly.

"I shall ring them immediately," she said.

"They aren't home," I told her.

Ilsa consulted her watch, holding it up very close to her eyes in order to make out the numbers because the watch was tiny, the face no larger than a dime. Once I had asked Ilsa why she did not get a bigger watch, one that she could simply glance at the way that other people did, but she said that that was precisely the reason—that one should never get into the habit of glancing at one's watch. "Please excuse me, my dears. I see that it is time to visit my apothecary," she said, and she stood and left the room.

"What is her apothecary?" I asked Martin, whispering, and he whispered back that he did not know but that perhaps she was referring to the bathroom.

We were quiet then, studying Ilsa's kitchen in a way that we had not been able to do when she was present. There was only one window, a single pane that faced a cement wall. This accounted for the dreariness, this and the fact that the room was tiny, three or even four times smaller than our kitchen. When I commented on this to Martin, he said, "I think that Ilsa's kitchen is the perfect size. You know what she always says— that she gets lost in our kitchen." But his tone was defensive, and I knew that he was disappointed as well.

"There's no island," I said suddenly. Our parents' kitchen had not one island but two, which Ilsa had given names. The one nearest the stove she called Jamaica and the other, Haiti, and when we helped her cook, she would hand us things, saying, "Ferry this cutting board over to Haiti," and "Tomatoes at the south end of Jamaica, please." Once, during a period when she had been enamored of religious dietary restrictions, she had announced, "Dairy on Jamaica, my young sous chefs. Meat on Haiti," and we had cooked the entire meal according to her notions of kosher, though when it came time to eat, she had forgotten about the rules, stacking cheese and bacon on our hamburgers and pouring us each a large glass of milk.

From the other room, we heard a sound like maracas being rattled, which made me think of our birthdays because our parents always took us to Mexican Village, where a mariachi band came to our table and sang "Happy Birthday" in Spanish. We heard water running and then the parrot screaming obscenities again as Ilsa passed through the living room and back into the kitchen. She had put on a hat, one that we had not seen before, white with a bit of peacock feather glued to one side.

"This has been an absolutely splendid visit, but I must be getting the two of you home," she said. "Gather your things, my goslings." But we had come with nothing save the spices, which now sat in a pool of brown liquid, and so we had no things to gather.

When we arrived home that afternoon, our father was already there, waiting for us at the dining room table, where he sat with the tips of his hands pressed together forming a peak. He did not ask where we had been but instead told us to sit down because he needed to explain something to us, something about our mother, who would not be coming home that day. "You know that your mother works for your grandfather?" he began, and we nodded and waited. "Well, your grandfather has done something wrong. He's taken money from the bank."

"But it's his bank," I replied.

"Yes," said my father. "But the money is not his. It belongs to the people who use the bank, who put their money there so that it will be safe."

Again, we nodded, for we understood this about banks. In fact, we both had our own accounts at the bank, where we kept the money that we received for our birthdays. "He stole money?" I asked, for that is how it sounded, and I wanted to be sure.

"Well," said my father. "It's called embezzling." But when I looked up embezzling that evening, I discovered that our grandfather had indeed stolen money.

"And what about our mother?" Martin asked.

"It's complicated," said our father, "but they've arrested her also."

"Arrested?" I said, for there had been no talk of arresting before this.

"Yes," said my father, and then he began to cry.

We had never seen our father cry. He was, I learned that day, a silent crier. He laid his head on the table, his arms forming a nest around it, and we knew that he was crying only because his shoulders heaved up and down. I sat very still, not looking at him because I did not know how to think of him as anything but my father, instead focusing on the overhead light, waiting for it to click, which it generally did every thirty seconds or so. The sound was actually somewhere between a click and a scratch, easy to hear but apparently difficult to fix, for numerous electricians had been called in to do so and had failed. I had always complained mightily about the clicking, which prevented me from concentrating on my homework, but that day as I sat at the table with my weeping father and Martin, the light was silent, unexpectedly and overwhelmingly silent.

Then, without first consulting me with his eyes, our custom in matters relating to our parents, Martin slipped from his chair and stood next to my father, and, after a moment, placed a hand on my father's shoulder. In those days, Martin's hands were unusually plump, at odds with the rest of his body, and from where I sat, directly across from my father, Martin's hand looked like a fat, white bullfrog perched on my father's shoulder. My father's sobbing turned audible, a high-pitched whimper like a dog makes when left alone in a car, and then quickly flattened out and stopped.

"It will be okay," Martin said, rubbing my father's shoulder with his fat, white hand, and my father sat up and nodded several times in rapid succession, gulping as though he had been underwater.

But it would not be okay. After a very long trial, my mother went to jail, eight years with the possibility of parole after six. My grandfather was put on trial as well, but he died of a heart attack on the second day, leaving my mother to face the jury and crowded courtroom alone. Her lawyers wanted to blame everything on him, arguing that he was dead and thus unable to deny the charges or be punished, advice that my mother resisted until it became clear that she might be facing an even longer sentence. Martin and I learned all of this from the newspaper, which we were not supposed to read but did, and from the taunts hurled at us by children who used to be our friends but were no longer allowed to play with us because many of their parents had money in my grandfather's bank and even those who didn't felt that my mother had betrayed the entire community.

We missed her terribly in the beginning, my father most of all, though I believe that he grieved not at being separated from her but because the person she was, or that he had thought she was, no longer existed, which meant that he grieved almost as though she were dead. There was some speculation in the newspaper about my father, about what was referred to as his "possible complicity," but I remain convinced to this day that my father knew nothing about what had been going on at the bank, though whether it was true that it was all my grandfather's doing, that my mother had been nothing more than a loyal daughter as her lawyers claimed—this I will never know. Martin was of the opinion that it shouldn't matter, not to us, but I felt otherwise, particularly when he came home from school with scratches and bruises and black eyes that I knew were given to him because of her, though he always shrugged his shoulders when my father asked what had happened to him and, with a small smile, gave the same reply: "Such is the life of a fairy." My father did not know how to respond to words like *sissy* and *fairy*, nor to the matter-of-fact manner in which Martin uttered them, and so he said nothing, rubbing his ear vigorously for a moment and then turning away, as was his habit when presented with something that he would rather not hear.

Of course, as Ilsa walked us home from her cottage that day, we had no inkling of what lay ahead, no way of knowing that the familiar terrain of our childhoods would soon become a vast, unmarked landscape in which we would be left to wander, motherless and, it seemed to us at times, fatherless as well. Rather, as we walked along holding hands with Ilsa, our concerns were immediate. I fretted aloud that our parents would be angry, but Ilsa assured me that they were more likely to be worried, and though I did not like the idea of worrying them, it seemed far preferable to their anger. There was also the matter of Ilsa herself, Ilsa, who, even with her hat on, seemed unfamiliar, and so Martin and I worked desperately to interest her in the things that we saw around us, things that would have normally moved her to tears but which she now seemed hardly to notice. Across our path was a snail that had presumably been wooed out onto the sidewalk during the previous day's rain and crushed to bits by passersby. I stopped and pointed to it, waiting for her to cry out, "Death, be not proud!" and then to squeeze her eyes shut while allowing us to lead her safely past it, but she glanced at the crushed bits with no more interest than she would have shown a discarded candy wrapper.

289

As we neared our house, I could see my father's car in the driveway. "Can we visit you again, Ilsa?" I asked, turning to her.

"I am afraid that that will not be possible, children," she said. "You see, I will be setting off very soon—really any day now—on a long journey. I suspect that I may be gone for quite some time."

"Are you going to see the ocean?" I asked. At that time in my life I could not imagine anything more terrifying than the ocean, which I knew about only from maps and school and movies.

"Yes," she said after giving the question some thought. "As a matter of fact, I believe that I will see the ocean. Have you ever seen the ocean, children?" Martin and I replied that we had not.

"But you must," she said gravely. "You absolutely must see the ocean."

"Why?" I asked, both frightened and encouraged by her tone. "Why must we?"

"Well," she said after a moment. "However can you expect to understand the bigness of the world if you do not see the ocean?"

"Is there no other way?" Martin asked.

"I suppose there are other ways," Ilsa conceded. "Though certainly the ocean is the most effective."

"But why must we understand the bigness of the world?" I asked.

We were in front of our house by then, and Ilsa stopped and looked at us. "My dear Martin and Veronica," she said in the high, quivery voice that we had been longing for. "I know it may sound frightening, yet I assure you that there have been times in my life when the bigness of the world was my only consolation."

Then, she gave us each a small kiss on the forehead, and we watched her go, her gait unsteady like that of someone thinking too much about the simple act of walking, her white hat bobbing like a sail. At the corner she stopped and turned, and seeing us there still, called, "In you go, children. Your parents will be waiting," so that these were Ilsa's final words to us—ordinary and rushed and, as we would soon discover, untrue.

Critical Essay

Characterization as a Foil in "The Bigness of the World"

Characterization is the presentation of the characters. It is the art of creating characters for a narrative. Characters may be presented by means of description, through their actions, speech, or thoughts. In most stories, writers devote much of the space of a story, to the characterization of the protagonist. However, in "The Bigness of the World", the title story of Lori Ostlund's award winning short story collection, *Ilsa*, there is a very impressive characterization of some minor characters.

The story is about IIsa, whom the Koeppe family hires as the babysitter for the children of the family, and the elder sister, Veronica, is the narrator of the story. The narrator's serious mother and father, a bank vice president and a "PR Czar" are very different from Ilsa, so different that they are, Ilsa being one extreme, just the other extreme of character.

Ilsa is very patient with the children. She is always there waiting for the kids when they arrive home from school. She prepares snacks when they are hungry. She helps them with homework and asks about their days. If the children have any questions, it is Ilsa that they go to for answers.

Unlike Ilsa, the parents of the children are often impatient with them in their respective ways. The father is always too occupied with his work to afford time and attention to his children.

I believe that he wanted to understand us, wanted to know, for example, how we viewed the world, what interested or frightened or perplexed us, but this required patience, something that our father lacked, for he simply did not have enough time at his disposal to be patient, to stand there and puzzle out what it was about his business card that we did not understand.

While the father's impatience with the children is understandable and even acceptable, on account of his busy work, their mother's impatience with them, deriving largely from her violent temper, causes the children quite a lot of pain and misery.

... if I failed to unload the dishwasher within two hours after it finished running or lied about completing a school assignment, she moved swiftly into punishment mode and became indignant when I feigned surprise.

The contrast between Ilsa's patience with the children and their parents' impatience with them is made manifest when the narrator, one of the children, comments that "Ilsa, while she was from here, was not, as my mother was fond of saying, *of* here, which meant that she did not become impatient or embarrassed when we occasionally cried as well. In fact, she encouraged it." It is then easy to see the characterization of the minor characters in the story has been integrated into the characterization of the protagonist, for such characterization serves mainly to delineate a very patient character of the protagonist rather than to impress readers with the parents' impatience, for, in terms of characterization, Ilsa's patience with children is much reinforced by their parents' impatience with their children.

Such contrast of characterization is manyfold and multiple to double and redouble the reinforcement of the presentation of the protagonist. A seemingly superfluous, yet possibly very meaningful, contrast between the characterization of the minor characters and the protagonist is how Ilsa and the mother are dressed. Ilsa loves to be dressed in a way that is doubtlessly unorthodox, unprofessional, and very individual.

Ilsa wore colorful, flowing dresses and large hats that she did not take off, even when she opened the oven door to slide a pizza inside or sat eating refrozen popsicles with us on the back deck. Her evening hats were more complicated than the daytime hats, involving not just bows but flowers and actual feathers and even, on the hat that Martin and I privately referred to as "Noah's Ark," a simple diorama of three-dimensional animals made of pressed felt. Martin and I considered Ilsa's hats extremely tasteful, a word that we had heard our parents use often enough to have developed a feel for. That is, she did not wear holiday-themed hats decked with Christmas tree balls or blinking Halloween pumpkins, although she did favor pastels at Easter. Still, Ilsa's hats really only seemed appropriate on the nights that she sang opera, belting out arias while we sat on the sofa and listened. Once, she performed Chinese opera for us, which was like nothing that we had ever heard before and which we both found startling and a little frightening.

The external appearance reveals in a large part the internal world. From the way Ilsa is dressed one might find it quite easy to understand her unique and quirky character. With such an overall understanding of Ilsa, one is well-prepared to be introduced to, as one goes on to read the story, a character who is "absolutely petrified" of abbreviations and math and "deeply afraid of" mold on bread and cars with power windows. Ilsa's way of dressing is almost akin to an obvious footnote to a character that is imaginative, constantly crying, Chinese opera-imitating, toothbrush-borrowing lunatic.

In the same fashion, the children's mother is dressed in a way that is also very telling of her character, which is, according to the narrator herself, "in sartorial contrast to Ilsa".

My mother, in sartorial contrast to Ilsa, favored tailored trousers, blazers, and crisply ironed shirts, and when my father occasionally teased her about her wardrobe, pointing out that it was possible to look vice presidential without completely hiding her figure, my mother sternly reminded him that the only figures she wanted her clients thinking about were the ones that she calculated for their loans.

The contrast, as employed in the previous instance, serves again to reinforce the characterization of the protagonist in the story, Ilsa. The mention of the word "contrast" makes explicit the author's deliberate use of the contrast of the characters for the benefit of the protagonist.

The contrast between the protagonist and the minor characters, in terms of characterization, develops with the development of the story and becomes more subtle and theme-revealing. The narrator's mother is good at numbers, which is a metaphoric way of saying that she is shrewd and fond of calculating.

My mother, who kept track of numbers for a living, liked that Weight Brigade promoted a strict policy of calorie counting and exercise, which she thought of in terms of debits and credits, though I suspect that what she liked most of all was the easy sense of achievement that she felt there among women who struggled terribly, and often unsuccessfully, with their weight.

Making use of such a metaphor, the author goes on naturally to give a rather lengthy description of how Ilsa is afraid of numbers, or math, as very well exemplified with Ilsa's confusion of "more pieces" of pizza and "more pizza".

The contrasting use of the metaphor helps greatly with the presentation of the more fundamental quality of the protagonist's character and helps the author convey the most important message of the story.

Throughout the story, the characterization of some minor characters serves as a foil for the characterization of the protagonist. Such presentation of the minor characters in the story aims at the ultimate presentation of the protagonist, who would otherwise be less vividly, impressively and dimensionally presented.

ID[1]

Joyce Carol Oates (1938–)

"For an *eiii-dee*," they were saying. "We need to see Lisette Mulvey."

This was unexpected.

In second-period class, at 9:40 A.M., on some damn Monday in some damn winter month she'd lost track of, when even the year—a "new" year—seemed weird to her, like a movie set in a faraway galaxy.

It was one of those school mornings—some older guys had got her high on beer, for a joke. Well, it *was* funny, not just the guys laughing at her but Lisette laughing at herself. Not mean-laughing—she didn't think so—but like they liked her. "*Liz-zete*"— "*Liz-zette*"—was their name for her, high-pitched piping like bats, and they'd run their fingers fast along her arms, her back, like she was scalding hot to the touch.

They picked her up on their way to school. The middle school was close to the high school. Most times, she was with a girlfriend—Keisha or Tanya. They were mature girls for their age—Keisha especially—and not shy like the other middle school girls. They knew how to talk to guys, and guys knew how to talk to them, but it was just talk mostly.

Now this was—math?—damn math class that Lisette hated. It made her feel so stupid. Not that she *was* stupid. It was just that sometimes her thoughts were as snarled as her hair, her eyes leaking tears behind her dark-purple-tinted glasses—*pres-ciption* lenses—so that she couldn't see what the hell the teacher was scribbling on the board, not even the shape of it. Ms. Nowicki would say in her bright hopeful voice, "Who can help me here? Who can tell us what the next step is?" and most of the kids would just sit on their asses, staring. Smirking. Not wanting to be called on. But then Lisette was rarely called on in math class—sometimes she shut her eyes, pretending that she was thinking really hard, and when she opened them there was one of the three or four smart kids in the class at the board, taking the chalk from Nowicki. She tried to watch, and she tried to comprehend. But there was something about the sound of the chalk clicking on the board—not a *black* board, it was green—and the numerals that she was expected to make sense of: she'd begin to feel dizzy.

Her mother, Yvette, had no trouble with numbers. She was a blackjack dealer at the

---

1   Joyce Carol Oates, *The Museum of Dr. Moses* (Ecco Press, 2010), pp. 1–20.

Casino Royale. You had to be smart, and you had to think fast—you had to know what the hell you were doing—to be a blackjack dealer.

Counting cards. This was forbidden. If you caught somebody counting cards you signaled for help. Yvette liked to say that one day soon she would change her name, her hair color, and all that she could about herself, an drive out to Vegas, or to some lesser place, like Reno, and play blackjack in such a way that they'd never catch on—counting cards like no amateur could do.

But if Lisette said, "You're going to take me with you, Momma, okay?" Her mother would frown as if Lisette had said something really dumb, and laugh. "Sweetie, I'm just joking. Obviously, you don't fuck with these casino guys."

Vegas or Reno wasn't where she'd gone this time. Lisette was certain of that. She hadn't taken enough clothes.

In seventh grade, Lisette had had no trouble with math. She'd had no trouble with any of her school subjects. She'd got mostly B's and her mother had stuck her report card, open like a greeting card, to the refrigerator. All that seemed long ago now.

She was having a hard time sitting still. It was like red ants were crawling inside her clothes, in her armpits and between her legs. Stinging and tickling. Making her itch. Except that she couldn't scratch the way she wanted to—really hard with her fingernails, to draw blood—and there was no point in just touching where her skin itched. That would only make it worse.

The ridge of her nose, where the cartilage and bone had been "rebuilt"—a numb sensation there. And her eye—her left eye, with its tears dripping out. *Liz-zelte's crying! Hey—Liz-zelte's crying! Why're you crying, Liz-zz-zette?*

They liked her, the older guys. That was why they teased her. Like she was some kind of cute little animal, like—a mascot?

First time she'd see J.C. (Jimmy Chang—he'd transferred into her class in sixth grade), she'd nudged Reisha, saying, "Ohhhh," like in some MTV video, a moan to signal sex-pain, though she didn't know what that was, exactly. Her mother's favorite music videos were soft rock, retro rock, country and western, disco. Lisette had heard her in the shower singing moaning in a way she couldn't decipher—was it angry or happy?

Oh, she hated math class! Hated this place! Sitting at her desk in the row by the windows, at the front of the classroom, made Lisette feel like she was at the edge of a bright-lit room looking in—like she wasn't a part of the class. Nowicki said, "It's to keep you involved, up close like this," so Lisette wouldn't daydream or lose her way, but it had just the opposite effect. Most days Lisette felt like she wasn't there at all.

She swiped at her eyes. Shifted her buttocks, hoping to alleviate the stinging red ants. Nearly fifteen damn minutes she'd been waiting for the teacher to turn her fat back so that she could flip a folded-over note across the aisle to Keisha, for Keisha to flip over to J.C., in the next row. This note wasn't paper but a Kleenex, and on the Kleenex a lipstick kiss—a luscious grape-colored lip stick kiss—for J.C. from Lisette.

She'd felt so dreamy blotting her lips on the Kleenex. A brand-new lipstick, Deep Purple, which her mother knew nothing about, because Lisette, like her girlfriends, wore lipstick only away from home, and it was startling how different they all looked within seconds—how mature and how sexy.

Out of the corner of her eye she was watching J.C.—J.C., stretching his long legs in the aisle, silky black hair falling across his forehead. J.C. wasn't a guy you trifled with. Not J.C. or his "posse." She'd been told. She'd been warned. These were older guys by a year or maybe two. They'd been kept back in school, or had started school later than their classmates. But the beer buzz at the back of Lisette's head made her careless, reckless.

J. C.'s father worked at the Trump Taj Mahal. Where he'd come from, somewhere called Bay-Jing, in China, he'd driven a car for some high government official. Or he'd been a bodyguard. J.C. boasted that his father carried a gun. J.C. had held it in his hand. Man, he'd fired it!

A girl had asked J.C. if he'd ever shot anybody and J.C. had shrugged and laughed.

Lisette's mother had moved Lisette and herself to Atlantic City from Edison, New Jersey, when Lisette was nine years old. She'd been separated from Lisette's father, but later Daddy had come to stay with them when he was on leave from the army. Then they were separated again. Now they were divorced.

Lisette liked to name the places where her mother had worked. They had such special names: Trump Taj Mahal, Bally's, Harrah's, the Casino Royale. Except she wasn't certain if Yvette still worked at the Casino Royale—if she was still a blackjack dealer. Could be Yvette was back to being a cocktail waitress.

It made Lisette so damn—fucking—angry! You could ask her mother the most direct question, like "Exactly where the hell are you working now, Momma? "And her mother would find a way to give an answer that made some kind of sense at the time but melted away afterward, like a tissue dipped in water.

J.C.'s father was a security guard at the Taj. That was a fact. J.C. and his friends never approached the Taj but hung out instead at the south end of the Strip, where there were cheap motels, fast-food restaurants, pawnshops, bail-bond shops, and storefront churches, with sprawling parking lots, not parking garages, so they could cruise the lots and side streets after dark and break into parked vehicles if no one was watching. The guys laughed at how easy it was to force open a locked door or a trunk, where people left things like, for instance, a woman's heavy handbag that she didn't want to carry while walking on the boardwalk. Assholes! Some of them were so dumb you almost felt sorry for them.

Lisette was still waiting for Nowicki to be distracted. She was beginning to lose her nerve. Passing a lipstick kiss to J.C. was like saying, "All right, if you want to screw me, fuck me—whatever— hey, here I am."

Except maybe it was just a joke. So many things were jokes— you had to negotiate the more precise meaning later. If there was a later. Lisette wasn't into thinking too seriously about later.

She wiped her eyes with her fingertips, like she wasn't supposed to do since the surgery. *Your fingers are dirty, Lisette. You must not touch your eyes with your dirty fingers. There is the risk of infection.* Oh, God, she hated how both her eyes filled with tears in the cold months and in bright light, like the damn fluorescent light in all the schoolrooms and corridors. So her mother had got permission for Lisette to wear her dark-purple-tinted glasses to school. They made her look cool—like she was in high school, not middle school, sixteen or seventeen, not thirteen.

"Hell, you're not thirteen—are you? You?" one of her mother's man friends would say, eyeing her suspiciously. But, like, why would she want to play some trick about her *age*? He'd been mostly an asshole, this friend of her mother's. Chester—*Chet.* But he'd lent Momma some part of the money she'd needed for Lisette's eye doctor.

This morning Lisette had had to get up by herself. Get her own breakfast—Frosted Wheaties—in front of the TV, and she hated morning TV, cartoons and crap, or, worse yet, "news." She'd slept in her clothes for the third night in a row—black T-shirt, underwear, wool socks—dragged on her jeans, a scuzzy black sweater of her mother's with *TAJ* embossed on the back in turquoise satin. And her boots. Checked the phone messages, but there were none.

Friday night at nine her mother had called. Lisette had seen the caller ID and hadn't picked up. *Fuck you, going away. Why the fuck should I talk to you?* Later, feeling kind of scared, hearing loud voices out in the street, she'd tried to call her mother's cell phone. But the call hadn't gone through. *Fuck you. I hate you anyway. Hate hate hate you!*

Unless Momma brought her back something nice, like when she and Lisette's father went to Fort Lauderdale for their "second honeymoon" and Momma brought back a pink-coral-colored outfit—tunic top, pants. Even with all that had gone wrong in Fort Lauderdale, Momma had remembered to bring Lisette a gift.

Now it happened—and it happened fast.

Nowicki went to the classroom door, where someone was knocking and—*quick!*— with a pounding heart Lisette leaned over to hand the wadded Kleenex note to Reisha, who tossed it onto J. C.'s desk. J.C. blinked at the note like it was some weird beetle that had fallen from the ceiling, and without glancing over at Keisha or at Lisette, peering at him through her tinted glasses, with a gesture like shrugging his shoulders—J.C. was so *cool*—all he did was shut the Kleenex in his fist and shove it into a pocket of his jeans.

Any other guy, he'd open the note to see what it was. But not Jimmy Chang. J.C. was so accustomed to girls tossing him notes in class, he didn't have much curiosity about what it was that the snarl-haired girl in the dark glasses had sent him—or maybe he already had a good idea what it was. *Kiss-kiss. Kiss-kiss-kiss.* The main thing was that

J.C. hadn't just laughed and crumpled it up like trash.

By now Lisette's mouth was dry like cotton. This was the first time she'd passed such a note to J.C.—or to any boy. And the beer buzz that had made her feel so happy and hopeful was rapidly fading.

She'd had half a beer, maybe. Swilling it down outside in the parking lot, where the buses parked and fouled the air with exhaust, but the guys didn't seem to notice, loud-talking and loud-laughing, and she could see the way they looked at her sometimes: Lisette Mulvey was *hot*.

Except she'd spilled beer on her jacket. Beer stains on the dark-green corduroy, which her mother would detect, if she sniffed at them. Whenever she returned home.

This Monday, in January—it *was* January. She'd lost track of the actual date like she'd lost track of the little piece of paper from the eye doctor that her mother had given her, for the drugstore, for the eye drops. This her mother had given her last week, the last time she'd seen her, maybe Thursday morning. Or Wednesday. It was some kind of steroid solution that she needed for her eye after the surgery, but she couldn't find that piece of paper now, not in her jacket or in her backpack or in the kitchen or in her bedroom—not anywhere.

Nowicki was at the door now, turning to look at—who? Lisette? It was like a bad dream, where you're singled out—some stranger, a cop, it looked like, coming to your classroom to ask for *you*.

"Lisette? Can you step out into the hall with us, please?"

Next to Nowicki was a woman in a uniform—had to be Atlantic City PD—Hispanic features and skin color, and dark hair drawn back tight and sleek in a knot. Everybody in the classroom was riveted now, awake and staring, and poor Lisette in her seat was paralyzed, stunned. She tried to stand, biting at her lip. Fuck, her feet were tangled in her backpack straps. There was a roaring in her ears, through which the female cop's voice penetrated, repeating what she'd said and adding, "Personal possessions, please," meaning that Lisette should bring her things with her. She wouldn't be returning to the classroom.

So scared, she belched beer. Sour-vomity-beer taste in her mouth and—oh, Christ! — what if the cop smelled her breath?

In the corridor, a worse roaring in her ears, out of the woman's mouth came bizarre sounds. *Eiii-dee. If you are Lisette Mulvey, come with me.*

Eiii-dee, eiii-dee—like a gull's cry borne on the wind, rising and snatched away, even as you strained desperately to hear it.

Turned out there were two cops who'd come for her.

The Hispanic policewoman introduced herself: Officer Molina. Like Lisette was going to remember this name, let alone use it. The other cop was a man, a little younger than the woman, his skin so acne-scarred you'd be hard put to say if he was white.

Both of them looking at Lisette like—what? Like they felt sorry for her, or were disgusted with her, or—what? She saw the male cop's eyes drop to her tight-fitting jeans with a red rag patch at the knee, then up again to her blank terrified face.

It wouldn't be note-passing in math class that they'd come to arrest her for. Maybe at the Rite Aid the other day—plastic lipstick tubes marked down to sixty-nine cents in a bin. Lisette's fingers had snatched three of them up and into her pocket, without her even knowing what she was doing.

"You are Lisette Mulvey, daughter of Yvette Mulvey, yes?"

Numbly Lisette nodded.

Officer Molina did the talking. Lisette was too frightened to react when the policewoman took hold of her arm at the elbow, not forcibly but firmly, as a female relation might, walking Lisette down the stairs, talking to her in a calm, kindly, matter-of-fact voice that signaled, *You will be all right. This will be all right. Just come with us.*

"How recently did you see your mother, Lisette? Or speak with your mother? Was it today?"

Today? What was today? Lisette couldn't remember.

"Has your mother been away, Lisette? And did she call you?" Lisette shook her head.

"Your mother isn't away? But she isn't at home, is she?"

Lisette tried to think. What was the right answer? A weird scared smile made her mouth twist in the way that pissed off her mother, who mistook the smile for something else.

Molina said, "When did you last speak with your mother, Lisette?"

Shyly Lisette mumbled that she didn't know.

"But not this morning? Before you went to school?"

"No. Not—this morning." Lisette shook her head, grateful for something to say that was definite.

They were outside, behind the school. A police cruiser was parked in the fire lane. Lisette felt a taste of panic. Was she being arrested, taken to *juvie court*? The boys in J.C.'s posse joked about *juvie court*.

In the cold wet air, she felt the last of the beer buzz evaporate. She hated how the cops—both cops—were staring at her, like they'd never seen anything so sad or so pathetic before, like she was some sniveling little mangy dog. They could see the pimply skin at her hairline and every knot in her frizz-hair that she hadn't taken the time to comb or run a brush through, let alone shampoo, for four, five days. She hadn't had a shower either. That long, her mother had been away.

Away for the weekend with—who? That had been one of Momma's secrets. Could be a new "friend"—some man she'd met at the casino. There were lots of roving unattached men in Atlantic City. If they won in the casino, they needed to celebrate with someone, and if they lost in the casino, they needed to be cheered up by someone. Yvette Mulvey was the one! Honey-colored hair, not dirt-colored like Lisette's, in waves to her shoulders, sparkling eyes, a quick soothing laugh that a man wanted to hear—not sharp and ice-picky, driving him up the wall.

Lisette had asked her mother who she was going away for the weekend with and Momma had said, "Nobody you know." But the way she'd smiled—not at Lisette but to herself, an unfathomable look on her face like she was about to step off a diving board into midair—had made Lisette think suddenly, *Daddy?*

She knew that her mother was still in contact with her father.

Somehow she knew this, though Momma had not told her. Even after the divorce, which had been a nasty divorce, they'd been in contact. That was because (as Daddy had explained to her) she would always be his daughter. All else might change—like where Daddy lived, and if Daddy and Mommy were married—but not that. Not ever.

So Lisette had persisted in asking her mother, was it Daddy she was going away with? Was it Daddy? Was it? —nagging at Momma until she laughed, saying, "Hell no! No way I'm seeing that asshole again."

Her mother had gone away for the weekend. "I can trust you, Lisette, right?" she'd said, and Lisette had said, "Sure, sure you can."

Alone in the house meant that Lisette could stay up as late as she wanted. And watch any TV channel she wanted. And lie sprawled on the sofa talking on her cell phone as much as she wanted.

It was a short walk to the mini-mall—Kentucky Fried Chicken, Vito's Pizzeria, Taco Bell. Though it was easier just to defrost frozen suppers in the microwave and eat in front of the TV.

The first night, Keisha had come over. The girls had watched a DVD that Keisha brought and eaten what they could find in the refrigerator. "It's cool your mother's gone away. Where's she gone?"

Lisette thought. Possibly her mother had gone to Vegas after all. With her man friend, or whoever. This time year, depressing cold and wet by the ocean—the smartest place to go would be Vegas.

"She's got lots of friends there, from the casino. She's welcome to go out there anytime. She'd have taken me, except for damn, dumb school."

"So when did you last speak to her?"

The cops were staring at her now, waiting for an answer, as she was guilty faltering, fumbling. "Could've been, like, just yesterday—or the day before."

Her heart thumped in her chest like a crazed sparrow throwing itself against a window, like the one she'd seen in a parking garage once, trapped up by the ceiling, beating its wings and exhausting itself.

Yvette Mulvey was in trouble with the law—was that it?

The only court Lisette had been in was Ocean County Family Court. There, the judge had awarded custody to Yvette Mulvey and visitation privileges to Duane Mulvey. If something happened to Yvette Mulvey now, Lisette would be placed in a foster home. It

300

wasn't possible for Lisette to live with her father, who was a sergeant in the U.S. Army, and, last she'd heard, was about to be deployed to Iraq for the third time. *Deployed* was a strange word—a strange sound. *De-ployed.*

Daddy hadn't *meant* to hurt her, she knew. Even Momma believed this, which was why she hadn't called 911. And when the doctor at the ER had asked Lisette how her face had got so bruised, her nose and eye socket broken, she'd said that it was an accident on the stairs—she'd been running, and she'd fallen.

Which was true. She'd been running, and she'd fallen. Daddy shouting behind her, swiping with his fists—not meaning to hit her. But he'd been pissed. And all the things that Daddy had said afterward were what she'd wanted to hear; they'd made her cry, she'd wanted so badly to hear them.

"And your father? How recently did you see your father, Lisette?"

In the cruiser, the male cop drove. Molina sat in the passenger seat, swiveled to face Lisette. Her cherry-red lips were bright in her face, like something sparkly on a billboard that was otherwise weatherworn. Her sleek black hair shone like a seal's coat, her dark eyes shone with a strange unspeakable knowledge. It was an expression that Lisette saw often on the faces of women—usually women older than her mother—when they looked at her not in disapproval but with sudden sympathy, *seeing* her.

Lisette was uneasy with the expression. She'd seen it on Nowicki's face too. Better was the look of disgust, dismay.

Must've been two, three times that Molina explained to Lisette where they were taking her—to the hospital for the ID. But the words hadn't come together in a way that was comprehensible.

Eiii-dee. Eiii-dee.

"We will stay as long as you wish. Or not long at all—it's up to you. Maybe it will be over in a minute."

Molina spoke to Lisette in this way, which was meant to soothe but did not make sense. No matter the words, there was a meaning beneath them that Lisette could not grasp. Sometimes adults were uncomfortable with Lisette because they thought she was smirking, but it was just the skin around her left eye, the eye socket that had been shattered and repaired, and the frozen look of that part of her face because some of the nerve muscles were dead. "Such a freak accident," her mother had said. "Told her and told her not to—not to run—on the stairs. You know how kids are!" And half-pleading with the surgeon, though she already knew the answer to the question, "Will they heal ever? The broken nerves?"

Not broken but *dead.*

At the hospital they parked at the rear of the building. In a lowered voice Molina conferred with the male cop. Lisette couldn't hear what they were saying. She had no wish to hear. But she wanted to believe that the Hispanic woman was her friend and could be trusted. It was like that with Hispanic women, the mothers of her classmates—

mostly they were nice, they were kind. Molina was a kind woman, you could see how she'd be with children and possibly grandchildren. Weird that she was a cop and carried a gun—*packed heat*, it was said.

Lisette's mother knew some cops—she'd gone out with a cop. She'd said that the life of a cop was so fucking boring; once in a while, something happened and happened fast and you could be shot down in that second or two, but mostly it was very, very boring, like dealing blackjack cards to assholes who think they can win against the house. *You never win against the house.*

They were standing just inside the hospital, on the first floor by the elevators. People moved around them, past them, like blurs in the background of a photograph. It seemed urgent now to listen to what Molina was telling her as she gripped Lisette's arm again. Did Molina think that Lisette was going to try to escape? The male cop held himself a little apart, frowning.

What Molina was saying did not seem relevant to the situation, but later Lisette would see that, yes, everything that the policewoman had said was relevant: asking Lisette about Christmas, which was maybe two or three weeks earlier, and New Year's—and what had Lisette and her mother done over the holidays, anything special?

Lisette tried to think. Holidays wasn't a word that she or Momma would use. "Just saw some people. Nothing special."

"You didn't see your father?"

"No."

"When was the last time you saw him?" Lisette tried to think: he'd been gone by the time of the face surgery and the eye surgery. She'd been out of school. Must have been the summer. Like, around July Fourth.

"Not more recently than that?"

Lisette swiped at her eye. Wondering, was this some kind of trick like you saw on TV cop shows?

"On New Year's Eve, did your mother go out?"

Yes. Sure. Momma always went out, New Year's Eve.

"Do you know who she went out with?"

"No."

"He didn't come to the house to pick her up?"

Lisette tried to think. If whoever it was had come to the house, for sure Lisette had hid from him, just like she hid from Momma's women friends, and why? No reason, just wanted to.

Lisette, how big you're getting!

Lisette, taller than your mom, eh?

They took the elevator down. Down to the floor marked "Morgue".

Here the hospital was a different place. The air was cooler and smelled of something like chemicals. There were no visitors. There were very few hospital staff people. A female attendant in white pants, a white shirt, and a cardigan sweater told them that the assistant coroner would be with them soon.

They were seated. Lisette was between the two cops. Feeling weak in the knees, sick—like she'd been arrested, she was in custody, and this was a trick to expose her. Casually—for she'd been talking of something else—Molina began to ask Lisette about a motel on the south edge of the city, the Blue Moon Motel, on Atlantic. Had Lisette heard of the Blue Moon Motel? Lisette said no, she had never heard of the Blue Moon Motel. Ther were motels all over Atlantic City, some of them sleazy places, and she did not think—as Molina seemed to be saying—that her mother had worked at any of these motels, ever. If Yvette Mulvey had worked at the Blue Moon Motel, she'd have heard of it. She had not. Lisette said that her mother was not a motel maid or a cocktail waitress but a blackjack dealer, and you had to be trained for that.

Lisette said, like she was groping for a light switch, "Is Momma in—some kind of trouble?" A twisty little knot of rage in her heart against Momma. All this was Momma's fault.

Molina said that they weren't sure. That was what the ID might clear up.

"We need your cooperation, Lisette. We are hoping that you can provide… identification."

Weird how back at school she'd heard *eiii-dee*, not ID. It was like static was interfering, to confuse her. Like after she'd fallen on the stairs and hit her face and her head and she hadn't been able to walk without leaning against a wall, she'd been so dizzy, and she'd forgotten things. Some short circuit in her brain.

"Can you identify these? Do these look familiar, Lisette?"

A morgue attendant had brought Molina a box containing items, of which two were a woman's handbag and a woman's wallet. Molina lifted them carefully from the box, with gloved hands.

Lisette stared at the handbag and the wallet. What were these? Were they supposed to belong to her mother? Lisette wasn't sure if she had ever seen them before. She stared at the brown leather handbag with some ornamentation on it, like a brass buckle, and straps, and the black wallet, shabby-looking, like something you'd see on a sidewalk or by a Dumpster and not even bother to pick up o see if there was money inside.

Molina was saying that these "items" had been "retrieved" from a drainage ditch behind the Blue Moon Motel.

Also behind the drainage ditch was a woman's body—a "badly damaged" woman's body, for which they had no identification yet.

Carefully Molina spoke. Her hand lay lightly on Lisette's arm, which had the effect of restraining Lisette from swiping and poking at her left eye, as she'd been doing.

"The purse has been emptied out and the lining is ripped. In the wallet was a New Jersey driver's license issued to Yvette Mulvey, but no credit cards or money, no other ID. There was a slip of paper with a name and a number to be called in case of emergency, but that number has been disconnected. It belonged to a relative of your mother's who lives, or lived, in Edison, New Jersey? Iris Pedersen?"

Lisette shook her head. This was all too much—just too much for her to absorb. She didn't recognize the handbag and she didn't recognize the wallet—she was sure. She resented being asked. These items were so grungy-looking it was an insult to think that they might belong to her mother.

Close up she saw that Molina's eyes were beautiful and dark-thick-lashed, the way Lisette's mother tried to make hers, with a mascara brush. The skin beneath Molina's eyes was soft and bruised-looking, and on her throat were tiny dark moles. It did not seem right that a woman like Molina, who you could tell was a mother—her body was a mother's body for sure, wide hips and heavy breasts straining at the front of her jacket—could be a cop; it did not seem right that this person was carrying a gun, in a holster attached to a leather belt, and that she could use it, if she wanted to. Anytime she wanted to. Lisette went into a dream thinking that if she struck at Molina, if she kicked, spat, or bit, Molina might *shoot* her.

The male cop you'd expect to have a gun. You'd expect he would use it.

Daddy had showed them his guns, the ones he'd brought back from Iraq. These were not Army-issue but personal guns, a pistol with a carved wood handle and a heavier handgun, a revolver. He'd won these in a card game, Daddy said.

Maybe he hadn't brought them from Iraq. Maybe he'd got them at Fort Bragg, where he was stationed.

Lisette was saying that if her mother's driver's license had been in that wallet maybe it was her mother's wallet, but definitely she didn't recognize it.

As for Iris Pedersen—Aunt Iris—that was her mother's aunt, not hers. Aunt Iris was old enough to be Lisette's grandmother and Lisette hadn't seen her in years and did not think that her mother had either. For all they knew, the old lady was dead.

"We tried to contact her and the Edison police tried to contact her. But—"

An ID by someone who knew Yvette Mulvey well was necessary, Molina said, to determine if, in fact, the dead woman was Yvette Mulvey—or another woman of her approximate age. The condition of the body and the injuries to the face made it difficult to judge from the driver's license photo. Or from the photos on file at the casinos where Yvette Mulvey had worked.

Molina went on to tell Lisette that they had tried to locate her father—Duane David Mulvey—to make the ID for them, but he was no longer a resident of Edison, or, so far as they knew, of the State of New Jersey.

Lisete said, "My father's in the U.S. Army. My father is a sergeant in the U.S. Army. He used to be stationed at Fort Bragg but now he's in Iraq." And Molina said, "No, Lisette. I'm afraid that has changed. Your father is no longer a sergeant in the U.S. Army, and he is no longer in Iraq. The Army has no record of Duane Mulvey at the present time—he's been AWOL since December twenty-sixth of last year."

304

Lisette was so surprised she couldn't speak. If Molina hadn't been gripping her arm, she'd have jumped up and run away.

She was shivering. The corduroy jacket wasn't really for winter—this nasty wet cold. Momma hadn't been there that morning, scolding her, "Dress warm! For Christ's sake, it's January."

Another morgue attendant, an Indian-looking man—some kind of doctor—had come to speak in a low voice to the police officers. Quickly, Lisette shut her eyes, not listening. Trying to picture the classroom she'd had to leave—there was Nowicki at the board with her squeaky chalk, and there was J.C. slouched in his desk, hair in his face, and Keisha, who breathed through her mouth when she was excited or scared, and there was Lisette's own desk, empty—though now it was later, it was third period, and J.C. wasn't in Lisette's English class, but there was always the cafeteria. When the bell rang at 11:45 A.M, it would be lunchtime and she'd line up outside the doors, with the smell of greasy food, French fries, macaroni and cheese, chili on buns... Lisette's mouth flooded with saliva.

She smiled, seeing the purple lipstick kiss on the Kleenex, as J.C. would see it when he unfolded it—a surprise!

Her mother didn't want her to wear lipstick, but fuck Momma. All the girls her age did.

Last time she'd seen Momma with Daddy, Daddy had been in his soldier's dress uniform and had looked very handsome. His hair had been cut so short.

Not then but an earlier visit, when Daddy had returned from Iraq for the first time, Lisette's mother had covered his face in purple lipstick kisses. Lisette had been so young she'd thought that the lipstick kisses were some kind of wound, that her daddy was hurt and bleeding.

The times were confused. There were many times. There were many Daddys—she could not "see" them all.

There was the time Daddy took Momma to Fort Lauderdale. They'd wanted to take Lisette but it hadn't worked out—Lisette had had to be in school at that time of year. She'd gone to stay with her mother's friend Misty, who worked at Bally's. They were planning on ten days in Florida but Lisette's mother had surprised her by returning after just a week, saying that that was it, that was the end, she'd had to call the police when he'd got drunk and beaten her, and in a restaurant, he'd knocked over a chair he was so angry—that was it for her, no more.

Yvette had had man friends she'd met in the casinos. Most of them Lisette had never met. Never wished to meet. One of them was a real estate agent in Monmouth County—Lisette could almost remember his first name. It was something unusual, like Upton, Upwell...

The Indian man looked very young to be a doctor. Behind his wire-rimmed glasses, his eyes were soft-black, somber. His hair was black, but coarse, not silky-fine like J.C.'s hair.

He was leading the cops and Lisette into a refrigerated room. Molina had a firm hold on Lisette's hand. "We will make it as easy for you as we can, Lisette. All you have to do is squeeze my hand—that will mean yes."

Yes? Yes what? Desperately Lisette was picturing the school cafeteria, the long table in the corner where the coolest guys sat— J.C. and his friends, and sometimes certain girls were invited to sit with them. Today maybe J.C. would call Lisette over to sit with them—*Lisette! Hey Liz-zette!* —because he'd liked the purple-lipstick kiss, and what it promised.

"Take your time, Lisette. I'll be right beside you."

Then—so quick—it was over!

The female body she was meant to ID was not anyone she knew, let alone her mother.

This one had hair that was darker than Yvette's, with brown roots showing, and it was all matted like a cheap wig, and the forehead was so bruised and swollen, and the eyes—you could hardly see the eyes—and the mouth was, like, broken. You couldn't make sense of the face, almost. It was a face that needed to be straightened out, like with pliers.

"No. Not Momma." Lisette spoke sharply, decisively. Molina was holding her hand—she was tugging to get free.

This was the *morgue*; this was a *corpse*.

This was not a woman but *a thing*—you could not really believe that it had ever been a woman.

Only the head and the face were exposed. The rest of the body was covered by a white sheet but you could see the shape of it, the size, and it was not Lisette's mother—obviously. Older than Momma, and something had happened to the body to make it small—smaller. Some sad, pathetic, broken female, like debris washed up on the shore.

It was lucky the sheet was drawn up over the chest. The breasts. And the belly, and the pubic hair—the fat-raddled thighs of a woman of this age, you would not want to look at. Guys were quick to laugh, to show their contempt. Any girl or woman who was not good-looking, who was flat-chested or a little heavy—she had to walk fast to avoid their eyes.

"This is not Momma. This is no one I know."

Molina was close beside Lisette, instructing her to take her time. It was very important, Molina was saying, to make an *eiii-dee* of the woman, to help the police find who had done these terrible things to her.

Lisette pulled free of Molina. "I told you—this is not Momma! *It is not!*"

Something hot and acid came up into her mouth—she swallowed it down. She gagged again, and swallowed, and her teeth chattered like dice being shaken. She wanted to run from this nasty room, which was cold like a refrigerator but smelled of something sweet, sickish—like talcum powder and sweat—but Molina detained her.

They were showing her some clothes now, from the box. Dirty, bloodstained clothes, like rags. And a coat—a coat that resembled her mother's red suede coat but was filthy and torn. It was not the stylish coat that Momma had bought a year ago, in the January sales at the mall.

Lisette said that she'd never seen any of these things before. She had not. She was breathing funny, like her friend Keisha, who had asthma, and Molina was holding her hand and saying things to comfort her, bullshit things, telling her to be calm, it was all right. If she did not think that this woman was her mother, it was all right: there were other ways to identify the victim.

Victim. This was a new word. Like *corpse, drainage ditch.*

Molina led her to a restroom. Lisette had to use the toilet, fast. Her insides had turned to liquid fire and had to come out. At the sink she was going to vomit but could not. Washed and washed her hands. In the mirror a face hovered—a girl's face—in purple-tinted glasses, her lips a dark grape color. The scarring around the left eye wasn't so visible if she didn't look closely, and she had no wish to look closely. There had been three surgeries and after each surgery Momma had promised, "You'll be fine! You'll look better than new."

They wanted to take her somewhere—to Family Services. She said that she wanted to go back to school. She said that she had a right to go back to school. She began to cry. She was resentful and agitated and she wanted to go back to school, and so they said, "All right, all right for now, Lisette," and they drove her to school. The bell had just rung for lunch, so she went directly to the cafeteria—not waiting in line but into the cafeteria without a tray and still in her jacket, and, in a roaring sort of haze, she was aware of her girlfriends at a nearby table. There was Keisha, looking concerned, calling, "Lisette, hey—what was it? You okay?" and Lisette said, laughing into the bright buzzing blur, "Sure I'm okay. Hell, why not?"

Critical Essay

"ID": A Story of Interactivity of the Author, the Character and the Reader

According to phenomenological critic Wolfgang Iser, as people read a text, there are two factors which act as the stimulus to evoke their feelings, emotions, associations and memories, namely, determinate and indeterminate meaning. Determinate meaning refers to what might be called the facts of the text, certain events in the plot or physical descriptions clearly provided by the words on the page. In contrast, indeterminate meaning, or indeterminacy, refers to "gaps" in the text—such as actions that are not clearly explained or that seem to have multiple explanations—which allow or even invite readers to create their own interpretations. The interplay between determinate and indeterminate meanings, as people read, results in a number of ongoing experiences for them: retrospection, or thinking back to what they've read earlier in the text; anticipation of what will come next; fulfillment or disappointment of their anticipation; revision of their understanding of characters and events; and so on.

The short story "ID" by Joyce Carol Oates is a story that invites readers' interactivity with the author and the characters through various "gaps". These "gaps" work perfectly to arouse the desirous sympathy from the readers in the course of their retrospection, anticipation, inference and deduction.

The story is about a middle school girl named Lisette. One day, when Lisette was having math class, she was asked out by two cops to identify a "badly damaged" woman's body which was suspected to be her mother. There is no dramatic conflict nor complex characterization in the story. What impresses readers most is that in the story Joyce Carol Oates deliberately leaves many "gaps" for the readers to fill and invites readers' participation in its many possible interpretations.

The "gaps" in the story derive largely from the unreliable character Lisette herself. When the story opens, "some older guys had got her high on beer," and as a result, she was quite muzzy-headed. She had lost track of many things, "even the year—a 'new' year—seemed weird to her, like a movie set in a faraway galaxy."

What worsened the matter was the math class she was having. Lisette hated math class, which "made her feel so stupid." The clicking chalk and the dancing numerals on the board, working together with the beer, made her "begin to feel dizzy." Sitting in the class, while "[e]verybody in the classroom was riveted now, awake and staring, [and] poor Lisette in her seat was paralyzed, stunned."

Lisette, with "the beer buzz[ing] at the back of [her] head" and feeling "careless and reckless", couldn't remember the exact date when she saw her mother for the last time. The date she saw her father the last time was a mystery to her, too. For her, "[t]he time were confused. There were many times. There were many daddys—she could not 'see' them all." She felt like "static was interfering, to confuse her. Like after she'd fallen on the stairs and hit her face and her head and she hadn't been able to walk without leaning against a wall, she'd been so dizzy, and she'd forgotten things. Some short circuit in her brain." To Lisette, "many things were jokes—you had to negotiate the more precise meaning later. If there was a later. Lisette wasn't into thinking too seriously about later."

While Lisette is an unreliable character, failing to provide the necessary and essential information for readers to make any sensible decision, many other undeterminable facts supply the rest of the "gaps". Though Lisette could name the places where her mother had worked, "she wasn't certain if Yvette (her mother) still worked at the Casino Royale—if she was still a blackjack dealer. Could be Yvette was back to being a cocktail waitress." Her mother never gave her a definite answer whenever she asked her questions like "Exactly where the hell are you working now, Momma?" Her mother "would find a way to give an answer that made some kind of sense at the time but melted away afterward, like a tissue dipped in water." Lisette did not know with whom her mother had been away with, either, because "[t]hat had been one of Momma's secrets."

The biggest "gap" comes from the "badly damaged" woman's body. It was so distorted that it was almost beyond recognition. "This was not a woman but a thing—you could not really believe that it had ever been a woman." "[T]he forehead was so bruised and swollen, and the eyes—you could hardly see the eyes—and the mouth was, like, broken. You couldn't make sense of the face, almost. It was a face that needed to be straightened out, like with pliers."

The indeterminate meaning in the story, in the form of "gaps", invites readers' participation while they try hard to figure out what has really happened. However, the indeterminate meaning has to work together with the determinate meaning to avoid too wild and far-fetched interpretation. As in the case of the short story "ID", going together with the "gaps", there are irrefutable facts, or the determinate meaning, serving to guide readers to be on the right track in their interactivity with the author and the characters, to guarantee that they will arrive at the conclusion the author was desirous of.

Though damaged beyond recognition, readers are provided with sufficient information for the consolidation of the cold fact that the woman *was* Lisette's mother, even though the mention was made in a very random fashion. "The purse has been emptied out and the lining is ripped. In the wallet was a New Jersey driver's license issued to Yvette Mulvey, but no credit cards or money, no other ID. There was a slip of paper with a name and a number to be called in case of emergency, but that number has been disconnected. It belonged to a relative of your mother's who lives, or lived, in Edison, New Jersey? Iris Pedersen?"

It is an ingenious writing technique on the part of the author to invite readers' participation and meanwhile guide their participation precisely towards the desirous response. With what is determinate, readers can easily determine what seems otherwise to be indeterminate. The more Lisette is trying to deny the fact that the dead woman was her mother, the more readers are convinced it *was* her mother. When the poor girl "stared at the handbag and the wallet", wondering "[w]hat were these? [w]ere they supposed to belong to her mother?" and unsure if "she had ever seen them before", readers, ironically instead of the girl herself, are already very certain that these are indeed her mother's items. It is a reader's response artistically achieved in that readers are manipulated to make the desirous response without feeling being manipulated.

The climax of the story comes when what is indeterminate becomes absolutely determinate: her mother's death. When Lisette was led to the morgue and shown the corpse, a moment when readers expect everything to be clarified, she, however, desperately refused to take it as her mother's corpse, rendering the matter indeterminate again. In her logic, largely misled by her reluctance to face the cruel fact of her mother's death, the body, with "[o]nly the head and the face were exposed", was "Older than Momma, and something had happened to the body to make it small—smaller." It could only belong to "[s]ome sad, pathetic, broken female, like debris washed up on the shore" and definitely not her momma. She encapsulated her sadness, shock and disbelief in the exclamation that "This is not Momma. This is no one I know." When the cop who was close beside her asked her to take her time, she pulled free of her and cried hysterically, "I told you—this is not Momma! It is not!"

It is a point of time when the indeterminate and determinate intermix and interplay with each other. It is also where the reader, the character and the author interact with each other for the ultimate revelation of the theme. At this point of time, in the course of reading the story, readers, guided by the author in a subtle and yet traceable way, have already reached their conclusion. It is very likely that they might have stopped arguing with the girl about the undeniable fact of her mother's death and might be, instead, shedding their sympathetic tears profusely for the unfortunate girl as she was feeling "[s]omething hot and acid [coming] up into her mouth—she swallowed it down" and "gagged again, and swallowed, and her teeth chattered like dice being shaken. She wanted to run from this nasty room, which was cold like a refrigerator but smelled of something sweet, sickish—like talcum powder and sweat."

The "ID", either the story or the character in the story, is not so difficult to determine had there not been so much interactivity of the reader, the character and the author. With such complications, the author was given the space and time to ladle out in an unhurried way her sympathy for the girl, reflection on life, and inclusion of the reader and herself in the huge admiration for the courage to live in an unwelcoming world.

Key to Exercises

Unit 1 1-5 CDABA 6-10 CCCAD 11-15 CADCA
Unit 2 1-5 DABCC 6-10 ABDCA 11-15 BDABD
Unit 3 1-5 DABDA 6-10 CCBDB 11-15 DABBA
Unit 4 1-5 CBADB 6-10 ABDCA 11-15 DCACD
Unit 5 1-5 CDDAB 6-10 DCABD 11-15 CABAD
Unit 6 1-5 CBDAB 6-10 CADCA 11-15 DDBCB
Unit 7 1-5 DBDBA 6-10 CBDAB 11-15 BCBBA
Unit 8 1-5 BADBD 6-10 CBBDA 11-15 CDCAC
Unit 9 1-5 ABDDD 6-10 ADDBA 11-15 BCCBD
Unit 10 1-5 ADCDB 6-11 DCAAC 11-15 CCBAB
Unit 11 1. sturdy 2. enchanting 3. libidinous 4. façade 5. glittering 6. contempt
7. plausible 8. splendid 9. vanish 10. umber
Unit 12 1-5 BDCBB 6-10 DBACB

图书在版编目（CIP）数据

　　美国短篇小说选读与文本批评 / 杨春编著 . -- 北京：
社会科学文献出版社，2025.1. --（中国社会科学院大
学系列教材）. -- ISBN 978-7-5228-4392-6

　　Ⅰ . I712.074

　　中国国家版本馆 CIP 数据核字第 2024V2M631 号

·中国社会科学院大学系列教材·

美国短篇小说选读与文本批评

编　　著 / 杨　春

出 版 人 / 冀祥德
责任编辑 / 赵　娜
责任印制 / 王京美

出　　版 / 社会科学文献出版社·群学分社 （010）59367002
　　　　　　地址：北京市北三环中路甲29号院华龙大厦　邮编：100029
　　　　　　网址：www.ssap.com.cn
发　　行 / 社会科学文献出版社 （010）59367028
印　　装 / 三河市东方印刷有限公司

规　　格 / 开　本：787mm×1092mm　1/16
　　　　　　印　张：20　字　数：446千字
版　　次 / 2025年1月第1版　2025年1月第1次印刷
书　　号 / ISBN 978-7-5228-4392-6
定　　价 / 128.00元

读者服务电话：4008918866